Cold Cold Heart

"Chilling and satisfying." —*People*

"This unusual take on a serial-killer novel offers a most-welcome exploration of traumatic brain injury and what it is like to be a survivor." —*Booklist* (starred review)

"Hoag's narrative explodes with an unexpected but believable conclusion. A top-notch psychological thriller." —*Kirkus Reviews*

"[A] chilling psychological thriller." —*Publishers Weekly*

"An unforgettable read." —*RT Book Reviews*

"Ms. Hoag weaves the intensifying plot in *Cold Cold Heart* with the expertise of a master seamstress blind stitching the facts, moving through multiple characters' voices, taking readers on a journey into the inner depths of her characters' minds, and in Hoag style, delivering a walloping ending." —*Pittsburgh Post-Gazette*

The Boy

"Every Tami Hoag book is deviously plotted, compulsively page-turning, with dead-on dialogue and twisted characters. You're in the hands of a master with Tami Hoag."
—*New York Times* bestselling author Lisa Scottoline

"[A] tightly plotted whodunnit . . . prepare to gasp." —*People*

"Thoughtful, character-driven . . . Hoag keeps the twists and turns coming all the way to the shocking conclusion."
—*Publishers Weekly*

"You're going to be staying up late at night as the pages turn with this one."   —*New York Journal of Books*

The Bitter Season

"A masterful tale of two colliding cases that become one tightly coiled plot, *The Bitter Season* is Tami Hoag at her down-and-dirty best. Authentic, dark, and intense, this is a portrait of flawed characters on both sides of the law that will surprise you and make you laugh as you double-lock your doors."
                     —*New York Times* bestselling author Tess Gerritsen

"Tami Hoag is simply one of the best. And *The Bitter Season*—engrossing, atmospheric, and taut with suspense—is the work of a writer at the top her game. A chilling psychological thriller!"
                          —*New York Times* bestselling author Lisa Unger

"Tami Hoag gives us a female detective who's sharp-witted and gutsy as she deftly weaves two cases together for one heart-stopping finale. I couldn't put it down."
                       —*New York Times* bestselling author Carol Goodman

The 9th Girl

"Cannily plotted and peppered with some of the sharpest dialogue in the business."   —*Entertainment Weekly* (A–)

"Outstanding! Tami Hoag continues to set the standard for excellence in her genre."   —*Suspense Magazine*

"Hoag's prose is martial-arts quick and precise, her humor is high-voltage, and her insights into the misery of high school, the toxicity of divorce, and the extreme psychosis of a serial killer are knowing and thought-provoking. . . . One of her very best."
                                                           —*Booklist*

Down the Darkest Road

Secrets to the Grave

Deeper Than the Dead

Also by Tami Hoag

Novels

The Boy
The Bitter Season
The 9th Girl
Down the Darkest Road
Secrets to the Grave
Deeper Than the Dead
The Alibi Man
Prior Bad Acts
Kill the Messenger
Dark Horse
Dust to Dust
Ashes to Ashes
A Thin Dark Line
Guilty as Sin
Night Sins
Dark Paradise
Cry Wolf
Still Waters
Lucky's Lady
Sarah's Sin
Magic

Short Works

The 1st Victim

TAMI HOAG

Cold Cold Heart

DUTTON

DUTTON

An imprint of Penguin Random House LLC
penguinrandomhouse.com

Previously published as a Dutton hardcover and a Dutton mass market edition

First Dutton trade paperback edition: October 2021

THE LIBRARY OF CONGRESS HAS CATALOGUED
THE HARDCOVER EDITION OF THIS BOOK AS FOLLOWS:

Names: Hoag, Tami, author.
Cold cold heart / Tami Hoag.
ISBN 978-0-525-95454-5 (hardcover)
pages ; cm
1. Missing persons—Investigation—Fiction. 2. Cold cases
(Criminal investigation)—Fiction. 3. Post-traumatic stress disorder—Fiction. I. Title.
PS3558.O333C65 2015
813'.54—dc23   2014035865

Dutton trade paperback ISBN: 9781101984468

Printed in the United States of America
1st Printing

Book Design by Leonard Telesca

Cold Cold Heart

Prologue

She should have been dead. After everything he had put her through, she should have died hours before. There had been many moments during the ordeal when she wished she would die, when she wished he would just end the unimaginable suffering he was inflicting on her.

He had done things to her she could never have imagined, would never have wanted to know one human being could be capable of doing to another. He had abused her physically, sexually, and psychologically. He had abducted her, beaten her, tortured her, raped her. Hour after hour after hour.

She didn't really know how much time had passed. Hours? Days? A week? The concept of time had ceased to have any meaning.

She had tried to resist physically, but she had learned resistance was rewarded only with pain. The pain had surpassed anything in her most terrible nightmares. It had surpassed adjectives and gone into a realm of blinding white light and high-pitched sound. Eventually, she had ceased to fight and had found that in seemingly giving up her life, she was able to keep her life.

Where there is life, there is hope.

She couldn't remember where she had heard that. Somewhere, long ago. Childhood.

At one point during the attack she had called for her mother, for her father. She had been overwhelmed with the kind of pure fear and helplessness that stripped away maturity and logic and self-control, reducing her to a screaming mass of raw emotion. Now she couldn't remember ever being a child. She couldn't remember having parents. She could remember only the sharp pain of a knife carving into her flesh, the explosion of pain as a hammer struck her.

She had tried to resist the overwhelming desire to break down mentally, to give herself over and drown in the depths of hopelessness. It would have been so much easier to just let go. But he hadn't killed her. Yet. And she wouldn't do the job for him. She continued to choose life.

Where there is life, there is hope.

The words floated through her fractured mind like a ribbon of smoke as she lay on the floor of the van.

Her tormentor was driving. She lay directly behind his seat. He was happily singing along with the radio, as if he didn't have a care in the world, as if there wasn't a beaten, bloody, half-dead woman in the back of his van.

She was more alive than he knew. In giving up fighting, she had reserved strength. In giving up fighting, she had stopped him short of rendering her completely incapacitated. She could still move, though there was something wrong with her coordination and every effort set off nauseating explosions of pain. Her head was pounding. It felt like her brain might burst out of her skull—or maybe it already had.

She faded in and out of consciousness, but she could still form thoughts. Many were incomplete or incoherent, but then she would muster as much will and focus as she could, and something would make sense for a second or two.

The cold floor beneath her was numbing some of the pain that wracked her body. The blanket he had thrown over her to hide her offered a cocoon, a place to be invisible. Her wrists were only loosely bound together in front of her with a long, wide red ribbon. He had positioned her with her elbows bent, her hands tucked beneath her chin as if in prayer.

Prayer. She had prayed and prayed and prayed, but no one had come to save her.

He had all the power, all the control. He had killed before, many times, and gotten away with it. He believed he was invincible. He believed he was a genius. He believed he was an artist.

He said she was to be his masterpiece.

She didn't know what that meant. She didn't want to find out.

The van hit a pothole in the road, jarring and rocking. She wanted to brace herself, to lessen the movement of her broken body, but the ribbon tied around her wrists prevented her. She strained against it for a few seconds, then stopped trying. The effort made her nauseous. As she rode the wave of the nausea, nonsensical words and images tumbled through her battered brain like the colored glass pieces in a kaleidoscope. As her consciousness dimmed, the glass shards of thought settled in a heap in her mind. The seductive voice of death whispered to her. She could just let go. She could go before she found out what he had in store. It would be so much easier.

The tension started to seep out of her body. Her hands relaxed . . . and she felt the satin ribbon loosen around her wrists. . . . She put her concentration to the task of working a hand free.

Where there is life, there is hope. Where there is life, there is hope . . .

"You're gonna be a star, Dana," he called back to her. "That's what you always wanted, right? Network news. Your face on televisions all across America? You'll have that now, thanks to me. It won't be the way you imagined it, but you're gonna be famous."

He cursed as the van hit another deep pothole. Dana's body bounced painfully on the van's floor. The pain rolled through her like a violent wave. She turned to her left side, curling into the fetal position, and tried not to cry out, not to make a sound, not to call attention to herself.

Next to her, the collection of tools he had brought along bounced and rattled in their open tote. Not considering her any threat to him at all in her semiconscious, beaten, broken state, he hadn't bothered to put the tote out of reach. His ego allowed him to disregard her. She was little more than an inanimate object to him now. Her purpose was as a prop to prove his point: that he was smarter than any of the many law enforcement officers who were looking for him.

They had offended him, crediting him with a murder that was sloppy; a careless crime, supposedly his ninth victim. He would show them his true ninth victim. He would present her to them as a work of art, tied up with a bright red ribbon.

He was a serial killer. The police and the media called him Doc Holiday. These were facts Dana had known before he had abducted her. She didn't fully grasp any of the details now. The story had been boiled down to this: He was a predator and she was prey. And if she couldn't pull herself together and make one valiant effort, she would soon be dead.

She had to do something.

She had to summon as much will and life as she had left. She had to form a coherent thought and be able to hang on to it for just a moment. She had to fight through the pain to find the physical strength to execute that thought.

It all seemed so hard. But she wanted to live. The fire of life had burned down to an ember inside her, but she wouldn't let it go out without a fight.

Her brain ached at the effort to form and hold the thought.

Her body protested and resisted the signals to move.

Under the blanket, her right hand trembled uncontrollably as she reached toward the tote.

In the front seat, he was still talking out loud. He was a genius. He was an artist. She would be his masterpiece. The media wanted to credit him with a victim who looked like a zombie? He would give them a zombie.

Dana pulled her legs up toward her chest and shifted her weight, turning onto her knees.

Where there is life, there is hope.

Her head swam; her thoughts tumbled. She had to fight so hard to stay in the moment.

She would have only one chance.

He laughed at his own joke. He glanced in the rearview mirror as if to see if she had heard him.

His smile died as his eyes met the eyes of his zombie.

With all the strength she had left in her body, Dana swung her arm and buried the screwdriver to the hilt in his temple.

Then everything went black, and she was falling and falling and falling into a darkness that swallowed her whole.

1

January
Hennepin County Medical Center
Minneapolis, Minnesota

She woke screaming. Screaming and screaming and screaming. Loud, long, terrible screams that tore up her throat from the
depths of her soul.

She didn't know why she was screaming. There was no emotion
attached to it, not pain, not fear. She seemed completely detached
from the noise coming out of her.

She had no awareness of her body. It was as if the essence of her
being had taken up residence inside an empty shell. She couldn't
feel. She couldn't move. She couldn't see. She didn't know if her eyes
were open or closed or gone.

She could hear the commotion of people rushing around her. She
didn't know who they were. She didn't know where she was or why
she was there. The people were shouting. She couldn't really understand what they were saying. Only one frantic voice penetrated as it
shouted: *Dana! Dana! Dana!*

The word meant nothing to her. It was just a sound.

Like the screams coming from her own throat, these words were just sounds. She continued to scream and scream and scream.

Then a sinuous sensation of warmth spread through her, and the screaming stopped, and she ceased to be aware of anything at all.

"I KNOW THIS WAS upsetting for you, Mommy."

Lynda Mercer was still shaken and shocked by the sound of her daughter's screams, screams that had come from Dana's unconscious body lying perfectly still on the bed.

Dr. Rutten motioned for her to take one of the two seats in front of his desk. He took the other, choosing not to put a professional distance between them.

In his midfifties, Rutten was Dutch, fit, and bald, with large, kind, liquid brown eyes. It was his habit to be close when he spoke to the anxious parents and spouses of patients, to reach out and touch with a large, reassuring hand. While the tactic could have seemed a phony, contrived intimacy, his kindness was genuine and very much appreciated. He was a rock for his patients and their families. He took her hand and gave it a squeeze.

"After all the years I've spent studying the human brain, and with all the technology we've developed to help us in our study of the human brain, the one thing I can tell you with certainty is that there is no certainty with a brain injury," he said.

"We can define the specific type of injury Dana has sustained. Based on our experience, we can attempt to predict some of the effects the injury might produce, some of the changes we might see in her personality, in her memory, in possible physical impairments. But there are no hard-and-fast rules about how her brain will react to the trauma."

"She was screaming and screaming," Lynda murmured, her trembling voice barely more than a whisper. "Was she in pain? Was she having a nightmare? All the machines were going crazy."

She could still hear her daughter's screams. She could still hear the shrill beeping and shrieking of the alarms on the monitors. Dana's heart rate had gone from a normal rhythm to a pounding pace. They had recently taken her off the ventilator, and she gulped air like a fish out of water.

"The screaming is extremely disconcerting to hear, but not an uncommon occurrence for people with brain injuries at this stage of their recovery as they begin to climb their way out of their unconscious state," Rutten assured her. "Sometimes they moan or cry hysterically. Sometimes they scream.

"Why does this happen? We believe this is caused by a misfiring of signals within the midbrain as it tries to cope and reroute itself. Neurons are firing, but the impulses are landing in strange places. Also, there can be heightened fight-or-flight responses caused by external or internal stressors, resulting in panic or combativeness."

"People scream when they're in pain," Lynda murmured.

Regardless of the neurologist's explanation, she couldn't escape the idea that her daughter was locked in a deep, unending nightmare, reliving the things a monster had done to her. Not just the skull fracture that had led to brain surgery to remove bone fragments, but also facial fractures, broken fingers, broken ribs, a fractured kneecap. Contusions and abrasions colored her body and her face. The killer the press called Doc Holiday had literally carved into her flesh with a knife.

Imagined scenes from the nightmare flashed through Lynda's mind like clips from a horror movie. Ligature marks burned into Dana's wrists and ankles indicated she had been tied down. She had been tortured. She had been raped.

"We immediately upped the amount of pain medication Dana is receiving," Rutten said. "Just in case some of that was the result of pain, but that may not be the case at all."

"I shouldn't have left her," Lynda whispered, a wave of mother's guilt washing over her.

She had left Dana's room for just a moment, needing to stretch her legs. Just a walk to the end of the hall, to the family lounge to get a cup of coffee. As she walked back, the first scream split the air and pierced her heart.

She had dropped the coffee and run to the room, flinging herself into the melee of scurrying hospital staff. She had shouted her daughter's name over and over—*Dana! Dana! Dana!*—until someone had taken hold of her shoulders from behind and pulled her out of the way.

Dr. Rutten squeezed her hand again, pulling her out of the memory to focus once more on him. The corners of his mouth curved subtly in the gentlest smile of understanding and commiseration.

"I'm a father myself. I have two daughters. I know how it tears at a parent's heart to think their child is suffering."

"She suffered so much already," she said. "All the things that animal did to her . . ."

Dr. Rutten frowned. "If it gives you any comfort, she probably won't have any memory of what happened to her."

"I hope not," Lynda said. If there were a God, Dana would remember nothing of her ordeal. But then, if there were a God, none of this should have happened at all.

"Will it happen again?" she asked. "The screaming?"

"It might. Or it might not. She could drift in and out like this for a long time, or she may become fully conscious tomorrow. She has been saying words these last few days. She's been responsive to vocal commands. These are positive signs, but every brain is different.

"The kinds of injuries Dana sustained can mean she may have difficulty organizing her thoughts or performing routine tasks. She may become impulsive, have trouble controlling her emotions or empathizing with other people. She may have difficulty speaking, or she may speak perfectly but not always be able to grab the right words from her brain.

"Damage to the temporal lobe of the brain may affect her memory, but how much? I can't tell you. She may have no memory of what happened to her. She may have no memory of the last ten years. She may not recognize her friends. She may not recognize herself. You may not recognize her," he said, unable to hide his sadness at a truth he had seen again and again.

"She's my daughter," Lynda said, offended. "She's my child. Of course I'll recognize her."

"Physically, yes, but she will never be exactly the girl you've known all her life," he said gently. "One thing I know is true in every case: The person you love will be changed from this, and that will be the hardest thing of all to accept.

"In a way, the daughter you had is gone. Even though she may look the same, she will behave differently, look at the world differently. But she is still your daughter, and you will still love her.

"You will have ahead of you a long and difficult road," he said. "But you will go down it together."

"But she'll get better," Lynda said, as if phrasing it as a statement instead of a question would make it so.

Dr. Rutten sighed. "We can't know how much. Every case is its own journey. This journey will be like driving at night. You can only see as far as the headlights reach, but you can make it the whole way nevertheless.

"You have to stay strong, Mommy," he said, giving her hand another squeeze. "You have to stay focused on what's positive."

Lynda almost laughed at the absurdity of his statement. "Positive," she said, staring at the floor.

The doctor hooked a knuckle under her chin and raised her head so she had to look him in the eye. "She shouldn't be alive. She survived a killer who had murdered who knows how many young women. She survived a car crash that could have killed her. She survived her injuries. She survived brain surgery. She's fighting her way back to consciousness.

"She should be dead and she's not. She's going to wake up. She's going to live. That's a lot more than I get to tell many parents."

*   *   *

THE WEIGHT OF HIS words pressed down on Lynda as she wandered the halls of the hospital. She needed to find a way to be positive. Dana would need that from her when she finally rejoined the world and they began her journey to recovery. But it was all uncharted territory, and thinking about the enormity of it was daunting.

She felt so tired and so alone, dealing with all of this in a strange, cold city where she knew no one. Her husband planned to come from Indiana on Fridays and go back Sunday nights. But even if Roger came to Minneapolis on the weekends, there was a part of Lynda that felt like he wasn't fully in this with her. Dana was her daughter, not Roger's. While Dana and Roger had always gotten along, they weren't close in the way Dana had been with her father before his death when Dana was fourteen.

Dana's coworkers from the television station came by but were allowed only short visits. The doctor wanted Dana to rest most of the time, to keep stimulation to a minimum to allow her brain time to heal. Her producer and mentor, Roxanne Volkman, brought a box of items from Dana's apartment so she could have some familiar things in her room—a perfume she loved, her iPod, a soft blue throw from her sofa, a couple of photographs.

Dana had been working at the station for only nine months. But even in that short time she had made a positive impression, the producer had told Lynda. Everyone appreciated Dana's sunny smile and go-getter attitude, but none of them knew her well enough to be much more than acquaintances.

The lead detectives assigned to Dana's case had come by to check on her progress. They would eventually want to speak to her, to find out if she could shed any light on the case. Even though the perpetrator was dead, there were still many questions left unanswered. Had Dana heard anything, seen anything, that might implicate the killer in other cases? According to Dr. Rutten, they would probably never find out.

The female detective—Liska—was a mother too. She brought Starbucks and cookies and lists of support groups for victims of crime and their families. They talked about the stresses and the joys of raising children. She asked Lynda what Dana had been like as a little girl, as a teenager. Lynda suspected that line of questioning was just a way to get her mind off the difficult present with stories of happier times.

The male detective—Kovac—didn't have as much to say. He was older, gruffer, and had probably seen more terrible things in his career than Lynda would ever want to imagine. There was a world-weariness about him, a certain sadness in his eyes when he looked at Dana. And there was an awkward kindness in him that Lynda found endearing.

In the aftermath of the crime there had been some public criticism of the police for not finding Dana or the killer sooner. Lynda didn't engage in it.

The local and national media had been all over the case as soon as it was known that Dana was missing. It was a sensational story: the pretty fledgling on-air television newscaster abducted by a serial killer. It was an even bigger story when she was found alive—if barely—and her captor was found dead. As far as anyone knew, she was his only living victim. They all believed she would have an incredible story to tell when she finally came to. They hadn't considered that she might not remember any of it. Lynda hoped she wouldn't.

Finally making her way back to Dana's room, she had no idea of the time of day or how many hours had passed since the screaming incident. As she went into the room she was surprised to see that the world beyond the window was already growing dim, as night seeped across the frigid Minnesota landscape. Darkness came early here this time of year. The pale, distant sun was gone by late afternoon.

The screens of the machines monitoring Dana's vital signs glowed in the dimly lit room, chirping and beeping to themselves. She appeared to be sleeping peacefully.

Lynda stood beside the bed, watching her daughter's chest rise and fall slowly. Her face was unrecognizable, swollen and misshapen, with centipede lines of stitches. Her head was bald beneath swathed gauze and the helmet that protected her in the event of a fall. Her right eye was covered with a thick gauze patch. The orbital bone and cheekbone had been shattered. The left eye was swollen nearly shut, and the black and blue seeped down into her cheek like a spreading stain.

Dana had always been a pretty girl. As a child she had been a pixie with blond pigtails and big royal-blue eyes full of wonder. She had grown into a lovely young woman with a heart-shaped face and delicate features loved by the camera. Her personality had accompanied her looks perfectly: sweet and optimistic, open and friendly. She had always been inquisitive, always wanting to dig to the bottom of every story, to research the details of anything new and unfamiliar.

Her curiosity had helped to shape her goals and had eventually led her to her career. Armed with a degree in communications, she had worked her way into broadcast news. She had only recently landed her first big job in front of the camera as a newscaster on the early-morning show of a small, independent Minneapolis station. She had been so excited to have the job, not caring at all that she had to leave her apartment at three A.M. to go on the air at four.

Lynda had worried about her going out alone at that hour. Minneapolis was a big city. Bad things happened in big cities all the time. Dana had pooh-poohed the idea that she could be put in jeopardy going from her apartment building the few dozen yards to her car in the parking lot. She argued that she lived in a very safe neighborhood, that the parking lot was well lit.

She had been abducted from that parking lot on the fourth of January, taken right out from under the false security of the light. No one had seen or heard anything.

Lynda had come to Minneapolis as soon as she heard of Dana's possible abduction. But she hadn't been able to see her daughter until she was brought to the ICU after the surgery, a tube coming out of her shaved head, attached to a machine to monitor brain pressure. Tubes seemed to come from every part of her, connecting to an IV bag and a bag of blood. A catheter line drained urine from her bladder to a bag on the side of the bed. The ventilator was breathing for her, taking one vital task away from her swollen brain.

Now the ventilator was gone. Dana was breathing on her own. The pressure monitor had been removed from her skull. She was still unconscious, but closer to the surface than she had been.

It had been eerie to watch her these last few days as her mind floated in some kind of dark limbo. She had begun to move her arms and legs, sometimes violently, to the point that she had to be restrained. And yet she wasn't awake. She responded to commands to squeeze the hand of the doctor, of the nurse, of her mother. But she wasn't awake. She spoke words that suggested she was aware of the physical world—*hot, cold, hard, soft*. She answered when asked who she was—*Dana*. But she didn't seem to recognize the voices of people she knew, some she had known for years, if not her whole life.

The physical therapist came every morning to prop Dana up in the chair beside the bed because movement was good for her. She would sit in the chair moving her arms and legs randomly, as if she were a marionette, her invisible strings being manipulated by an unseen hand.

But she had yet to open her eyes.

She stirred now, moving one arm, batting at Lynda. Her right leg bent at the knee, then pushed down again and again in a stomping motion. The rhythm of the heart monitor picked up.

"Dana, sweetheart, it's Mom. It's all right," Lynda said, trying to touch her daughter's shoulder. Dana whimpered and tried to wrench away. "It's okay, honey. You're safe now. Everything is going to be fine."

Agitated, Dana mumbled and thrashed and clawed with her left hand at her neck brace, tearing it off and flinging it aside. She hated the brace. She fussed and fought every time someone tried to put it on her. She tore it off every chance she had.

"Dana, calm down. You need to calm down."

"No, no, no, no, no, *no! No! No!*"

Lynda could feel her own heart rate and blood pressure rising. She tried again to touch her daughter's flailing arm.

"*No! No! No! No!*"

One of the night-shift nurses came into the room, a small, stout woman with a shorn hedge of maroon hair. "She has a lot to say today," she said cheerfully, checking the monitors. "I heard she was pretty loud this afternoon."

Lynda stepped back out of her way as she moved efficiently around the bed. "It's so unnerving."

"I know it is, but the more she says, the more she moves, the closer she is to waking up. And that's a good thing." She turned her attention to Dana. "Dana, you have to rein it in. You're getting too wild and crazy here. We can't have you thrashing around."

She tried to push Dana's arm gently downward to restrain her wrist. Dana flailed harder, striking the nurse in the chest with a loose fist, then grabbing at her scrub top. She rolled to her left side and tried to throw her right leg over the bed railing.

Lynda stepped closer. "Please don't restrain her. It only upsets her more."

"We can't have her throw herself out of bed."

"Dana," Lynda said, leaning down, putting her hand gently on her daughter's shoulder. "Dana, it's all right. You're all right. You have to quiet down, sweetheart."

"No, no, no, no," Dana responded, but with a softer voice. She was running out of steam, the brief burst of adrenaline waning.

Lynda leaned closer still and began to sing softly the song she had rocked her daughter to sleep with from the time she was a baby.

"Blackbird singing in the dead of night. Take these broken wings and learn to fly . . ."

The words touched her in a very different way than they had all those years ago. The song took on a very different meaning. Dana was the broken bird. She would have to learn to fly all over again. She would have to rise from tragedy, and Lynda was the one waiting for that moment to arrive.

Tears rose in her eyes. Her voice trembled as she sang. She touched Dana's swollen cheek in a place that wasn't black-and-blue. She touched the pad of her thumb ever so softly to her daughter's lips.

Dana let go a sigh and stilled. Slowly her left eye opened—just a slit, just enough that Lynda could see the blue. She was afraid to move, afraid to take a breath lest she break the spell. Her heart was pounding.

"Welcome back, sweetheart," she murmured.

The blue eye blinked slowly in a sea of blood red where the white should have been. Then Dana drew a breath and spoke three words that shattered her mother's heart like a piece of blown glass thrown to the floor.

"Who . . . are . . . you?"

2

Pieces of cheap jewelry. Locks of hair bound with tiny rubber bands. Human teeth. Fingernail clippings painted in confetti colors.

Nikki Liska looked through the photographs of the suspicious items found in the home and vehicles of Frank Fitzgerald—aka Frank Fitzpatrick, Gerald Fitzgerald, Gerald Fitzpatrick, Frank Gerald, Gerald Franks, and a couple of other names, according to the driver's licenses and credit cards they had found. The cops called him Doc Holiday.

Law enforcement agencies had attached him to nine victims in various states in the Midwest, four in the metro area alone. The supposed trophies from his victims indicated the victim count could be much higher. He had traveled the highways in a box truck for years, collecting antiques and junk for resale and kidnapping young women. He took them in one city, tortured them for days, and dumped their bodies in another state, another jurisdiction, complicating any investigation.

He had been too good at getting away with his crimes for law enforcement to believe murder was new to him. Men in their forties didn't wake up one day as sexual sadists and start killing women. The seeds for that behavior were planted early on, were nurtured and festered for years. Aberrant behavior began small—porn, window peeping, panty sniffing—and escalated over the years. The first kill usually happened in the man's twenties or early thirties. Doc Holiday had been thirty-eight when Dana Nolan buried a screwdriver through his temple and into his brain.

The items in the photographs were almost certainly trophies, remembrances of the kill. Something he could hold and look at and relive the crime. Sick bastard.

Nikki stared at the picture of the nail clippings—some long, some short, some acrylic, some with what looked like the dried remains of blood on the underside.

"That's just disgustingly weird," she said.

"Hmm?" Kovac asked, pulling his attention away from the wall-mounted television where the travel channel was beckoning viewers to explore winter in Sweden. No one else in the hospital lounge was paying any attention.

"We live in Minnesota," Nikki said, looking up at the screen. "Why the hell would we go to Sweden in the winter?"

"They have a hotel made entirely of ice," Kovac said. "Even the beds are made of ice."

"That's not a selling point for me."

"What are you looking at?"

"The nail clippings. That's so creepy."

"Doesn't beat suncatchers made of tattooed human skin."

They had seen that once, too. The killer had cut the victims' tattoos off their bodies and stretched the hide on little hoops to dry, then hung them in a window in his home.

"True," Nikki conceded. "But still."

"The teeth creep me out," Kovac said. "Sick fuck. I hope the lab can pull DNA out of them."

Kovac always looked like he hadn't slept in a night or two—a little rumpled, a little bleary-eyed. Harrison Ford after a three-day bender. His salt-and-pepper hair was thick and stood up like the pelt of a bear. He had ten years and half a lifetime of homicides on her.

"You think we'll ever know how many girls he really killed?" she asked.

He shook his head. "No. But maybe we'll get to identify a few more."

Like that was a good thing, Nikki thought, being able to call more parents and tell them their daughters weren't missing anymore because they had been abducted, tortured, raped, and murdered by a serial killer. How many times had she imagined what it would be like to be the parent on the receiving end of a call like that? Every case. Every single case.

She thought of her boys: Kyle, fifteen, and R.J., thirteen. She loved them so much she sometimes thought the enormity of that emotion would make her explode because she couldn't possibly contain it all within her. She was barely five feet five, but her love for her sons was the size of Montana and as strong as titanium. She would have taken on an army for them.

What if she answered the phone one day and the voice at the other end told her someone had beaten and strangled R.J. to death? She thought of Jeanne Reiser, the mother of their first Doc Holiday victim. Her grief and her pain had seemed to cut through time and space to reach all the way from Kansas like a lightning bolt over the phone lines.

What if someone called to tell her Kyle was in the hospital, clinging to life, the only known surviving victim of a sexual sadist? Nikki had been the first to speak to Dana Nolan's mother, Lynda Mercer. The split-second shocked silence on the other end of the line had seemed to Nikki as if the news had struck Lynda Mercer as hard as the hammer blow that had fractured her daughter's skull.

"If something like this ever happened to one of my boys . . . ," she said, shaking her head at the violent images that ran through it.

"I wouldn't want to be the guy who did it," Kovac said impassively.

She gave him a serious look. "I'd fucking kill him, Sam. You know I would. I'd kill him with my bare hands."

Kovac shrugged, his expression not changing at all. "I'll hold him down. You kick him."

"I wouldn't do it quick, either," she went on. "I'd beat every inch of his body with a steel rod, and slowly, slowly let his muscles break down from the lactic acid, and let his internal organs digest themselves in pancreatic fluid."

"Saw on him with a steak knife while you're waiting," he suggested. "And pour salt in the wounds."

"Fresh-ground sea salt," she said, glancing at a somber family having a quiet discussion at a table on the other side of the room. "Bigger granules take longer to dissolve and cut into raw tissue like ground glass."

Kovac raised an eyebrow. "You're perfecting this fantasy."

"Damn right," she said. "Someone messes with my kids, I'm going fifty shades of crazy all over them. And no one would ever find a trace of the perp. Not so much as a pubic hair."

"Fifty-five-gallon drum and forty gallons of sulfuric acid," Kovac suggested, using the remote control to scroll through the on-screen TV guide. "Mix the acid with concentrated hydrogen peroxide and make that piranha solution the ME told us about. That shit will dissolve anything.

"Do it at his house," he added matter-of-factly. "Seal the drum and leave it in the farthest corner of the basement. It could sit there for thirty years. No one would ever want to bother moving it."

They had probably had this conversation a couple of hundred times over the course of their partnership.

Nikki sighed and got up and wandered to the coffee machine. She was tired. She was tired of thinking terrible thoughts, but given what they had been working on since New Year's Eve, terrible thoughts were the norm. The abduction of Dana Nolan. The hunt for Doc Holiday. The gruesome murder of one of Kyle's school friends. And then, the discovery of Dana Nolan and the captor she had killed.

Nikki would never forget the sight of the once-perky young newscaster as the paramedics went to load her into the bus. She was unrecognizable, her face battered, cut, bloody, and grotesquely swollen. Her would-be killer had drawn a huge red smile around her mouth, making her look like an evil clown from a macabre nightmare. A red ribbon fluttered from her mangled left hand. Drifting in and out of consciousness, she had babbled over and over, "I'm his masterpiece."

Nikki checked her watch as the coffeemaker sputtered and spewed more fuel into her cup. They had been waiting for nearly an hour. An hour and three weeks since Dana had been rushed to the hospital. It seemed like a year ago—and it seemed like she had been working every hour of that year. She was exhausted. She wanted to go home and hug her kids, put on sweatpants and a big old sweater, curl up on the couch with them, and watch some silly blow-'em-up boy movie.

"Let's step out," Kovac murmured, throwing his cup in the garbage. He tilted his head toward the family across the room. A doctor with a too-serious expression had joined them at the table and was speaking to them too softly for the news to be good. The mother of the family started to cry. Her husband put his arm around her and whispered something in her ear.

Nikki nodded. She slung her bag over her shoulder, took her coffee, and followed her partner into the hall.

A large window looked out onto the dim world of winter's dusk: the darkening ash-gray sky, bare trees, dirty snow, wet street lined with slush. A restaurant across the street far below them beckoned the hospital's weary, hungry, emotionally raw refugees with a red neon light: COMFORT FOOD CAFÉ.

Nikki set her coffee cup on the sill and crossed her arms against the chill coming off the glass, thinking, *I need to change my life. I can't stand all the bad anymore.* She and Kovac dealt every day in death and depravity. Even now, though they were here to see a victim who had survived, the experience would not be a happy one. Dana Nolan would not be who she had been before her abduction. She wouldn't look the same. Her injuries were devastating and disfiguring. No one could say with any certainty how debilitating—or how permanent—the brain damage would be. And psychologically, Dana Nolan was broken in a way doctors couldn't fix.

Nikki turned her back to the window and looked up at Sam, who stayed facing the gloom.

"You know she's not going to remember anything," she said. "Even if she can, why would she want to?"

"We have to try," Kovac said. "Rutten said there's no way to know exactly what she'll remember and what she won't. Maybe something in one of these pictures will strike a chord. Maybe the only thing she'll remember is Fitzgerald telling her the names of his other victims.

"If you had a daughter missing, you'd want the cops to ask her," he said. "You'd beg Lynda Mercer to let you talk to Dana. There are families out there who need to know what happened to their girls."

"I know. You're right. If I was the mother of a missing girl, I'd do anything to find out what happened," Nikki said. "But if I was the mother of a daughter who had been tortured and brutalized and nearly killed, I'd do whatever I could to protect her."

"Dana is the lucky one," Sam said. "As fucked-up as that may be."

"That's about as fucked-up as it gets."

He studied her face for a moment. He knew her as well as anyone. Better.

"Look, I'd send you home to the boys and do this myself. But there's a good chance she isn't going to want anything to do with a man."

"It's okay," Nikki said, dodging his eyes. "I'm fine."

Kovac drew a long breath and let go a longer sigh.

He knew what she was thinking, and he knew why. After all these years, she was going to transfer out of Homicide. They had already had the discussion . . . over and over. She needed better hours and more time with the boys. She loved her job. She was good at her job. But her first job was to raise her sons. She knew too well that the time for that could be gone in a heartbeat.

"We need to do this soon," Kovac said. "Before she ships off to rehab in Indiana."

Although Dana had regained consciousness two weeks past and was reportedly doing well in relation to the things that had happened to her, Lynda Mercer had put them off again and again. Dana wasn't well enough to see anyone. Dana couldn't remain conscious or couldn't focus long enough to be asked questions. Communicating was exhausting for her. All of which was probably true, but excuses nonetheless.

It had been Nikki's job to crack the ice with Lynda, to impress upon her the necessity of their talking to Dana. Feeling like a traitor to the motherhood union, she had downplayed what they would be asking of Dana. All they wanted was for her to look at some snapshots of objects, see if she recognized any of them. What they really wanted was for that recognition to lead to a memory made during a traumatic event.

"Let's go check at the nurses' station," Kovac said. "If they're not ready for us by now, we'll come back in the morning."

"You're just trolling for a date," Nikki chided, bumping her partner with an elbow as they started down the hall, giving him a wry smile, trying to lighten the mood—hers as much as his.

"I've sworn off nurses," he growled. "They know too many ways to inflict pain."

DANA NOLAN WAS SITTING in a chair next to her hospital bed when they walked into the room, wearing a hospital gown and a hockey helmet. This was the first time Nikki had seen her conscious since the night they had found her near the Loring Park sculpture garden, her captor's van crashed into a light pole. Nikki had kept in touch with Dana's mother, stopping in at the hospital every few days to check on Dana's progress and to offer Lynda Mercer a little kindness from one mother to another.

Nikki had dealt before with victims who had suffered brain injuries. The process from coma to consciousness was arduous and unpredictable. Patients came up from the depths like deep-sea divers—slowly, stalling now and again to adjust to the new pressure. They could remain submerged just below the surface, near enough to see but not to communicate, or they could bob in and out, for days or weeks, responding to stimuli, even speaking, but not fully waking up.

In the movies, the heroine always awoke from a coma as if from a wonderful long nap, with bright eyes and rosy cheeks and a full head of beautifully brushed long tresses. And the worst trauma she faced was deciding whether or not Channing Tatum was really her husband. Dana had a much longer road ahead of her.

Some of the swelling had finally left her face, but she looked nothing like the pretty young woman who had greeted the early-rising residents of the Twin Cities on the first local newscast of the day. Bandages still swathed her skull, and a patch covered her right eye. The bruising in her face had faded from black to blue to a red-purple surrounded by a sickly shade of yellow. The cheekbone on the right side of her face appeared to be sinking. The right corner of her mouth drooped downward in a constant frown. Stitches marred her face like train tracks on a map.

"Sorry we kept you waiting," Lynda Mercer said, mustering a brittle smile.

She fussed with the thin white blanket covering her daughter's lap and legs, tucking it in around her, her movements quick and nervous. A pretty, petite woman in her late forties, she seemed to have aged years since she had arrived in Minneapolis the day of her daughter's abduction. She had lost weight. Her hair was dull, her face drawn, her skin sallow. Her blue eyes had a haunted quality Nikki could only imagine had come not only from worry for her daughter's recovery, but also from the inevitable thoughts of what had been done to her child. And now she and Kovac would ask to open the door on Dana's memory of that torture.

"Dana was pretty tired after her speech therapy this afternoon," Lynda said. "Weren't you, sweetheart?"

"Mom . . . don't." Dana tried to push her mother's hands away. Her movements were slow and as awkward as a drunk's. She fixed her one good eye on Nikki.

"Dana, this is Detective Liska," Lynda said. "Remember I told you she would be coming to see you? To talk about your accident."

Nikki traded a quick look with Sam. *Accident?* She stepped a little closer while Sam hung back.

"No," Dana said.

"Hi, Dana. It's good to see you awake. How are you feeling?"

The young woman looked at her with suspicion. "I don't . . . think you. Think?" Her eye narrowed as she searched for the word she wanted. "I don't . . ."

"Know," Lynda said.

Dana frowned. "I don't know you."

Her speech was labored and slightly slurred, as if pulled down and held back by the drooping corner of her mouth.

"Dana gets frustrated with her speech deficiencies, but Dr. Rutten says this type of aphasia is normal for someone with a brain injury," Lynda chattered. She couldn't seem to be still. She moved around like a sparrow darting from one branch to another.

"He said the brain is like a filing cabinet. And Dana's has been turned upside down and all the files have fallen out on the floor. It's hard for her to find the right file or to know what files should go where," she explained. "Sometimes she can't find the right word, but she can find a word close to what she means. Anomia, the speech therapist calls it."

"That has to be tough," Nikki said. "Especially for someone who uses words for a living."

"She's always been so articulate," Lynda said. "She won speech competitions in school. She was on the—"

"Don't talk . . . a-bout me," Dana said firmly, "l-ike I'm not where."

"Here," Lynda corrected.

"I'm sorry, Dana," Nikki said, taking a seat across from her. "I'm here to talk to you, not about you. Me and my partner, Sam."

The girl looked past Nikki's shoulder, squinting at Sam.

"Hi, Dana," he said. "Is it all right with you if I come in and sit down?"

She didn't answer right away.

"It's all right, sweetheart," Lynda said as she pulled up another chair. "Policemen are good."

Dana sighed impatiently. "I'm not a little . . . killed? K-illed?" She didn't like the word, though she seemed not to understand why. Her respiration picked up. Her right hand squeezed and released on the arm of her chair. "Not killed. No. No."

"Child," Lynda supplied.

"K-Kid," Dana said, scowling. "I'm not a . . . lit-tle kid. Stop treat-ting me like it."

Lynda's eyes filled with tears. The tip of her nose turned red. "I'm sorry, sweetheart. I'm only trying to help."

Dana pounded her hand down on the arm of her chair. "Stop! Stop it!"

"Please calm down," Lynda pleaded.

"I'm not . . . stu—stu-por. Stu . . . pid. I'm . . . not stupid!"

Lynda knelt down at her daughter's feet to beg forgiveness. "No, of course not, Dana. I don't think you're stupid. Please calm down. You don't need to get upset."

Dana clenched and unclenched her right hand. She was breathing hard and turning red beneath the bruises.

"I've watched you on television, Dana," Sam said, taking a seat, distracting her.

"I . . . don't know . . . wh-why," Dana said flatly.

"She's having a little trouble with her memory," Lynda said, stating the obvious. She hovered and fussed around her daughter like a new mother whose baby was just learning to walk. She wanted to catch every fall, to spare her child failure or injury.

"That's okay," Sam said to Dana. "You don't need to think about that right now."

"No. N-ot," Dana said, moving her head slightly left and right, hindered by the brace around her neck. Still agitated, she pushed her blanket off onto the floor. "Not o-kay. It's not o-kay."

"It'll all come back to you, sweetheart," Lynda said, picking up the blanket. "It's just going to take some time."

Her false cheer was almost as hard to listen to as nails on a chalkboard. Nikki's own level of tension ratcheted up as Dana waved away her mother's attempts to put the blanket back on her lap.

"Don't!" Dana snapped.

"Your friends from the station are going to bring some DVDs of you on the news," Lynda said, still talking to her as if she was a five-year-old. "Remember? Remember Roxanne told you she would do that? That'll be fun to see, won't it?"

"N-no. Stop it." Dana turned her face away, reached up with her good hand, tore the neck brace off, and threw it on the floor.

"Dana . . ."

"Lyn-da . . ."

Nikki reached down to retrieve the brace.

"She hates this thing," Lynda said, taking it. "She doesn't want anything around her throat."

Nikki looked at the bruising that circled Dana Nolan's throat.

She had been strangled—repeatedly, by the look of it. No doubt a game for Doc Holiday—choking her unconscious, then letting her come back, watching her "die" over and over, feeling the rush of godlike power as she came back to life. He hadn't intended for her to die of it. If Doc Holiday had wanted her dead, she would have been dead. Anything he had done to her had been just a game to satisfy his sick, sadistic fantasies.

"I don't like things around my throat either," Nikki said. "I don't even like turtlenecks."

"She's tired," Lynda said curtly, though she was clearly as close to the end of her rope as her daughter was. "We should probably just call it a day."

"Let's have Dana take a quick look at those photos first," Kovac suggested. "Then we can get out of your hair."

"I don't have any," Dana said without emotion. "Hair."

"Your hair will grow back, honey," Lynda said. "You'll be just as beautiful as before."

Nikki almost winced. She wondered if Dana had been allowed to look at herself in a mirror. She suspected not.

"We just want you to take a look at each of these photographs, Dana," she said, pulling the pictures out of her bag. "And tell us if anything looks familiar to you."

She shuffled the images of human teeth and fingernail clippings to the bottom of the stack in favor of the snapshots of individual pieces of jewelry, starting with a silver bracelet dangling with charms.

Dana took the picture with her good hand and frowned at it.

"Does that look familiar to you?" Nikki asked.

Dana stared at it. "N-no."

Nikki handed over another, this one of a necklace with a small cross.

Again Dana stared at the photograph, frowning, suspicious. Her respiration quickened ever so slightly. "N-n-no. Wh . . . why?"

"We're just wondering if you may have seen these things before," Kovac said, ignoring her question.

She turned her eye on him. "What's it . . . to do with my . . . accident?"

Kovac flicked a glance at Lynda Mercer.

"I think you should go now," she said stiffly. "Dana needs to rest."

"No," Dana said.

"Dana—"

"Lyn-da . . . No," she said again. She reached out her good hand toward Nikki for another photograph.

Nikki hesitated. Dana didn't know. Her mother hadn't told her that she had been abducted, that she had been tortured and raped by a serial killer. She knew she had been in a car accident. That was all. As a mother, Nikki knew she would have been tempted to do the same. As a cop, she had to hand over the next photograph: a necklace. A delicate silver-filigree butterfly dangling from a fine chain.

Dana stared at the photograph.

Sam leaned a little closer, studying her face. "Does that look familiar to you?"

She continued to look down at the photo. "T-tell me . . . why."

"It's not important, sweetheart," Lynda said. "It doesn't matter. We don't have to do this now."

Dana gave her mother a long look, then turned back to Nikki. "W-w-why?"

Nikki took a deep breath. She could feel the ice of Lynda Mercer's gaze . . . and the calm, steady heat of Kovac's. "It has to do with the other person who was in the accident," she said.

"I don't know . . ."

"You didn't know him, sweetheart," Lynda said impatiently. She went to reach for the photographs. Dana clutched them against her body.

"You're tired," Lynda said. "We can do this another time. It's not important. Let's get you into bed."

She started to reach out toward her daughter. Dana stopped her with three words: "You are . . . ly-ing."

"Dana . . ."

"Stop ly-ing to me!" Dana said loudly, struggling more with the words as she became more agitated. "What are th-ese things?" she asked Nikki, holding up the photographs.

Lynda grabbed them out of her daughter's hand. "That's enough. We're done with this."

She flung the pictures in Sam's direction and pointed toward the door. "Get out."

"Lynda," Nikki started, getting to her feet.

"How dare you?" Lynda Mercer hissed, turning on her, her face growing red, her eyes bright with tears. "How dare you?"

"Mrs. Mercer," Sam began, getting to his feet.

"T-t-tell m-m-me!" Dana shouted. Her upper body began to jerk slightly, forward and back. "T-t-t-tell t-t-t-te-ll me who h-h-e-e w-was!"

Nikki went to move toward her, to tell her to calm down, to tell her that there was no reason for her to get upset. The photographs were of some worthless trinkets she had probably never seen, and it didn't really matter if she had. No girls were going to rise from the dead because Dana Nolan had seen photographs of jewelry kept as souvenirs by a killer.

Suddenly Dana's head snapped back, her visible eye rolling back as her body went stiff. She seemed to fling herself from the chair to the ground, shaking violently.

"*Oh my God!*" Lynda shrieked.

"She's seizing!" Nikki yelled, dropping to her knees, grabbing hold of Dana Nolan's shoulders.

Kovac bolted for the door, calling for help.

Dana's body bucked and strained against Nikki's hold.

Lynda Mercer flung herself to the floor, striking out, shouting, and sobbing, "Get away from her! Leave her alone!"

Nurses rushed into the room, their focus on Dana. Lynda was pulled away to one side, Nikki shoved to the other. Then Kovac was behind her, seeming to hold her up with his hands clamped around her upper arms. As he drew her backward, the chaos swirled before her in a blur of blue scrubs and Dana's violently jerking body and Lynda Mercer's face as she cried out her daughter's name, the hate in the woman's eyes as she looked at them, screaming, "*You did this! You did this!*"

Sam pulled her out into the hall. She jerked away from him. "We did that!" she said, pointing at the room. "We did that!"

Kovac grabbed hold of her again, his face dark. "Stop it! We did not," he argued. "We showed her pictures of jewelry and asked her if she'd seen it before. We did not cause her to have a seizure."

"Would she have had a seizure if we hadn't come here?"

"The girl has a traumatic head injury, Tinks. People with head injuries have seizures. Besides, she wasn't upset with us. She was upset with her mother."

"You can't blame her mother for trying to protect her."

"I'm not blaming anyone for anything. I'm stating the facts. Lynda Mercer agreed to have us come and do this."

"Because I bullied her into it," Nikki said.

"You're not the bad guy here, Tinks. There is no bad guy. No," he corrected himself. He let go of her arms and stepped back, plowing his fingers through his hair.

"Doc Holiday is the bad guy," he said, calmer. "Let's not lose sight of that. We only came here to try to close the door on some of the misery he caused. I'm sorry Mrs. Mercer got upset. I'm sorry we didn't approach the conversation a little differently. I'm sorry this ever happened to that poor girl. Am I sorry enough?" he asked without sarcasm.

Nikki sighed. The truth of the matter was that there was no good to come of it all, no matter which way they played it.

"Don't be a martyr, Tinker Bell," Kovac said softly. "Life is hard enough."

Drained and exhausted, Nikki nodded. She glanced across the hall to the open door of Dana Nolan's room. The activity within had quieted. The seizure had passed or been subdued by drugs.

"No matter how bad her mother wants to protect her from the truth, she's going to find out," Kovac said. "Her friends know. She's going to ask them. Hell, the whole damn country knows. *Dateline* is going to be calling; *48 Hours* is going to come knocking. Every newsie vulture in America has already called our office."

"Tragedy," Nikki said. "The gift that keeps on giving."

"People eat that shit up with a spoon," Kovac said. "And the world keeps on turning."

"Survival of the fittest."

"Evolution is a bitch. And we're all caught in her teeth."

Nikki could feel the truth of that statement. She felt like she'd been mauled. She could only imagine how Lynda Mercer felt.

"We have to forgive ourselves, Tinks. Nobody else will."

She nodded and gave him a sorry excuse for a smile. "I guess that means I have to ask *you* for a hug."

"Oh, Jesus Christ," he grumbled, even as he took a step toward her and opened his arms.

Tears welled in Nikki's eyes as an overwhelming wave of sadness washed over her. She leaned into him, keeping her head down. She would pretend she wasn't crying. And he would pretend he didn't know that she was.

"Let's get you home, Tinker Bell," he said. "You need to hug your kids."

3

Dana drifted in and out of the shallowest depths of sleep. The sounds of the hospital had gone soft and hushed. The only light in the room was a soft blue-white glow that came from somewhere behind the bed and drifted across the room like fog to reveal the shadowed shapes of furniture.

She liked this time of day best. No one was poking or prodding her. She could relax without the pressure of her mother's eyes and expectations on her.

But even now there was a level of anxiety humming like an idling motor in the pit of her stomach. She didn't know why. No one wanted to tell her why. Everyone became anxious when she asked. They turned their eyes away when they answered. She didn't need to know now, they told her. She needed to heal. She needed to get stronger.

Her conclusion was that someone had died in the accident and no one wanted to tell her.

What if it was me?

What if she was dead? What if this was how a person passed from one life to the next? Maybe this was purgatory. Maybe she was in this painful state of limbo because she had caused someone else to die. If only she could remember.

She felt like her skull was a bucket full of holes, with memories running out like water, and she had nothing to catch them in. It seemed what remained in her memory was a collection of weird, random things, and she trusted none of them.

She knew Lynda was her mother. She had been told so. But the memories of family were dreamlike things concealed in shadow. Her childhood was just a jumble of scenes tangled together like a snarl of yarn.

She had had a career. People she worked with came to the hospital to see her. She knew them but she didn't. It was like meeting an acquaintance in an unexpected place. Her frame of reference was gone. The face seemed familiar, but she didn't quite understand why. She couldn't quite grab their names from her memory, just like she couldn't always find the words she needed to convey a thought.

The frustration of that was enormous and exhausting. She had no patience for her fumbling brain. She had no patience for anything. Every day in physical therapy she lost her temper for being clumsy and slow.

Everyone excused her. Everyone told her it was all right to fail. Everyone told her it would all come back to her, everything—her memory, her coordination, her personality, her sense of self. She hoped so, because not knowing the people who came to visit her was nothing compared to not knowing who she really was.

She had only pieces of an incomplete puzzle and couldn't yet see what the finished picture should look like. And every day, every moment of trying to put those pieces together, left every cell of her being drained and exhausted.

And yet now she couldn't sleep. Something had happened earlier. She remembered the police detectives. That memory stuck with her because she hadn't understood why they had been there. She remembered Lynda getting upset. She could still feel the residual vibrations of her own anger with her mother, though the cause of that anger eluded her. Then nothing.

She had lost time. She lay awake now in her hospital bed with mesh netting on either side of it reaching to the ceiling to catch her if she tried to climb out or fell in the night.

Her mother had fallen asleep in the reclining chair beside the bed. Dana stared at her, wondering if she would ever fully remember the life they had shared.

The lack of memory left her feeling alone and adrift on a dark sea of nothingness. The void's gentle waves finally lulled her to sleep. And as she slept, she dreamed of delicate pieces of jewelry floating in the air. And beyond the glittering objects she saw the faces of dead girls she had never known.

4

October
The Weidman Recovery Center
Indianapolis, Indiana

Dana woke as she always did: panting, drenched in sweat, her heart pounding in her chest; confused, and afraid of something she couldn't remember—a dream, a nightmare, a memory of the ordeal she had been through months earlier? She didn't know. All that remained was the emotional waste—fear, anxiety, apprehension. Without moving, she looked to one side and then the other of the dimly lit room to see if she was alone. She saw no one.

The world was dark beyond her window, but forty watts of amber security glowed on an end table in the corner, next to her chair. Beside the lamp was the book she had been trying to read for the past three weeks. She tried to read it before she went to bed at night when she was exhausted and her brain was full of fog, and she had to reread and reread to get the words to penetrate and make sense.

Had she tried to read the book last night? She wondered as she sat up and propped herself against the headboard. Had she slept a few hours or a few weeks? Was it a bad dream that chased her from her sleep, or a memory forever shrouded in a black shadow?

The questions and all the possible answers brought a flood of emotions. Fear, panic, grief, and anger came all at once, like a rushing wave inside her head.

That was in fact what the doctors called it: flooding. A tsunami of emotions that crashed through the injured brain, short-circuiting logic and the careful strategies the brain-injured person worked on every day in the attempt to put her life back on some kind of simple track.

Dana knew she had to stem the tide. She grabbed her four-by-six note cards off the nightstand and fumbled through them for the right one. As she found it, she called to mind Dr. Dewar's soothing voice:

1. *Breathe slowly, in through the nose and out through the mouth.*
2. *Concentrate on the mechanics of filling your lungs. Hold the breath for two beats, then exhale slowly. Four beats in, four beats out.*
3. *Work to find the connection between the mind and the body. Feel the energy in your toes, slowly moving up your legs. Move your fingers. Feel the energy slowly move up through your arms . . .*

If she could stay focused on the exercise, she could keep at bay the flood and all the debris that came with it. Sometimes she succeeded in this. Sometimes she didn't. Sometimes the flood crashed over her, and she panicked and froze, couldn't breathe, couldn't think, couldn't move. This time the flood receded slowly, leaving her feeling weak from the effort of fighting it.

She had been told time and again during her stay here that the key to success in dealing with her issues was all a matter of routine. If she could consistently repeat the routines of each day, the thoughts and actions would become automatic and she wouldn't feel so fatigued from having to remember every detail of every task.

She looked at the digital clock on the nightstand: 3:17 A.M. Shuffling through her note cards, she found the one she wanted, and she read through the same list of questions she asked herself every morning to establish her routine.

Where am I?
In my room.

Where is my room?
The Weidman Recovery Center.

Where is the Weidman Center?
Indianapolis.

Why am I here?
Because I have a traumatic brain injury.

Who am I?
Dana Nolan.

Who is Dana Nolan?

The last question wasn't on the card, but she asked it anyway. She wished she could answer with something other than the adjectives other people had given to her—sweet, bubbly, friendly, kind, helpful, sunny, always smiling, always laughing, perky, pretty.

Those words might have applied to her former self—"Before" Dana—but she felt none of them applied to her present self—"After" Dana. Her memories of the Dana Nolan other people described seemed like clips from a movie passing through her mind. In them, Dana Nolan was a character played by an actress, and Dana herself was just an observer watching the show, wondering if that actress was anything like what the tabloids wrote about her.

There was a strange disconnection between the person in the memories and the person she was now that was impossible to explain to anyone who hadn't experienced it. She couldn't describe it to the friends and family of that former self, the people who had come to visit during her months here at the center—some of whom she didn't remember from her past life at all. She could remember them now because she had their photographs in her iPhone along with a description of who they were and how she had known them, the last time she had seen them, key subjects they had spoken about.

They seemed hurt by her lack of ability to recognize them, as if she had a choice in the matter, as if she was deliberately snubbing them just to be a bitch.

Several of the people she had known and worked with in Minneapolis had come to visit once, then never again. They had come with a cheery, party attitude, bringing DVDs of their days in the newsroom with footage of Dana doing her job, of the staff at parties, things they wanted her to remember. But seeing her former self on television served only to upset her. She didn't remember being that girl. She didn't remember being happy and sweet. And she certainly didn't feel any connection to the pretty face with the sunny smile.

The pressure of her coworkers' expectations and their disappointment in her reaction to them had been too much for her. The emotional tidal wave had rolled over her, and she had become panic-stricken and violent, throwing things and shouting at them to leave.

They hadn't returned. Her mother, ever the diplomat trying to smooth over the jagged edges, had told her it was the distance that deterred them. Minneapolis was a long way away from Indianapolis. When Dana countered with the fact that airplanes regularly flew between the two places, her mother changed tacks to the fact that people in the news business were very busy and couldn't get away as much as they liked.

"We hardly saw you after you moved to Minneapolis," she pointed out. "You were so busy! Remember?"

No. She didn't remember. And that was the whole point, wasn't it? If she didn't remember those people, why should they remember her? They would rather stay in Minneapolis with the memories of Before Dana, the Dana Nolan they had known, than deal with the reality of After Dana, the Dana Nolan she was now.

Dana wished she had that choice. Or, if not that choice, then at least the ability to make them understand what it was like to live inside her head. But not even the doctors who worked with brain-injured people every day could truly get what that was like.

Tired of thinking about it, Dana pushed the covers back and got out of bed. Stiffness and aches growled and barked through her body like a pack of angry dogs. The fractures and lacerations and contusions had all healed, but their aftereffects remained. In particular her right knee and the once-mangled fingers of her left hand remembered what had been done to them even if Dana's brain didn't.

She went into the bathroom, turned on the shower, and climbed in under the hot water, remembering too late that she was supposed to take her clothes off first. She peeled off her now-sodden T-shirt and flannel boxer shorts and dropped them in a heap that immediately acted as a plug over the drain. The water began pooling around her feet as she shampooed her short hair, then washed herself, then shampooed her hair again, then washed herself. She rinsed and repeated not because the shampoo bottle said to, but because she didn't remember she had already done it.

Her thoughts were elsewhere. She was going home today.

The wet clothes were forgotten as she left the shower stall and went to the sink. The notes on the mirror told her to towel herself off, reminded her to brush her teeth, to comb her hair. Dana didn't look at the notes. Her attention was on the dripping-wet stranger staring back at her.

The first time she had been allowed to look at herself in a mirror after waking up from the coma, she had not been able to comprehend that she was seeing an image of herself. She didn't remember knowing anyone who looked like this. The face staring back at her was something from a nightmare or a zombie movie.

The right side of the bald skull was flat and pitched like the angle of a roof, a huge section of bone having been temporarily removed to alleviate the pressure on her swelling brain. The face was bruised and cut and stitched back together like an abused rag doll. The features seemed misshapen and asymmetrical. The right eye was covered with a patch.

Confused, Dana had stared at the creature in the mirror for a long while without saying anything. She looked from the unrecognizable face to her mother's worried reflection peering over its shoulder. But her mother was standing behind *her* with her hands on Dana's shoulders. It didn't make any sense. How could she be behind two people at once?

Slowly Dana had reached up and touched her mother's hand, felt the brush of fingers over fingers, skin on skin. She stared at the mirror, watching the image in the mirror mimic her movements exactly. Just as slowly, she lifted her hand away from her shoulder and reached toward the mirror. The monster in the mirror reached out toward her. Her fingertips touched the cold glass and the fingertips of the image at the same time.

Panic grasped her by the throat as realization dawned. She was looking at herself. The horror-movie image in the mirror was her own reflection. And she began to scream and scream and scream.

She didn't scream now as she stared at herself in the glass. She just stood there stiffly, staring as water dripped from the ends of her boy-short blond hair. This was what she looked like now. Just as her friends had been unable to recognize the personality that now occupied her brain, she was still unable to recognize the face that now masked the front of that brain.

The doctors, the nurses, the friends, the family—all told her not to be too upset, that there was still much healing to be done, that the plastic surgeons still had work to do. She would be as good as new, eventually, they told her. They said it so frequently and so emphatically, Dana knew it had to be a lie. The truth was never that hard to sell.

She reached out and swiped the gathering fog off the mirror with her hand, clearing a swatch of harsh reality.

Her right orbital had been shattered, and the cheekbone along with it. An implant had restored the cheek in order to give a foundation for the damaged eye area, but the eye drooped slightly, nevertheless, pulling from the brow bone down, making it look like that part of her face might have started to melt from the inside out. A madman's knife had carved a curved outline around the apple of her left cheek, gouging deep below the cheekbone, slicing flesh and muscle. A marionette line hooked downward from the right corner of her mouth.

Picasso couldn't have done a better job of distorting the female countenance.

Masterpiece. A voice whispered the word through her mind every time she stared at this reflection. *Masterpiece.* And every time she heard it, a fist of fear squeezed her heart.

She swiped a hand across the mirror again, wiping too low to again reveal the reflection of her face. Instead, in the spotlighted area of glass, framed by obscuring fog, was what she had come to call the Mark of the Devil. No matter how many times she looked at it, her heart's immediate reaction was always one big thump.

The number 9 had been carved in the center of her chest, from the base of her collarbone to the midpoint between her breasts. The number had a quality as sinister as the dark voice that drifted through her mind. Coiled like a snake at the top, the number's tail appeared to flick and twitch when she moved.

It must have looked shocking when she had been brought to the emergency room, a garish open wound, dripping blood. From a distance it had probably looked as if it had been hastily painted on her pale, delicate skin by a messy graffiti artist. Healed, the scar was raised and deep red and weirdly smooth to the touch. She touched it now, traced it with her fingertips.

Masterpiece.

She should have been dead. She should have been the ninth victim of a serial killer. But she had survived.

Why? For what?

To start her life all over again as someone she didn't know.

The mirror had fogged over again, and Dana realized the air in the bathroom had become a suffocating cloud of moisture. Water pooled around her feet. She looked down, confused, then turned toward the shower stall. She had left the water running. Suddenly she was aware of the sound of it like a pounding-hard rain. She had left her wet clothes to plug the drain. The room was flooding.

She knew the feeling.

"SO TODAY'S THE DAY. You're going home," Dr. Dewar said. "How are you feeling about that, Dana?"

"Great," Dana said without emotion, knowing her neuropsychologist would not be satisfied with her answer.

"Would you like to elaborate on that?"

"No."

Janelle Dewar sighed. She was a woman on the downside of middle age with a softly rounded figure always draped in flowing skirts and tunic tops and adorned with chunky art-fair jewelry. Her shoulder-length brown hair was thick and liberally threaded with gray. She was a kind, practical woman with the patience of a saint.

She had been working with brain-injured people her entire medical career. Nothing surprised her. Nothing threw her for a loop. She never judged. She never told patients they shouldn't feel one way or another. She was a rock, an anchor for people whose brains were pulling and pushing their emotions in all directions.

The idea of leaving Dr. Dewar and not having her steadying influence day in and day out terrified Dana. But what good would it do her to elaborate on that? It was time for her to leave the Weidman Center. That was that.

They sat in Dr. Dewar's cozy conference room—Dana, Dr. Dewar, and Lynda. Dr. Dewar preferred to call it her den, to give a less institutional impression, just as she preferred her patients to call her by her first name, so she seemed more like a friend than a physician. The office was furnished with comfortable oversize armchairs, a love seat, a coffee table. There were large, leafy plants near sliding glass doors that opened onto a small private garden courtyard.

Dana stared out the window. A steady, soft rain was falling from a drab gray sky. How did she feel about going home? She would be going back to the house she had grown up in. She felt like she would be expected to fit back into a life to which she no longer belonged. She worried her mother would expect her to fall into place like a missing puzzle piece, like nothing had ever happened or changed. But everything was different. Everything had changed.

She worried that people who had known her would look at her like she was a freak. She had been a story on the national news—the abducted newscaster, then the victim who killed the serial killer. People who had followed the story would know as many details about what she had endured as she did. How did she feel about going home to that? Apprehension and dread pressed down on her like an anvil.

"Dana?" Dr. Dewar prompted.

Dana pretended not to hear her.

Her mother tried to fill the awkward silence with awkward talk. "We're so excited to have Dana coming home. After everything she's been through, after all her hard work here, we'll finally have some time to be a family again, just be together, maybe take a vacation somewhere warm. It's a new beginning."

Under the sugary enthusiasm, her mother had to be as anxious as Dana was. Dana could hear the edge of it in her mother's voice. She could smell it beneath the cloying layer of perfume her mother had put on to mask any nervous perspiration. Lynda would be taking home her daughter, a virtual stranger.

"It *is* a new beginning," Dr. Dewar said. "And, as exciting as that may be, it's normal to also be a little apprehensive about this transition," she reminded them. "For both of you. There's going to be a period of adjustment. Don't make the mistake of setting unrealistic expectations. Don't put yourselves under that kind of pressure."

"No," Dana's mother said. "No pressure. No pressure at all. We'll take everything a day at a time. I just want to keep a positive outlook. We could have lost her. We're so lucky to still have her—"

"Don't talk about me like I can't hear you," Dana said.

"I'm not talking about you like you can't hear me. I'm telling Dr. Dewar how I feel," her mother said. "You can do the same. If you chose to participate, you wouldn't feel left out."

In her mind, Dana frowned, though it was doubtful anyone noticed. Her face had been carved into a permanent frown.

"I'm just saying I feel lucky to have you alive and with us," her mother said. "How do you feel?"

"I feel so lucky," Dana said so flatly that her answer was probably construed as sarcasm, though she wasn't sure if that was how she had meant it or not.

Her mother looked away, upset.

Dr. Dewar broke the tension. "Dana, what are you going to do each day when you get home?"

Dana felt herself freeze for a second as the answer eluded her. She felt ambushed. No one had told her there would be a quiz.

"Breathe," the doctor said softly.

Dana drew a breath and let it go.

"What are you going to do each day when you get home?"

"The same things I do here," Dana said. "Follow my routines. Implement my strategies."

"I've spoken at length with Dr. Burnette," Dr. Dewar said. "Do you remember who that is, Dana?"

Dana concentrated on her phone, clicking through a series of commands, bringing the name *Burnette, Dr. Roberta* up from her contacts list. She read aloud the note she had made to go with the name. "Dr. Rob-erta Bur-nette is the thera-pist I will be working with when I get home. She received her under-grad-uate and doc-tor-ate degrees at Purdue Univer-sity."

It frustrated her that she still stumbled over multisyllabic words when reading aloud. She recognized and understood the words, but there was still a slight disconnect getting them translated from vi-sual recognition to speech. She looked up at Dr. Dewar to gauge her response.

The doctor arched an eyebrow, a smile tugging at one corner of her mouth. "Someone's been busy on the computer."

"I have," Dana said, missing the intended humor.

"Dana's always been a research fanatic," her mother said. "She was born to be a reporter."

"I'm glad you're back at it," Dr. Dewar said. "Curiosity is a great sign. It tells me you're making strides to overcome your adynamia. You're rediscovering your passion for something."

Dana said nothing. She had taken it as an assignment to find out about the new therapist. Research was work, not passion. Research was a strategy against being taken by surprise. But she kept that to herself. Adynamia—her apparent lack of motivation and enthusiasm—was her enemy. It was always the first topic of conversation in her evaluations, the stumbling block that impeded her from progressing toward normalcy.

Dana felt the words *adynamic* and *bored* should be considered interchangeable. Eight months into rehab, she was bored and list-less. As much as the frightened, apprehensive part of her wanted to cling to the routine and familiarity of this place, another part of her craved stimulus and wanted to move on to life beyond the walls of the Weidman Center. The internal conflict left her feeling impatient and irritable.

"Her office is only about half an hour from our house," her mother said. "I can run you down there and go do my errands—"

"I can drive myself," Dana said. "I have a car. I can drive a car."

Her mother frowned. "I don't think that's a good idea, sweetheart—"

Dana shot her a hard look. "I don't care what you think."

"Dana . . ."

"Lynda . . ."

"If the route isn't too complicated, it should be fine for Dana to drive herself," Dr. Dewar said.

"See?" Dana said.

Her mother frowned harder.

"Go together the first few times," Dewar said. "Then start with short drives close to home on your own."

"I'm definitely going with you to start," Lynda said firmly. "And that's the end of it."

"I'm not sixteen," Dana grumbled.

"No," Dr. Dewar said. "You're not sixteen. You have a brain injury. Cut your mother some slack. She needs to see that you can do things for yourself, Dana. That's only fair."

"I don't want to be fair," Dana said without emotion. "I want to be normal."

Her mother pressed a hand to her lips as tears welled up in her eyes. She looked away, out the window, not wanting to face the truth—that her daughter wasn't normal, that she might never be considered "normal" again.

"You have a new normal now," Dr. Dewar said. "And you'll build a new normal every day. You've got a mountain to climb—both of you. And you do that one step at a time. There will be many days when you feel you're taking one step forward only to fall three steps back. You just have to keep trying. That's all you can do. Use the tools we gave you here at the center, and do the best you can every day."

5

Dana was quiet as they started the long car ride home through the rolling southern Indiana countryside. The rain had stopped, but swollen gray clouds still crowded the sky. Fall was sweeping down from the north on a blustery wind. The grass was still a vibrant green, but shades of red and orange rippled through the trees. The leaves on the white birch trees fluttered like golden spangles as they passed.

For a while she tried to look out the window at the countryside, but the dips and turns in the road upset her equilibrium, and nausea forced her eyes forward. She fidgeted in her seat, tugging on the shoulder strap.

"How long until we get there?" she asked, hoping the answer would be sooner rather than later.

Her mother sighed. "About an hour and a half."

"Did I ask you that already?"

"That's okay, sweetie. I don't mind."

"I don't mean to keep asking the same thing over and over."

"I know you don't."

"I'm sure it's really annoying. I would be annoyed if I had to listen to someone ask the same questions over and over."

"It's all right, honey," her mother said. "I don't care if you ask the same question a million times."

"Of course, if someone asked me the same question over and over, I might not remember that they had asked already," Dana pointed out. "So I guess that's the bright side."

"That's one way of looking at it."

"I should write down in my phone what I already asked so I can check to make sure I haven't already asked it."

She pulled her iPhone out of the pouch of her oversize pink hoodie and flicked a finger across the screen to the notes icon and began to type.

QUESTIONS ASKED
3:17 PM   Q: How long 2 home?
A:

She couldn't remember the answer.

Frustrated, she heaved a sigh. She felt stupid, though she knew she wasn't. She was intelligent, had always been an A student and an overachiever. The fact that her short-term memory came and went didn't make her less intelligent. It just made her feel that way—which made her think other people would feel the same way about her. They would think of her as brain-damaged. They wouldn't want to be around her because the idea made them uncomfortable. Everyone had loved Before Dana. No one would have chosen After Dana.

"Why didn't Roger come today?" she asked.

She looked at her mother, gauged the beat of silence, the deep breath, the way her hands tightened and relaxed on the steering wheel.

"Did I ask you that already too?"

The forced little smile. "It's okay."

Dana looked down at her phone and typed.

3:26 PM   Q: Y didn't Rgr come 2 get me?

"Roger wanted to come today," her mother said, "but he had commitments."

ANSWER: He didn't want to.

"Then he didn't really want to come, did he?" Dana said without emotion. "If he really wanted to come, he wouldn't have made other plans, would he?"

"That's not true, Dana," her mother said. "Roger's running for reelection, and he's still running the business. He has a busy schedule that isn't always under his control. That doesn't mean you're not important to him."

"Just that other people are *more* important," Dana pointed out. "It doesn't matter. I don't like him anyway."

Her mother's jaw dropped. "Dana! That's not true!"

"Lynda! I'm pretty sure it is."

"You and Roger have always gotten along!"

"But I don't think I like him," Dana insisted.

"I don't know why you'd think that. You just don't remember; that's all. He's been like a father to you since you were fourteen. He's been there for everything since your dad died—your school activities, graduation, college, moving you to Minneapolis. You don't remember any of that?"

Dana shrugged. Her memories of Roger Mercer were as ady-namic as she was. They evoked no strong emotions in her. He was simply present in the pictures in her mind and the photographs on her phone. When she looked at those images, she couldn't say what she felt about him. But she knew she didn't like the man who had come to see her during her stay at the Weidman Center. He had shown up exactly once a month for a few hours on a Sunday. He had come out of duty and nothing else as far as Dana was concerned. He didn't know what to say to her. He didn't want to look at her. He grabbed any excuse to leave the room—a phone call, a coffee run, the men's room, to check on the baseball game on the television in the visitors' lounge. Maybe he had been close to Before Dana, but he wanted nothing to do with After Dana.

She supposed she couldn't blame him. She would have preferred Before Dana as well, but she didn't have a choice.

"You're just tired," her mother declared.

"Am I?"

"Like Dr. Dewar said: Leaving the center is a big step. It's a positive step, but it's stressful, too. You have a lot of emotions swirling around inside of you—good and bad."

"Not really," Dana lied. "I'm adynamic, remember? I don't have emotions."

If her mother was going to say something, she swallowed the words back and kept her eyes on the road. One of the emotions Dana had just denied having bit her in the conscience. Guilt.

She *was* tired, physically and mentally. She *did* feel the stress of taking this step. The Weidman Center was a safe place. Everybody knew her there. Everyone knew what to expect from her and of her. They were all used to looking at her. They didn't know Before Dana. People back home *only* knew Before Dana. The idea of introducing them to After Dana made her sick to her stomach.

What would people in the real world know about flooding or adynamia or any of the other strange storms that went on in the mind of someone who had been damaged the way she had been damaged? Nothing. The only people who could understand it were people who had gone through it—and the loved ones who had shared the experience.

Like her mother.

"I'm sorry," Dana murmured.

Her mother shook her head. Tears filled her eyes and choked her voice. "You don't have anything to be sorry for."

Dana slid down in her seat and stared at the road ahead, uncomfortable with the notion of having to deal with her mother's emotions as well as her own.

"How long before we get home?" she asked.

Her mother sighed. "About an hour . . ."

SHE COULD SEE THE sunlight hitting the surface of the water far above her, diluting instantly as it tried to penetrate the depths. She swam toward it. Up. Up. Kicking. Reaching. But something held her back like an unseen arm across her chest. It pulled on her from behind, slowing her down, drawing her backward away from the light and the air and freedom.

Her composure burst like a balloon within her, like her lungs exploding, flooding her with ice-cold panic. In the next instant she broke the surface of consciousness, literally throwing herself into the present. She cried out as she struggled against the hold of the seat belt and shoulder strap. Her arms flung out before her, hands clawing at the dashboard of a car.

"*No! No!*"

"Dana! Dana!" Her mother's voice shouted her name frantically as the car swerved to the shoulder and stopped hard. "Dana, it's all right! It's all right, sweetheart!"

Still not fully in the present, Dana batted away the hand that reached toward her. She sucked in air in great choking gulps. Her pulse roared in her ears.

"Calm down. Calm down," her mother said over and over, her voice trembling. "You're all right. It's all right. You're safe."

Dana thought her heart would gallop out of her chest like a runaway horse. She could smell her own fear in the cold sweat that drenched her clothing. Her mind scrambled for the list of things to do to calm herself.

Slow your breathing.
Be conscious of your pulse.
Take stock of your surroundings.

Slowly the world began to come into focus. She was in a car. It was daylight. The radio was playing softly. They sat on the side of a road that bordered a neighborhood on one side and a wooded field on the other.

"You're all right, sweetheart," her mother said again, reaching over to touch Dana's shoulder and stroke a hand down her arm. "You just had a bad dream. You're safe. We're almost home. You're all right."

She sounded as if she was trying to calm a panicked animal.

She is, Dana thought.

She shrugged off her mother's touch, irritated by it, irritated and embarrassed by the situation. She pulled her hood up, wanting to close herself off.

"You had a bad dream."

"Yes."

"It's over now. You're all right. We're almost home, sweetheart," her mother said, reaching out again to touch her.

Dana shied away, crowding herself against the car door, scowling. "Just go. Let's go. Don't make such a big deal."

Lynda sat back behind the wheel and sighed, then put the car in gear and eased back onto the road.

"Are things starting to look familiar?" she asked.

"I guess," Dana murmured, looking at the houses as they turned into a neighborhood.

Lovely brick houses of complementary styles sat on large landscaped lots. Pumpkins and mums and happy scarecrows decorated front steps and front yards. Ghosts of memories slipped through Dana's mind. She had been the little girl in pigtails riding her pink bike down the street. She had been the girl walking the dog, the teenager sitting with her friends on the park bench, talking fashion and boys. All that seemed like something from a movie, from someone else's life.

They turned onto a cul-de-sac lined with vehicles—three of them news vans wrapped in advertising for their stations, satellite dishes perched on the roofs.

"Oh no," Lynda muttered under her breath.

Dana felt her mother tense. It didn't occur to her why. It didn't occur to her that she would be considered news. She knew she had been a headline in Minneapolis in January, but she had spent the last nine months—her entire After Dana life—in hospitals living with medical staff and other brain-injured patients with little connection to or interest in the rest of the world.

Her attention was on the bouquet of pink balloons that adorned a copper mailbox at the end of the street. The house beyond that mailbox was home—a large brick house with blue shutters and interesting rooflines and a yard to showcase the talents of Mercer-Nolan Landscape Design.

They pulled into the driveway, drawing alongside a black Mercedes SUV with a red, white, and blue sticker in the back window: REELECT MERCER/STATE SENATE. The front door of the house swung open and Roger came out to meet them followed by a younger man Dana didn't recognize.

Roger looked like a man an ad agency would choose to star in a commercial for real estate or home insurance—tall, handsome, with dark hair swept back and Clark Kent glasses. His smile was broad and white. He came around the hood of the car and opened Dana's door.

"Welcome home, sweetheart!" he said cheerfully, leaning toward her. "How was your drive down?"

"I don't know," Dana said. She stared down at the clasp of her seat belt, momentarily stumped as to how to open it. "I wasn't there."

"She fell asleep," her mother qualified, reaching over the console with impatient hands to unfasten the belt.

"What are those people doing here?" Lynda snapped, her irritation directed at her husband. "They have no business being here now."

"I don't control the media, Lynda."

"How did they find out Dana was coming home?"

"I don't know," he answered with sarcasm. "Maybe a dozen pink balloons tied to the mailbox isn't a good way to keep a secret."

"Can you fight later?" Dana asked. "I want to get out of the car."

Roger offered her a hand to help her out of the vehicle. She straightened slowly as she got out, stiff and achy from the long ride, but she let go of Roger's hand quickly, nevertheless.

She cut a glance at the other man, who stood behind her stepfather. He looked to be in his thirties, with a blocky build and a doughy face. He was buttoned up and professional in a jacket and tie, his thin brown hair combed flat to his head. He stared at her with carefully concealed shock. Dana could see it in his eyes and instantly disliked him for it.

"Who is he?" she asked bluntly, tugging the edges of her hood forward.

Roger glanced over his shoulder. "Wesley Stevens. He's helping run my campaign."

"Why is he here?"

Roger forced a laugh. "So many questions!" He moved to hug her. "Welcome home, sweetheart."

Dana stepped back against the car, frowning. "You already said that. Don't touch me. I don't like to be touched."

His frown was fleeting, and he quickly turned around even as his eyes darted to the left, looking for witnesses. "I'm sorry, honey. I just want to give you a hug. I'm happy to have you home. We've missed you!"

"Then you should have come to visit me more," Dana said with simple logic.

"I wish I could have."

"How does it feel to have your stepdaughter home, Senator? How does it feel to be home, Dana?"

Dana turned toward the source of the questions. The reporter was standing at the end of the drive maybe a dozen feet behind her mother's car—a petite blonde with a professional smile that wavered badly as Dana faced her.

"How does it feel to be home?" she asked again.

Dana stared at her. They were about the same size. The reporter's hair was cut in a shoulder-length bob, just as Dana's had been before it had been shorn off in the hospital. Her blue wool blazer could have come straight from Dana's own closet.

Oh my God, I used to be her, she thought.

Beside the blonde stood her cameraman. The camera was rolling, sucking the moment of revelation in to spew it out to the home viewing audience of southern Indiana and northern Kentucky.

Dana felt rooted to the spot, unable to turn away. She wanted to disappear. She wanted to pull her hood over her face and vanish, but she couldn't seem to move.

A second reporter and a second cameraman appeared, and then a third pair.

They all seemed to speak at once, their questions coming in a wave of language rushing toward her even as her emotions began to flood her mind from within.

Dana, how are you?
How do you feel?
What—? Where—? How—? Who—?
Dana— Senator— Doc— Casey— Holiday— Grant— Senator— Dana— Mercer— Dana, Dana, Dana!

The words all ran together and tumbled over one another, ceasing to make any sense. Panic began to close a hand around her throat. And all the while she continued staring at the blond reporter—the girl who reminded her so much of herself, of who she had been. The young woman's features were so like hers—the shape of her face, the tip of her nose, the color of her hair. Her intent expression was so familiar it was as if Dana was somehow creating it, generating that intensity from her own emotion.

In a trick of her damaged brain, the girl became her. She wasn't a stranger who happened to look like her. She *was* Dana. She was Before Dana, and After Dana was suddenly staring into the face of her past.

Her whole body began to shake from its very core outward.

"Stop it," she said, so softly she wasn't even certain she had spoken out loud. Then the voice came stronger. "Stop it. Stop it!"

Without realizing what she was doing, she took a step forward, and then another, reaching out toward the image of herself.

"*Stop it! Stop it!*"

The faces of the reporters loomed larger, distorted, their mouths tearing open. Questions turned to screeching, discordant sound.

"*Stop it! Stop it!*" Dana shouted.

Like in her dream about the water, something caught her from behind, dragging her backward. A strong arm banded across her chest, pulling her back. Dana reacted on instinct, grabbing at the arm, fighting to pry it away. Her feet came off the ground as she was lifted and turned, and suddenly she was in her mother's arms and being turned again and pushed in the direction of the house.

Behind her she could hear a man's voice booming with authority. "That's enough, folks! Please! I'm sure you can understand this is family time. Senator Mercer's daughter is just out of the hospital. She's exhausted. She's overwhelmed."

"We're thrilled to have Dana home at last," Roger said loudly. "But please have some respect for our privacy."

Dana felt herself propelled through the front door into the foyer, her body on some kind of self-defense autopilot, moving to escape the mob even as her brain was still swimming in the noise and emotion.

Dana! Dana! Dana!

She twisted and turned and ran backward out of her mother's reach, banging into a hall table and knocking over a vase of fresh flowers. Water cascaded to the floor, splashing on the tile. The sound of crystal shattering seemed as loud as a bomb.

"Dana!" her mother shouted. "Calm down! Calm down!"

Dana shied sideways and ran into the powder room, yanking the door shut behind her, cutting off the sound and the motion and the madness. With trembling hands, she turned on the faucet, scooped up the water, and splashed it over her face. She repeated the process again and again, slopping the water down the front of her hoodie, all over the vanity, and onto the floor.

"Dana?" her mother called, tapping on the door. "Are you all right, sweetheart? Please open the door."

The question was absurd, Dana thought as she stood staring into the ornate gold-framed mirror above the vanity. Was she all right? Nothing was right, least of all her. She had just had a meltdown in front of news cameras. News cameras in the driveway of her home, where she was supposed to feel safe and secure.

Why did they care that she was home? Her newsworthiness should have died with the man who had victimized her.

Welcome home, she thought as she stared at herself in the mirror.

Her mother knocked again, harder. "Dana? Answer me!"

Forgetting to turn the faucet off or dry the water from her face, Dana stepped back and sat down on the toilet, her legs feeling like rubber beneath her as the adrenaline subsided.

The door flew open and Lynda burst in looking frightened and frantic and pale.

"Honey, are you all right? Are you okay?"

She started to lean in, to reach out, to touch and fuss, and Dana couldn't stand the thought of it.

"Stop!" she said, holding her hands up to block her mother's advance. "Just stop it! Oh my God! Leave me alone!"

Lynda pulled back, looking hurt and at a loss. She didn't know what to say. She didn't know what to do. The faucet was still running in the background. She crossed her arms and held on to herself as she struggled to calm her own emotions.

"Are you all right?" she asked again with forced calm.

"I'm tired," Dana said softly. All the emotions tumbling inside her, and she chose the simplest physical excuse. She didn't have the energy to address the rest of it. Better if she just shut down. Better for everyone.

Her mother turned off the faucet, pulled a hand towel off the towel bar, and handed it to her. "Dry your face, sweetheart."

Dana pressed the towel to her face, then wound her hands into it and held it in her lap, leaning forward, resting her forearms on her thighs. She wanted to put her head down and go to sleep right there. Maybe when she woke up she would be someplace else and all this would have been a bad dream. She wondered how many times a day she had had that thought since this second life had begun.

"I can't believe the nerve of those people," Lynda said, looking out the door, as if the reporters might have come inside to wait in the hall. "How dare they show up here? They're nothing but vultures."

"I used to be one of them," Dana pointed out.

"You were never like that," her mother argued. "Pushy and rude. You were never like that."

"They're just doing their jobs," Dana said in automatic defense of her former colleagues, even though she didn't want them here either. "They have assignments."

"I'd like to know how they got this assignment. If Wesley had anything to do with it, he's getting a piece of my mind. Mr. Campaign Manager," she muttered. "It's none of their business—someone coming home from the hospital. After everything you've been through. What did they think? That you would want to give a press conference in the driveway?"

"I guess I'm news."

Dana thought of the blond girl in the driveway thrusting a microphone, asking a question. She had been that girl, getting the answers, getting the story. Now she *was* the story. *Shoe Meets Other Foot: Details at Five.*

"You're not a headline," her mother said. "You're my daughter. I don't want them upsetting you. Don't be angry with me for wanting to protect you. I'm your mom. That's my job."

She reached out and brushed Dana's wet bangs out of her eyes.

"I'd wrestle a grizzly bear for you, you know," she said with a soft smile.

Dana tried to smile back. It was something her father had always promised—that he would wrestle a grizzly bear for her. After his death, her mother had taken up the mantle of bear slayer.

"They don't have any right to come here," her mother said. "It's time for us to get our lives back. They have no right to intrude on that."

But they wouldn't get their lives back, Dana thought. There was no getting back what had passed. They could only move forward and hope for the best. Forward looked like a long hike up a steep hill at the moment. The idea of it drained what little energy she had left.

"I need to lie down," she said. "Can I lie down now?"

"Of course, sweetie," her mother said, holding out her hand to help Dana up. "Your room is all ready for you. Just the way you left it."

"Great," Dana said. "Now all I have to do is find it."

6

When Dana woke with a start, the world beyond the windows had grown dim. Warm amber light puddled beneath the small alabaster lamps on the nightstands. A soft pink blanket swaddled her in warmth. The big bed was like an ivory cloud beneath her. She felt like she was in a wonderful cocoon.

As always when she woke, she had no idea where she was. To head off the panic, she looked to the nightstand for her four-by-six cards with her familiar questions and instructions. There were no cards. She tried to remember the questions.

Where am I?
Not the Weidman Center.

Without moving, she looked around to take in the details of her surroundings and try to process them. Across the room, near the windows, sat a writing desk with feminine lines and curved legs. On the desktop sat a computer, a dictionary, a pink ceramic mug filled with pens and markers. Behind the desk, ivory-painted built-in bookcases were filled with books and framed photographs and the mementos of a young girl.

Where am I?
My room.

Where is my room?
Home.

She looked down as something stirred among the soft folds of the blanket. A black-and-white cat snuggled up against her stomach.

"Tuxedo!"

The cat awoke, yawning and blinking. He rolled and stretched and purred and yawned, then looked up at her with a self-satisfied cat smile and began purring like a small engine, kneading the covers with white-mittened paws. Dana stroked a hand over him, soaking in the sensation of peace that simple action gave her.

She had rescued the cat from a shelter in Minneapolis after interviewing the shelter director on the early-morning news show she had anchored. Tuxedo had been one of three cats brought along to promote an adoption event. He had spent the remainder of the day snoozing in an open desk drawer, curled up in a cashmere cardigan.

Dana had only a vague memory of the story—and her mind may well have pieced that memory together out of the details other people had given her. Until her mother had brought a framed photograph of Tux for her to keep in her room at the Weidman Center, she hadn't remembered having a cat. But stroking his glossy fur brought back a strong, familiar feeling of peace and contentment.

Across the room, the door cracked open and her mother peeked in.

"Just checking," she said, letting herself in. "Did you sleep well?"

Dana nodded as she sat up and leaned back into a mountain of frilly pillows. Tux immediately resituated himself in her lap, chirping and trilling as he curled into a ball.

Her mother sat down on the edge of the bed and reached over to scratch the cat's ears.

"He's missed you."

"I missed him."

"I think Roger is allergic to him," her mother confessed with a little smile.

"Too bad for Roger," Dana said without sympathy.

"That's what I told him. The girl and the cat are a package deal," she said. "Dinner's on the way from Anthony's. I ordered all your favorites."

"What are my favorites?"

"Meatball ricotta pizza with mushrooms. Baked ziti. The big salad with chickpeas and red onions and tomatoes, with red wine vinaigrette. And garlic bread with cheese."

"What if those aren't my favorites anymore?"

"Then we'll find you new favorites."

So many things were different now. She had lost her taste for certain foods and craved flavors she had never cared about before. Her injury had taken away even the simplest of familiar small pleasures. She had to rebuild everything from scratch, even her likes and dislikes.

"It's all going to be fine, honey," her mother said. "The only important thing is that you're home. Who cares if you don't like chickpeas anymore? If you can't stand the smell of my perfume, just tell me. It doesn't matter."

"I can't stand the smell of your perfume anymore," Dana said. "Seriously."

Her mother smiled and laughed. "I'll throw it out tonight—even though you gave it to me for Christmas. What else?"

"I'll let you know," Dana said, finding a little smile of her own. "I'm not crazy about that sweater either."

They laughed together, something that would have seemed unlikely earlier in the day. Her mother patted her cheek.

"I love you."

"I love you too," Dana said. "I'm sorry if it doesn't always seem like I do."

"You don't have anything to apologize for, sweetheart," her mother said softly. "You have one thing to concentrate on: getting better. I don't want you to worry about anything else, okay?"

Dana nodded.

Her mother got up from the bed, busying her hands by folding the pink blanket. "Now, you should freshen up. Dinner will be here soon. And Frankie and Mags are coming too. Do you want me to help you unpack?"

"I can do it," Dana said automatically, a decision she regretted almost as soon as her mother left the room with Tuxedo tagging after her in hopes of a meal.

She opened her two suitcases and emptied the contents onto the bed and was immediately overwhelmed by the questions of what to put away where, what should go on hangers and what should go in drawers. Deciding the best decision was no decision, she abandoned the task and went into her bathroom to check herself out in the mirror.

She had changed out of her drenched pink hoodie for a gray hoodie before lying down, and now she looked like she had just crawled out of a laundry basket. Wrinkles creased the top, but she couldn't bear the idea of having to pick something else to change into. Her short hair was sticking up in all directions. Her solution was to put up her hood and call it good enough. There would be no television cameras at dinner, no strangers to judge her.

Still, she felt nervous. She tried to tell herself no one was going to expect anything special from her. It wasn't as if she hadn't had dinner with her mother and Roger before, or that she hadn't seen her aunt Frankie since everything that had happened. Frankie and her partner, Maggie, had been regular visitors to the Weidman Center. But it was somehow different because she was now home for good.

This was the first day of the rest of her life. What if she didn't pass the test of behaving like a normal person at dinner? What if she couldn't find her way to the bathroom? What if . . . what if . . .

What if she couldn't find her way to the kitchen?

The idea would have seemed ridiculous to most people. She had grown up in this house. How could she not know where the kitchen was? But she hadn't navigated this house in a long time, and even if she had gone from room to room ten times today, there was no guarantee she would remember the path without having written it down.

She snatched up her iPhone from the nightstand, brought up the notes app, and typed:

DIRECTIONS: from my room to the kitchen

Her bedroom was located on the lower level of the house along with a large family room, giving this floor the feeling of being its own apartment. Both rooms faced out onto a large flagstone patio scattered with lounges and cushioned chairs that invited guests to relax around tables or the fire pit. Beyond the patio, a green area sloped away to woods.

After spending her childhood in a bedroom down the hall from her parents, Dana had been so excited when, at sixteen, she had been allowed to move downstairs, giving her the extra privacy and independence every teenage girl wanted (and giving her mother and Roger, who were newly married, the extra privacy they wanted as well).

Dana left her room and turned right, going toward the light-filled family room. Her mother, no doubt, had turned on the fat ginger-jar lamps that squatted on the end tables beside the big overstuffed leather sofa. A stone fireplace dominated the end wall, with a huge television hanging above the thick mantel.

A gracious curving staircase led the way up to the first floor, where Dana paused to recalculate. Turn right? Turn left? From where she stood she could see the front door, the door to the powder room, the staircase that curved upward to the second-floor bedrooms. She stood quietly, taking in the details, listening carefully, trying to call up memories.

Left. Turn left. She made the note on her phone and continued down a hallway that opened to a formal living room on one side and a dining room on the other. She could hear voices now. Women's voices. Familiar voices. She paused and listened.

"I saw it on the television at the gym. I couldn't believe it! How did they know Dana was coming home today?"

"I don't know. Roger said I shouldn't have put the balloons on the mailbox."

"Oh, for God's sake! What a dick! He puts the blame on you? Like you don't have enough stress?"

"But he probably has a point—"

"Don't defend him, Lynda! How dare he do that to you? And you know darn well it was probably Wesley Stevens who tipped off the newspeople. Anything for a media moment. Please tell me he's not coming to dinner. He clings to Roger like he's made of Velcro."

"Wesley is not coming to dinner. Family only," Lynda said. "And Roger didn't want what happened in the driveway, Frankie—"

"Well, it got him on television, didn't it? And it didn't cost a dime. *And* it's a news bit, so no equal time for the opponent. I hear this senate race is too close to call."

"I'm not going to believe Roger had anything to do with that. He feels terrible that Dana was upset."

"I feel terrible that Dana was upset, too," a third voice chimed in. Frankie's partner, Maggie. "Dana is where our focus should be, Frankie. The look on her face . . . broke my heart."

"What that newscaster had to say made me want to break her face," Frankie said. "And bringing up Casey Grant. What the hell? That was years ago! Why bring that up now? Nobody knows what happened to Casey. Leave it alone, for Christ's sake. Even if there was some connection, what possible difference could it make now?"

"Can we not talk about it?" Lynda said impatiently. "Dana's going to be coming up here any minute. I don't want her hearing any of this. She doesn't need to be reminded about this afternoon, and she certainly doesn't need to be reminded about Casey. It's her first night home. That's stressful enough for her. Let's just be happy and positive we have her back."

Someone sighed.

"You're right," Frankie said. "I'm sorry. It just made me so fucking angry."

"Let it go, Frankie."

"I will. I am. It's gone. See? Happy face! Now, where's my niece? I want to welcome her home."

"She had a nap," her mother said, "but she's up—at least, she *was* up. That's not to say she might not have forgotten about dinner and gone back to bed."

"How is she?" Maggie asked.

"She seems better now that she's rested. She just got overwhelmed by all that madness in the driveway."

"Understandably so. I felt overwhelmed just watching."

"It scares me when that happens to her," her mother admitted. "I don't know where her mind goes. It's like she doesn't even recognize me."

"Don't take it personally, Lynda," Frankie said gently. "The brain's first instinct is to protect itself. That fight-or-flight response is the strongest thing we have. I'm sure it's only more so in Dana, considering everything she went through."

"I don't even want to imagine what would be left of my mind," Maggie said. "I don't think I could have survived what that madman did to her. I really don't. She's so brave."

"Should I go get her?" Frankie asked. "I'll go get her."

A chair scraped against the floor.

Dana stepped backward one step, two steps, not wanting to get caught eavesdropping.

"Hey there, sweetheart!"

The voice was behind her, big and deep, startling her even as she stepped backward into its owner—Roger.

Her heart leapt into her throat, and she spun around, tripping over her own feet.

Roger grabbed her upper arms, catching her, holding on to her.

"Wrong way!" he said, smiling, laughing.

In the dim light of the hallway he looked sinister, towering over her. Dana tried to turn, to wrench out of his grip.

"There she is!" Frankie said, coming out of the kitchen. "I was just coming to find you! Welcome home, Li'l Dee!"

And then she was out of Roger's grasp and into Frankie's hug and being swept out of the hall and into the kitchen.

"We're so excited to have you home!"

Maggie came across the room, smiling, reaching out. She was all soft lines and gentle curves—the body of a yoga enthusiast and a dancer, while Frankie was the feminine version of Dana's father: compact, athletic, angular. Frankie had a handshake that could make a man wince, and the trademark rectangular Nolan smile and stunning blue eyes. In contrast to her partner's long dark hair, Frankie kept her hair in a punkish platinum crop that always sported a new splash of color, purple being the current choice.

"Come sit," Frankie said, herding her toward the harvest table, which sat in an alcove of windows. "We get to wait on you tonight."

"What would you like to drink, Dana?" Maggie asked. "We brought sparkling cider to celebrate. Does that sound good?"

"Yes, thanks."

Dana slipped around to the far side of the table, putting her back to the windows. She worked to slow her racing heart and racing mind by slowly taking in the familiar room, focusing one by one on the things she recognized—the antique white cupboards, the big island with the dark granite top, the copper pots that hung from the iron pot rack. On the counter a giant pottery cat dressed as a butler stood upright holding a menu board that read: LYNDA'S KITCHEN.

Maggie set a champagne flute on the table in front of her. Dana dutifully took a sip of the sparkling cider.

"So," Dana said. "Did anybody catch me on the news? Was I the lead or the human interest story?"

Everyone froze for an almost comic second. Frankie glanced at Dana's mother as if asking silent permission to comment.

Lynda frowned. "Can't we just let that go for the evening?"

"Like it never happened?" Dana asked.

"Yes, exactly like that. I have no problem with that. Denial can be a wonderful thing."

"Then I have to be the elephant in the room?" Dana said. "Everybody has to walk around on eggshells and pretend I didn't have a big meltdown in front of multiple TV cameras? I'd rather not. Might as well acknowledge the madness—mine and theirs. People still think I'm news, so I'm news," she said. "There must not be much going on in the world today."

"There's never anything much going on here," Frankie said. "This is rural Indiana. The crop report is news. You survived a horrific ordeal, Dee. That would make you a headline anywhere. Here you're going to be ranked right behind the Second Coming of Christ."

"Did I miss that while I was away?" Dana asked.

Frankie laughed. "No. The biggest thing you missed was the scandal of the Sweet Corn Festival Queen getting caught half-naked in a car with the high school baseball coach. You definitely beat that, Dee."

"People are fascinated with stories of survival," Maggie said. "As intrusive as it seems to us, you can't blame them."

"Yes, I can blame them," Lynda argued. "My daughter is not a curiosity."

"Sure I am," Dana said. "I'm a freak. Look at me."

Her mother scowled harder. "Dana . . ."

"Lynda . . ."

"People are ghouls who slow down when they drive by car wrecks," Frankie said. "It's lascivious voyeurism."

"I don't think that's all of it," Maggie countered gently, taking the seat next to Dana. "I think people hear Dana's story, and they want to know what does she have inside her that got her through it. They wonder if they would have that kind of strength and determination if they found themselves in that situation."

"I think people are slugs who have no lives, and they like to look at the tragedies of other people so they can somehow justify their own choices to merely exist," Frankie said.

"I think you're both right."

The women turned and looked at Roger as he opened a beer and poured it into a pilsner glass.

Frankie made a face. "Spoken like a politician."

"Nothing is black-and-white," Roger said. "And we live in this age of instant stardom through electronic media. People all over the world know Dana's story. They've become attached to her. They've invested in her emotionally. They want to know more."

"They should mind their own business," Lynda grumbled as she dug silverware out of a drawer and dumped it on the island next to a stack of plates.

"That's not going to happen, Lynda," Roger said. "And we might as well face it. We've had calls from *48 Hours, 20/20, Dateline . . .*"

Dateline. There was irony, Dana thought. She had aspired to be on *Dateline* as an on-air personality. Now *Dateline* was calling her to be the subject of a story.

"If we ignore them, eventually they'll go away. And next week something horrible will happen to someone else, and *they'll* be news," her mother said as the doorbell rang.

"That's probably *Dateline* now," Frankie said. "Roger, you get it.

Maybe you can sidetrack Lester Holt onto a story about Indiana politics. Get some more bonus airtime."

Roger frowned.

"I'm hoping it's the pizza," Maggie said. "I'm starving. How about you, Dana? You've had a long day. You must be hungry."

Dana shrugged. "I don't know. Maybe."

"Sometimes she has trouble distinguishing between hunger and fatigue," her mother said.

"Don't talk about me," Dana said irritably. "God, that's so annoying. I'm right here."

"And we're glad for it," Frankie said, taking the seat on the other side of her. She reached an arm around Dana's shoulders and gave her a squeeze. "We're all so happy to have you home, Li'l Dee. Don't give us too hard a time for fussing over you and protecting you like we're a whole pack of mama bears. It's all because we love you so crazy much."

The pungent aroma of garlic preceded the food coming into the kitchen. Frankie began chanting "Pi-zza! Pi-zza!" as she popped up out of her chair to help. Maggie got up as well, going to the island to help organize the dishes.

They had ordered enough food for an army. Roger came back into the kitchen, arms full of Anthony's bags, followed by the deliveryman with the pizzas.

Dana remained in her seat, her focus on the delivery guy. He looked familiar, but she couldn't place him because she didn't know any pizza deliverymen. Her brain repeated that truth over and over as she tried unsuccessfully to find another context for him. There was something familiar about the angle he held his head at, the set of his shoulders, the line of his jaw.

He kept his head down as he mumbled the amount due and handed a rumpled bill to Roger. His dark hair was military short, and he wore an army jacket with the collar flipped up.

She didn't know anyone in the military. She didn't know anyone in the military, and she didn't know any pizza delivery guys—two strikes in her literal brain—but still, she felt the vague pull of recognition.

"Don't be cheap with the tip, Roger," Frankie prodded. "They had to send the military to get through your media mob outside."

Roger gritted out a smile. "The reporters are gone, but I always support our troops, Frankie."

"Your voting record says otherwise," Frankie muttered. She shot a sly look at the delivery guy. "Direct deposit is the way to go anyway, right, soldier? Skip the political red tape and put cash in hand."

"Yes, ma'am," the deliveryman mumbled, his head still down. He took the extra five Roger handed to him with a quiet "Thank you, sir."

As he started to turn away, Frankie put a hand on his arm.

"Hang on," she said. She turned to dig through a purse on the counter, muttering, "Jesus Christ, Roger. Five bucks?"

She came up with a ten and held it out.

"Thank you, ma'am."

Dana's eye caught on the name tag on the chest of the jacket as he turned to accept the bill: Villante.

A strange mix of recognition and apprehension snaked through her. Fragments of memories flickered through her head like shooting stars, there and gone. High school. The name of a friend—her best friend—Casey. Frankie had mentioned Casey. A reporter in the throng outside the house had called out the name *Casey*. Casey Grant. As Dana looked at Villante the delivery guy, the name that came to her mind was *Casey*.

Something cold and powerful surged through her, driving her to her feet.

"I know you," she said.

He shot her a sideways glance, brows slashing low over dark eyes.

"I know you," she said again, more firmly this time. She pulled her phone out of the pouch of her hoodie and snapped a picture of him.

"I have to go," he mumbled, turning away from her, turning to leave.

"John," Dana said. "John Villante."

She came around the table, following him as he left the kitchen.

"I remember you," she said as he pulled open the front door and bolted for the car parked at the curb.

"I remember you," she said. "You killed my best friend."

7

The memories came rushing and tumbling over one another, caught up in an avalanche of emotion. He ran from them. He bolted and ran like a coward, out of the beautiful house, across the manicured yard, away from the specter rising from his past.

He ran to the ridiculous-looking car he drove for Anthony's—a VW Beetle wrapped in restaurant advertising and made to look like a tomato, right down to a green plastic stem and leaves sprouting from the roof. He slid behind the wheel and started the engine, glancing back at the house, half expecting the inhabitants to come pouring out of it in pursuit of him.

The ghost still stood in the open doorway, staring out at him. *I know you. You killed my best friend.*

Her words had penetrated his head and echoed off the walls of his skull. *I know you. You killed my best friend. I know you . . . I-I-I-know-know-know-you-you-you . . . killed-killed-killed . . .*

He threw the car in gear and hit the gas. As soon as he had escaped the cul-de-sac he began to question what had just happened. He half hoped at least part of it had been conjured up by his mind, part memory, part hallucination. His heart was pounding and he was drenched in cold sweat, the same as when he woke from his other nightmares.

The car's tires screeched as he turned out of the neighborhood onto the main road. He turned right instead of left—away from town instead of toward it. The VW's small engine protested his heavy foot on the gas pedal with a cartoonish high-pitched roar as it grudgingly pushed the speedometer past sixty.

John wished for more horsepower. He felt the need to get away faster than the Tomato Bug could take him. He needed to be alone. Fuck the Mercers and Dana Nolan. Fuck his job and his boss and his boss's bitch of a wife. The idea of returning to the restaurant with all its noise and chaos just added to the sick feeling in his stomach. He had to get away.

Of course, there was no escape, not truly. He couldn't escape what was in his head. He couldn't escape his past. He couldn't escape the present. The memories chased him from within. And now the memory of Dana Nolan's face chased him as well, down Forest Hill Road to Kanner to the dirt service road that ran through the woods to the cluster of sheds and garages tucked up alongside the edge of the state park.

A single dull light cut the darkness, illuminating the outlines of the buildings that housed maintenance equipment—tractors and mowers, tools and whatnot. The buildings were locked up tight behind a high fence topped with razor wire to keep out vandals and thieves. The gate was shut and bound with chains and padlocks. A big sign warned of video surveillance and the promise of prosecution of trespassers.

He pulled into the gravel parking area outside the fence and swung the car around to face the road, back end to the fence so no one could come up behind him. He just needed to be still and alone for a bit, to take the tangle of memories and emotions and straighten them out in a line to make sense of them.

He had recognized the name *Mercer* on the delivery slip and had recognized the home when he had pulled up in front of it. But he had not expected anyone there to recognize him. Most people were

focused on their food and getting their correct change. They didn't care who was standing on the other side of the bags and boxes. Besides that, it had been, what? Seven, eight years now? He had been a kid the last time any of those people had seen him. It had never occurred to him that Dana might be there.

You killed my best friend . . .

Dana Nolan. He never would have recognized her if he hadn't heard her name spoken, if he hadn't heard her voice, if she hadn't said his name. He remembered her being pretty: long blond hair and a heart-shaped face, big blue eyes and a beautiful smile. A cheerleader. The princess of this and the captain of that. Top of the class. Editor of the school paper. Little Miss Perfect. Too good for the likes of him, which meant her best friend, Casey, was also too good for him, too good by association—though Casey had felt otherwise.

He hadn't seen Dana Nolan since the summer after they graduated. The summer Casey Grant disappeared, never to be seen again. He had gone off to the army, off to war. He hadn't come back here—would never have come back here if things had worked out differently. Glad to be gone, he hadn't kept up with local news. Even since he'd come home, he did his job and minded his own business. His only focus was to make enough money to try to go someplace else.

You killed my best friend . . .

She didn't look like that girl anymore. The person who had stood in the Mercers' kitchen, staring out at him from inside the tunnel of a hood, bore little resemblance. She was the *Walking Dead* version of the Dana Nolan he had known, thin and scarred, with haunted eyes. He had no idea what had happened to her. Maybe she had been in a car wreck, put her face through a windshield or something.

Regardless of what she looked like, he hadn't expected to see her there. She had grown up and gone, like anyone with ambition and opportunity did. Miss Most Likely to Succeed had gone off to college and gone from there to make something bigger of herself than

anyone left in this town ever could—or so he imagined. And yet, there she was, accusing him.

You killed my best friend . . .

John jumped as his phone started buzzing and vibrating in the cup holder between the bucket seats. The caller ID showed one word: *WORK*. That would be Paula Tarantino, calling to bitch at him for being slow, or worse, to say Dana Nolan had called to complain about him. He could hear Paula's screechy nasal voice shrieking, *She said you killed her best friend! I should fucking fire you!*

God, he hated Paula. He hated everything about her, from her leathery tan to her spray-starched peroxide blond bouffant to the pickled-sour expression that twisted her thin-lipped mouth into a puckered knot. He couldn't imagine how Tony hadn't strangled her by now. He had been tempted himself to put his hands around her throat and choke her until her bug eyes popped out of her bloated face.

The thought disturbed him now, on the heels of Dana Nolan's accusation. Could he really strangle a woman? He had a violent nature. He had been told that his entire life. He was the son of a violent man. The apple never fell far from the tree—at least not in the minds of people in a small town. The military had been the only place for him to go. Jail or the army had been his choices. The army could channel his rage. He could make himself useful to his country as a weapon.

But he wasn't useful anymore. A tour in Iraq and one in Afghanistan. Years strung together by battles and deaths, deployments and medals thrown in a box. One well-placed improvised explosive device had ended his service. The IED explosion and the ride in the Humvee as it cartwheeled across the barren landscape had scrambled his brain inside his head, and here he was, back in Indiana with nothing and no future, driving a VW Bug made to look like a tomato, delivering pizzas like a sixteen-year-old kid.

The depression pressed down on him now, always worse when he was tired or stressed. There seemed to be no bright side to his life even on his best day, and this was not his best day. Today he had seen a ghost and been accused of murder, and as his phone began to buzz and vibrate again, he had to think he had probably lost his job as well.

Headlights turned off Kanner and came toward him down the dirt road. A spotlight flooded the Tomato Bug, making him squint as the car pulled off the road and parked cattywampus in front of him, blocking his exit like a bully at the locker room door. A sheriff's deputy rounded the hood of the cruiser and came toward him with a Maglite flashlight held high, the way cops did, so they could quickly flip it over and use it for a club.

John ran down the window and heaved a sigh.

"What're you doing out here, son?" the deputy asked. John couldn't see his face behind the glare of the light, but from that angle, he seemed tall and thick around the middle from the bulletproof vest under his shirt.

"Nothing, sir," John said.

"Nobody's getting a pizza delivered out here."

"No, sir."

"Then why are you here?"

"Just needed a minute," John said. "I had to take a leak, sir."

"And you come all the way out here to do it?"

John didn't answer.

"Maybe you've got some other kind of delivery to make," the deputy suggested.

"No, sir."

"I need to see your license and registration."

People came out here all the time to make exchanges of all kinds, John knew. He'd bought his share of weed and alcohol out here when he was in high school. Crystal meth had become the drug of choice of area dealers. No doubt they used this spot as well. And kids probably still came out this way to park and exchange bodily fluids, as they had done for generations.

He dug the Tomato Bug's registration out of the glove box and handed it through the window along with his driver's license.

"John Villante?" the deputy said with an incredulous tone of voice. "Maybe you better get out of the car."

John took a big breath but stifled the sigh. He could feel his patience burning down like the sizzling fuse of a firecracker. He climbed out of the car, keeping his hands out to the side, away from his body.

"I thought you joined the army."

"Yes, sir, I did."

The deputy changed the angle of the light so that the glow touched his own face. "Tim Carver. Deputy Carver now."

Oh Jesus. This night just gets better and better.

Tim Carver. Captain of the football team, Mr. All Everything. Dana Nolan's high school boyfriend. They had played together, he and Tim Carver—football, basketball, baseball. Their girlfriends had been best friends. But he and Carver had never really gotten on. Tim Carver was a leader, from a good family, had been destined for bigger things—West Point, to be precise. It had been a big deal all over town when Carver got accepted to the Point. John didn't ask him how he had ended up in a deputy's uniform.

He had the sudden thought that Dana Nolan had sent Carver after him, and the thought quickly festered into anger. All these years had passed. He had gone and served his country, had been respected by his peers, yet just like that he could be reduced to feeling like the outcast kid from high school all over again.

"What are you doing out here, John?"

"Like I said, I had to take a leak."

"I don't like you being out here. You and I both know a whole lot of nothing good goes on out here at night."

John shrugged. "You want to search me, go ahead. I got nothing for you."

"How long you been back in town?"

"A few weeks."

Carver gave him a long look. "Nobody's going to be happy you came back here, John."

John said nothing. He had as much right to come back as anybody. All the same, he wouldn't have if he'd had any other place to go.

He had always resented Tim Carver—resented his better-than attitude, his smug assuredness that the world was his for the taking. Tim Carver had been going places in the big world outside of Shelby Mills. And yet, here he was, Mr. West Point, a Liddell County deputy prowling the back roads of nowhere, telling John he shouldn't be here. Fuck him.

John wanted nothing more in that moment than to grab Carver's head and slam his superior face down on an upthrusting knee. He wanted to spew obscenities and throw his fists and turn the valve wide open on the pressure his temper was building inside his head and chest. Who the fuck was Tim Carver to lord it over him?

In the cup holder of the Tomato Bug, his phone was buzzing and jumping again.

Fucking Paula.

His level of anxiety cranked up a notch.

"You got anything in this car you shouldn't have?" Carver asked.

"No, sir."

"Then you won't mind if I have a look, right?"

"Nope," John said, already formulating his denial for the joint he had stashed. It wasn't his. Someone else had driven the car. Or it probably belonged to that Mexican kid at the car wash . . .

Carver wouldn't believe him. They had both been out on this road buying weed and smoking it back in the day. Not that anybody would have believed John's version of the story.

Carver shined his Maglite into the car and went from window to window, sniffing like a bloodhound. The car reeked of pizza, the pungent aromas of tomato sauce and oregano overpowering a single little joint of marijuana.

Carver's shoulder-mounted radio crackled with gibberish from a dispatcher. Bigger trouble was brewing elsewhere in Liddell County.

He shined the light directly in John's eyes and stepped back toward his cruiser. "All right. I've got to go. I suggest you do, too, John."

"I will."

"Stay out of trouble . . . if you can."

John chewed down hard on a big *Fuck you*. He watched Carver get back into the cruiser and drive away, then got back into the To-mato Bug and followed him down the service road. He kept to the speed limit, in no particular hurry to get either a ticket or back to Anthony's.

He looked over as he passed the illuminated carved sign for Bri-dlewood Estates, wondering what might have gone on in the Mer-cer house, what was going on there right now. Was Dana Nolan thinking about him? Talking about him? Telling anyone who would listen how she knew he must have done something terrible to Casey Grant all those years ago?

He wished he hadn't had to come back here. But he had nothing, and nowhere else to go. Here he had a place to live, anyway, and a job . . . for the moment.

He turned down the alley, parked behind the restaurant, and went in the back door, into the noise of clanging pans and shouted orders, the smell of oregano and tomato sauce. He hated the noise and the bustle. It unnerved him. He couldn't stand to be in such a small space with so many people and so many voices.

Paula came storming down the narrow, dark hallway like a heat-seeking missile, her face sucked into a tight, ugly fist of angry fea-tures.

"Where the fuck have you been? Why don't you answer your fucking phone? What the fuck is wrong with you?"

John ducked his head against the barrage. Paula sounded like New Jersey and looked like Danny DeVito in a platinum fright wig.

"Are you fucking deaf, John?" she shrieked, stopping just short of colliding with him.

"No, ma'am," he muttered.

"We've had orders sitting here waiting for you!"

"I'll take them now."

"No! No! It's too late. Tony had to take them himself because you weren't fucking here to do your fucking job! I would fucking fire your ass if it was up to me!"

John wanted to shove her away. The hall was too narrow and too hot, and Paula was too close and too loud and too aggressive. He tried to step away from her, but she closed the distance.

"In fact, I *am* going to fire you. You're fired! You hear that? You're fucking fired! You want your job back? You can go crawling to Tony and beg for it! And if he knows what's good for him, he won't take you back. We've got a business to run. We've got a reputation to keep. And if you can't manage a simple delivery job, and you can't manage to answer your goddamn phone, then you shouldn't be here."

"I'm sorry," he mumbled.

He hated apologizing to her. Not because he wasn't in the wrong, but because she was such a raging bitch. This was how she was all the time, always ragging on people, belittling everyone who worked for her. She did it to her husband as well. She especially loved going after men, making them feel small and powerless because she knew they wouldn't fight back.

John wanted to punch her in the face so hard she would fly backward all the way down the hall, through the crowded restaurant, and out the front door like something from a cartoon. But he couldn't do that. At least he had sense enough to know he couldn't do that, no matter how much he wanted to.

"I'm sorry you were in the war and whatever," she went on, "but that's no excuse—"

Abruptly, John turned away. He had to go. Now, before he really did lose it. No excuse? Too bad he almost died for his country. Too bad he would probably never be right in the head ever again. None of that compared to the importance of delivering pizza.

"Don't you turn your back on me!"

John kept walking. Paula kept ranting, but he ceased to hear the words. His pulse was roaring in his ears as he went out the door, past the Tomato Bug, and across the alley to where he had parked his truck in the vacant lot next to a welding shop. He couldn't hear anything but his own anger and embarrassment jeering at him, filling his skull with white noise.

The truck's engine grudgingly rumbled to life, and he pulled out of the lot, down the alley, and onto the side street. He kept off the main roads, hoping to avoid cops. The left taillight had been out since before he joined the army. His old man refused to fix it or pay any of the boxful of traffic tickets he'd accumulated in John's absence. He kept them instead, like a collection of something that somehow entertained him, occasionally using one to light a fire or squash a bug.

He was three-quarters drunk, sprawled in his recliner watching professional wrestling, when John walked into the run-down little ranch-style house they lived in on the outskirts of town. The stink of cigarettes, sour sweat, and bourbon permeated the room.

The old man popped one eye open a little wider, glancing over his shoulder. "You get fired yet?" he asked in a voice that was half gravel, half phlegm.

John said nothing. The rotten old bastard asked the same question every night, just as he had when John had been sixteen and mowing lawns for pocket money. He had always taken a perverse delight in his son's failures, happy to crawl atop his own child's fallen ego and crow. Christ knew he was generally too drunk to climb any higher.

John cut him a look as he passed, disgusted as always by the sight of his father. Mack Villante was forty-seven going on sixty-two, his body pickled and aged by alcohol and bitterness. His face was hard and carved with lines, leathered from the sun, the tan a stark contrast to the white Fu Manchu mustache and crew cut. The beer belly was a permanent feature, and as hard as stone, no doubt with a liver to match. He was a big ham-fisted man, still capable of great strength and great violence, but not when he was like this— too intoxicated to stand up straight or speak without slurring his words.

He laughed at John's silent disapproval of him.

Fuck you, John thought. *Fuck you, old man.* But he didn't say it. He had learned long ago not to pick a fight with a drunk. He stuffed that anger in with the rest, in with the bubbling, seething potful of it inside him. With every minute that passed he felt more and more like a volcano ready to blow.

Going into his bedroom, he shrugged out of his coat and flung it on a chair, stripped off his T-shirt, and shucked off his pants. Locked in the Tomato Bug with pizzas for hours at a time, everything he wore to work reeked of oregano and sausage.

He threw on sweatpants, a clean T-shirt, and a hooded sweatshirt. Sitting on the edge of the narrow bed he had slept in most of his life, he pulled on running shoes. He ignored his phone buzzing in the pocket of his discarded coat. Probably Tony Tarantino calling to second his wife's decision to fire him. He could never reconcile the Tony who had fought in the First Gulf War with the pussy-whipped version who was his boss. *Ex*-boss.

Fuck them both.

The old man was snoring with his mouth hanging open as John passed back through the living room on his way outside. Maybe tonight would be the night he died in his sleep or choked to death on his own vomit. Good. The world would be well rid of him. John would be well rid of him. Better an orphan than the son of Mack Villante. How many times had he thought that growing up? Every day of his life.

He bolted out the door into the night and started running. He needed to run to blow out some of the pent-up energy and the pent-up anger, and the rage at this place and this world, and the memories that weighed him down and plagued his sleep. He ran to clear his head, and he ran to exhaust himself. He didn't care that the night was black with only intermittent glimpses of the moon. It didn't matter that the wind was picking up or that it brought with it raw, cold rain. He welcomed the cold and the wet against the heat of his temper. He only ran harder into the dark, welcoming the jarring reality of footfalls on pavement and cold air sawing into hot lungs.

His mind went other places as he ran—to Iraq, to Afghanistan, to basic training, to high school. He saw men he had served with, men who had died, men without limbs, men without heads. He saw Dana Nolan as she had been and Dana Nolan as she was. Damage, damage, damage. Nothing got better. Life just got worse, harder, uglier.

He wanted it to change. He wanted to make it change. He wanted to beat the world with an angry fist and smash it into a million pieces. But in reality he couldn't do anything about it. He was helpless and worthless and a burden on society. He had no strength. He had no power. He had all he could do to get from day to day without fucking something up, without wanting to kill himself or someone else.

All he could do was run into the night and hope the night would swallow him whole.

8

You killed my best friend.

Killed wasn't the word she wanted. She meant something else. She searched her brain for the right word or something close to it. Not *killed. Hurt.* No. She went through a list: *Killed, hurt, dead, gone. Gone.* Casey Grant was gone. What did that mean exactly? Why was she gone? Where had she gone? What did John Villante have to do with her being gone?

Dana felt a door fall ajar in her memory. It opened just a crack on rusty hinges. She tried to peer inside, but as in much of her memory, the view wasn't clear. The memories were bright in places, foggy in others. Parts of the pictures were missing, like lost pieces from a puzzle.

She remembered Casey now, could see her face as clearly as if she'd seen her just an hour ago: big brown eyes and a bigger smile, long dark hair that fell like a silk curtain around her slender shoulders. They were about the same size, two sides of a coin, best friends since grade school. They had been like sisters, attached at the hip. There were framed photos of the two of them on the bookcases in her bedroom.

Dana remembered so much about Casey now that she remembered her at all. How strange that she hadn't thought of her friend in all these months. Not once. How could she forget her best friend?

How could she not remember the last time she'd seen her? How long had it been? Years, she thought. College and internships and the start of a career ago. They had been children. She was an adult.

She felt guilty and unnerved at once—guilty for forgetting her friend, unnerved that so much time could have passed. Her focus these last months had been so completely and solely on herself, on getting from one moment to the next, that no one else had mattered to her. She had lived in relative isolation, in a place that held no past for her. It was tough to reminisce without a memory or a catalyst to spark a memory. But to not even have a thought about someone she had been so close to disturbed her.

"What happened to her? What happened to Casey?" she asked, looking from her mother to her aunt to Maggie.

Her mother was upset and angry. Frankie didn't seem to know what to say. In the background, Roger frowned into his beer.

"Can we just have our dinner and talk about this later?" Lynda asked. "The food is getting cold."

"I'm not hungry," Dana said.

"You don't remember that you're hungry," her mother corrected her. She picked up a plate from the stack on the island and began to arrange food on it. "You have to eat, Dana. You haven't had anything since lunch. Your brain can't function if you don't feed it."

"Okay," Dana said. "While we break for dinner, let's pretend I didn't just accuse someone of murder. We can pick up the conversation after the cheesecake."

"There was no murder," Roger said.

"That anyone knows of," Frankie added.

"I can't believe Anthony's sent that boy to our house," Lynda muttered.

"He was never charged with anything," Roger pointed out. "No one knows that there was even a crime committed."

"I didn't recognize him," Maggie said. "I didn't know he went into the military."

"Those were probably his two choices," Roger said. "The army or end up in jail for something. He was always in trouble, that kid. Just like his old man."

"But you said there was no crime—" Dana started.

No one was listening to her. They all had something to say, and they said it all at once. Their chatter tumbled together until they sounded like a flock of birds squawking, none of it making any sense to her.

Frustrated, Dana climbed on top of the table, stood up, and shouted, "Would someone answer me?"

"Oh my God, Dana! Get down from there!" her mother ordered, hurrying across the room, the color draining from her face. "Get down before you fall!"

"Could someone please answer my question?" Dana asked again. "What happened to Casey?"

Frankie reached up toward her. "Come on, Li'l Dee, get down from there. You're going to give your mom a heart attack."

Dana raised her hands out of reach. A vague dizziness began to tilt the table beneath her as she looked down.

"Tell me," she said. "Tell me what happened to Casey. Where is she? Did he do something to her? John Villante—did he do something to her? Why would I think that?"

"Dana, please get down," her mother said. "Your balance isn't that good, sweetheart."

"I don't need balance," Dana snapped. "It's a table. The table is flat."

Even as she said it, she glanced down again, her vision tripping over the edge of the table to the floor.

"What happened to Casey?" she asked again.

Frankie stepped up on a chair and then onto the table.

"She's missing, Dee," she said, reaching up and taking hold of Dana's wrist. "Casey's been missing since the summer after you graduated. You don't remember that?"

"No, I don't remember that," Dana said defensively, trying half-heartedly to pull her arm away from her aunt's grasp. "I don't remember what happened to *me*. What do you mean, she's missing? Missing—like someone took her? Did someone do something to her? John Villante—did he do something to her?"

"Nobody knows what happened," Roger said. "She just disappeared."

"Like I disappeared?" Dana asked quietly.

No one wanted to make eye contact with her.

As quickly as the strong emotions had assaulted her, they washed away like water down a drain, leaving her feeling weak. Slowly, she sank down to sit on the tabletop, her legs folding beneath her.

She had disappeared. She had no memory of it, but she looked at the outcome every day in the mirror. She knew what had happened to her because she had been told. Maybe those same things had happened to Casey. Maybe worse.

She let Frankie and her mother help her down off the table and slipped quietly onto a chair. The conversation went on around her as dinner was served. Casey had not been getting along with her mother that summer. Some people thought she might have run away. There had been sightings reported over the years, in Indiana, Ohio, Kentucky, and as far away as Florida. None had led anywhere, but that didn't mean Casey wasn't out there somewhere. There was still hope.

"Where there's life, there's hope," Dana murmured, picking at the toppings on her pizza. As she said it, a shiver went through her. She didn't know why.

No one seemed to hear her.

They didn't talk about the obvious other choice—that Casey was dead, that someone had taken her and killed her, that she had met a terrible end at the hands of someone she knew or someone she didn't know. The world was full of evil. It happened all the time. Dana was the exception that proved that rule. Her family stepped around that truth like it was a pile of broken glass.

"But she's probably dead," Dana said, raising her voice so they had to hear her. "That's what no one is saying. Someone probably killed her. Just say it. We're all thinking it."

Roger frowned. "There's no proof of anything."

"So we're just going to pretend that it's not a possibility?" she challenged. "By not saying it, are you assuming it won't occur to me? I'm brain injured, not stupid."

"No one thinks you're stupid," Roger said impatiently.

"Naïve, then. Casey is missing and probably dead. There's nothing real to suggest she's alive. Chances are she's not," she said. "It's not like I don't know how that happens. I'm also aware that Santa Claus isn't real. So no need to tiptoe around that one either."

"The sarcasm isn't necessary, young lady," Roger said stiffly.

Dana bristled. "Don't scold me. I'm not a child. I'm not *your* child."

Her mother gasped. "Dana!"

"We're just trying to be careful of your feelings, Dee," Frankie said.

"You might want to consider returning the favor," Roger muttered.

"It's been a long day," Lynda said. "I'm sure Dana is tired."

Dana groaned in frustration. "I'm right here!"

"Forgive us for not quite knowing how to deal, Dee," Maggie said, the quiet voice of reason. "We're all in uncharted territory here."

Dana frowned. "I just want everyone to be normal."

No one pointed out that she wasn't normal. She wasn't the Dana they remembered, the sweet, sunny, happy Dana. No one had to say it; it was written on their faces. It hung in the air like a foul odor.

Suddenly, Lynda struck the table hard with an open hand. The *crack!* made everyone jump.

"That's enough!" she shouted. Her face was angry and drawn, the dark circles beneath her eyes accented by the overhead lighting. "I'm done with this conversation. We are done talking about this. Does everyone understand me?"

No one spoke.

"I want this to be a nice, pleasant family dinner welcoming Dana home. Is that too much to ask? Huh?" She looked from one face to the next. "We are no longer talking about violence or death or missing girls or what happened to Dana. Period. Is everybody clear on that? We're happy. We're happy to have Dana home."

Tears filled her eyes as she looked at the carefully blank faces around the table.

She's fragile, too, Dana thought. This day had been as difficult on her mother as it had been on her. She felt selfish and childish for not having thought of it sooner. Her life had been all about herself all day, every day for months now. Just as she hadn't remembered Casey, she hadn't given much thought to anyone else, either.

Frankie banged a hand on the table and popped up from her seat. "Let's have some fun, Goddamnit! This is a celebration!"

She snatched up her champagne flute and proposed a toast.

"To Dee. As corny as this may sound, today really is the first day of the rest of your life, Li'l Dee, and we're all so grateful to be a part of it. Welcome home."

They toasted and drank, and the subject moved to plans for the next day and the days after. Dana would start with the new therapist. She would start training with Frankie at the gym, furthering the work she had done in physical therapy at the Weidman Center. Maggie talked about showing her the benefits of yoga. Roger excused himself. Lynda seemed to have run out of things to say.

Dana felt the weight of the day press down on her until she pushed her plate aside and put her head down on the table, effectively ending the party. Exhausted, she tuned out and said nothing as her mother insisted on walking her down to her room. She didn't want to brush her teeth or take a bath or have a cup of tea. She didn't want to change out of her clothes or even turn down the covers.

"At least let me put these things away for you," her mother said, reaching for one of the piles of clothing Dana had dumped on the bed earlier.

"Mom, no," Dana said, gently tugging a T-shirt out of her hands. "It's okay. Really. I just want to go to sleep. This stuff can wait."

Lynda's eyes misted with tears. "I just want to take care of you. I know how lucky I am to have the chance. Don't spoil my fun all the time," she added, mustering a little teasing smile as she reached up and brushed at Dana's cheek with a thumb. "You have pizza sauce on your face. You should wash up."

"I'm too tired," Dana said. "Besides, maybe I'll want a snack in the middle of the night."

Lynda licked her thumb and scrubbed the offending stain away. "Mom's prerogative. You'll have to go hungry." She leaned in and kissed the spot. "Sleep well, sweetheart."

Dana shoved aside the piles of clothing, not caring that half of it fell to the floor, crawled onto the bed, pulled the pink blanket over her, and closed her eyes. Her body felt so heavy she could hardly move. She expected the physical and emotional exhaustion to drag her beneath the surface of consciousness like an undertow. She wanted to drown in it.

But while she longed for the nothingness of sleep, the faces and voices of the day continued to spin through her head like an unending newsreel.

She didn't want to see it. She didn't want to hear it. She fought to shut it down, trying to implement strategies she had learned at Weidman—visualization, relaxation, biofeedback techniques. The images and noise were stronger than her will to be rid of them.

Finally giving up, she sat up in the bed, turned on the television, and started flipping through the channels. The effect was no different from what was going on in her head—snippets of this, snatches of that—with the exception that the voices and faces belonged to strangers . . . until they didn't . . . until the face on the local news was the face that stared back at her in the mirror every morning.

Everything seemed to freeze in that moment—the chaos in her mind, the beating of her heart, the breath in her lungs. She had seen herself on television many times—the old Dana, Before Dana. After Dana didn't belong on-screen. After Dana was the still photo that stopped the viewer's eye and kept him tuned to the channel the same as a photograph of a car wreck might. The station would probably get phone calls from viewers complaining about the shock value of her scarred face.

The reporter was the blond girl, the girl Dana had transformed into herself as she had stood staring at her in the driveway that afternoon. Kimberly Kirk. With both images side by side—Kirk's animated face and the flat still photo of herself—the contrast was extreme. Beauty and the Beast.

As Dana stared, mesmerized, Kirk told viewers that Dana had no comment when asked if she thought the man who had abducted her could have also abducted her best friend, Casey Grant, seven years before.

Dana hadn't even heard the question that afternoon. There had been too many voices, too much commotion. Casey Grant was a name from another lifetime. Hearing the question now shocked her, the shock bringing with it a huge logjam of emotions she couldn't even begin to penetrate. She had to try to peel the feelings away a layer at a time to identify and try to deal with them one by one.

Outrage and disgust at the prurient sensationalism. Offense at the intrusiveness, the willingness to breech a personal boundary and reach into her memory. What had happened to her was her own experience. She didn't owe anyone the right to know anything about it.

Which was just the opposite of what she would have said as a reporter. As a journalist she would have said that people had invested in her story and had a right to know the truth about that story. And she would have pressed to get the answers to her questions, just as Kimberly Kirk had done.

Anxious and upset, Dana got up from the bed, displacing the cat, and began pacing back and forth across the width of the room, in front of the windows and French doors that led out to the patio.

Now that she had heard the question about Casey, she couldn't unhear it. It ran in a continuous loop through her brain. Could the man who had abducted her have taken her best friend seven years ago? Could the man who had ended her life as she knew it taken Casey seven years before anyone had ever heard of Doc Holiday?

The idea seemed ridiculous on the face of it—that Doc Holiday could have come to Shelby Mills, Indiana, all those years ago and taken Casey Grant, then years later abducted her best friend from a city hundreds of miles away. The odds against that kind of coincidence had to be astronomical. And yet, the possibility was like a snake that slithered into her imagination, cold and slick, accessing the deepest reaches of her most primal fears.

Could he have watched them both, stalked them both when they were eighteen and just getting ready to experience life? Had he chosen one over the other for a reason or by chance? Had he later chosen Dana knowing, wanting to compare them? If he hadn't, was he now in hell laughing at the joke that people might consider him so brilliantly diabolical?

Dana had no organic memory of the man who had abducted and tortured her. No image of his face existed in her mind. She hadn't seen a single photograph of him. She didn't want to. Better that she didn't know what he looked like. Better that she couldn't remember. It could only be worse for the monster to have a face to haunt her nightmares.

But while she had avoided the photographs that would have humanized him, she had sought out the articles that had chronicled his history. She knew Doc Holiday was a middle-aged man with half a dozen aliases who had spent many years crisscrossing the Midwest collecting and selling antiques and junk. He was known to have killed women in Illinois, Iowa, Minnesota, Kansas, Wisconsin, and Missouri. Why not Indiana? Those cases had all come in the past few years. And while he had marked Dana as his ninth victim, the authorities suspected there were probably more victims than they could officially give him credit for, possibly many more.

Dana couldn't help but wonder now: What if she might have seen him that summer after graduation? He might have pulled off the interstate and had a meal at the Grindstone truck stop, where Casey had waitressed part-time in the summer. Dana had gone there nearly every afternoon. What if Casey had waited on him? What if Dana had seen him? And if she had, had she remembered him? Had there been a moment of recognition years later as he grabbed her and threw her into his van?

The answer had to be no. Things like that only happened in the movies. Which meant the evil that had touched her life couldn't be contained to a single entity—Doc Holiday. But she had already known that.

Roxanne Volkman, her friend and mentor at the television station where she had worked in Minneapolis, had explained to her the circumstances that had led to her abduction. Dana had been reporting on the story of a Jane Doe homicide victim that had turned out to be a local teenager, Penelope Gray. For a time, the authorities had suspected the girl was the ninth known victim of Doc Holiday. In the end, a stranger abduction and serial killer had turned out to be the farthest thing from the truth. Evil had lived much closer to home for Penny Gray.

That conversation with Roxanne came back to Dana now as if they had only just had it, even though she hadn't thought of it once in months. Dana had been among the first to report the possible link between the elusive serial killer and the gruesome discovery of the girl's body on New Year's Eve. When the victim's identity had become known, Dana's interest had only increased. With the station shorthanded due to the holidays and a rampant flu bug, she had lobbied hard with Roxanne to be able to do more on the story than just report on it from behind the desk on the early-morning news. She had begged for and gotten the extra field assignment as part of the around-the-clock coverage of the story.

And the reason she had been so interested and pushed so hard to get that assignment, Roxanne had reminded her, was that she once had a friend go missing and never come home.

Her coverage of the Penny Gray story had captured the interest of Doc Holiday.

"Oh my God," she whispered now, sinking down onto the chair behind her desk.

She had asked to cover Penny Gray's story because of Casey and had ended up in the clutches of a killer—a killer who might have ended her friend's life seven years ago.

No wonder the news media was so hot for the story. It was tailor-made for television: a tale of good and evil as intricately woven as a fine tapestry, as twisted as a Gordian knot.

As a journalist, she would have given her right arm for a story like that to dig into. As a victim, she didn't want to share any part of it with anyone.

And as the best friend of a missing girl . . . ?

She looked at the blank black screen of her computer. She could turn it on and in a matter of seconds see the face of the man who had ruined her life and maybe spark a memory that could solve a seven-year mystery.

She stared at her dark, ghostly reflection in the screen, as a cold fear spread through her chest. *Seven years,* she thought. Whatever had happened to Casey had happened long ago. What was the point in knowing the worst? Better to leave it alone and let hope, however slim, live, right? If she was dead, she was dead. Nothing could change that. If she was alive, then Doc Holiday had nothing to do with her disappearance.

In her exhaustion, her damaged mind toyed with her. Her reflection shivered and shuddered, taking on dimension, radiating energy. Dana sat back, trying to get away from it.

Save yourself, little coward, it said.

"So what if I do?" she asked back.

Better to leave her own memory blank, she thought. She didn't want to know more about the man who had abused her. Knowing more wouldn't change what had happened. It would only make the forgetting more difficult. And more than anything, she wanted to forget—or not to remember, to be more accurate.

The reflection's eyes glowed red. *You can never escape yourself.*

"You're not real," Dana said.

I'm as real as you are. I live in your head. You can't get away from me.

In defiance, Dana rose and turned her back on the computer, coming face-to-face with a photograph in the bookcase, one of her younger self and Casey Grant. Best friends forever, each with an arm around the other, the two girls mugged for the camera, silly at sixteen, dolled up for a school dance. Dana: blond and blue-eyed. Casey, so pretty with her dark hair and sparkling dark eyes and wide smile. They looked as happy as they could have possibly been, clueless about the cruelties life held in store for both of them. They'd had no thought in that moment that life wouldn't always be exactly what they wanted. It hadn't occurred to either of them that everything could change in the blink of an eye.

"Stay that way," Dana murmured, as if those girls could hear her, as if she could somehow bend space and time and warn them, and change it all.

If that were possible, I wouldn't be here now and this wouldn't be real, she thought. Then this reality would be nothing but a bad dream from which she could awake. God, how she wished that could be true.

You can never escape yourself, her own voice whispered within the walls of her mind.

Something touched her from behind, and she gave a little shriek as she spun around, expecting to face her specter from the computer screen, thinking it might have crawled out of the machine onto her desk. But there was nothing there but her cat, Tuxedo, sitting with his head tipped quizzically to one side.

Shivering from the stress and the fatigue, Dana wrapped her arms around herself and walked away. She went to stand at the French doors and leaned her forehead against the cool glass, staring out at the patio. The area was aglow with subtle lighting tucked beneath the shrubbery. She could see only to the edge of the landscaping. Beyond that was nothing but blackness . . . and whatever lived in blackness—the evil she would have warned her younger self to fear.

As she stood there staring out, she imagined that evil embodied, an entity staring back at her, waiting to reach out and touch her. She imagined she could feel its gaze on her, greedily drinking in the sight of her from just out of her range of vision. That was what evil did, what predators did—watched and waited, patient for an opportunity, ready to spring when the victim wasn't looking.

Fear rippled down the back of her neck, and she shuddered. That evil knew her, had already had her. It could want more of her.

An icy cold seeped through her, running down her arms and legs like water, sliding back up her chest like a cold, bony hand, fingers wrapping around her throat, cutting off her air.

The trembling began deep within, working its way to the surface like an earthquake.

You can't escape. I'm inside you.

A little mewling sound of fear escaped her lips. Hands shaking, she fumbled with the deadbolt, fully expecting that evil thing to rush out of the darkness, across the patio, to yank the door open before she could secure the lock.

Tears welled up in her eyes and turned her vision to liquid. She yanked the curtains closed and backed away from the door, her breath catching hard in her throat as she banged into the desk, turned and bumped into an upholstered chair.

She scurried to the bed—to high ground—put her back up against the headboard, and curled herself into a quivering knot, arms bound around legs, knees tucked against chest—the position she always assumed to ride out the storm of panic.

She held tight to herself, shaking and crying. And even as she choked on the fear, in the back of her mind lingered the mocking thought that she should be used to this by now. This terror threatened to swallow her whole on a nightly basis. But that knowledge didn't lessen the trembling or the sensation of not being able to breathe. And just because she hadn't died of it the night before didn't mean it wasn't real tonight.

Tonight might be the night the faceless evil that stalked her mind took physical form and finished the job started months ago. Because, even though Dana had no conscious memory of it, she knew better than anyone what evil was capable of doing.

AND IN THE NIGHT, beyond the reach of the lights, the watcher stood in the woods, wrapped in the blackness, and sighed in disappointment as the girl closed the drapes . . .

9

The sound of the screams pierced her eardrums like the point of the knife. The knife traced patterns in the girl's flesh like a fine red pen. The red was blood that fell in drops like tears from her eyes. Big brown eyes full of terror and pain, and something that struck even harder—accusation.

Not my eyes, Dana thought.

Not my blood.

Not my pain.

And yet, she felt trapped there, frozen in hell, unable to move, as if she was the one tied to the table.

"You should have seen him coming," the girl said calmly. "I died for nothing."

"You're not dead."

The girl smiled a dark, cruel smile. "I'm as dead as you are."

"I'm alive."

The girl began to laugh. She arched her back and strained against the ties that bound her wrists to the table, laughing and laughing.

"Stop it!" Dana shouted. "Stop laughing!"

The girl paid no attention to her. The sound of her laughter seemed to multiply and echo until Dana felt surrounded by it. Then the laughter gave way to choking. The young woman's long dark hair transformed to a mass of writhing snakes. She turned her face toward Dana and her eyes changed from human eyes to elliptical reptilian slits, glowing green and red.

Dana sucked in a breath to scream but couldn't release the sound, couldn't release the air from her lungs. She tried to turn away, to move away, to run away, but she couldn't move. Something invisible and oppressive held her in place in a grip as strong as iron.

The demon's face turned red as it began to choke. Its body convulsed with effort as it choked and gagged, trying to dislodge something from its throat.

Suddenly a tiny hand emerged from the mouth, fingers curling and uncurling. Another round of choking forced a tiny arm to thrust out. Then Dana watched in horror as a baby was born from the mouth of the demon, emerging on a sea of blood, falling to the floor. It looked up at Dana, and she tried again to scream as she stared down into her own face.

Terror propelled her from the nightmare, flinging her to consciousness, flinging her upright in the bed, flinging her from the bed. She scrambled to get her feet under her, slipped and fell to her knees as her stomach twisted and heaved. She grabbed the wastebasket from beside the desk and vomited into it again and again.

The nightmare image burned the insides of her eyelids: her own face looking up at her, attached to the body of a newborn infant covered in blood. She pressed the heels of her hands hard against her eyeballs, pressing until all she could see were starbursts of color on a field of black. But the images only went deeper into her psyche.

She couldn't unsee the baby or the face of the girl turned demon bound to the table—Casey Grant. Pretty Casey with her long dark hair and big brown eyes transformed into something demonic and terrifying.

Shaking uncontrollably, drenched in sweat, Dana alternated between sucking in air and retching into the wastebasket.

I'm as dead as you are . . . I'm as dead as you are . . . Casey's words from the dream echoed inside her head.

"Stop it. Stop it," Dana said again and again. "I'm alive."

She looked around as her heart rate slowed and her breathing gradually returned to normal. The television on the wall above her dresser was whispering to itself. She had left all the lights on. Bored with her histrionics, Tuxedo sat in a pile of clothes on the foot of the bed, licking the toes of an upraised hind paw.

Mustering some strength, Dana got up from the floor, took the wastebasket into her bathroom, flushed the contents, and washed out the plastic cylinder, then washed her hands and face and brushed her teeth. She didn't have the energy to strip off her sweaty clothes or shower.

The digital clock on her nightstand read 3:27 A.M. She had been abducted from the parking lot of her apartment building around 3:15 in the morning, on her way to work. She woke up nearly every night around the same time, as if to somehow ward off potential danger in her dreams. Too late tonight.

She felt like she'd been run over by a truck. But as tired and drained as she was, she had no desire to try to return to sleep, where this new nightmare lay in wait. She tried to interpret the dream as she sat down in her desk chair.

It was obviously Casey being held by Doc Holiday. Tied down as Dana had been told she had been tied down. It had taken months for the ligature marks to fade from her ankles and wrists. Casey was telling Dana she should have seen the monster coming. Why? Because she had seen him before?

It was only a dream, she told herself, spun out of all the things she had been thinking about earlier. It didn't mean anything. Yet she still felt disturbed by it. She couldn't shake the creepy aftereffects.

Dr. Dewar had told her the subconscious mind couldn't distinguish between an experience that was real and one that was vividly imagined. The brain's physiological reaction was the same, hence the pounding heart, the rapid breath, the sweating, the sense of dread. *A stupid design flaw on the part of Mother Nature,* Dana thought. *A waste of adrenaline.*

But even knowing the logical explanation, she couldn't shake the feelings. She couldn't stop seeing the baby. What deep psychological twist did that represent? That somehow Casey's tragedy had given birth to something within her?

She had pursued the Penny Gray case in part because of Casey. Maybe somewhere in the back of her mind she had imagined her coverage of that case propelling her forward in her career.

Or it was just a creepy dream conjured up by a damaged, tormented, overtired brain fueled by meatball ricotta pizza.

She wished she could have accepted the last explanation. Guilt wouldn't allow it. The guilt that came from having pushed Casey's story to the far reaches of her memory. If Casey had been her inspiration to pursue her career in journalism, then Casey's story should have remained important to her.

Dana looked up at the photographs on the shelves behind her again, the emotions attached to those images stirring inside her: delight, silliness, love—each facet of happiness that comprised the simple joy of youth. The emotions prompted her memories of those times like sparks firing a long-dormant engine.

She had spent the better part of a year just trying to remain in the present, to survive and fight to drag her broken self forward from zero. She hadn't chosen to forget Casey or their friendship or the tragedy that had taken her friend from her. She had set those things aside out of necessity to focus on rebuilding herself. But those memories were pieces of the puzzle, too, and the time had come to get them back.

Taking a deep breath and letting it go, she reached out and turned on the computer.

"DID YOU SLEEP WELL, sweetheart?"

"Sure," Dana mumbled as she shuffled into the kitchen.

She was still wearing the clothes she had gone to bed in. They were wrinkled and damp with sweat. She had pulled her hood up and hid herself as deeply as possible within the tunnel, trying to keep the dark circles beneath the bloodshot eyes hidden from her mother's eagle eye.

She had started nodding off at her desk around five and had grudgingly curled up on the bed and pulled herself into a tight little ball around a pillow clutched for security. Sleep had come in torturous fits and starts, a few minutes at a time, never deeper than just below the surface. Her heightened sense of danger never allowed her the luxury of a deep, restful slumber. On constant alert, that part of her brain was convinced she had to be able to wake and bolt and run for her life in a matter of seconds.

That same paranoia prevented her from taking the sleeping pills Dr. Dewar had prescribed. Even though she knew in her logical mind that she was safe behind locked doors, the primal instincts were too strong to override. When she was in that state of hypervigilance, she couldn't help thinking, what if she took the pill and fell asleep and couldn't wake up? What if she couldn't wake and escape a physical threat? What if she couldn't wake and escape the horror of her nightmares?

At Weidman she had learned all kinds of tips and strategies to help her relax and sleep. None of them quite translated to real life once the fear had dug its hooks in. The trick was to implement the strategies *before* the panic set in, but they never seemed necessary until *after* the panic set in.

Keeping her head down, she slid into a chair at the big table. She could feel her mother's eyes on her like a pair of heat-seeking missiles.

"I made that egg casserole you used to like," Lynda said. She brought the pan to the table and dished a scoop onto the plate in front of Dana. "Don't forget you have your first appointment with Dr. Burnette today."

Which meant she would have to take a shower and find something to wear that she hadn't slept in or on or thrown on the floor for the cat to make into a nest. The prospect was daunting on no sleep. She found her thoughts paralyzed at the decision of where to start, what to do first. Would she remember how to run her shower? Could she manage it without flooding the entire lower level of the house?

And, provided she surmounted the obstacles of getting ready and actually made it to the appointment, what would this new doctor know about her? What would she expect? What did Dana want her to know? What should she be willing to share? Would she be able to trust this woman? What if she didn't like her? What if they didn't like each other?

The questions swirled around like angry bees inside her sleep-deprived, fuzzy mind.

At least the doctor was a woman. She seized on that thought, cutting a look at Roger. He sat at the far end of the table, ignoring her, his interest absorbed in a newspaper. He was probably still angry with her for what she'd said at dinner. He had a capacity for sulking that usually prompted her mother to fuss around him like a nervous toy dog. Before Dana would have tried to distract him with some happy chatter. After Dana had no interest in pandering to him.

"Eat your eggs before they get cold," her mother said, taking her seat at the near end of the table.

Dana picked at the food, sniffing at a forkful, tasting the tiniest experimental bite.

The television on the wall opposite the table was tuned to the local morning news, a network affiliate out of Louisville. The male/female anchor team had shared the news desk for years with a pleasant, easy, back-and-forth style. Dana had grown up watching them and found something comforting in seeing them again, like seeing old friends. She checked the clock and used the remote to up the volume. Top of the hour. Hard news would lead.

The male anchor began with a serious expression. "And in Shelby Mills, Indiana, last night, a nineteen-year-old female was reportedly attacked and sexually assaulted while walking home from her job as a waitress at the Grindstone Café and truck stop. The victim, whose name is currently being withheld—"

Lynda grabbed the remote and hit the mute button. "We don't need to hear about that," she declared, scowling.

"It's news," Dana said.

"It's bad news. I don't want to hear bad news."

"Just because you don't want to hear it doesn't stop it being true."

Roger snapped his newspaper and peered over the top. "Don't you think your mother has had to deal with enough?"

"What's that supposed to mean?"

"It means you could start the day without arguing with her."

"We aren't arguing," Lynda said. "Can we just have breakfast?"

"A girl was raped last night," Dana said, staring at her stepfather. "We're supposed to pretend that didn't happen?"

"We don't have to talk about it over our eggs," he said.

"Is that what you said when it happened to me?" Dana asked. "I guess I owe you an apology for being so inconvenient and inappropriate as to be a victim of a violent crime."

Her mother sighed. "Dana . . ."

Roger's face darkened with anger, but he wouldn't quite look at her. He never did. He couldn't deal with her disfigurement. That was why he hadn't come to see her more than he had to during her recovery despite the fact that he was in Indianapolis all the time.

It hurt her more than she wanted to admit, and in that moment Dana felt an acute and painful longing for her father. The ghost of the little girl in her owned the certainty that Daddy would have somehow still found her to be the most beautiful girl in the world, scars and all.

Roger folded his newspaper and set it aside, pushing back from the table. "I have to go. I have a meeting with Wesley."

"God," Dana said as he left the room, "he doesn't even bother to deny it."

"That's not fair," her mother said.

"Not fair to who?"

"Roger has taken a very hard line on crime, and he's promoting victim advocacy because of what happened to you."

But was that out of conviction or was it a convenient campaign issue? Dana wondered. His sudden great compassion for crime victims hadn't been extended to her personally. Frankie's criticism of Roger from the night before came back to her now, her assertion that the media scene in the driveway had been good free publicity. Was that what she was to him now? A free ticket to get on the news? Was Roger now meeting with his campaign manager to think of more ways to capitalize on the notoriety of being stepfather to the only living victim of a serial killer?

The idea stung more than she wanted it to.

Appetite gone, Dana turned her attention back to the mute television screen as she picked at her now-cold eggs. They were rolling video of a manager from the Grindstone standing in the parking lot outside the café, frowning grimly as he spoke. The truck stop was located maybe ten minutes away, on the edge of town near the interstate.

Casey had worked part-time at the Grindstone that last summer.

The coincidence gave Dana a chill. The memory of the feeling she had experienced last night while standing at the French doors to her patio came back to her now—the sense that something evil had been lurking in the darkness, staring at her.

Something evil *had* been lurking. It just hadn't come for her this time.

She wondered if it had followed her here, if Doc Holiday had been a vehicle, a host, and the evil had passed from him to her. Now she had brought it home with her, and it had gone out into the darkness last night to stalk another victim.

It was a stupid notion, she knew, but she couldn't shake the feeling that came with it.

She reminded herself that Shelby Mills was a growing community within commuting distance of Louisville, a big city with big-city problems. While her hometown had been a safer place when she was a child, people here locked their doors now and took the keys out of their cars. Guns and drugs were too readily available, and consciences were seemingly in shorter supply than they had been in the last millennium. Burglaries, theft, and drug-related crimes were not uncommon.

But violent crime was still rare enough to be shocking. And to have news of a sexual assault greet her on her first morning home was unnerving. The lack of sleep along with the post-traumatic stress had stirred her paranoia. Then she had spent nearly two hours reading articles about Casey's disappearance seven years past.

Even seven years ago, the sheriff's office had not been without suspects in Casey's disappearance. The making, buying, and selling of methamphetamine had become a huge problem in the area. Rumors had gone around that Casey might have crossed paths with someone in the drug trade. She had known kids who dabbled in it. A classmate of theirs had died because of crystal meth. After that Casey had talked about becoming a counselor for people with addictions.

She might have unknowingly stumbled onto a deal going down or might have simply been spotted by a ruthless opportunist from that world who had seized the moment. The drug world and the world of sex trafficking were bound together like kudzu vines. She could have been taken by one and turned over to the other for profit.

People had wanted to zero in on John Villante as the prime suspect because he was the boyfriend with a bad reputation, but singling him out also answered a simple human need for evil to have a face and a name. If her boyfriend did it, then the evil was contained within Casey's own circle of acquaintance.

Everyone feared random acts of violence, the bogeyman who struck without reason or warning. The boyfriend was the answer that made people feel safe. Better to blame someone they knew than to think evil could have pulled in off the interstate to strike like a snake and leave. But Dana knew firsthand that happened all the time.

It could have just as easily happened in Shelby Mills that summer Casey Grant went missing as it had in Columbia, Missouri, nearly two years ago when Doc Holiday had abducted Rose Reiser from outside a convenience store when she was en route to college in St. Louis. Her body had been found days later, cast into the snow along a truck route in Minneapolis.

It could have happened again last night to a nineteen-year-old waitress walking home from a late shift at the Grindstone Café. Doc Holiday may have been dead and gone, but Dana knew the world would never run out of men willing to take his place. From the dawn of time to the end of time, the world would never run short of cold, cold hearts.

10

What the hell were you thinking, John? You can't just drive off in the middle of your shift! What the fuck?"

Tony Tarantino tossed his hands up in the air and turned around in a circle like a man doing a bad folk dance. They stood in the alley behind the restaurant, hemmed into a corridor by the Dumpster on one side and the Tomato Bug on the other. The smell of garlic cooking was already in the air as the kitchen started to prepare for the day's business.

John stood sideways, trying to minimize the claustrophobic effect of the tight space. Even leaving himself an exit route, he still felt trapped. Across the alley, the welding shop was in full operation; the sounds of the torch and metal on metal skated across his nerves like razor blades. He wanted nothing more than to bolt and run, but he stood his ground and took his boss's abuse.

Where he had probably once been described as a fireplug, Tony now more resembled the corner mailbox—square and stout with stubby legs and a big mouth. A steady diet of pizza and bread sticks had packed the fat on since his retirement from the Marine Corps. John had seen the photographs of his days in Desert Storm and other global hotspots. He had once been a badass. Now he was just an ass, just another pussy-whipped middle-aged guy with a mortgage and a bitchy wife and a couple of spoiled, ungrateful kids.

"And then we get a call from Senator Mercer's wife, having a shit fit that we sent you there in the first place," he went on, red-faced. "Why the hell did you take that delivery?!"

Because that's my job, John thought, but he didn't say it. What good would it do him to point out that he had been the only delivery guy available and that it would have been Paula having the shit fit if he had refused to take it? Of course, now he wished he had done just that. Then the bitch could have fired him before he had the chance to embarrass himself and before he had the chance to let Dana Nolan call him a killer and dredge up a thousand memories he didn't want to have. He could have avoided going on the radar of the Liddell County Sheriff's Office, courtesy of Tim Carver.

"Roger Mercer is running for office, for Christ's sake," Tony ranted on. "He's a fucking state senator! Do you have any idea how many fucking pizzas we deliver to his campaign office? Or how many we deliver to Mercer-Nolan Landscaping, for that matter?"

"No, sir."

"More than your fucking weight in fucking gold!"

He huffed and puffed and threw in a "Jesus Christ!" for emphasis.

John just shoved his fists harder into the pockets of his fatigue jacket and hunched his shoulders against the onslaught. He was an old hand at weathering tirades. He'd been riding out his father's since as long as he could remember. No drill sergeant could dish out what John Villante couldn't take. The army had been a piece of cake by comparison.

"So am I fired?" he asked quietly, looking down at his boots.

He had already been wondering what he might do next, where he might find someone willing to hire him to do something, anything. Jobs were scarce in general. Scarcer still for him.

Any prospective employer checking his record would find he had a psych discharge from the army. They wouldn't care what exactly that meant. And if they dug a little deeper, they would find out he had done five months in the brig for assault prior to the psych discharge. No one would want to hear about how he had lost seventeen buddies in two tours of duty—five at once in the incident that had given him his head injury. They wouldn't want to take the time to understand the depression, the PTSD, the attempts to self-medicate, the doctors' attempts to overmedicate him. No one would care about the details.

Of the few jobs available to him, there were bosses who would thank him for his military service like good patriots but refuse to hire him for the very same reason. He was a trained killer just out of the VA hospital with a head injury and a history of psychological problems. How could they risk having him around?

And of the jobs available to him, there weren't that many he could tolerate. He couldn't be in the midst of too many people. He couldn't handle the chaos of multiple conversations going on around him. The noise was magnified and reverberated inside his skull until he thought his head would explode. He couldn't be surrounded by people, couldn't have people behind him. They got too close, moved too fast. His instinct to react, to protect himself, was too quick. His self-defense skills honed in army combatives training were too dangerous.

At least working at Anthony's he was able to come and go, to walk away from the noise. Paula was a cunt, but he could take a small dose of her, then leave. The waitresses ran interference for him as much as possible, bringing his deliveries out to the Tomato Bug so he could avoid her altogether much of the time.

Tony jammed his hands on his hips and huffed and puffed some more. John awaited the verdict, stoic in his resignation. He could already hear his old man gloating.

"Fuck," Tarantino said, but without the bluster.

John glanced at him without raising his head.

"Paula's got me by the balls on this, kid," he said. "I didn't know anything about that missing girl. That was before we came here. But Paula saw it on the news last night after the Mercer woman gave it to her with both barrels over the phone. She went fucking ballistic on me!"

"I don't know what happened to Casey Grant," John said.

Tony held his hands up. "I'm not saying that you do. I'm not saying you did anything to her. I'm sure you didn't. I think you're a good kid, John. But this is a small town. Word spreads like a fucking grease fire." He held his hands up as if framing his new motto. " 'Anthony's: Killer pizza delivered by a murder suspect.' I can't have that."

John didn't bother pointing out that no one knew for a fact that Casey Grant was dead, let alone a murder victim. Nor did he point out that he was an actual killer, that he had killed numerous people in two wars, yet he was being judged for an imagined death. Irony would not be his friend in this fight any more than Tony Tarantino was his friend.

"And then we see on the news this morning some waitress got raped last night leaving the Grindstone—"

Heat flashed through John, burning his face and the back of his neck. His fists tightened to stone in his coat pockets. "I'm no rapist, sir."

"I didn't say you were! But someone attacked that girl, and now people are going to be freaked-out."

Tarantino sighed like a man with chest pains. He pulled out his wallet and fingered out two hundred-dollar bills, thrusting the money at John with sheepish embarrassment. "Take this for now. To tide you over. I'll find you another job. I promise."

John looked at the money with disdain. "I don't need your handout, sir."

"Yes, you do," Tony blustered, shoving the cash at him. "Take the goddamn money. Buy yourself a different coat, for Christ's sake. One that doesn't have your fucking name on it."

John glanced down at the patch on the army-issue jacket he had worn to serve his country. The name tag had already begun to come loose at one corner, the broken thread twirling up out of the fabric like a tiny filament corkscrew. He grabbed hold of the tag, tore the name off in one violent motion, and threw it on the ground. Then he pulled himself to full height and looked down his nose at Tony Tarantino with his hundred-dollar bills clutched in his fat hand.

With as much dignity as he could muster, he said, "Fuck you, sir."

And he turned and walked away.

"John. John!" Tony called.

John kept walking toward his truck. The thought struck him that he could have taken the money and gotten his taillight fixed. Behind him he could hear the scuffle of Tony's sneakers on the crushed asphalt.

"Come on, kid," Tarantino said. "Don't be so fucking proud."

He grabbed hold of John's arm from behind. John spun around, throwing off his boss's hold and shoving him backward all in one motion. Automatically, his left arm came up and back, cocked and loaded, fist ready. Fear flashed in Tarantino's eyes.

John pulled himself back, pulled his anger inward. He lowered his arm. "I don't have much to be proud of, sir," he said, "but I'll hang on to it."

He climbed in the truck and coaxed the engine to life. As he pulled out and headed down the alley, he glanced in the rearview mirror to watch Tony Tarantino standing there with his hands on his hips, growing smaller and smaller along with his opportunities.

He didn't know where he was going. God knew, he didn't have anyplace *to* go. He drove around town trying to organize his thoughts, trying not to wonder how much shittier his life could get, trying not to let the anger take control.

The truth was, he knew exactly how shitty life could get. Life could blind you, maim you, take your legs, take your arms, blow your face off your head but leave you alive. He'd seen all of those things. He knew more broken people than whole ones. Even most of those who appeared intact were shattered inside.

Sometimes he thought the men whose seventeen names he had tattooed down his back were the lucky ones. He had had their names etched into his skin to carry their memories with him. Many times he had wondered if they would have rather he hadn't. Hadn't they suffered enough in their own lives? Now they had to be witness to his failures and to the rejections of the people they had all signed up to serve.

He drove past the elementary school and the high school, unable to call up a single good memory from his time in either place. He had been a good athlete and had known success in several sports, but in his present state of mind he could remember only conflicts and betrayals and disappointments.

His senior year, he had been offered a football scholarship to Indiana State at Terre Haute. But then Casey had gone missing and the cops had been all over him. Suddenly he had been a villain in every newspaper and on every television in the state. He was the troubled loner boyfriend of a town sweetheart, the kid with a history of violent run-ins, the son of a bully, abandoned by his mother. There was clearly something wrong with him. Who knew what darkness lay in his heart?

The scholarship offer had been withdrawn. The military had been presented as his only honorable option. Better to get the hell out of Dodge before the detectives could pin something on him.

Truth to tell, the army suited him. He liked the structure of it. He had felt a greater sense of family with the men he served with than he had ever known at home. Nobody in his unit cared who he had been. They had all come there to reinvent themselves in one way or another.

He missed it. He missed it badly. Not the war, but the rest of it. When the army had cut him loose, he had lost everything—his career, his family, his home, his future, his sense of self-worth. The sense of betrayal and rejection was like a deep bruise that never healed. He had given everything, had done everything asked of him. He had been awarded medals for his bravery and his valor. He had been wounded in his efforts to give his all, and because of that, because he had sacrificed for the cause, the very organization that had asked that sacrifice of him had turned its back on him. He was broken because of the army, and the army didn't want him because he was broken.

His head injury had been misdiagnosed for a long while after the IED incident. He hadn't appeared to be that badly hurt. The damage was hidden inside his skull and had manifested itself in blackouts and bad decisions, outbursts of rage, debilitating headaches, frightening mood swings. His efforts to self-medicate with alcohol had only magnified the problems.

An altercation with a superior had landed him in the brig for assault. The headaches had moved him from the brig to the hospital. In the hospital, a psychologist had diagnosed him as bipolar, and that had been the end of his career. The hill had continued to go down from there, and here he was, back in Shelby Mills, starting over at less than zero.

It was a wonder he was alive, considering. Most days he wasn't sure life had been the best choice. And then he would think of the names on his back and the fact that those men had had no choice at all.

He drove away from downtown, past the picturesque old watermill complex that had given the town its name. The original Shelby Mill building had been transformed years ago into a posh restaurant with a hotel adjacent in a setting of wooded gardens. He had eaten in that restaurant once in his life: on the night of his senior prom with Casey, an awkward double date with Dana Nolan and Tim Carver. He had worried the entire time he would use the wrong fork or spill something or say something stupid.

The memory of that awkward apprehension came back to him

now to mingle with the anger and the frustration and the shame and all the rest of it that constantly simmered inside him; a flood of emotion, all of it angry and bitter and dark. Every time it came, he thought he would drown in it. It swamped his brain and swelled in his chest, the rage building and building. The faces swam in it—Tony Tarantino, Paula, Tim Carver, Dana Nolan, Casey—their expressions masks of disapproval and disdain.

Goddamn them all. Who were they to judge him? They didn't know him. No one had ever known him. No one had ever taken the time to see who he really was. No one. Not the people he worked with, or the people he went to school with. Not his father—least of all that wretched son of a bitch who had called him a loser and a quitter his whole life. Not his mother, who hadn't stuck around long enough to know him past the age of eight.

The emotions in full boil now, he pulled into the driveway of his house and got out of the truck, breathing hard, his heart pounding. He went into the garage via the side door, stripping off his coat and casting it aside, not caring where it fell. He pulled his sweater over his head, balled it up, and flung it. His pace quickened as he crossed the floor until he was running at the old heavy leather punching bag that hung from a ceiling joist.

He launched himself at the bag from five feet out, slamming his shoulder into it, absorbing the pain, welcoming the pain as it exploded through his chest and neck and down his back. The bag swung away, sending him past like an angry bull sidestepped by a matador.

John turned and came back swinging, bare knuckles connecting hard with the cracked leather and the patches made of duct tape. Left, right, left, right. One-two, one-two. Left hook, right hook, left hook, right hook.

He grabbed the bag in a clinch and drove his right knee into it as hard as he could again and again, then switched his stance and brought the left knee up once, twice, three times, four times.

With every punch, with every knee, his breath left him on a hard, guttural sound. He sucked in oxygen tainted with the smell of stale grease and gasoline. His pores opened and sweat beaded on the surface of his skin despite the chill of the fall air. As he worked the bag, the sweat ran down his back, across the seventeen tattooed names, and soaked the back of his pants.

He threw his hands until the muscles of his arms were bulging and heavy, the veins popping. He twisted into the hooks until the taut, ripped muscles that wrapped around his rib cage and stretched across his belly were burning and quivering with fatigue. He threw knees until it felt like his boots were made of lead.

When his hands hurt too much to connect another punch, and his knuckles were raw and bleeding, he switched to throwing elbows, imagining the strikes connecting to the faces of everyone who had ever looked down on him—Tony, Paula, Tim Carver, Dana Nolan; the list went on and on . . .

The emotions poured out of him like toxic steam, bitter and acrid. He could taste it like metal in his mouth. The feelings came up from the depths of him like bile. And when his body was spent, and his knees gave out, and he lay in an exhausted heap on the dirty floor, the last of the emotions drained out of him in his tears.

11

"What if I don't like her?" Dana asked for what was probably the fourth time in fifteen minutes.

"What if you do?" Lynda asked back. "What if she's the coolest person you've ever met?"

Dana didn't answer. Her mood was stuck on pessimism. It felt better to be angry than apprehensive.

She had managed to shower and brush her teeth but had refused to make much more of an effort than that. No makeup. No jewelry. She had left her hair wet and had dressed from a pile of clothing that had fallen to the floor during her fitful sleep—a pair of baggy jeans and an oversize black hooded sweatshirt.

Before Dana had been all about her looks, all about the wardrobe and what her clothing said about her. What her current look said about her was that she didn't give a damn. Her post-incident wardrobe consisted of T-shirts and hoodies, sweatpants, yoga pants, and jeans. After Dana was the Anti-Dana. Why should she try to impress people with her looks when her looks had been taken from her? Why seek approval when all she would get was pity? What did any of that superficial bullshit matter anyway?

She certainly didn't care to impress Dr. Roberta Burnette. She hated the idea of starting the process of therapy all over again. She didn't want to have to tell her story again or be asked how she felt about it.

The stupidest question of all time: How did she feel about having her life destroyed? How did she feel about having been raped and tortured?

To distract herself, she opened her photos app and looked at the picture she had taken of John Villante the night before.

He scowled at her in a sideways glance, straight dark brows pulled low over narrowed dark eyes. He had an angular face pulled taut over high cheekbones and a square jaw. Even set in a hard line, his mouth was, for lack of a better word, beautiful, with a full lower lip. He could have been a Calvin Klein model, sullen and angry, selling designer underwear and sexuality on the pages of *GQ*.

He had always had a chip on his shoulder but never had much to say. Dana had never really approved of him as a boyfriend for her best friend. Casey could have done so much better than an angry boy from the wrong side of town. She remembered him thinner, lean and hungry looking, with an unruly head of dark wavy hair that looked silly when she tried to attach it to the image of the man on her phone screen.

That was the difference. He had been a boy then. He was a man now. In her memory of before, John Villante was a teenage boy, a troubled loner who never quite fit in. Years later, he was a man, a soldier—or had been, at least. Whatever innocence he had possessed had been shorn away along with his hair. The anger and resentment he had carried as a boy had had seven years to harden into bitterness.

Seven years changed everyone. Dana wondered what Casey would have been like now. She had talked about becoming a social worker to help kids, or maybe to work with people with drug and alcohol abuse issues. She had always been a caretaker.

Outside of school, they had both volunteered at the local food bank and helped out with the kids' reading program at the public library. But where Dana had felt fulfilled in doing her civic duty, Casey had always made it more personal. It hadn't been enough to stock the shelves at the food bank. She had to befriend the little kids of the families who came there. It hadn't been enough to read to children during story hour at the library. She had to mentor a little girl as well. It hadn't been enough to volunteer at the animal shelter. Casey had to feed half a dozen feral cats that lived in the woods at the edge of her neighborhood.

Casey had always taken in strays . . . like John Villante. They had started dating the fall of their senior year. Bubbly, sunny Casey and the agent of gloom.

"Do you want me to go in with you?"

Dana looked up, surprised to see they were no longer in Shelby Mills. Lost in thought, she had missed the drive to the northern suburban reaches of Louisville. They had pulled into a parking lot adjacent to a long old two-story brick building that had once been a train station. The ground floor was filled with galleries and boutiques, places to eat and have coffee.

"I can do it," Dana said automatically.

"I know you can do it," Lynda said. "That's not what I asked you."

Dana said nothing as she stared at the unfamiliar building. What if she couldn't find the directory? What if she couldn't find the elevator?

"Come on. We'll go find the elevator," her mother said, getting out of the car. "I see opportunities for retail therapy. I'll check those out while you're with Dr. Burnette. You can text me when you're finished and I'll meet you. Does that sound like a plan?"

Relieved, Dana nodded. She took a photo of the building from their parking spot and made a note for future reference, then opened her parking app and set it to find the car later. Then she took a deep breath to brace herself for the next task at hand: opening herself up to the stranger who would want to drag all her ugly secrets out into the light.

"I KNOW WHAT YOU'RE THINKING," Dr. Burnette began as she took a seat in a leaf-green upholstered cube of a chair near the bank of windows. Barefoot, she curled her long legs beneath her with the grace of a deer. She was dressed in gray yoga pants and a fitted fuchsia T-shirt that showed off an athlete's body. Her bare arms were smooth and long, sculpted in lean muscle.

"You're thinking: What's this crazy-looking black woman gonna do for me? I've done told my story more times than I ever want to, and now I have to start all over and do it again, and that's gonna hurt, and I'm gonna hate it, and fuck this shit.

"Am I right?" Burnette asked.

Dana just stared at her, not sure what to think. This was not Dr. Dewar, Mother Earth, with her pseudo-hippy skirts with sitar music playing in the background. Roberta Burnette was thirtysomething with a trendy urban vibe about her. She wore her hair in short braids all over her head with a random assortment of colored beads woven in. Her ears were pierced with moonstone gauges that seemed to change color every time she moved her head.

"I know I'm right," she said. "And I'll tell you why I know I'm right. Because I've been the one sitting right where you're sitting, thinking all the same things," she said, her voice growing softer. She paused at that, giving Dana a moment to absorb what she had said, waiting for a reaction.

Dana didn't blink.

"I know this isn't easy," Burnette continued. "It's like you already built a house out of Legos and somebody has taken it all apart and you have to start over, and the last thing you want to do is start from scratch because that means the first thing you have to do is walk around in your bare feet, stepping on all those damn Legos.

"I have a six-year-old nephew," she confessed. "I know all about stepping on Legos."

Still Dana said nothing. Legs tucked beneath her, she burrowed back as far as possible into the corner of the love seat, which was the bark-brown counterpart to the chair Burnette occupied.

The room had a Zen quality to it—a polished old plank floor, sage-green walls, furnishings with clean, simple lines, and uphol-stery fabrics with organic colors and textures. One wall of simple built-in shelving displayed books and a collection of colorful, heavy glass sculptures with smooth, rounded shapes. While there were sev-eral lamps on tables around the room, only the lighting in the book-cases was turned on to spotlight the art pieces. Natural light filtered in through the tall windows that overlooked a cobblestone yard where people strolled or sat on park benches or at café tables, sip-ping coffee.

Dana stared out at them, envying their seemingly simple lives. From the corner of her eye she could see Burnette flip open a file folder to consult whatever notes were kept inside. She peered at Dana over the purple rims of her reading glasses.

"It doesn't say anything in here about you being mute. Is this something new? Nod for 'yes.' Shake your head for 'no.'"

Dana took her time responding, staring at the doctor with no expression for a moment before shaking her head slowly within the confines of her hood.

"Good, because talk therapy tends not to be the way to go with someone who doesn't talk," Burnette pointed out with an arched brow, her full lips kicking upward at one corner.

Dana held her silence again.

Burnette drew in a long, dramatic breath. "Much as I love the sound of my own voice . . ."

"What happened to you?"

"Ah . . . ," the doctor said softly to herself, pleased to have finally gotten a response. "Well, they tell us in shrink school not to share these personal things, but the people who wrote those textbooks have never been victims, and they don't know what it's like to sit down on a couch across from a stranger who wants to poke and prod inside their minds and tell them what they should and shouldn't feel. That's just bullshit, if you ask me. It made me angry when I was going through it, and I vowed I would never do that to anyone. So I will tell you right up front that I've been a victim, and while I didn't have your exact experience, we have some common ground."

"What kind of victim?" Dana asked again, her curiosity muscling past her determination to be uncooperative.

"I went to college on a track scholarship, had a goal to make the Olympic team. I was good enough, too," Burnette said. "But late one night I was in the parking lot of a convenience store waiting for a friend to pick me up, and I got pulled into a car and taken for a ride by two guys who didn't care how fast I could run four hundred yards. The second they got hold of me, it didn't matter anymore."

"They raped you?"

"They did. And used me for a punching bag. And stabbed me. And held a knife to my throat. And at one point, when I tried to get away, one of them tackled me, and I blew out my knee," she said. "So when you tell me something and I say I understand how you feel, I really do. I get how hard this is, Dana. I know how much you lost."

"They didn't carve your face up like a Halloween pumpkin."

"No, they didn't, but I spent a year rehabbing a knee that never worked right again. And I spent a lot longer than that trying to come to terms with the anger, and the panic, and the nightmares, and the rest of it. We both lost big dreams, you and I."

"And this is where you tell me I should still consider myself lucky, and that I can still have a great life," Dana said, the familiar resentment sour on her tongue.

"You *can* still have a great life," Burnette said, unfazed by her sarcasm. "You will. You didn't fight that hard to stay alive for nothing. You stuck it out for a reason."

And if I had known what the aftermath would be like, would I have fought as hard? Dana wondered.

If she had known about the endless anxiety and the physical pain, the struggle to sleep, and the exhausting ordeal of relearning life minute by minute, would she have fought as hard?

"Where there's life, there's hope," Dr. Burnette said.

The words snapped Dana out of her thoughts.

"You know how this works," Burnette said. "You've been doing it every day since this happened to you. You survive this minute, and then the next minute, and then the minute after that. Each minute has the potential to be better than the last."

"Or just as bad," Dana countered. "Or worse."

"Or better," the doctor insisted with the quiet, firm resolve of someone who had had this conversation many times before. "I know you're feeling overwhelmed. Just the step of moving from Weidman back home is a big deal. But I saw your homecoming on the news last night. That was a whole lot of crazy to deal with that you probably didn't expect."

Dana replayed the scene in her head, the surprise, the frustration, the chaos, the flood of emotions . . .

"What happened to me happened months ago," she said. "It's over. He's dead; I'm not. There's nothing left to say about it."

"You're the only living survivor of a serial killer. That will make you news for the rest of your life."

Dana frowned and looked away, arms crossed tight over her chest. She wanted to deny it, but she knew she couldn't. She would forever be the asterisk in the accounts of Doc Holiday's exploits as the one that got away. She didn't want the attention. The irony wasn't lost on her—the girl whose goal had been the spotlight didn't want the spotlight.

"They asked me about Casey," she said. "I didn't know what they were talking about," she confessed. "Casey was my best friend since grade school. She disappeared the summer after we graduated. I didn't remember that. How could I not remember that?"

"It was out of context," the doctor said. "You've spent the last few months working like a dog just to get your brain to function in the moment. Don't expect it to turn on a dime and redirect its efforts to something from the past."

"She was my best friend," Dana said again. "We were like sisters."

"Dana, you've just been through your own abduction and every horrible thing that went along with that crime. It doesn't surprise me at all that you may have blocked out the abduction of your friend," Burnette said gently. "Those are two horrific events. And to your mind they are essentially the same recurring event viewed from two different perspectives. Your brain is trying to protect you from that. It doesn't make you a bad person that you didn't remember."

But does it make me a bad person that I don't want to think about what might have happened to her? Dana wondered. *Does it make me a bad person that I don't want to remember the man who did this to me, even if remembering could help solve Casey's mystery?*

She kept those questions to herself even as the horrific images from her nightmare flashed through her head: Casey as the victim and the demon, taunting her, tormenting her . . .

"I can't even remember what happened to me," she said.

"You may never," Burnette said. "Or it may come back to you in bits and pieces."

"I think I have some memories from the days before . . . But I don't know how much of that is real and how much of it my brain has pieced together from other sources—or just made up completely.

"I don't remember him at all," she said. "I can't see him. I don't want to see him."

"You don't have to."

"But how can I be so terrified of something I have no memory of?" she asked. "And how can I move past something I can't remember?"

"Because the brain stores emotional memories and the physical details of what happened in two separate places. This is oversimplifying, but in a sense your mind doesn't want you to remember the details of that trauma," Burnette said. "And the brain injury makes it easier to pull that off. You've got a built-in excuse to not remember. But whether you consciously remember it or not, that experience, and the emotion attached to it, is a part of you. It's just deeper than you can readily access."

"I don't want to access it," Dana said. "Everybody wants me to remember. They want to know every gory detail."

"Unfortunately, that's human nature. It's entirely your call what you want to share, Dana. And how you feel about that may change over the course of time. Some victims find it cathartic to talk about their experiences. Some find it empowering to share their stories in a way that might help others. Some just want to move on."

"I want to move on," Dana said impatiently.

"Fair enough. But don't think that means you don't have to deal with the effects of what happened. You don't have to access the physical details to address the emotional damage within yourself. You can't escape your own experience."

"I don't know about that," Dana said. "I hardly recognize who I used to be. It's like that girl is someone I met once a long time ago. I'm someone different now."

"That doesn't mean she's not still a part of you," the doctor said. "She always will be.

"But let's focus forward," she suggested. "You want to move on. So do you have a plan? What are you going to do with yourself?"

Dana shrugged and nibbled at a ragged cuticle. "I don't know. So far today I managed to take my clothes off *before* getting into the shower. That might be the highlight. My mother tells me that should be enough. She says my job now is healing."

"Healing is ongoing," Burnette said. "But I don't think that's going to be enough for you. It's Mama's job to protect you. You're her baby, and she's not going to be quick to forgive the world for hurting you. She's going to want to keep you in the nest. That's understandable. It's even okay for a while. But that's not going to be good for you long term. You need a goal. You're a fighter, Dana. You need something to fight for."

Dana didn't think she would have described her Before self that way. A worker, yes. Ambitious, yes. Goal oriented, yes. But a fighter? No. Before Dana had been a rule follower, a diplomat. She had thrived on making people proud of her, on meeting and exceeding expectations. But a fighter? Someone who kicked and scratched and fought to win? No. She hadn't needed to be.

"What do I have to fight for?" she asked. "I'm an unemployable newscaster living in my mother's basement."

"When you woke up in the hospital, you had a goal to get out of the hospital. When you went to the Weidman Center, your goal was to get well enough to go home. Now you're home. You need a new goal. And when you reach that goal, you'll need another goal. Does that sound like a plan?"

"It sounds like a lot for someone who got lost on the way to the kitchen last night."

"They don't have to be big goals. A small one each day. They're like handholds and toeholds as you climb the bigger mountain. Ultimately, you will get to the top of the mountain, but in the moment you only need to focus on the next ledge."

"Yesterday I dumped all my clothes out of my suitcase into a pile, then couldn't cope with what to put in drawers and what to hang on hangers," she confessed.

"So your first goal is to put away one thing, then another thing, then another. Eventually, the pile goes away and the job is done."

"'Brain-Damaged News Girl Empties Suitcase. Film at Eleven,'" Dana said sarcastically.

"Nine months ago you were in a coma."

"Ten months ago I was a morning news anchor."

Dana looked out the window again, at the people walking up and down. Burnette waited patiently.

"I loved my job," Dana confessed after a moment. "Yesterday, standing there in the driveway, looking at that reporter, the blond girl . . . I saw my face. I literally saw my face on her body. That should have been me asking someone else the questions. It's so unfair."

"Yes, it is," Burnette agreed. "Life is completely unfair. That's no news flash, is it? You lost your dad when you were young, right? Your best friend disappeared when you were barely out of school. No one has seen her since. You know firsthand that bad things happen. You've no doubt reported on stories of child abuse, rape, murder.

"It's no surprise to you that life isn't fair. You just never thought you'd be the one getting the shit end of the stick again. Neither did I," the doctor confessed. "I had my life all planned out. I was going to win a gold medal and have my picture on a Wheaties box, and get a million-dollar Nike sponsorship, and go on to be a star for ESPN."

"You still could have gone into broadcasting," Dana said. "You're a beautiful woman."

"Thank you, but my life took a different turn. After what happened to me, I fell down a deep, dark rabbit hole. Depression, anxiety, post-traumatic stress—the whole nine yards. It was a long climb out of that, and on the way, I learned a lot about myself and what I really wanted to do with my life—which is help other people out of their rabbit holes.

"So maybe you can't be in front of a camera anymore," she said. "That doesn't mean you don't still have skills. Dr. Dewar told me you like doing research on the computer. So you start by researching subjects that interest you. Maybe you end up doing research for news stories. Maybe you end up becoming a writer. Start with writing a blog. Or maybe this journey takes you on a whole other path. I don't know. But I do know if you don't have a destination, you'll never go anywhere.

"I want you to think about that for next time—after you've organized your closet," Burnette said, unfolding herself from her chair. "What's your first goal going to be?"

Dana got up, chewing her lower lip as she thought about her answer, smiling a little when she did. "Finding the elevator."

The doctor smiled with her. "I'll help you with that one."

Burnette padded barefoot across the room to a door that exited directly into the hall within sight of the elevator.

"None of that was in your bio," Dana said, lingering in the doorway. "What happened to you. None of that came up when I researched you."

"I had a different last name then," Burnette confessed. "I was a different person. Just like you were."

"Which you is better?" Dana asked.

"I've learned to love them both. You will too."

"Will I?"

"When you were in the hands of a killer, your goal was to get out alive, and you achieved that goal," Dr. Burnette said. "After that, I wouldn't bet against you, girl."

I hope so, Dana thought as the elevator descended, dumping her back into the world. But as she caught the shocked glances of people passing by, she had nothing but doubts.

12

A Liddell County sheriff's cruiser was waiting at the end of the street when Dana turned onto the cul-de-sac.

After her appointment with Dr. Burnette, she had decided her goal for the day would be to take a small step toward independence by driving home. If she could prove to her mother that it was possible for her to get from point A to point B without getting lost or crashing into someone or something, she would begin to build her case to get her own car back. After a minor glitch in that she had no idea how to start her mother's Mercedes, she had succeeded with the aid of the navigation app on her phone, only mixing up right and left twice.

She was feeling very pleased until she saw the sheriff's car. In that instant, the bottom dropped out of her stomach and an old feeling that was attached to an old memory came rushing up through her, taking her breath away.

Suddenly she was fourteen, sitting in the backseat with Casey, giggling and laughing, excited to get home to show Daddy the dress she had bought for their father-daughter dance at the country club. It was a fall day, just like this day—a little chilly, a little blustery, but the sun was shining and the sky was blue. It was too pretty and too perfect a day for something bad to happen, but something bad *had* happened.

A county cruiser had been parked at the curb in front of the house. The deputy standing beside it with his arms crossed looked grim. Roger paced the length of the patrol car, agitated, running his hands back through his hair again and again.

From that memory, Dana's mind went back to the last time she had seen her father that same morning. He had made breakfast, as he did every Saturday. Even though the weekends were busy at the nursery, he insisted on his family time. Ed Nolan's Saturday mornings consisted of cooking breakfast for his daughter: chocolate chip pancakes, bacon, and scrambled eggs. Sacred time.

Dana remembered she had chattered nonstop that morning about the big day she was about to have with her mom and Casey and Casey's mom. They were headed to Louisville for shopping and lunch, manicures and pedicures. She was looking for a dress like one she had seen in a magazine. She had shown the picture to her father, and he had told her she would make that dress look special, not the other way around, because she was the most beautiful, special girl in the world. She could still feel his arms around her as he hugged her tight and kissed the top of her head.

He had come out of the house to wave them off as they backed out of the driveway. She could see him in her mind's eye like she was looking at a movie. Her father waving with one hand, the other hand hanging on to the collar of Moose, their chocolate Lab. She could see her father's face, as clear and sharp as a photograph—his wide, rectangular smile, his piercing blue eyes crinkling at the corners. He was a compact, athletic man with more stubble on his square jaw than hair on his close-shaved head. Even without hair he was as handsome as a movie star.

It was the last time she had seen him alive. He had been found dead that afternoon. An accident, they said. No one knew really what had happened. There had been no witnesses.

They knew he had taken Moose and gone pheasant hunting by himself in the late morning. He and Roger—his best friend and business partner—owned seventy-five acres of hunting property a few miles east of town—a rugged mix of woods and open fields bordered on the south by bluffs that dropped off to the river. Speculation was that, for whatever reason, he had ventured too close to the edge of the bluff and had fallen to his death. Some hikers had found his body, still warm, but too late.

"Dana? Dana? Dana!"

Dana came back to the present, turning to her mother, indignant. "What?"

"We're sitting in the middle of the street."

"Oh."

She had stopped the car a good fifteen yards short of the driveway. She pulled ahead, only glancing at the deputy who had gotten out of the cruiser. He was holding a bouquet of pink and white flowers.

"Tim!" her mother exclaimed, getting out of the car. "Oh, my goodness!"

"Hey, Miss Lynda. How's your day today?"

"Oh my God! What a wonderful surprise! I had no idea you were a deputy! Dana, look who it is! Tim Carver! For heaven's sake!"

Dana got out of the car, rearranging her hood, hiding herself in the back of it. She looked across the roof of the car at the deputy. He was medium height, broad shouldered and slim hipped, built to wear a uniform. He turned and looked at her, a wide white smile firmly held in place, blue eyes shining, set off by laugh lines.

"Dana," he said.

Dana stared at him as he came around the car. Tim Carver, her high school sweetheart. Of course she recognized him . . . now that she did. She remembered his easy smile, the hint of good-natured mischief in his eyes. She had no memory of him becoming a deputy—or a grown man, for that matter. She hadn't seen him in years—not that she could remember, anyway.

They had broken up the summer after graduation. She remembered that. It wouldn't have been practical to try to keep the romance going. She was off to college in the fall. He was headed to West Point with much fanfare—something Roger had helped to orchestrate. Then Casey had gone missing, and nothing else that summer had mattered.

They hadn't stayed in touch after they had left Shelby Mills. Dana had gotten caught up in her new life at school. There had been a new boyfriend—whose name and face she couldn't recall now. She had lost track of Tim Carver.

"Welcome home," he said, holding the flowers out to her.

Dana accepted the bouquet, looking at it like she had no idea what to do with it.

Her mother broke the awkward silence. "Tim, how long have you been a deputy?" she asked, coming around the hood of the Mercedes to stand with them.

"Five years now," he said. "Not all in Liddell County, though. I started up in DeKalb County for two years, but I wanted to come back home, you know."

"You've been back three years and you haven't looked us up?" Lynda said. "Shame on you!"

"Well, you know," he hemmed and hawed, ducking his head. "Time gets away. Busy with the job and all."

"How are your folks?"

"They're well, thanks. My dad is with a firm in Lexington now."

"And your mother?"

"Moved back to Texas. My sister's down there in Austin."

The Carver family had come to Shelby Mills from Texas, Dana remembered. Tim had joined her seventh-grade class. He had never entirely lost the twang of Texas in his voice.

"The last I remember, you had gone off to West Point," Lynda said. "You were going into the military."

He nodded, looking a little uncomfortable, Dana thought.

"Yes, ma'am. Well, it didn't quite suit me," he said. "After what happened with Casey, I kept thinking I would rather go into law enforcement, and . . . well . . . here I am."

"You're losing your hair," Dana blurted out.

Her mother gasped. "Dana!"

Dana frowned. "Well, he is."

"I can't very well deny it," he said, chuckling, running a hand back over his head. Dana remembered him with a full head of fine blond hair. He wore it cropped short now, not trying to hide the fact that his hairline at his temples had receded markedly.

"Dana sometimes says things without thinking now," Lynda explained.

"Don't talk about me like that!" Dana snapped. "Like I'm a fucking moron or something."

Her mother arched an eyebrow. "Case in point."

Dana made a show of turning away from her, giving her full attention to Tim.

"I look different, too," she admitted.

"I'd know those pretty blue eyes anywhere," he said with a kind smile.

"You always were a charmer, Tim," Lynda remarked.

"Well, ma'am, that's easy around beautiful ladies."

"I'm not beautiful," Dana said flatly.

"Why don't we go inside?" Lynda suggested, taking the bouquet from Dana's hands. "Can you stay for a cup of coffee, Tim?"

"Yes, ma'am. Thank you. I'd like that. I'm not on duty for a while yet."

"You and Dana can catch up."

Her mother turned to go to the house. Tim reached out as if to put his hand on Dana's shoulder. She twisted away.

"Don't touch me," she snapped. "I don't like to be touched."

Surprised, he stepped back, raising his hands. "Sorry."

"It's not your fault," Dana said, turning away.

They went inside, into the kitchen to sit at the big table, Dana at one end, Tim with his back to the wide expanse of window. Dana looked past him, past the deck that stepped down in levels to the flagstone patio, and beyond to the gentle green slope that rolled down to the woods. A deer stood in the clearing looking up at them, then flicked its tail and dashed away.

Dana wished she could dash away. What was she supposed to say to him? What kind of small talk was a person supposed to make after they'd looked into the face of evil and barely snatched their own life out of the jaws of doom? Were they supposed to talk about high school after that? Was she supposed to ask him if he had married, if he had a family? She didn't care.

"So are you married, Tim?" her mother asked, as the coffee machine hissed and spat into a cup. She busied herself at the sink, snipping the stems of the flowers, putting them into a vase.

"No, ma'am," he said. "Married to the job, as they say."

"That's not very romantic," Lynda said as she brought the bouquet to the table.

"All things in their own time," he said. "I'm on a serious career track with the sheriff's office. I passed the detective's exam recently. I'm just waiting on an opening in the department.

"You know, I had the best girlfriend," he said, nodding toward Dana, eyes twinkling. "I haven't found another girl who could fill those shoes."

"I remember you now," Dana said dryly. "You were always full of shit."

"Dana!" her mother scolded.

"Who? Me? Not at all!" Tim protested with a laugh. "That's the God's honest truth, Dana. You ruined me for other girls."

"Cream or sugar for your coffee, Tim?" Lynda asked.

"No, thank you, ma'am. Black is fine."

"Dana, would you like a coffee?"

"Do I like coffee?"

"You did this morning."

"No, thank you," she said, feeling stupid.

"I'll leave you two alone to chat, then," her mother said, setting Tim's steaming mug on the table in front of him.

Dana drew a quick breath to tell her not to go but stopped herself. Tim had been her first crush, her first kiss, her first young love. He had been her best friend after Casey. She should be able to have a conversation with him.

He sighed as Lynda left the room.

"I can't say how sorry I was to hear what happened to you, Dana," he said quietly. "I can't even imagine what you went through."

"I don't remember it."

"None of it?"

"No."

"Thank God."

"For what?" she challenged. "If there's a God, he let a sexual sadist kidnap and torture me—after he'd already killed who knows how many girls. God gets a big pat on the back for that?"

His eyes widened a little. He only knew Before Dana, sweet Dana, happy Dana, the diplomat, the good girl. *Welcome to After Dana,* she thought. *Damaged Dana. Unfiltered Dana.*

"I guess I didn't think of it that way," he said.

"Nobody thinks of it that way. But the God that lets me forget the details is the same God that let it happen in the first place. So forgive me if I'm not entirely thankful to a higher power."

He raised his hands in surrender. "Hey, I don't blame you. You have every right to be bitter. People just want to make sense of things that can't be made sense of. You and I both know there's not always an answer to be had. We learned that with Casey. Seven years and we still don't know what happened."

"Did you really become a cop because of her?"

"Yes, ma'am, I did. I watched the investigation and the searches and all when Casey went missing. I was a part of that, just as you were. It stuck with me," he said. "And I read that you were reporting on the murder of a teenage girl when you got abducted. The newspaper said you were putting in extra hours because you had lost a friend from high school."

"Casey had a big impact for someone who isn't even around."

"More than she could know."

"Do you have anything to do with her case?"

"Not directly. The original detective—I don't know if you remember him—Dan Hardy—he retired a couple of years ago. The case got reassigned," he explained. "It's just been sitting, cold, truth to tell—until now. There hasn't been anything to go on."

"I heard there had been sightings of her in different places," Dana said.

"Reports here and there," he said. "Nothing panned out. People see the story on the news or on some reality crime show, and they want to help or they want to feel important. They think they see the person, or they just flat make it up. None of those leads went anywhere."

"And now?"

"The detective in charge is going to want to talk to you about the possible connection to the man who attacked you," he said. "I told him I know you. I figured it might be easier coming from me."

It might be easier coming from an old friend with a wink and a smile and a bouquet of pink flowers, Dana thought, looking at the vase her mother had set on the other end of the table.

"You don't have to try to suck up to me," she said bluntly. "Just ask."

"I'm not trying to suck up to you, Dana," he said, offended. "I can't bring flowers to a friend? I thought that was the gentlemanly thing to do."

"I don't have anything to contribute to your case," she said. "I don't remember anything about the man who took me. I don't have any memory of what he looked like."

"Would you be willing to look at a photo array?"

"No," she said flatly. "What good would it do? I have no memory of him at all. You want to put a face into my mind so I can convince myself I might have seen him that summer before Casey disappeared?"

"No, that's not—"

"Because that would make it easier on everybody, wouldn't it?" she suggested. "Everyone could assume Doc Holiday took Casey and killed her, and that's the end of it. Her body will never be found, but we'll have a conclusion to the mystery. Case closed. Everyone can just get on with life."

"Nobody's looking for an easy way out," he said with frustration.

"Everybody's looking for an easy way out," Dana declared. "And why not? It's been seven years. An easy, made-up answer would be better than not having an answer at all, right? The parents of missing children always say the worst thing is not knowing."

"I'm sure Casey's mama would sooner have her daughter alive anywhere than think she's dead," he countered.

"Have you asked her? Has anybody asked Mrs. Grant if she ever saw that man before? Am I the only person in a town of ten thousand people who might have seen him?"

"No. Mrs. Grant moved away years ago, to Hawaii, I heard. But you and Casey were practically joined at the hip. Maybe this creep would have approached the two of you at the Grindstone or at someplace like that," he said. "He preyed on young women. He frequented truck stops. Casey worked at the Grindstone. It's not outside the realm of possibility that he came there.

"I mean, I know you all weren't getting along right before Casey disappeared, but—"

"We weren't?"

"No," he said. "You were having some kind of a girl spat. You don't remember that?"

"No."

Dana tried to think back. All the ready memories of Casey were happy ones—the two of them smiling and laughing, having fun, being girls.

"It was about John Villante, as I recall. Casey and him had a big falling out; she was probably going to take him back," he said. "That's what you and Casey usually fought about. Villante's back in town, by the way. I ran across him last night."

"I know," Dana said absently, still trying to dig for the memory.

"Maybe you don't recall that you and I broke up that summer," Tim mused, flashing a comically hopeful look. "That could work out for me."

"I remember that," Dana said without regard for his ego.

"Dang." He pretended disappointment, then took a sip of his coffee.

"You wouldn't want me now, anyway," Dana said quietly. "I'm not the girl you used to know."

He propped his forearms on the table, leaned down, and looked at her hiding inside the black hood of her sweatshirt. She felt trapped at the back of a cave with no exit.

"I think she's probably still in there somewhere," he said softly.

Dana shoved her chair back from the table and stood up. "No. She's not. You should go now. I'm tired."

"Okay, well, I need to be getting to work anyway," he said, pushing his chair back from the table. He fished his wallet out of his hip pocket, pulled out a business card, and laid it on the table.

"You call me," he said. "For any reason at all. If you have something to tell me, if you just want to talk, or . . . whatever. I'm told I'm a reasonably entertaining dinner companion."

"I'm not very social anymore," Dana said as they walked to the front of the house.

"That's all right. I recall we had some pretty nice times doing nothing much at all. God knows I can talk enough for the both of us."

"You talk a lot," Dana said. "And I blurt out things I shouldn't. That could be entertaining for someone."

He paused on the front step. Dana pulled her phone out of her pouch and snapped a picture of him.

"It helps my memory," she said.

He nodded but glanced away, like maybe he didn't want her to see something in his face, like sadness or pity.

"I know the circumstances aren't anything we would have asked for," he said. "But I really am glad to reconnect, Dana. We were good friends. It's been too long."

"Thanks for the flowers."

"You're welcome. I'd give you a hug, but I know you don't want that," he said. "I am a hugger, if you recall, so . . ." He pointed to his temples and smiled. "I'm hugging you up here. It's a good one. Visualize if you care to."

"Maybe later," she said, finding a little smile to give back to him.

"That smile is nice to see," he said softly. "You go have a rest. And lock your doors. It's not as safe here as it used to be."

"No," Dana said. "Turns out it never was."

13

He pulled the cruiser to the curb in a yellow zone on the curve near the ER entrance and parked.

The Liddell Regional Medical Center was a bigger name than facility. While the name brought to mind a sprawling complex, the medical center was in fact a respectable modern small hospital that served the basic needs of the area. If you needed your appendix out, this was the place. If your wife was having a baby, the maternity ward was nice. If you got your lip busted in a bar fight, the ER staff could stitch you up just fine. Aside from the normal maladies and misadventures, all major and exotic diseases and traumas were deferred to one of Louisville's many outstanding medical facilities just a short helicopter hop or ambulance ride away.

"Hey, Deputy Carver."

"Hey, Jeannine," he said, waving to the plump middle-aged red-head at the reception desk as he came through the ER doors.

"Are you stopping by to keep me company?"

"As pleasant as that would be, I'm afraid I'm here on business," he said, but he went to the counter nevertheless. It always paid down the road to cultivate friendships in a small town. He was a frequent visitor to the ER, coming in to interview drunken brawlers, overdose cases, accident victims, and the like. He made it a point to treat the staff well.

Jeannine Halston frowned, leaning toward him, arms on the counter. "That poor girl from last night," she said, her voice hushed so as not to be overheard by any of the bored, uncomfortable people sitting in the waiting area. "I heard she got beat real bad. Kay O'Dell said she looks like she went five rounds with Floyd Mayweather."

"I didn't know you and Kay were boxing fans."

"Do you have any suspects?"

"I can't tell you that."

"I don't know what she was thinking, walking home at that hour," she said. "Nothing good happens around the Grindstone after midnight. Hookers in and out of those truck cabs. Drug deals going down in the parking lot."

Tim arched a brow. "Sounds like maybe we should deputize you, Jeannine. You've got your finger on the pulse of crime in Liddell County."

"Maybe you should."

"Can you tell me what floor my victim is on?"

"She's on two. I heard you answered the call. I was off last night. Was it as bad as they say?"

"I don't know what they're saying, but there's sure as hell no good kind of assault. No matter what it looks like, it's all bad for the victim."

"Did she see the man? Did she know him?"

"All will be revealed in the full measure of time," he said, drifting away from the counter. "You'll probably know before me, anyway. See you later, Jeannine."

He took the stairs to the second floor because he didn't want to end up looking like the man who was standing at the nurses' station, scowling as he read over a report.

"Isn't the maternity ward on the third floor?" Tim said, winking at the nurse behind the counter. "Oh, Walt, that's you!"

"Very funny, Carver," the detective said. "I'll have you know this belly runs in my family."

"I gotta think that belly don't run anywhere."

Tubman patted his stomach like it was a faithful dog. "This here is a lifelong achievement, son."

On the high side of his fifties, Tubman looked like a cross between Teddy Roosevelt and a walrus. He had come to the Liddell County Sheriff's Office from Indianapolis about the same time Tim had, looking for a less hectic pace on the downside of his career.

"This belly represents the accumulation of years of expertise in the culinary arts of fried food and pastry."

"A man should have something to show for his efforts," Tim said. "How's our victim?"

"She's been sedated most of the day, but Trish here tells me she seems fairly alert now."

"She's just about due for her pain meds," the nurse said. "You should talk to her now because she'll be out of it after that."

"Let's do it," Tim said.

The nurse preceded them into the room, speaking to her patient in a soft voice, explaining who the men were and why they were there, then slipped out quietly.

April Johnson lay propped up in the bed, her head best resembling a giant rotting tomato—misshapen, discolored, oozing. She had taken a beating like a punching bag in a boxing gym full of rage-a-holics.

She was—had been—pretty enough in a plain sort of way. Young and not terribly bright, she had poured coffee for Tim at the Grindstone on many occasions. Tim had to think she made decent tips because she had a cute figure and she liked to flirt a little in a sweet, innocent way.

She wouldn't be flirting with anyone anytime soon. Even once the bruises faded and the swelling subsided, it was going to take a few weeks to get her some new teeth.

"Hey, April," he said. "Deputy Carver here."

He introduced himself because he doubted she could see him very well with two black eyes swollen nearly shut.

"It's good to see you awake," he said.

She had been drifting in and out of consciousness when he had first arrived on the scene the night before. She was lucky to have been found. The assumption was that her assailant had followed her from the truck stop down a footpath that cut across a wooded lot and came out about three blocks from the trailer park where she lived. The path had been there forever. Adults had been warning kids not to cut through that lot for as long as Tim could remember. And for that long and longer, people hadn't listened. It was the shortest distance between two desired points.

The attack had taken place at the halfway point on the trail, the place where the light from the truck-stop parking lot on one end and the streetlight at the other end was dim and diffuse, the charcoal-gray light of a bad dream. That spot on the path was as far from the opportunity of a witness as possible.

April had been initially attacked on the path, then pulled off the trail behind a thicket of wild blackberry bushes, where her assailant had sexually assaulted her. He had left her there, facedown in the dirt and loam. She had dragged herself back toward the parking lot of the Grindstone, not quite making it. If not for a trucker too lazy to walk to the building to use the john, she would probably have been there all night. April Johnson owed her life to a guy who had decided to take a leak in the woods behind his big rig.

She didn't acknowledge Tim in any way.

"April, Detective Tubman and I need to ask you some questions. Do you think you can answer for us?"

She sighed. "Can-n't hard-ly t-alk," she said, the words all but unintelligible. Her jaw didn't move. The sound had to find its way around broken teeth and swollen lips and came out in a wet whisper he had to bend down to hear.

"We'll try to keep to yes-or-no questions. If you can't talk, maybe make a gesture with your hand. Thumbs up for yes. Like that."

"April, did you get a look at the man who did this to you?" Tubman asked.

"Nnn-o-o. D-ark. Mmmm-asssk."

"He wore a mask?" Tubman scribbled in a little notebook. "A ski mask?"

"C-cam-mo."

"Camouflage?"

"Y-yes."

"Was he a big guy?" Tim asked. "Tall?"

She made an impatient gesture with her hand, calling attention to the angry red scratches the brambles had etched into her skin as she had crawled and dragged herself toward help. She was tougher than he would have given her credit for. You never knew about people until they were tested by adversity.

"Was he bigger than you?"

She raised her thumb.

"Was he heavyset?" Tim asked. "Did he have a big ol' belly like Detective Tubman here?"

"Nnn-no."

"Did he say anything to you before or during the attack?" Tubman asked.

"Nnn-nooo. Just starr-ted hit-ting mm-me."

"Could he be anyone you know, April?" Tim asked. "Someone angry with you?"

"Wwwhy?" she asked. "Why wwwould any-body . . . No."

"Can you tell us anything about him, April?" Tubman asked. "Anything at all?"

She didn't respond for so long, Tim thought she might have passed out or died. Finally she sucked in a deep breath and said, "So . . . st-rong . . . Angry. So . . . so . . . ang-ry."

She began to cry then, a strange, soft, mewling sound that was both piteous and eerie. Her hand scratched at the bed, balling the white sheet into her fist.

"Hurts," she said on a moan. "It hurts."

The door opened and the nurse slipped back into the room, dragging a cart loaded with medications.

Tim and Tubman went back into the hall. Tubman scribbled in his notebook as they waited for the elevator. Tim rested his hands on his belt.

"So she was attacked by an angry, average guy in a mask," Tubman said. "That narrows it down."

"A camo ski mask," Tim stipulated.

"So we're looking for a turkey hunter—or any guy with a Cabela's catalog," Tubman said. "We've tracked down most everybody that was in the Grindstone last night. People remember April leaving because she said good-bye. Nobody saw anyone follow her out."

"So the guy was in the parking lot."

"Or he knew she would be cutting through that lot at that time, and he was lying in wait."

The elevator opened and a pair of square, middle-aged women in pastel track suits got off, one with a bouquet of flowers, the other with a bag of knitting. Coming to sit with a sick loved one. Maybe they were related to April Johnson, and they would sit in her room and watch game shows on TV, and talk about nothing, and pretend it was all normal while April breathed in and out through her broken teeth.

"Then she wasn't just an opportunity; she was a target," Tim said as they got on the elevator and the doors closed behind them. "In which case he must know her."

"He was wearing a mask. Maybe because he didn't want her to recognize him."

"A ski mask is pretty standard equipment for your average rapist."

"Maybe so," Tubman conceded, "but I think he knew April Johnson would be on that trail. And I think you have to be from here to know about that trail in the first place."

"So he's somebody who has it in for April. Why?" Tim asked. "She's a sweet girl. Not too bright, but not the kind to piss people off."

"Rejected suitor?"

"She's been pining away for Tommy Lynn Puckett, whose worthless bony ass is sitting in our own fine jail right now for driving on a suspended license."

"Does Tommy Lynn have any enemies who might want to take out their frustrations on his girl?"

Tim shrugged. "Other than April, I don't think there's a person in Liddell County—or the world, for that matter—who gives two shits about Tommy Lynn Puckett, including his own mama."

They got off on the first floor and Tubman took a detour to the vending machines down the hall from the waiting room.

"You were on patrol last night," he said, feeding a couple of bills into a machine and punching buttons for a cappuccino. "Was anything going on?"

Tim shook his head. "Naw. Not really. I heard there was a bit of a media circus over at Senator Mercer's house in Bridlewood. You know, because Dana Nolan came home. But I wasn't over there."

"I saw that on the news." Tubman sipped his coffee and made a face, though whether the look was prompted by the taste or by his memory wasn't clear. "Poor girl looks like an extra from the *Walking Dead*."

"That was hard to see," Tim admitted. "Dana was a pretty girl, never a hair out of place. She always had everything in her life lined up just so. She'd make a goal and have a plan, and go right down the checklist until she achieved whatever it was. No deviation from the plan, ever. Rigid, I guess you could say, but she got where she wanted to go."

"Sounds like a bitch."

"No, no. As sweet as she could be. Unless you rocked her boat, then, man, she'd cut a person off like a dead limb. Boom! Just like that. Done."

"Is that the voice of experience talking?"

"Me? No," Tim said, looking pensive. "We split up because it was time; that's all. We were each going our own directions. We were kids, for crying out loud. Who stays with their high school girlfriend all their life?"

"About two-thirds of people around here."

"Well, me and Dana were destined for bigger things."

"Yet, here you both are," Tubman pointed out.

Tim shrugged. "Life takes some funny twists. I stopped by to see her today, and I asked her about the Doc Holiday thing," he said. "Asked did she remember seeing him back when Casey Grant went missing."

"And?"

He shook his head. "She says she doesn't remember anything that happened to her, doesn't remember what the guy looked like. Doesn't want to."

"Not even if it helps her friend's case?"

"Does it, though?" Tim asked. "Casey's gone. If that guy took her, she's dead and gone. Either way, we don't get Casey back."

"We could get a lead, though."

"A lead on a dead man."

"Sounds good to me," Tubman said. "In fact, that would be the best of all worlds if we could put the victim with a known serial killer who is now dead. The state wouldn't even have to go to the expense of a trial. It'd be like virtual justice."

"The best of all worlds for you is putting a teenage girl with a serial killer? That's cold, man."

"I'm not wishing it on her. I'm just saying. If she's dead, she's dead. I'd like to close that case. That's all."

"Well, you'll have to do it without Dana Nolan," Tim said. "Unless I can get her to soften up."

Tubman smiled and patted him on the shoulder. "I have faith in you, my young, handsome friend."

Tim laughed. "I hope you're good at holding your breath. She all but threw me out of the house for even bringing up the subject today. I wouldn't expect her to change her attitude anytime soon. In the meantime, though, I did see someone last night you might want to have a conversation with."

"Who's that?"

"John Villante. He was Casey Grant's boyfriend. I hadn't seen him since that summer. I heard he got packed off to the army, but he's back. He's a delivery guy for Anthony's Pizzeria. I came across him out by the state park last night, sitting in the parking lot back by the maintenance buildings. Said he wasn't doing nothing, just sitting there gathering his thoughts, but you and I both know the kind of stuff that goes down back there."

"Refresh my memory. Does he have a record?"

"Juvenile shit when we were kids. Since then . . . I don't know. Like I said, the last I knew he was in the army."

"Drugs?"

"He liked to smoke a little weed as I recall, but I don't know what else. I can tell you the boy had a short fuse and quick fists. I'm sure you know from reading the file that Detective Hardy liked him for Casey's disappearance, but nothing ever came of it. You have read the file, right?"

Tubman made a face like he was passing gas. "Yeah. A seven-year-old disappearance with no victim and no evidence? I'm all over that."

"Well, John Villante was the key person of interest. Now he's back in town and a girl gets raped and beaten . . ."

"Was he violent with the Grant girl?"

"I never saw any bruises on her, but they had one of those breakup/makeup relationships. They had a blowout right before she went missing."

"What about?"

Tim shrugged. "I wasn't privy to it. Dana and I had already split up by then and I was busy with other things. I do remember Dana was fed up with the never-ending drama. Casey and John would break up. Casey would go running to cry on Dana's shoulder. Dana must have told Casey a hundred times to dump that loser, but Casey always took him back. They had a kind of Romeo and Juliet syndrome, Casey and John. Star-crossed lovers. She was going to be the one to save him from . . ." He shrugged as he searched for what might have made sense to an eighteen-year-old girl. "His upbringing, his bad attitude, his . . . whatever."

"You mean their families didn't get along?"

"Casey's mom didn't like John. And nobody gets along with his old man. Mack Villante is the most contrary, mean, nasty son of a bitch you'd ever want to come across. He's been a guest of the county more than a few times. He'd probably have a rap sheet as long as my arm if people weren't too scared of him to press charges."

"So maybe the apple didn't fall far from the tree," Tubman said. He tossed back the last of his coffee and dropped the cup in the trash. "See if you can't get John Villante to come in for a chat."

14

They looked so young in the photographs. Dana turned through the pages of her high school yearbook, reading the things her classmates had written in their farewell to childhood. The usual sentimental tripe of teenagers: *I'll never forget you! We'll always have S.M.H.S.! Best Friends Forever! Rock on!*

Rested after a short nap, she had pulled the book from the shelves and propped herself up against the pillows for a trip down memory lane, hoping her memory would participate. Tuxedo joined her on the bed, curling himself into a purring knot of fur up against one of the piles of clothing Dana had yet to deal with. The yearbook seemed a better choice than organizing the clothes, despite what Dr. Burnette had said about setting a goal to put her stuff away.

There had been 173 kids in Dana's graduating class. If their names hadn't been printed beneath their photographs, Dana thought she probably couldn't have recalled more than a dozen at a glance. The faces were familiar. The photographs that put them in context with activities like cheerleading, the school newspaper, and yearbook staff helped trigger memories. Once one memory was triggered, others with the same cast followed.

She had had many acquaintances in school, but only a few really close friends. She had always been a creature of schedules and lists and goals. So much time had to be allotted to her studies, so much to clubs, so much to activities, so much to her friendships. The balance had to be maintained so she could achieve the level of success she wanted in each area.

It hadn't made sense to her to try to be besties with a gaggle of girls. She had structured her friendships in tiers. Casey was her best friend. Nichole Findlay had been her—and Casey's—second-best friend. Then came a tier of girls and guys she knew through classes and activities, with whom she had been friendly but not close.

As she thought back on the meticulously organized girl she had been, Dana felt a strange mix of familiarity and distance. She thought of the Dana in the photographs as someone she used to know rather than someone she was or had been. And yet, there were photographs that triggered strong memories and strong feelings that were deeply, intrinsically *hers*.

Tucked among the pages was a strip of black-and-white photobooth photos of her and Casey. Side by side, cheek to cheek, one light, one dark, smiling and laughing, making faces and cutting up for the camera. As she stared at the pictures, a cavernous sense of grief yawned open inside her, and Dana could picture herself, tiny, teetering on the edge of it, ready to fall into the abyss of sadness and longing.

"I miss you, Case," she murmured to the dark-haired girl in the photographs. And she felt it, really felt it, like a heavy pressure on her chest. She missed her friend, the girl she hadn't thought of in months until last night.

Tim said she and Casey hadn't been getting along at the time of Casey's disappearance. It made her sad to think that they had wasted time being angry, not knowing that their time was about to run out. A spat over Casey's relationship with John Villante, Tim suggested. It wouldn't have been their first disagreement on that subject, but it would have been their last.

John was dark and moody and overly sensitive. He didn't like

Casey's friends—which, of course, rubbed Dana the wrong way. Casey had been her best friend long before she had ever wanted anything to do with boys. And Dana prided herself on being a good and loyal friend. That was the whole point of having a few close friendships as opposed to many casual ones—so she could be the best friend possible. Who was John Villante to criticize her? What did he know about being a good friend? He didn't have any friends . . . except Casey.

Dana turned another page of the yearbook, and another, taking in the photographs. John and Tim as football stars, as basketball stars. Sometimes they got along; sometimes they didn't. There was a picture of Casey and herself in their cheerleader outfits. Casey under the caption "Most Friendly." Dana and Tim under the banner "Most Likely to Succeed." Herself and Tim decked out as homecoming royalty, and another photo of them looking serious as student government leaders.

Tuxedo popped his head up and meowed seconds before the light rap on the door. Dana's mother poked her head into the room.

"I thought you might still be sleeping," she said, letting herself in. "Did you get some rest?"

"Sure," Dana answered, not interested in mentioning that her sleep had been peppered with fragmented memories and dreams like scattershot fired from another dimension. All the changes in the last two days, all the newly remembered faces, all the fresh suggestions of what she should do and who she could be—all of it was overloading the circuits of her brain.

"That was quite a surprise to see Tim again," her mother said, sitting down on the edge of the bed. "I guess we just lost track of his family. You weren't seeing him anymore, and both of you had gone away to school . . . I had heard his parents were splitting up, but . . . I guess there was no reason to keep in touch."

"I didn't stay in contact with him either," Dana said. "I don't think he stayed in touch with me. I don't remember that he did."

"He wasn't too happy when you broke up with him. I don't imagine he felt a need to keep in touch."

Dana frowned. "But we were both going away that fall. We both knew that was the end."

At least that was the way she was remembering it.

Her mother picked a T-shirt off the pile of clothes and began to fold it. "Young men have tender egos. That summer was supposed to be his time to shine. You tarnished that for him a little bit breaking up with him when you did."

"Boys are such babies," Dana said, the words falling strangely, as if a much younger version of herself had spoken them. "I was supposed to just be his arm candy all summer, then wait for him to pick the moment to break up with me when it was convenient for him?

"That's just stupid," Dana declared. "He always wanted everything to be his idea."

"He was a little full of himself that spring," her mother recalled. "But I remember that he could be very sweet, too, and he always had a great sense of humor. I always thought he would go far."

"He went far and came back," Dana said. "That doesn't make sense to me. He was all about his big career in the military. Remember?"

He had been in every parade for fifty miles that summer. The big West Point cadet riding around in the back of a Cadillac convertible, waving to the crowds.

"Sometimes big plans look better from a distance," her mother said, folding another top. "Maybe the reality of that bigger life just wasn't a good fit for him. I'm sure that wasn't easy to admit or accept.

"But he decided he wanted to come back here and make a difference," she said. "I like what that says about him. Casey's disappearance inspired him to a career that he feels strongly about. He's dedicated to it and ambitious. It doesn't sound like he settled for something. He just made a different choice."

A mischievous smile turned one corner of her mouth. She cut Dana a sideways glance as she made a neat stack of the T-shirts. "And he's still pretty darn handsome, thinning hair notwithstanding."

"So I'm sure he has all the girlfriends he wants," Dana said flatly. "Good for him."

"I'm not suggesting that," her mother said. "But there's no reason you can't enjoy his friendship or his company. He made a point to come here and welcome you home."

"Mom, don't go there. Really."

"The two of you were friends for a long time. You know each other. You're comfortable together. It would be nice for you to have that friendship again. He could always make you laugh. I'd like to hear that again."

Dana said nothing but reached for a T-shirt from the pile and folded it. She hadn't given any thought to having any kind of social life. Her focus was on her immediate self, on healing and therapy and finding something to do with her life. She hadn't thought about having friends, male or female. She hadn't thought about reconnecting with the world in a social way. The idea made her uncomfortable. She wasn't ready. She wasn't sure she would ever be ready.

"He came here to ask me about Doc Holiday," she said. "The flowers were a bonus."

Her mother's back stiffened. Her expression hardened. "He did what?"

"He did his job."

Dana pulled a purple hoodie from the pile. Tuxedo rolled onto his back and batted at the dangling hood strings with his white-mittened paws.

"He asked me if I remembered seeing Doc Holiday around here before Casey went missing," she said, and shrugged. "I don't know what Doc Holiday looked like. I can't remember him. I don't want to remember him."

"You don't have to," her mother said. "I don't want you to."

"You're the only one," Dana said, folding the sweatshirt and setting it aside. She pulled a jewelry pouch from the pile of belongings and dumped the contents in her lap.

"Tim said Casey and I weren't getting along before she disappeared," she said. "Do you remember that?"

Her mother's brow knitted as she tried to recall. She smoothed her hands over the folded sweatshirt in her lap and sighed. "The usual teenage drama. There was plenty to go around. Breakups, makeups. I couldn't keep up. You had broken up with Tim. Casey always had some drama with her boyfriend. You were upset because Casey was upset. Or you were upset with Casey for being upset. But you never stopped being friends. Casey stayed overnight here the night before she went missing."

Dana tried to pick a necklace from the jumble of jewelry. The chains of several necklaces had somehow woven themselves into a knot. She couldn't tell which chain belonged to which charm bristling from the knot like the elaborate spines of some fantasy sea creature—a cross, a heart, a butterfly, a flower with a tiny pearl in the center.

"I was out of town," her mother said. "I was in Florida. Grandma was having surgery. I remember Roger complaining over the phone that two teenage girls was more than he could cope with."

"Roger's a dick."

"Dana!"

"Well, he is."

"That's not true," her mother argued. "I don't know where this sudden animosity is coming from."

"I don't think it's sudden," Dana said. "I think I just don't have good impulse control anymore."

"That's a fact. Maybe Dr. Burnette can help you with that. See if she can work on your sudden use of bad language, too."

"I don't think she'll be helpful with that," Dana said as she continued to fuss with the necklaces.

The necklace with the cross had been a gift for her confirmation when she was fourteen. The heart had been a gift from Casey. The flower with the pearl had belonged to her great-grandmother on her father's side. The butterfly . . . She didn't recognize the butterfly.

She tried to pick the necklaces apart with her fingertips, tried to loosen something into a single recognizable thread—a task not unlike trying to make sense of the jumble of memories and thoughts in her mind.

"That's a mess," her mother said. She reached out a hand. "Let me hold it while you untangle."

Dana dropped the ball of chains in her mother's palm and used two hands to fuss with the necklaces, working the butterfly necklace free. She held it up to the light and studied the pendant, a butterfly rendered in intricate silver filigree.

"That's beautiful," her mother said. "Where did you get that?"

"I don't know," Dana murmured, staring at the butterfly as it turned in the light, a strange sense of apprehension stirring within. "I don't remember ever having this."

Her mother reached out and fingered the end of the chain. "It's broken. See where the latch is?"

Dana examined the chain. The latch was in place and fastened, but two inches down from the latch, the chain separated. As she looked more closely, she could see that the links had not pulled apart but had been cut.

"That was in the bag," her mother said. "I remember that was in the bag of your belongings at the hospital. You must have been wearing it when they found you. They must have cut the chain off in the ER that night."

Dana closed her hand around the butterfly, the points of the tiny wings digging into her palm, and a low current of anxiety hummed through her, though she didn't know why. She opened her hand and looked at the marks that crossed the lines of her palm and wondered if somehow the necklace had made a similar impression on her life. Had it meant something to her? Had someone given it to her as a token of affection or to mark an occasion, as the other necklaces in the pouch had? They were all things with memories attached.

But as she set the necklace aside on her nightstand, she had the uneasy feeling that she might not want to remember this one, even if she could.

"What do you think happened to Casey?" she asked, taking the rest of the necklace knot from her mother to work at freeing the small heart.

"I don't know," her mother said, getting up and taking the stack of tops to the closet. "I guess I want to believe she ran away. No one ever found evidence to the contrary. For her mother's sake, I hope that's what happened."

Dana followed her into the spacious walk-in and watched her sort the T-shirts and hoodies, arranging them neatly on the shelves.

"Then again, I wouldn't wish that not-knowing on anyone, either. It's a terrible thing—not knowing where your child is. Is she alive? Is she in pain? The wondering, the speculation—it's terrible. I can't imagine living with that year after year. I don't think I could stand it."

"Would you rather know I was dead?"

"No! Of course not!"

Dana shrugged. "That's the alternative."

"I would rather nothing bad happen in the first place."

"But it did," Dana said. "It happened to Casey *and* to me. That's weird, isn't it?"

"It's a terrible coincidence."

"Or not. If the same man took us."

"I don't know why we're having this conversation," her mother said, frustrated. She turned and left the closet, walking away from the issue. "He's dead. It's over. I don't see the point in wondering about it. It's time for everyone to move forward."

"Has Casey's mom moved forward?" Dana asked, following her.

"I don't know. I haven't heard from Caroline in years. She moved to Hawaii."

"But you used to be friends."

"We were friends because our daughters were friends," she said. She picked up an empty suitcase from the floor, put it on the foot of the bed, and zipped it shut, her movements quick and efficient. "After you went away to college . . . It was just too hard."

Dana sat down beside the suitcase. "Too hard for who?"

"For both of us. The things we had in common were you girls and your activities. Then suddenly I had a daughter and Caroline didn't. It was just too hard for both of us."

"Did you feel guilty?" Dana asked, more interested in having her questions answered than in her mother's discomfort with them.

"Of course I felt guilty. I had my perfect, smart, beautiful daughter, and Caroline . . . didn't. How could I not feel guilty about that?"

"But you abandoned her," Dana said without thought.

Her mother looked like she'd been slapped. "I did not!"

"You didn't want to be around her because you felt guilty, so you stopped being her friend. You just said so."

"She didn't want to be around me, either," she pointed out, taking the suitcase to the closet and setting it inside. "Why would she? So she could be reminded of what she'd lost? I tried to be there for her those first few months, but I could never say the right thing. I never knew what to do to help. She was living through something I couldn't even imagine."

"But now you know."

"Yes. Now I know," she said quietly as she came back to the bed and sat down beside Dana. "And I know there wasn't anything I could have done to make it better for Caroline, because there isn't anything that makes losing a child better. There's nothing anyone can say or do that makes that okay or less than what it is. Nothing.

"People try to give you some kind of comfort or some kind of divine explanation for what's happening, and they can't," she said. "There is no explanation for evil. Bad things happen. They don't happen for a reason. We have to deal with them as best we can. It doesn't help to have someone try to tell you there's some kind of greater plan," she said. "Why would anybody tell a parent that?"

"I don't know," Dana said. "Maybe it makes them feel like it can't happen to them if the plan was meant for someone else."

"Maybe."

"Didn't you think that when Casey went missing? Better her than me? Doesn't everybody think that when they see a tragedy?"

Her mother looked at her for a long moment as she processed the thought. She reached out a hand and stroked Dana's short-cropped hair like she was delivering a blessing.

"Everybody but a mother," she said softly, tears misting her eyes. "Better me than you, little one. There's nothing in this world or any other I wouldn't protect you from if I could. If only we got to choose."

"Only the bad guy gets to choose," Dana said. "The rest of us are just pieces in his game."

"Not anymore. No more," her mother whispered, shaking her head. "Never again."

But even as her mother pulled her close and held her tight, Dana knew she couldn't make that promise and keep it. The world was full of people with bad intentions. Her mother wanted to ignore that fact. She wanted to believe that once evil had touched their lives and they had somehow survived, they would now be immune, as if they had survived a disease and developed antibodies against reinfection.

Dana knew that wasn't true. She could still imagine the oily residue of evil on her skin. She could still smell it in her dreams. She could still sense it lurking just beyond the reach of the light as day faded beyond her window. She could still feel the pull of its energy, daring her to fight or to run.

She didn't want it to touch her. She didn't want to go near it. But at the same time, she kept seeing Casey's face from the terrible dream, confronting her, ridiculing her.

You should have seen him coming . . . I died for nothing . . . I'm as dead as you are . . .

She closed her eyes and saw the bloody infant that looked up at her with her own face. What did it mean? That she had become who she was at Casey's expense? That she had pursued her career and found success because of what had happened to her friend? Had her own suffering at the hands of Doc Holiday somehow been payback for that? Or was finding the truth about what had happened to Casey her chance at redemption?

That was a challenge she didn't feel strong enough to accept. But even as she hid in the refuge of her mother's arms, she had the terrible feeling it was a challenge she wouldn't be able to escape.

15

In Shelby Mills, if a man wanted a job that paid cash with people who asked no questions, he went to the truck stop out by the interstate and hung around in the parking lot on the west side of Silva's Garage. George Silva, a man who had built his life up from the dirt, let day laborers gather there around the picnic tables his mechanics used on their break time. The only rule was that no one make any trouble.

First thing in the morning and at the end of the day, people would come looking to hire. The work offered was simple physical labor—digging ditches and heavy lifting, farmwork, and the like. The jobs might last a day or a week or as long as it took to pick all the apples in an orchard. They were generally the kinds of jobs that didn't require much more than a strong back. They were the kinds of jobs that didn't require customer relations skills, or speaking English, for that matter. There were no benefits and there was no withholding. Pay was flat cash money.

Most of the men who showed up at this spot were Hispanic with dubious documentation. Or they were local guys a little down on their luck, maybe just out of jail for petty stuff, or guys that drank too much from time to time who needed work between benders.

John joined them reluctantly late in the day. He had no faith that

Tony Tarantino would come through with another job for him. That would require an effort on Tony's part—something Paula would squash like a bug. And seeing how she carried Tony's balls around in a tiny little jar in her handbag, that would be the end of that.

John parked his truck under the trees at the edge of the parking lot and went around to sit on the tailgate, staying away from the picnic tables and the other men. He hadn't come for camaraderie or commiseration. He didn't want to draw any attention or invite any conversation. He pulled his ball cap low over his eyes and hunched his shoulders up around his ears, his hands jammed in the pockets of his jacket.

Anxiety stirred in his belly as he waited. From where he sat he could see his father's black Chevy Avalanche parked in the line of cars by the garage. The old man worked as a mechanic for Silva. He would get off work between four and five, then go to the bar across the street and drink boilermakers until he was feeling good and mean. At some point in the evening he would come back to the truck stop, go to the Grindstone for dinner or for a piece of pie.

John didn't want his father seeing him here. He didn't want to have to hear the old man crowing over the fact that he had gotten fired from Anthony's. He didn't need to hear the I-told-you-so bullshit. His father had been calling him a failure his whole life. It pissed John off no end that every once in a while the rotten bastard turned out to be right.

Right now he was a loser. He was a failure. His father called him a quitter, but he had never been that. People quit on him, not the other way around. That had always been the case. His mother had quit on him. Teachers had quit on him. Casey had quit on him. The army had quit on him. But here he was, coming back for more.

Half a dozen Hispanic guys were hanging around one of the picnic tables. One of them had brought along a portable radio that was playing Mexican polka music as the men chatted and laughed. After a few initial glances, they paid no mind to John.

He checked his watch and hunkered down a little deeper into the upturned collar of his coat. Four forty-seven. Guys were starting to wander out of the mouth of Silva's Garage. He could hear his old man's voice from across the parking lot—not the words, but the tone of it—and then the laughter of several men.

John willed him not to look his way, as if that would do any good. He was in no mood to take shit from his father. Just the possibility got his blood up. His brain raced ahead, running the worst possible scenario: Mack spotting him, making a beeline across the parking lot, laughing out loud, telling everyone in earshot that he'd seen it coming, that his loser kid had lost his job. He would go on saying that John was such a loser, he even failed at being a pizza deliveryman. And now here he was, come begging for the shit jobs usually tossed to fucking wetbacks.

As he listened in his mind to his father's hate-filled racist diatribe, John could feel the pressure building inside his head until he couldn't hear at all, until his vision flushed red. He could see himself running at the old man. He could feel the tension in his upper arm as he drew his fist back and the release as he let it fly like a stone being hurled from a catapult. He could feel the sweet pain sing up his forearm all the way to his shoulder as his knuckles crushed the old man's nose.

He knew once he started, once the gate was thrown open on his hatred, he wouldn't be able to stop. He would keep punching and punching and punching until someone pulled him off. And he would sincerely hope that wouldn't happen until the son of a bitch was drowning in his own blood.

His heart was pumping now. His vision was narrowing, telescoping in on the man across the parking lot. His fists clenched hard in the pockets of his coat.

If he didn't break this train of thought now, it was going to be too late. That truth cut through the hot haze in his brain like a knife.

He wasn't sure he cared.

He wasn't sure it wouldn't be worth it.

And then a car door slammed and a small child's voice shattered the pounding of his pulse inside his head.

"Papi! Papi!"

A dark-haired little girl of five or six dashed away from an old Toyota toward the picnic tables, her face bright with joy as she ran toward her smiling father.

John slipped off the tailgate and walked around the front of his truck. This edge of the parking area was bordered by a wooded lot nobody ever bothered clearing out except for a trail that cut through, a shortcut to the nearest neighborhood. Three steps in and he would disappear.

Still watching the parking lot, he stepped in among the trees. He watched as his father got into his truck, backed up, and turned around. The Avalanche paused for a moment, Mack Villante looking in the direction of John's truck. John held his breath, then let it out as his father drove forward, headed across the road, more concerned with getting a drink than wondering about his own son.

John watched him go, thinking that he had to scrape something together. He had to get a job and save enough money that he could get the hell out of Shelby Mills, out of his father's house. He didn't feel as if he had a future, but he sure as hell didn't want to keep living in his past.

Something rustled in the brush behind him, and he spun around, crouching low, arms up, hands out in front of him, ready to defend or attack as need be. He scanned his surroundings left to right and back and saw no one. Then the brush moved again at ten o'clock, down low, and he dropped his gaze.

A dog lay in the brush maybe fifteen feet away, watching him intently, some kind of German shepherd cross by the look of it, with a thick dark coat and bright eyes.

John squatted down, eyes on the dog, hand outstretched. The dog lowered its head and flattened its ears. Leaves rustled behind it, as if it must have been wagging its tail.

"I won't hurt you," John said quietly.

The dog whined and cried but stayed where it was. John took a step toward it, and the dog came up in a crouch and stepped backward. It was young, or starved, or both. Lean and ribby, tucked up in the flanks. In need of care but not wanting to trust anyone who might give it.

I know how you feel, John thought, but he made no move to reach out again. What the hell would he do with a dog? His old man would never have it at the house. John knew that from hard experience. He had tried a couple of times to have a pet when he was a kid. He wouldn't let himself remember what had happened to them. He could only recall the emotions attached to those memories: heartbreak, grief, hatred.

He turned his back on the dog and walked back out to the parking lot.

A truck from Mercer-Nolan Landscape Design had pulled into the area near the picnic tables. A thick-bodied man in his fifties got out wearing jeans and a uniform shirt and heavy work boots. The Hispanic guys gathered around him.

"I need some strong backs for heavy lifting," he was saying as John hustled up to the group. The man holding the little girl on his hip translated into Spanish for the others.

The Mercer-Nolan guy eyed John. His name was embroidered over his shirt pocket: Bill Kenny. "Can you lift, soldier?"

"Yes, sir."

"Six forty-five in the A.M. We pick up here or you can get yourself to Mercer-Nolan if you know where it is."

"Yes, sir," John said. "Thank you, sir."

"Thank you for your service," Bill Kenny said, extending a hand.

John hesitated a second, then pulled his hand out of his coat pocket and reached out.

Bill Kenny frowned at the sight of his swollen, bruised knuckles and battered flesh.

He gave John a hard look. "You been fighting, son?"

"No, sir."

"The hell. I know a busted-up fist when I see one."

John stuffed his hand back in his pocket and hunched his shoulders. "Just hitting a bag, sir."

"You don't have sense enough to wear gloves?"

"Didn't have any."

Kenny clearly didn't believe him. John said nothing more. The frustration was like a busted-up fist in the center of his chest, pounding and pounding. What the hell difference did it make to this jerk if he wanted to knock his knuckles on a bag or a brick wall?

"I won't have troublemakers," Kenny warned.

"No, sir," John said. "I'm not. I swear, sir."

Kenny gave him a long look, then turned to the Hispanic guy who had translated and told him the same thing about pickup in the morning, saying he would take three of the six men. He pointed to the ones he wanted.

As he spoke, a Liddell County Sheriff's Office cruiser pulled into the parking area and rolled slowly toward them. The Hispanic guys exchanged nervous glances. John kept his head down, his gaze narrowed on the cop car as it came to a stop and the deputy climbed out. Tim Carver.

"Is there a problem, Deputy?" Bill Kenny asked with a bit of an edge in his voice, unappreciative of the interruption and the implied threat of authority. Crew bosses had been picking up day laborers, legal and not, in this parking lot for years. It was just the way things were done. Nobody messed with the system.

"Not at all," Carver said, thumbs hooked in his belt as he walked up. "I just need to have a word with Mr. Villante here."

"For what?" Kenny asked.

Carver smiled. "For none of your business, sir."

Kenny scowled. "Is he wanted for something?"

"Not that I'm aware of."

"No, sir," John said emphatically.

"I just have a couple of questions for him," Carver said. "John and I went to school together. This man here was the best tight end in three counties. Hands like butter and legs like a Kentucky Thoroughbred."

Bill Kenny looked suspicious of the story. He jammed his hands on his waist. "Tell me now if he's going to jail. I just hired him for tomorrow. If you're gonna take him, I'll replace him right now."

John's heart thumped in his chest. He didn't dare look at Tim Carver, or Bill Kenny, for that matter.

"No need for that," Carver said. "I'm not going to interfere in you hiring a veteran, Mr. Kenny. Especially when your alternative is probably not in possession of the proper credentials, right? You hire John, here. Made in the U.S. of A. And as I recall, he'll work like a damn mule."

He looked at John and tipped his head away from the group. "Let's just step over here for a minute, John. I need to ask you something."

He put his hand on John's shoulder as they turned and walked toward the truck. John moved to the side, deftly stepping away from the contact.

Carver got a peevish expression. "What ever happened to the concept of the comfort of the human touch?" he asked.

John chose not to answer. He turned and faced Carver, hands jammed down in his pockets, his right shoulder pressed against the side of his truck, as if he needed it for an anchor.

"I spoke with Tony Tarantino," Carver said. "He told me they had to let you go."

John said nothing.

His old teammate shook his head. "I told you coming back here was a bad idea, John."

"You tracked me out here to say I told you so?"

"No."

"How did you know I'd be here?"

He shrugged. "This is where men come when they got nowhere else to go, job-wise. I give you credit for trying."

John didn't want his pat on the back, literally or figuratively. His head was hurting now, a huge sense of pressure pushing outward, as if his skull had suddenly become too small for his brain. It pressed against the backs of his eyes and the base of his neck.

"What do you want from me?" he asked.

"Do you know a girl named April Johnson?"

"No."

"You're sure."

He said it as if he already knew the answer was something other than what John had said. John tried to think. Was that the name of some girl they'd gone to school with? He didn't have a social life. It wasn't like he had a long list of girlfriends, or friends of any sort, for that matter.

"She's a waitress at the Grindstone."

John shrugged. "Maybe. I don't know."

"No," Carver said. "I'm telling you. She's a waitress at the Grindstone. I'm told you go there fairly often."

"Who told you that?"

"Do you?"

"I go there sometimes." The coffee was strong and the pie was good, and it was a cheap place to eat when he was sick of the food he snuck at Anthony's.

"April," Carver said. "She's about nineteen, dark hair, cute figure, pretty enough. You don't remember her?"

"Why?"

"Where'd you go last night after work?"

"Home."

"Alone?"

"Why?"

"Mrs. Tarantino fired you last night," Carver said. "I have to think you might have been a little angry. Or a lot angry."

"You can tell me what this is about," John said, "or we're done talking."

"You shouldn't take an attitude with me, John. I'm gonna be the closest thing you've got to a friend here. The detective in charge of this case wants me to bring you in for a talk."

"What case?"

"April Johnson was assaulted last night cutting through these very woods after work. Somebody beat the ever-living shit out of her and raped her."

Heat flashed through John from the top of his head, down his arms, down his legs. "You're calling me a rapist?"

Carver held his hands up. "I didn't call you anything, John. I asked you where you were last night."

Anger ran like a fire along his nerve endings. Anger and fear. This wasn't the first time he'd been accused of something. He knew how this would go. He'd get hauled in to the sheriff's office, someone would tip off a reporter. The next thing would be a media feeding frenzy, and then the public outcry.

No one would care that he was now a decorated war hero. To the people who had been here seven years ago, he would still be the boyfriend of a girl who had disappeared, never to be seen again.

There was a part of him that wanted to bolt forward and knock Tim Carver flat, then jump in his truck and get the hell out of Shelby Mills, out of Liddell County, out of Indiana.

A low growl rumbled beside him, distracting him, and he looked down and to his left. The young dog had crept out of the woods and come to stand near him. It stared at Tim Carver without blinking, hackles raised.

Carver looked at the dog, frowning. "You'd better have control over your dog."

"It's not my dog," John said.

"Really? Then I'm calling Animal Control to come and get it. That thing looks mean."

John took a step toward the dog and said, "Git!"

The dog scurried backward to the edge of the woods and stood there.

"I don't know," John said. "Seems like he's maybe a good judge of character."

"Ha-ha. Be glad they sent me," Carver said. "Another deputy might have just hauled your ass in and shot that dog for a cur. I'm giving you an opportunity here, John."

"An opportunity to what?"

"To get out in front of this thing."

"There is no *thing* to get in front of," John said. "I don't know anything about that girl."

He pulled his truck keys out of his coat pocket.

Carver's eyes went straight to the damaged hand—the red, swollen knuckles, the lacerated flesh.

"What'd you do there, John? Go a few rounds with a tree trunk?"

"Something like that."

"You gonna tell me I should see the other guy?"

"There was no other guy."

"Sure looks to me like someone got a beating," Carver said. "And I've got a girl lying in the hospital looks like she went the distance with Mike Tyson."

"Then maybe you ought to go looking for him," John said. "I haven't done anything wrong."

"If you haven't done anything wrong, then you probably won't mind if I have a look inside the cab of your truck."

"I mind," John said. "You want to look in my truck, you can get a warrant."

"That attitude's not gonna help you any, John."

John went to the back of the truck and dropped the tailgate. As he backed away, the dog came up to investigate, sniffing, then jumped up into the bed of the pickup.

"I thought you said that wasn't your dog," Carver said.

John closed the tailgate. "He's not, but if he's willing to stick up for me, I'll do the same for him."

"You always were loyal."

Which was more than he could have said for Tim Carver, who had routinely cheated on Dana Nolan their senior year of high school. But he didn't say that. It was none of his business how Tim Carver defined loyalty.

"Am I free to go?" he asked.

Carver frowned. "I can't say that you won't be hearing from the detective on this case. He's the same one working Casey Grant's case. He thinks you're a guy he should talk to."

"Yeah? Where'd he get that idea?"

John pulled the door open and got into the truck. Carver came and stood beside the cab, looking in.

"I didn't write the history book, John," he said. "It is what it is. You can cooperate or not. I'm just giving you the heads-up here. You'd do better for yourself if you didn't make every single thing in your life so goddamn hard."

"Yeah, well, I guess that's just me," John said. He pulled the truck's door shut and started the engine.

"It always was," Tim Carver said, shaking his head. "It always was."

16

Are you sure you don't want us to drop you off at the gym?" Dana's mother asked. "Frankie's teaching classes until nine; then she'll bring you home."

"I don't need a babysitter," Dana said as she watched her mother dig a lipstick out of her purse and apply it, looking at herself in the entry-hall mirror. "I'm not eight years old."

"I don't think you need a babysitter," her mother said, looking at her via the mirror. "I thought you might not feel comfortable being home alone."

"I'll be fine," Dana said. "You look nice."

In her smart tailored navy-blue suit and pearl necklace, she looked conservative and professional, like she could have just as easily been the Mercer running for state office. She turned around and smiled.

"Thank you, sweetheart. You know how I hate these political dinners. I'd rather stay home with you. We could make popcorn and watch some old movies."

"Lynda?" Roger's voice boomed down the stairwell. "Where are my cuff links?"

"In the little jeweler's envelope on your dresser! I got them fixed, remember?" she called back. She looked at Dana and rolled her eyes, as if to say *Men!*

"Got it! Thank you!"

She turned her attention back to Dana. "There's baked ziti left over from last night in the refrigerator. Just reheat it in the microwave. And there's salad. Please remember to eat."

"I will."

"And don't forget to take your meds," she said as the doorbell rang. "You'll probably be in bed by the time we get home. These things drag on and on. I can't wait for this election to be over."

Dana stepped to the side, out of direct view, as her mother opened the door.

"Wesley," her mother said, stepping back to allow Roger's campaign manager into the foyer. "Are you our chauffeur for the evening?"

"I guess so. I want to go over some talking points with Roger on the way. The opposition is trying to bring up the gay marriage issue again."

He glanced over at Dana and came toward her with a serious expression and an outstretched hand. "Dana, I'm Wesley Stevens. We didn't get properly introduced yesterday."

Dana looked at his stubby hand, meeting it reluctantly with her own. Not expecting to see a stranger in her home, she had put on a long-sleeved thermal T-shirt and felt naked now without a hood to pull up and hide inside.

Stevens was in a dark suit and white shirt with a prep-school striped tie. His jacket didn't want to hang properly—too snug in the biceps and not quite right in the shoulders—a fit that suggested he worked out more than the average man.

"I'd actually like to sit down and have a conversation with you, Dana," he said. "I'm sure Roger has told you we've had a lot of interest in you from the prime-time news magazines. They all want to do your story. You can—"

"No," Dana said, yanking her hand back. She couldn't resist the urge to wipe her palm on her jeans. His hand was clammy and soft, and the idea of a stranger touching her made her want to go take a shower.

Stevens bit down on his professional smile. "I'm sure you'll want some time to settle in here at home, but when you're ready—"

"No."

Dana's mother stepped between them. "Wesley, why don't you go start the car? We'll be right out."

Wesley looked up as Roger came down the stairs in a charcoal suit and oxblood tie, his crisp white shirt a stark contrast to his tan. He looked successful and confident. He didn't so much as glance at Dana.

"Wesley, did you bring those notes we made this morning?"

"Yes, and I made a few more."

"We'd better hit the road, Mrs. Mercer," Roger said, pulling a topcoat out of the hall closet. "There's a rubber chicken dinner waiting with our names on it."

Dana's mother kissed her cheek and rubbed the lipstick off with the pad of her thumb. "Call if you need me. Or call Frankie. She can be here in ten minutes."

"I'll be fine," Dana assured her, following her to the door.

She watched as they backed out of the driveway in Roger's SUV and drove away. Glad to have them gone, she shut and locked the door and went to the kitchen to fix her dinner. She turned the oven on, got the ziti out of the refrigerator, put some on a plate, and stuck it in the microwave, then walked away and forgot about it as she stared out the big window.

Her mind was a kaleidoscope of the memories she had dug up that afternoon after Tim Carver's visit. Now that she had opened those doors in her mind, she couldn't seem to close them. Faces, voices, feelings, sights, sounds, all swirled around and around.

She didn't want to think about her own story, the story Wesley Stevens wanted her to present to America on prime-time television. She had spent the last nine months living that story every moment of every day. Now that she had rediscovered her past, it was almost a relief to focus on Casey's story—a thought that came with a mix of emotions that ran the gamut from guilt to obligation. In her own mind, at least, she could turn the spotlight away from herself to her friend, whose story had lain dormant all these years.

Her mother had told her that Casey had stayed over the night before she disappeared. They had undoubtedly sat at this table and had dinner. Dana sat now and imagined the two of them at the other end of the table, eating and talking and laughing. They would have spent the rest of the evening downstairs in the family room, watching movies, braiding each other's hair, doing each other's nails. Roger had spoken to her mother over the phone that night, complaining that two teenage girls were too much for him to handle. Whatever differences she and Casey had been having that summer must not have been that bad.

It seemed stupid that they would have been fighting about the boys in their lives when their lives were poised to move beyond Shelby Mills and high school sweethearts. The boys would have been moving on as well.

While Dana had always been the more goal and career oriented, and Casey had ultimately wanted to settle down and have a family, they had always talked about going off to college together. They couldn't wait to get away from small-town life, to make new friends, to experience campus life, to spread their wings and have adventures. But that fall Dana had gone off alone . . . and made new friends, and immersed herself in campus life, and spread her wings. And Casey had been nothing but a memory. The guilt and shame that came with that thought was palpable and sour in her mouth.

Dinner forgotten entirely, Dana left the kitchen and went back downstairs to her room and brought the computer screen to life with a jiggle of the mouse. Dr. Burnette wanted her to have a direction, and Dana felt the need for it as well. She wanted the comfort of a task, something to focus on that wasn't herself. Researching a story was something she had always been good at. Digging for details and gathering facts made her feel like she was moving toward something, like a bloodhound on a scent. If ever she had needed to feel some small sense of accomplishment, it was now.

She sat down at the desk and called up one of the old news articles about Casey's disappearance, one she had read earlier, scanning for the name of the detective in charge of the case—Dan Hardy. The photo from one of the news conferences showed Hardy, a big, heavyset man with a formidable frown set beneath a bushy mustache. What Dana remembered most about him as she browsed the articles was that he was intimidating. He had a way of looking at a person that would make them feel guilty of something even if they weren't.

Tim had said Hardy retired and another detective at the sheriff's office had taken over the case. But, while that detective would have all the files and reports, Hardy would be the one with firsthand memories of what had happened.

She grabbed her phone and stared at it while she tried to screw up her nerve—or talk herself out of it. When she was a reporter, cold calls had been an everyday task, but even as she dialed information and asked for Dan Hardy's phone number, her nerves were jangling so badly she thought she would probably just hang up if he answered. But then the phone on the other end of the call was ringing, and suddenly a low, gruff voice said, "Hardy."

Dana swallowed hard, her mouth instantly as dry as a desert. "Detective Hardy, my name is Dana Nolan," she began. Her heart was pounding. "I don't know if you remem—"

"I remember you. I'm retired, not senile."

"Oh, good, um," she stammered, embarrassed that she was nervous. "I have some questions for you. About my friend Casey. Casey Grant. The girl who—"

"I know who Casey Grant is," he said. "You have questions. Ask them."

Oh God. Where did she begin? "I'm having trouble remembering what happened to Casey, and—"

"We don't know what happened to Casey."

"I mean, I don't have a clear memory of the things that went on," Dana corrected herself. "I'm hoping you might be willing to talk to me. Or if I could read over my interview with you—"

"All right. Come over."

"Oh. Uh . . . um . . . Thank you," she said, surprised he had agreed so easily when he seemed like such a disagreeable person. "When would be a good time for you—"

"Now. Tonight."

"Um . . . uh . . . ," she stammered. "I was thinking maybe tomorrow—"

"I won't be around tomorrow. I'm here now. Come tonight."

Unable to stammer out an excuse, Dana scribbled the address he gave her on a pink Post-it. Hardy hung up before she had a chance to thank him or put him off.

She set her phone aside and stared at the address, her heart thumping. He wanted her to come to his house. The idea brought a wave of anxiety—not because she was afraid of him. Dan Hardy was—had been—a trusted law enforcement officer. He was hard-nosed and intimidating, but she didn't think he would harm her. It was the getting to him that put a fist of panic in her chest.

If she was going to see him tonight, she had to get herself to his house. Her mother wasn't here to take her. Frankie was teaching classes at the gym. She needed to go now, before she could lose her nerve or change her mind, or before her mother could talk her out of it.

She had argued with her mother earlier in the day that she should be able to drive herself around. This was her chance to exert her independence and prove that she was capable. Her car was sitting in the garage. She hadn't driven it since the day she was abducted. But she had driven her mother's car home from Dr. Burnette's office, and that had gone well enough. There was no reason she shouldn't be able to drive to Detective Hardy's house ten minutes away.

Before she could talk herself out of it, she entered Hardy's address into the navigation app on her phone. She pulled on a hoodie over her T-shirt, grabbed a notebook and pen off the desk, and headed for the garage.

Upstairs, turn left, go through the kitchen, go through the laundry room . . .

Her car keys were hanging on the key rack beside the door from the laundry room into the garage. She recognized the big white plastic Hello Kitty on her key chain. She grabbed the keys and went into the garage, looking for and finding the buttons that opened the big doors.

The dark-green Mini Cooper—her college graduation gift from Roger and her mother—sat in the farthest bay. It had been so long since she'd been in it that it felt strange to slide behind the wheel. She took a moment to look over the gauges and find the ignition. She started the engine and sat there listening to it purr.

Heart beating a little too strongly, she turned on her navigation app on her phone and set her mind on following the voice commands as she backed slowly out of the garage. That was all she had to do, she told herself—follow instructions—and she would get there. No big deal.

To the end of the street. Turn right. Proceed point seven miles. Turn right.

She was so intent on following the orders given by the faceless female voice, she didn't realize she was going only about twenty miles an hour. A car behind her honked and pulled out and passed her, the driver giving her a dirty look as he passed.

Dana kept her attention on the road. The disembodied voice was sending her away from town rather than toward town. She didn't like that. The streetlights ended at the next left turn. And suddenly there was no more pavement, no more planned developments, and she was driving up and down the hills of a gravel road with heavy woods on either side, going toward the river.

Anxiety stirring in her gut, Dana began to question her impulsivity. It was one thing to get lost in town. It was something else to get lost out here. She was going to the home of a former sheriff's detective, but it wouldn't matter that she trusted him if she ended up taking a wrong turn and found herself in the secluded yard of a drug dealer.

People lived out here for a reason: because they didn't want to be bothered. There were marijuana-growing operations out in these backwoods. Abandoned hunting camps were sometimes taken over by meth dealers as cookhouses. And then there were the men who lived alone for the simple reason that it wasn't safe for other people to live with them.

The anxiety built and turned and swelled up the back of her throat. The woods seemed to loom up on either side of the road, the tree limbs reaching up and out like bony arms with skeletal fingers. Dana gripped the steering wheel until she could feel her pulse throbbing in her hands. *Turn around, go back, turn around, go back*—the words bounced and echoed inside her head.

She jumped as the voice of the navigation app said, "In point four miles, turn left."

Another turn. How many times had she turned? How many lefts? How many rights? What the hell had she been thinking, coming out here?

But even as she questioned her judgment, she made the left turn, as instructed.

"Your destination will be on your right," the voice said pleasantly.

Dan Hardy's modest log home sat in a clearing, a small oasis of warm light shining through multipaned windows. The detective stood on the front porch like a sentry, with a massive dog standing at attention on either side of him.

Dana sat in the car looking at the man and the dogs, wishing she hadn't come. Once she started this, once she got out of the car and engaged this man, she felt like there would be no turning back.

"You have arrived at your destination," the navigation voice said.

And then she was getting out of the car, her notebook clutched against her.

The photographs in the old newspaper articles she had found online showed Hardy as a big man, heavyset, with a ruddy face that suggested he might be just one big, bloody steak away from a massive heart attack. As Dana stopped at the foot of the steps, she realized that the man standing on the porch bore little resemblance to those photographs. In his sixties now, he was easily fifty pounds lighter, his face much narrower and pale under the yellow bug light. This man was bald. The mustache looked similar but was heavily peppered with gray.

What if this wasn't the man? What if this wasn't the place? It wouldn't have been the first time the navigation app had taken her to the wrong address. What if she had just put herself in danger because she hadn't taken the time to think through the possibilities?

She stood frozen as her heart raced and her brain flooded with emotion and confusion.

"You've got the right place," he said in that same low, gruff tone she remembered from the phone. "I look a little different from the last time you saw me. Cancer," he said by way of explanation. "I've got chemo tomorrow. That's why you had to come tonight. Once they pump me full of that toxic shit, I'm no good for days after. Come on in."

Dana looked from Hardy to one stone-faced guard dog to the other.

"Don't mind them," Hardy said, holding the front door open. "They're on duty. A person needs a couple of good dogs out here. The neighbors leave something to be desired."

The dogs watched her intently as she climbed the steps to the porch but made no move toward her. But as she passed them, they jumped to attention and charged down off the porch, their barking like cannon fire.

Dana gave a little involuntary shriek and dashed into the house, banging into Hardy's back. He turned and caught hold of her by the shoulders, and she realized that, despite the extreme weight loss, he was still a big man, big boned, with big hands that felt strong enough to crush her like a soda can. He looked down at her with fierce dark eyes, and she jerked backward, out of his grasp, banging her head against the doorframe.

"I'm sorry. I'm so sorry," she stammered, scrambling to regain some semblance of her composure, fighting the urge to bolt out the door and run back to her car. She clutched her notebook to her chest as if to keep her heart from leaping out.

Hardy's expression didn't soften. He made no effort to put her at ease. He studied her, his hard gaze making her feel naked and exposed. She pulled her hood forward around the sides of her face.

"You came looking for me," he reminded her. "I didn't drag you out here."

"Yes," Dana said, her voice too breathy. "Thank you for seeing me."

As much to escape his scrutiny as anything, she glanced around, taking in the large open space of the main room. A stone fireplace took up one end, with the head of a trophy elk mounted above the mantel. Dead animals of all descriptions adorned the log walls— ducks, pheasants, deer, antelope, wild boar. All seemed to stare back at her with the same cold, black eyes as the man who had killed them.

"As I recall," Hardy said, "your daddy was a hunter."

"You knew my father?"

"I investigated his death," he said. "You were hardly more than a little girl then."

"It was an accident," Dana said, uneasy. "Why were detectives involved?"

"Just because something looks like an accident doesn't mean it is," he said. "A man ends up dead at the bottom of a cliff, somebody had better make sure he didn't have help getting there."

"Did you think someone murdered him?"

Dana felt like she'd fallen down a hole into a surreal alternate universe. She had come here to talk about Casey, not her father. She had never questioned the circumstances of her father's death. She didn't remember anyone ever suggesting his death hadn't been an accident.

"There wasn't any evidence of foul play," Hardy said. "No witnesses. Looked like he just got too close to the edge of that bluff and lost his footing. It was real dry that fall. The ground was hard; the shale was loose." He set his hands at the waist of his baggy jeans and shrugged. "Shit happens. I'd say you know all about that concept. If you didn't then, you do now.

"Always did find it strange, though," he added. "We never found his dog. What the hell happened to that dog?"

Dana had no answer. The trauma of losing her father had taken precedence over everything else at the time, but not only had she been a child who had lost her father; she had also lost a treasured pet, the dog that had provided a shoulder for her to cry on over the small hurts of childhood. She remembered asking her mother at one point what had happened to Moose, and Roger had scolded her for thinking about the stupid dog when they had just lost her father, her mother's husband, and his best friend and partner.

Eventually the assumption was made that the Labrador retriever had run off when her father had fallen to his death. Moose had been a gorgeous, big, obviously purebred dog. Someone had probably picked him up on the road and kept him, ignoring the tags on his collar. But Hardy's question threw a sinister light on the disappearance of Moose.

Dismissing the topic, Hardy led the way down a short dark hall and turned right into a small home office crowded with file boxes, filing cabinets, a gun safe, a desk, and a long folding table loaded down with more boxes and files. The wall above the desk displayed framed commendations, certifications, diplomas—the remnants and mementos of a long career in law enforcement. The wall above the folding table was covered in whiteboard. The whiteboard was crowded with photographs and news clippings and what looked like the manic scribbling of a madman.

It took a moment for Dana's brain to process what she was looking at. As realization dawned, a chill went through her, down her spine, down her arms and legs, and a sudden nausea swirled through her stomach and rose in the back of her throat.

Her eyes went to the photographs. Too many photographs. Formal and casual. Posed and candid. Casey in her senior portrait. Casey in her cheerleader outfit. Casey in short shorts, holding a sign for a charity car wash. Casey as a little girl. Casey as a prom princess.

A shrine to a girl missing seven years, built by a man no longer a detective.

17

She was a pretty girl, wasn't she?"

Dana shied sideways and spun around to face him, realizing too late that he had now cut off her escape route to the door. Her heart was pounding wildly. He could probably see it fluttering like a trapped bird at the base of her throat. She wanted to panic. She wanted to scream. She knew she couldn't do either.

Slowly, she slipped a hand into the pocket of her hoodie, reaching for her phone, only to find it wasn't there.

"Was?" she said. "She's missing. She's not dead."

"Do you really believe that?" Hardy asked.

"She's alive until someone proves to me that she's not. There have been sightings—"

"I'll tell you right now that girl is dead," he said. "And she's probably been dead since the day she went missing."

"People survive horrible things," Dana said, hating the tremor in her voice. She had to blink to fight back the tears that threatened to rise in her eyes.

"You know all about that, don't you?" Hardy said quietly.

She wanted to bolt and run, but he blocked her way out the door. Behind her a big plate-glass window looked out on the yard. Security lights illuminated the clearing between the house and the woods beyond. The yard was being patrolled by a pair of massive guard dogs. Even if she could have gotten past Hardy and out of the house, she would never make it to the car.

The sense of dread and panic swelled in the base of her throat until she thought she would choke on it. Hardy stared at her like a big cat waiting for a mouse to run. Her right hand closed around the pen she had clipped to her notebook. She could try to use it like a dagger. If she got him in the eye or the throat . . . She had no memory of it, but she had stabbed Doc Holiday in the temple with a screwdriver. She could do it if she had to.

"Are you afraid of me, little girl?" he asked, amused at the prospect. "Afraid of an old man with cancer?"

He wasn't that old, Dana thought, and how did she know he had cancer? Because he had told her? She had put herself in danger by accepting an image of this man she had created in her own mind. He had been a sheriff's detective; therefore, he must be a good and decent person. He was retired; therefore, he must be old and harmless. He had cancer; therefore, he must be weak.

The truth was that he was bigger and stronger than she was, and he was enjoying making her afraid.

"Why do you have all of this?" she asked, glancing at the wall covered with photographs and notes and news clippings. "You're not a detective anymore."

"It's the one case I never solved that sticks with me," Hardy said.

He stepped closer, his hands on his hips, his attention on the collage of photographs mounted on the wall. "I spent days and weeks and months investigating her case. Years. A man spends that much time with a victim, she becomes like his daughter and his sister and his lover all in one. I'm not letting go of that. What else do I have? I've got no family. I've got no career. I won't have a life much longer."

"But another detective took over the case when you left," Dana said.

Hardy made a sour face. "Tubman. Fat, lazy bastard. It's my case. I have a copy of every single piece of paper in that file. If anybody's going to solve it, it's going to be me. She's my girl."

Dana looked from one side of the whiteboard to the other, taking in the notes Hardy had made in harsh, hard-slanting handwriting, using his own personal shorthand, abbreviations, and cryptic symbols. In her nervous state, her brain on the brink of flooding, the letters and numbers and arrows and lines combined into an indecipherable mishmash that began to turn and spin as she stared at it. Desperate for a focal point, she looked at the long timeline that ran across the lower third of the board. It began with the day Casey went missing.

> *9:00 AM Vic & D Nolan dprt Mercer res in Vic's vehicle*
> *9:15 AM Girls stop @ Grindstone breakfast*
> *10:00 AM Vic & D Nolan arrive @ Mercer-Nolan Lndscp*

Dana's summer job had been to help around the nursery, watering plants, working in the gift shop, helping at the checkout. Sometimes Casey would go with her in the morning before she had to go to her own job at the Grindstone in the afternoon. They would talk while Dana dragged the hoses around through row after row after row of colorful annual flowers and terraces of potted rosebushes.

They were forever getting in trouble because the summer months at the nursery were crazy busy and the place was swamped with customers. There was no time for gossiping teenage girls lollygagging in the aisles. The frustrated manager would occasionally root Roger out of his office, and he would give them a few terse words and send Casey on her way.

Roger hadn't gone into work that day. Dana remembered now he had stayed home with a migraine—no doubt brought on in part by having to tolerate the shrieks and giggles and endless chattering of two teenage girls the night before.

> *10:15 AM (aprx) Vic and D Nolan seen arguing. Vic leaves the premises.*

"What did we argue about?" she asked.

"I don't know," Hardy said. "You told me you weren't arguing," he said. "You told me Casey left because she wasn't feeling well. You lied."

"I'm not a liar!" Dana protested. "If I said Casey wasn't feeling well, she wasn't feeling well."

"You lied about not arguing with her. Another employee told us they witnessed the two of you getting into it near the employee restrooms."

"They're mistaken," Dana said stubbornly. "Or it wasn't really a fight."

"Everybody lies," Hardy said. "Everybody lies to the cops. The question is why? Why did you tell that lie on that day?"

"Stop saying I lied! Casey and I didn't fight. My mom said we were having some kind of disagreement about our boyfriends. Maybe we had words about that, but Casey was my best friend. I loved her like a sister. I just thought her boyfriend was holding her back; that's all."

"Call it whatever makes you feel better about yourself," Hardy said, stepping back to lean against his desk. "You don't want to believe you had harsh words with your friend, then never saw her again. That's okay—unless what you fought about was relevant to her disappearance. In that case, you're hindering an investigation at best, and at worst you're an accessory to the crime."

"If I knew something that would help Casey, I would have told you."

"That wasn't your call to make. What an eighteen-year-old girl thinks might be relevant to a criminal investigation and what actually might be relevant are two different things," he said. "Cases get broken all the time on small details that might seem to mean nothing to the person who mentions them. It might be a tiny discrepancy in someone's story—a time that doesn't jibe, a name that doesn't ring a bell. It might be a piece of evidence that seems irrelevant to the person who has it—a note, a photograph, a cigarette butt, a piece of jewelry. Every little thing is part of the puzzle. It's the detective's job to put the pieces together to complete the puzzle. But we can't complete the puzzle if we don't have all the pieces."

Dana stared at the whiteboard and the note on the timeline that said she and Casey had argued. She couldn't believe that she would have held anything back that might have helped the case, but now she couldn't remember the details at all. What might have seemed insignificant then couldn't even be held up for scrutiny now.

"You weren't the only one who thought that about the boyfriend," Hardy said. "Young Villante had trouble written all over him."

"But you never arrested him."

"Can't arrest somebody without evidence. Villante claimed he hadn't seen Casey for a couple of days before she went missing. We never found anything or anyone to contradict that. We know from Casey's cell phone records she called him around one in the afternoon the day she disappeared. She left a message telling him she wanted to see him that evening. He claims she never showed. She also spoke to Tim Carver that day shortly after she left the nursery. To complain about you, he said."

Dana frowned, not liking the idea of her friends talking about her behind her back. If she had been hard on Casey, it was only because she wanted the best for her. Casey had always been too quick to fall for a sob story and take in the wounded and the abandoned, a habit that always hurt her in the end.

"She was mad at me for breaking up with Tim," she said. "She kept trying to get us back together."

"Yeah? Well, good judgment on your part," he said. "Carver was quite the little prick back then. Mr. Ambition. Too good for the likes of this town. Karma kicked him in the balls, didn't she? Got his ass chucked out of West Point."

The comment stopped Dana short. "He told me he decided it wasn't for him."

"That's an easy decision when you've been asked to leave."

That would be like the Tim she remembered, Dana thought, always spinning the tale to reflect well on himself.

"Turns out he otherwise wasn't as smart as he thought he was," Hardy said. "He flunked out."

That wasn't like Tim at all. He had always been a good student and a clever politician, winning over his teachers with his wit and humor. But West Point wasn't Shelby Mills High. The expectations at the Point were of the highest order, and certainly no one skated by on looks and charm. Still, she couldn't imagine him flunking out.

But after leaving West Point, he had chosen to come back to Indiana and go to the police academy. And he had chosen to come back to Shelby Mills when he could have gone anywhere with no one here the wiser. She liked what that said about Tim Carver the grown man. He had to have eaten his share of humble pie over his failure at West Point, but here he was, working his way up the ranks in the sheriff's office.

"You said over the phone you wanted to see your statement to me," Hardy said. "Why?"

"I have a head injury. My memory is coming back, but it's sketchy. Casey was my best friend. I feel like I should remember every detail, but I don't. Maybe if I could find all the pieces, I could put that puzzle together now. Maybe I would look at something differently now, see something I didn't see back then."

"Like Doc Holiday?" he asked, moving away from the desk again.

He seemed too close in the cramped space. The astringent antiseptic scent of his aftershave burned her nostrils. Dana stood her ground, wishing she could get to the other side of him, nearer to the door.

"I don't have any memory of him. I don't remember any of it," she said. "So don't bother asking me if I think Doc Holiday took Casey, because I don't know."

"That would be a hell of a coincidence," Hardy said.

He pulled a pair of half-glasses out of the breast pocket of his denim shirt and perched them on his nose as he turned toward his desk and opened a file folder lying on top of a pile.

"Then again," he said, "you and I both know real life is far stranger than fiction. Fiction has to make sense in the end. There's plenty of shit goes down in the real world no book editor would ever believe in a novel. It doesn't matter how impossible, improbable, coincidental, anything might be in the real world. Reality doesn't have to make any damn sense at all."

He swiveled his desk chair around to face her and lowered himself into it like a man in pain. A fine film of sweat coated his face. He drew in a slow breath and let it out carefully.

"When I heard that theory was being tossed around," he said, "that maybe Doc Holiday was around here back when Casey went missing—I reached out to someone I know with the FBI," he said. "They've got a team coordinating the local agencies that think they might have Doc Holiday victims. They're going back years, laying out timelines. Turns out he was part owner of a junkyard near Terre Haute since 2005. Which means he had a base three hours away from here.

"There are a few people in the county who deal in antiques and junk who claim to have run across him at flea markets and auctions and the like. So, yeah, he could have passed through here," he said. "He could have stopped at the Grindstone. I don't know of anyone who could testify to it, but Casey Grant could have served him a piece of pie. He could have taken a shine to her and somehow got her into his truck. All of that could have happened."

"Do you think that's what happened?" Dana asked.

He looked across the narrow room at the timeline. "I don't know. She never made it to work that day, but her car was in the parking lot. Where'd she go? Nobody saw anything. Did Doc Holiday snag her out of the parking lot with nobody seeing a damn thing? That's what he did to you, right? Caught you in the parking lot, pulled you into his vehicle—"

"I don't remember," Dana said quickly, but her heart rate increased a beat; anxiety tightened her throat as if she was reacting to a memory she swore she didn't have.

"That's the story," Hardy said. "That was his MO. He grabbed a girl in Missouri out of a convenience store parking lot. Picked up a girl in Milwaukee at a truck stop. He grabbed you in the parking lot of your apartment building when you were on your way to work."

"But you thought John did something to Casey," Dana said. "That's what everybody thought."

He shrugged. "We didn't know about Doc Holiday then. And it's a known fact that most personal crimes are committed by people who were known to the victim. Despite your experience, stranger abductions are relatively rare. Most people are done in by so-called friends and loved ones; their reasons are simple: money or sex, and variations on those themes.

"The significant other is always a prime suspect. Casey and John hadn't been getting along. She was probably going to dump him, right? That was what you wanted. You dumped your boyfriend. You wanted her to dump hers."

"It wasn't like that," Dana protested.

"Wasn't it?" Hardy arched a brow. "You were quite a bossy little thing."

"You didn't know me," Dana said, irritated by the picture he was painting of her.

"You were supposed to go off to college together, right?"

"Yes. So?"

"So it's a lot more fun going to college as two single girls than having one of you tied to a boyfriend," he said. "Especially a boyfriend like young Villante. Maybe that's what the two of you argued about. Maybe you were pressing her to break up with him. Maybe she was telling you to go fuck yourself. Or maybe that's why she wanted to see him that night—to tell him it was over."

That was the theory most people had latched onto at the time. But nothing had ever come of it.

"But seven years later he's still walking around free."

"Like I said before, we never had any evidence he did anything to her. Was an angry eighteen-year-old boy smart enough to pull off the perfect crime? That doesn't seem very likely. Did he seem like a criminal mastermind to you?"

She thought about John Villante, about the boy she had seen in the yearbook photos. Overly sensitive, easily offended, often brooding, sometimes angry. Casey had helped him to keep his grades high enough to stay in sports.

"No."

"Now we hear about Doc Holiday," Hardy said. "We weren't looking for a serial killer back then, so we didn't see one."

Once again he took a big breath and blew it out slowly, looking away from her. He pulled open a desk drawer and came up with a pack of Marlboros and a lighter.

"Should you be smoking?" Dana asked.

He hung a cigarette on his lip and gave her a sardonic look as he lit up.

"I'm gonna die, little girl. I might as well enjoy myself while I can."

He pulled a document out of the folder he had opened and handed it to her. "Here's a copy of your statement, for what it's worth. Read it over. Maybe you'll remember the answers you should have given me."

Dana took the report and tucked it into her notebook without looking at it.

"Seven years after the fact," Hardy said. "People forget things—faces, names. Waitresses at the Grindstone have come and gone. Is anybody going to remember seeing Doc Holiday? Maybe only somebody who has a reason to—like you."

THE TROUBLE WAS, DANA thought as she drove away from Dan Hardy's property, while she might have been the one person with a reason to remember Doc Holiday, she was also the one with every reason to forget him.

Her head was throbbing as she tried to focus on the road and on the voice of the navigation app. She wanted to blink her eyes and be magically back home and not have to wonder if she had turned left instead of right. The up and down and twist and turn of the country roads were making her nauseous. And suddenly there were lights behind her.

She couldn't have been much more than a mile gone from Hardy's cabin in the woods. She hadn't seen another vehicle on the drive out here. The way the woods closed in on the sides of the road made her feel like there couldn't be another human being for miles, and yet, she knew there were others. One was right behind her.

It was a truck, she thought. The headlights seemed to loom over her little Mini. Too close. Much too close.

The speedometer told her she was going thirty miles an hour. It felt like she was doing seventy. She was afraid to step on the gas. It had been too long since she had driven on gravel, too long since she had driven at all. Yet the bigger vehicle behind her seemed to want to push her along—or push her over.

If she went in the ditch, what could she do? Nothing. She had no weapon. She had nowhere to run. She had no idea where she was or if there might be anyplace to get help. The idea of running back to Hardy's place—and Hardy's dogs—was as terrifying as any other option in the pitch-black night. For all she knew, Hardy was in the truck behind her. She tried to remember another vehicle in his yard, but she couldn't.

She jumped as the navigation voice said, "In three hundred yards turn right."

The voice was so calm. Dana's heart was racing. She was trembling. Her fingers tightened on the steering wheel in a death grip. She jumped again as the phone rang, the musical ringtone interrupting another instruction from the faceless female directing her.

She let it ring. She couldn't take her hands off the wheel to pick up the phone. She couldn't take her eyes off the road or the rearview mirror to see who was calling. What difference would it make who was calling if she crashed and died, or crashed and was taken by whoever was in the pickup behind her?

She turned at the intersection and held her breath, eyes on the rearview mirror. For a moment it seemed the other vehicle would go in a different direction. She had been panicked for no reason. She would have to learn not to be so paranoid, she told herself.

And then the headlights turned in her direction, and the truck came roaring up behind her, so fast Dana thought it would hit her.

Tears spilled down her cheeks as she stepped on the gas. She began to hyperventilate as the car seemed to lose purchase on the loose gravel and started to skid into the next curve in the road.

"In point five miles turn right," the voice said.

"How can you be so fucking calm?" Dana shouted, straightening the wheel.

Behind her, the truck moved to the left, as if to come alongside her. On the seat beside her, her phone rang again.

"Shut up!" Dana shouted. It was all too much—too much happening at once, too much sound, too much movement, too much pressure.

"In three hundred yards turn right."

She hit the gas, sobbing now, desperate to get to the intersection. The next road was paved. There would be streetlights soon, and houses.

She barely slowed down to make the turn, her tires squealing as she straightened onto the new road.

The pickup stopped at the intersection.

Eyes on the rearview mirror, Dana drifted into the other lane. The blast of a horn brought her attention back just in time to miss hitting an oncoming car head-on.

She looked in the mirror again. Nothing. No lights behind her. No truck following her.

She immediately told herself she had probably never been in danger. It was just her imagination conjuring a bogeyman out of the shattered remnants of her memory.

But she was still shaking as the sign for the Bridlewood development came into view.

18

The flood of adrenaline gone, Dana wanted to curl into a ball and go numb.

Almost home. You're almost home . . .

She would park her car and slink into the house and downstairs to her room and her bed . . .

But as she turned onto her street, it looked like there might be a party going on at the end of the cul-de-sac. Cars choked the driveway and lined the curb. A news van sat cockeyed. People were milling around in the street.

It probably had to do with Roger and the fund-raiser he and her mother had attended, Dana thought, annoyed as she abandoned her car in front of a neighbor's house. She pulled up her hood and walked toward her house, head down, eyes up, notebook clutched to her chest.

Two of the cars near the driveway were sheriff's cruisers. Deputies were trying to control the scene. She recognized the blonde from the local news trying to set up a shot in the front yard, and she felt both irritated and anxious. She was exhausted. Her brain felt like it had been wrung out like a sponge. All she wanted was to go to bed, but she was going to have to run a gauntlet to get there.

She looked around for Roger or his campaign manager so she

could give someone the evil eye. Before she could find him, she spotted Tim Carver in conversation with another deputy. Head down, she went to him as the other deputy turned away.

"Can I get a police escort to my door?" she asked.

He started to dismiss her with the wave of a hand, then did a double take, eyes wide. He glanced around to see who might be looking, then leaned down toward her and spoke to her in a harsh whisper. "Jesus, Dee! Where the hell have you been?"

Dana took a step back. "Excuse me?"

He glanced around again for witnesses as he herded her off to the side of the street, then leaned down and all but stuck his face inside the hood with her. "Every deputy in the county is out looking for you."

"What? Why?"

"The order came straight from the sheriff himself. Your aunt Frankie came by to check on you and found the garage wide open. Your car was gone, there was food left out in the kitchen, the stove was on, there was a faucet running. No sign of you—"

"Oh no," Dana groaned, a sick feeling of embarrassment and failure churning in her stomach.

It would have looked like she had been taken.

She had thought she could slip out of the house, see Hardy, come back, and have no one the wiser, that she could just come and go from her home like a normal human being. But she wasn't a normal human being. Sidetracked by her thoughts, she forgot about things like running faucets and dinner half started. She hadn't thought to close the garage door because she had needed all her attention on backing out of the driveway.

"And why the hell haven't you answered your phone?" Tim asked.

Because she couldn't concentrate on driving and her phone at the same time. And she had forgotten her phone in the car when she went into Hardy's house. When she had come back out, all she wanted was to leave. She hadn't checked the phone for voice mail or text messages.

"Where were you?"

"I had to go see someone," she said.

"Well, you might have thought to tell somebody."

But who would she have told? Her mother would have stopped her going. Frankie was busy teaching classes. Hardy had told her she had to come see him tonight. In her too-literal brain with her fresh obsession on what had happened to Casey, she hadn't considered other options. Impulsivity was a side effect of her brain injury. She often spoke and acted long before the logical part of her brain could think things through.

"Deputy Carver?" a woman's voice called. "Could we get a moment with you on camera?"

From the corner of her eye Dana could see the blonde coming toward them with purpose. She turned her back to the woman, hunching her shoulders, wishing she could disappear.

Tim held a hand up to ward the reporter off. "Not just now, Miss Kirk. I'll be with you in a minute."

"Is the sheriff coming?"

"He's on his way with the Mercers."

"Oh God," Dana groaned again. She felt like she was fourteen and caught out after curfew. Now she would have to face her mother and Roger with news cameras capturing every moment. She wanted to pull her hood over her face and disappear for real.

Another cruiser came roaring down the street, lights rolling. The car pulled over behind the news van, and a dark SUV—Roger's SUV—pulled up hard beside it.

Wesley Stevens came out of the driver's side and made a beeline for Kimberly Kirk. Roger came out of the passenger's side looking grim and angry, demanding to know who was in charge.

Tim clamped a hand on Dana's shoulder and moved her with him as he stepped forward.

"Everything's all right, Senator Mercer. Everything's under control."

The back passenger's door of the SUV opened and Dana watched as her mother scrambled out, tripping and falling to her hands and knees as she tried to rush forward.

"Dana! Dana!"

Dana stepped toward her, then froze as the scene began to overwhelm her—the lights, the cameras, people shouting, people rushing toward her.

Tim let go of her and hurried to help her mother up from the pavement.

Crying, disheveled, hands dirty, skirt torn at the hem, Lynda accepted his hand up but immediately pushed past him.

"Dana! Oh my God! Oh thank God!"

Sobbing, she threw her arms around Dana and squeezed so hard Dana thought she might suffocate. The earth seemed to tilt beneath her feet, and the crowd pressed in on them. She had to close her eyes tight against the harsh glare of handheld lights as a television camera zoomed in on them.

"Mom, I'm so sorry!"

"Thank God you're safe!" her mother said over and over, touching her face, brushing back her hair, then hugging her tight again and again.

Dana tried to lean back out of her mother's death-clutch embrace just to gasp for air. A cacophony of sound assaulted her eardrums—the roar of her pulse, her mother's sobbing voice, Kimberly Kirk's insistent questions, the general din of the crowd around them. And then she found herself moving, swept along with her mother, up the driveway, surrounded by uniformed deputies.

A wave of people followed them into the house and into the formal living room—Roger, Wesley Stevens, Frankie, Maggie, Tim, the sheriff.

"I was worried sick!" her mother said, pursuing her, reaching out for her again.

"Mom, please stop," Dana said, twisting away. "Please stop touching me. I feel like I can't breathe."

Still in panic mode, her mother looked stricken. "Do we need an ambulance?" She looked to her husband, wild-eyed. "Roger, she can't breathe!"

"No! No!" Dana said. "That's not what I meant! I—I just n-need . . . um . . . um . . ."

Overwhelmed, she couldn't find the word. Not finding the word only added to the flood of anxiety and frustration. She clamped her hands on top of her head as if she might be able to squeeze the rest of the sentence out of her brain.

"This wasn't supposed to happen!" she said, tears rising, the pressure in her head building as she tried to hold them back.

"Dee, we were all worried," Frankie said, perching herself on the fat rolled arm of the sofa. "I got here and I didn't know what to think. Your car was gone, the garage was open, the house looked like you left in a hurry. You didn't answer your phone. I texted your mom to ask if you had told her you were going somewhere. She said no."

"We all jumped to the worst conclusion," Maggie said.

"I was only going to be gone for a little while," Dana said. "I never thought anyone would know, let alone send out a search party. I'm so embarrassed."

"Sheriff Summers was at our table at the dinner," her mother said, lifting a hand in the direction of Summers, a lean, middle-aged man in a pressed uniform. "He saw how upset I was. You never said anything about going out. What were we supposed to think?"

They weren't supposed to think anything because Dana had never imagined them knowing she was gone.

"We just got you back, Dee," Frankie said. "You really can't blame us for freaking out."

"Especially after that waitress was attacked last night," Maggie added. "There is a rapist running around loose. Isn't that right, Tim?"

Tim crossed his arms over his chest and nodded solemnly. "That is true. At the moment, we have no strong suspects. And it was a brutal attack on that girl. I have to say, Dee, I got here and had a look around, and I was concerned too."

"I've got extra manpower on the case," Sheriff Summers said. "But until we have a suspect in custody, I would advise women to be cautious going out alone at night."

"Where the hell were you?" Roger demanded, unable to contain his temper another minute. He had jerked his tie loose and stood with his hands on his hips, his suit jacket open.

"I had to see someone," Dana said weakly, dreading the can of worms that was about to get opened and spilled out in front of all these people.

"Who?"

She didn't want to say, knowing Hardy's name would only open another line of questioning, and she was already exhausted and embarrassed and wanted nothing more than to go crawl into bed and pull the covers over her head.

"Am I supposed to be a prisoner here?" she asked. "No one told me. Maybe you should have left a guard."

"How dare you cop an attitude with me?" Roger's face was red with temper. He seemed big and imposing as he took an aggressive step toward her. "You scared your mother sick!"

"I'm sorry! I said I was sorry!" Dana cried. She sat down on the large leather ottoman and curled over, covering her face with her hands.

"Roger, that's enough!" her mother snapped, coming to sit beside her, wrapping an arm around her shoulders. Dana made no objection to her touch this time.

"Jesus, Roger," Frankie grumbled. "Could you be a bigger dick?"

He blew out a breath. "I'm sorry. I'm sorry I shouted. I'm upset."

"That doesn't give you the right to shout at Dana," Frankie lashed out. "Why don't you go back outside and talk to the press. That should brighten your spirits."

"Frankie, that's not fair," Dana's mother said.

"Don't defend him, Lynda. I'm not going to stand here and listen to him browbeat my niece. It's not Dana's fault she can't remember to shut off the stupid faucet. I'm sure it wasn't her plan to create a panic tonight."

"But she did," Roger said.

Dana glanced up to see Roger plow his hands back through his thick hair, his eyes closed as if against some internal pain. Behind and around him stood the sheriff and Tim and Wesley Stevens, all looking uncomfortable to be witnessing the family drama.

"I'm sorry," Roger said again. "But you're not living through this in the same way Lynda and I are, Frankie."

"If there weren't cops here right now, I would come over there and kick you as hard as I could," Frankie said, offended. "She's my flesh and blood."

"You weren't sitting at that table tonight watching your wife go from zero to full-blown hysteria because she didn't know where her daughter might be," he said. "You didn't see the panic grow with every unanswered phone call and text. That's upsetting to me, Frankie. And what could I do about it besides ask Sheriff Summers for help? Not a damn thing."

"Oh, well," Frankie grumbled. "I guess that should give you license to be a complete and total asshole to Dana. Forgive me. What was I thinking?"

"I don't need you coming into my house and insulting me," Roger said. "Maybe you should go now, Frankie."

Frankie advanced on him, looking like she was ready for a fistfight. Dana wouldn't have bet against her despite the almost comical difference in their sizes.

"Don't threaten me, Roger," Frankie said. "As far as I'm concerned, this isn't your house. This was my brother's house. Eddie's house, Eddie's wife, Eddie's daughter. You just happen to live here. So back off my niece."

Roger gave her a cold glare and turned away, throwing his hands up as if to signal he was done with the conversation, conceding the fight to Frankie.

"What was so urgent that you ran out like that, Dee?" Tim asked, turning the attention back to Dana.

"It wasn't urgent. I just left," Dana said, miserable. "I decided I had to go and I left. I didn't mean to leave the stove on or the faucet or whatever. I didn't think of any of that stuff. I'm sorry, I just didn't."

"Who did you need to see?"

She sighed, resigning herself to the idea that she wasn't going to get out of having to explain and weather their reactions. Everyone was looking at her, waiting for the big revelation.

"Detective Hardy," she confessed. "I wanted to ask him some questions about when Casey went missing. I'm trying to piece together my memories and fill in the blanks. I thought he might be able to help. I left my phone in the car when I went in his house."

"That couldn't have waited until tomorrow," Roger said. He shook his head in disbelief at what he clearly viewed as impulsive, irresponsible behavior.

Dana didn't try to answer him. He wouldn't understand that when Hardy had told her she had to come tonight, her brain took that literally. She hadn't meant to be irresponsible.

"Casey Grant?" Wesley Stevens asked. "The girl that disappeared back when?"

"She was Dana's best friend," her mother said, giving her a little squeeze around her shoulders.

"I know the story," he said, dismissing her and turning to his boss. He spoke softly. "I don't see any reason to bring that up in our statement to the media. We'll just say she took a drive and didn't realize people were looking for her."

Roger nodded.

"I think we can chalk this evening up as nothing more than an unfortunate miscommunication—or lack of communication," Sheriff Summers said. "Let's just be grateful Dana is home safe, and we can call it a night—except you, Deputy Carver," he said, turning to Tim. "I believe you've got a shift to get back to."

"Yes, sir," Tim said. He went to Dana and bent down close, resting a hand on her shoulder. "I'm glad you're safe, Dee."

"Thanks."

He leaned in closer as if to kiss her cheek and whispered in her ear, "I'll see you later."

Dana stared at him, confused, as he gave his regards to her mother and Roger, then followed the sheriff out the front door. The tension in the room dispersed as Roger and Wesley walked out after the other men.

Frankie clapped her hands. "Well, that was fun," she said sarcastically.

"You were out of line saying that to Roger," Dana's mother said, but without much force, as if she'd said the same line so many times over the years it had become nothing more than a token objection.

"I don't care," Frankie said. "I didn't say anything that wasn't true. I'm not going to stand around and let him bully Dana. Fuck him. I don't owe Roger Mercer a damn thing."

"Roger was upset because he saw how upset I was."

"Don't make excuses for him, Lynda."

"But you're never fair to him, Frankie! Roger has been very good to us—"

"Oh, for Christ's sake! You make it sound like he took you in off the street! You didn't need him. Eddie left you the house, half the business, insurance. Roger made out like a fucking bandit!"

"Frankie, that's enough." Maggie put a hand on her partner's arm. "It's probably time for us to go."

Frankie made a face. "That's code for 'Shut up now, Frankie.'"

"Yes. Shut up now, Frankie," Dana's mother said.

"I'm sorry," Frankie said. "I didn't want to upset you, but you know I'm not going to stand by and let him yell at Li'l Dee. Not happening."

"I'm sorry I ruined everyone's night," Dana said, getting to her feet.

Frankie gave her a hug. "Don't beat yourself up, Dee. You didn't mean to do anything bad. We just love you so much we couldn't cope with the idea of losing you again."

"I love you guys too," Dana said, swiping at a stray tear on her cheek.

"Are you all right, sweetheart?" her mother asked.

"I'm fine," she said, almost laughing at the absurdity of the statement. "I'm a brain-damaged idiot who sparked a manhunt by forgetting to turn off a faucet. It's all good."

"Dana . . ."

"Really, Mom, I just want to go to bed. I'm sorry for all the confusion."

She'd had enough of people, enough of the day. Her head felt like it weighed a thousand pounds. She didn't want to think about the mess she'd made on her first foray toward independence. She wanted to be alone in the quiet sanctuary of her bedroom, shutting out her own thoughts one by one.

She was so tired she made two wrong turns getting there.

She put her notebook on the desk and went into the bathroom, where she had to stand at the sink and read the note cards she had taped to the mirror to remember her bedtime rituals. *Wash your face with cleanser. Brush your teeth WITH TOOTHPASTE. TAKE YOUR MEDS!*

Too tired to even decide which of the steps she could leave out, she performed the tasks with as little thought as possible. Her hoodie smelled of nervous sweat. She went into her closet, pulled it off and dropped it on the floor with her jeans, and replaced the outfit with a big Indianapolis Colts T-shirt and a pair of plaid flannel pajama bottoms.

As she emerged from the closet, she stopped dead, then ran back-ward, gasping for air, reacting in fear before her conscious mind even realized there was a man standing outside her patio doors.

Her brain scrambled to process what it was taking in.

A man at the door.

Waving.

Smiling a sheepish smile.

Tim.

Her heart was pounding so hard Dana thought it might explode in her chest and drown her in her own blood.

"Oh my God!" she said, opening the door. "What the hell are you thinking? Don't ever do that to me again!"

"I told you I was coming," he said without apology.

"No, you didn't!"

"I said, 'I'll see you later.' Just like old times."

"What?"

"When I used to bring you home from a date and say good-bye in front of your folks, then sneak around down here."

"That was years ago!" Dana said, even as pieces of those memo-ries came back to her. "I didn't remember that! I didn't know what you were talking about!"

He made a pained face. "Ouch. That's a blow to the old ego."

"Screw your ego!" Dana snapped. "You scared me. Don't ever do that again!"

"I'm sorry! I'm sorry!" he said, holding his hands up in surrender. "I'll never do it again. I promise. Let's calm down and have a seat."

"What do you want, anyway?" Dana asked, too agitated to sit. She paced back and forth beside the upholstered chair, arms wrapped tight across her chest. "I'm tired."

"I want to talk to you about Dan Hardy."

"What about him?"

"You shouldn't have gone out there by yourself, Dee," he said. "That guy ain't right in the head."

"Now you tell me."

"He didn't retire because he wanted to go fishing," he said. "It was suggested to him by the sheriff. There were rumors about him and an underage girl over in Clarksville. Nothing ever came of it, but still . . ."

"What kind of rumors?"

"The kind that don't end well."

Dana sank down on the chair, pulling her legs up, wrapping her arms around her knees. She thought of the sick feeling of dread she'd felt, trapped in Dan Hardy's office as he seemed to delight in frightening her.

"Tell me what that means," she said quietly.

Tim took a seat on the ottoman in front of her, forearms resting on his thighs. "There used to be a . . . place . . . over that way, out in the sticks . . ."

"What kind of a place?"

He glanced away, looking uncomfortable. "A . . . uh . . . a whore-house, for lack of a more genteel word. A girl known to have been working there disappeared, then turned up a couple of days later wandering naked down a dirt road, beat to hell. She wouldn't talk. Never did talk. She OD'd on heroin as soon as they let her out of the hospital."

"What did Hardy have to do with it?"

"He knew the place, knew the girl, had developed an obsession with her, according to the woman who ran the place. He had tried to physically remove her from the house against her will at one point a month or so before. No one ever knew if he had anything to do with what happened to her, but when she died, he lost it. He had a breakdown. That was pretty much the end of his career."

"He wasn't prosecuted?" Dana asked.

"Nope. There was never an arrest. There wasn't any evidence against him—or anyone else, for that matter. What happened to that girl was a straight-up mystery. Still is."

"Do you think he did something to her?"

He shrugged. "Doesn't matter what I think. All that matters is what can be proved, and nobody could prove anything. But what I can tell you is Dan Hardy is not a stable individual. We're going to have to look at him for what happened to that waitress last night."

Dana felt sick to her stomach to think that she might have put herself in jeopardy going to see a man she had thought of as above reproach because of his profession. She didn't want to think about what could have happened. Doc Holiday had been a peddler of antiques and junk. People who had known him had described him as jovial, friendly, kind. No one had suspected him of being a monster. They didn't come with labels.

"So how is there a whorehouse operating in the county without getting shut down?" she asked. "And if this girl was underage, why didn't anybody remove her and put her in the child welfare system?"

"Nobody knew how young she really was until late in the story. As for the whorehouse, it's gone now. It's not like it was a storefront business. It was sort of . . . unofficial, you might say."

"I might say that's a load of crap," Dana said with disgust. "It existed because men allowed it to exist. Men are unbelievable. Everything in your lives is about sex and control and power."

"You can't judge—"

"A man beat my head in with a hammer because it got him off," she said. "I think I'm a pretty good authority on the subject."

He looked away from her and sighed, as if her statement had hit him physically. "I'm sorry, Dee. I'm real sorry. But he wasn't me. You can't lump us all together."

Can't I? Dana thought, suddenly remembering the feeling of a hot surge of jealousy and anger toward him. He had been a notorious flirt back in high school. She had confronted him once about rumors he was fooling around with a girl from Levine.

"What did Hardy have to tell you?" he asked.

"He told me you flunked out of West Point," she said bluntly, in part to punish him for the memory she'd just had.

He looked down at the floor, the muscles in his jaw flexing. He had never taken it well when someone called him on his shit, she remembered. The happy-go-lucky Texas-country-boy facade could disappear in the snap of two fingers.

He swallowed back his temper and nodded. "My grades weren't what they should've been," he admitted. "My head wasn't in my studies. I didn't want to be there and, consequently, they didn't want to have me."

"It all worked out."

"That's the way I look at it," he said. "What else did Hardy have to say? You didn't go out there to talk about me."

"No," Dana said. "He has everything about Casey's disappearance tacked up on a wall in his office—timelines and notes and questions, and all these old pictures of Casey." A shudder went through her at the memory. "It's creepy. He's obsessed. He said he has a copy of every single piece of paper from the case."

"I can't say I'm surprised," Tim said. "He's like a crazy old dog with a bone. He worked that case for five years and never got an answer. That has to grind on him like nothing else."

"I asked him for a copy of my statement from when he interviewed me," Dana said. "I thought reading it might open up those memories."

"Did he give it to you?"

"Yes. But he said I didn't tell him the whole truth. He thinks I held something back," she confessed. "I argued with him. I would never have held back anything that could have helped Casey."

"No, you wouldn't have."

"Even if Casey and I were fighting, I loved her," she said, tears rising. "I would never have done anything that could have hurt the chances of finding her."

"No," Tim said. "You were like sisters. You could get pretty cold when you were angry, but I don't think you would have done anything to hurt Casey, directly or indirectly."

"I wouldn't have!" Dana said, offended at the tiniest sliver of possibility left in his statement.

"No. Don't mind Hardy," he said. "He's a jacked-up old lunatic. All he ever lived for was mind-fucking people, if you'll pardon my language. Don't take anything he says to heart, Dee. Christ only knows what kind of toxic mind-altering substances he's using out there in the boontoolies. There's no telling what's going on in his head. He's fixing to die, is what I hear. Too bad he doesn't just get on with it."

Dana shrugged and picked at a loose thread on the hem of her pajama bottoms, frowning. "I don't know. We were kids when Casey disappeared. We thought we knew everything. What if I decided it wasn't important to tell him some detail, and it turned out to be the one thing that could have meant everything?"

"Like what?"

"I don't know," she whispered. Tears came in a sudden flood, filling her eyes, spilling down her cheeks. "I wish I knew. I wish my brain worked. There are things I remember clearly, and other things not at all."

"Hey," Tim said softly. He reached out and put a hand on her shoulder. "Don't cry, Dee. It's not worth it. If you'd known something, you would have said something."

She deftly shrugged his touch away like a cat slipping out from under a hand, her intolerance stronger than her need for comfort. He pulled his hand away and sighed.

"It's not worth tormenting yourself that some minor detail could have turned the tables," he said. "Real life isn't an episode of *CSI*.

"Casey's gone. She isn't coming back," he said. "Whatever happened back then, whatever you said or didn't say, isn't going to change that. Let it go. You said yourself, that's why everyone wants to know if Doc Holiday took her. Everyone just wants to put it to rest. There's no good outcome to be had at this late date."

Dana wiped the tears from her cheeks with the tail of her T-shirt. "And if it wasn't Doc Holiday? Then what? Someone took her away from us, Tim. If she's dead, then someone killed her, and that person is walking around having a life, and Casey isn't. Don't we owe it to her to do something about that?"

"If I thought there was a hope in hell," he said.

"That's a great attitude from law enforcement."

"I'm just trying to be practical here with regards to what you're putting yourself through, Dee. The case has been open and active for seven years, and it hasn't been solved yet. Short of finding Casey herself or Casey's body, or getting a confession from someone who might have done her harm, there's no reason to think it's going to be solved. We don't always get an ending with these things, let alone a happy one. You know better than me; your personal story is a rare exception."

She did know that truth better than most people. But she also knew her story would have ended very differently if she hadn't kept fighting for herself. If she had quit, she would have been dead now.

"Put it away for tonight, Dee," Tim said, getting up from the ottoman. "Get some rest."

Dana went to the door to let him out.

"Lock up behind me," he said, stepping out to the patio.

"I will."

He watched her turn the deadbolt, then gave her one of his aw-shucks smiles and pointed to his temples.

"I'm hugging you up here," he said.

Dana waved him away and closed the drapes against the night and whatever might be lurking in it.

19

You're not my dog. Do you get that?" John said as he pulled half a cheeseburger from the takeout bag and put it in a bowl he had brought out from the kitchen.

The young shepherd tipped its head sideways, dark eyes shining bright with curiosity. It licked its lips and whined a little, dancing in place, wanting to come forward and take the food but too afraid to do so.

John went to the end of the pickup's box, sat down, and leaned back, watching the dog stick its nose in the direction of the bowl and sniff, then whine and dance and lick its lips again.

Knowing his old man wouldn't bother to wonder where he was, John had parked behind the garage, where the pickup couldn't be seen from the driveway. He had heard his father's truck pull in some time ago, heard the truck's door slam, then the house door slam. Home from the bar, drunk and well fed, the old man wouldn't come back outside. He wouldn't check behind the garage. He wouldn't notice the security light on at the back of the building. There wasn't anything back here of interest but a couple of dead 1950s vintage car carcasses he never got around to fixing up and the dilapidated shed where he kept his yard tools and assorted junk car parts and other crap that should have been thrown out two decades ago.

John watched the dog crouch down and stretch its neck out as far as it could, then snap up the half-eaten cheeseburger, bun and all. It carried its prize back to the old blanket John had put in the corner of the truck box, up behind the cab, out of the wind, and ate it in three gulps. It never took its eyes off John.

This was the stray's second meal of the evening. John had gone through the local drive-through and picked up a bag of ninety-nine-cent cheeseburgers to feed both himself and the dog, and a large order of onion rings for himself. Leery of letting the dog gorge himself, he had doled out the first burger in two halves. He pulled another burger out of the crumpled bag and took a bite out of it, not caring that it was now cold and tasted like grease and old leather. He'd eaten enough army rations that anything tasted better.

He tossed the other half to the dog.

"There you go, trouble," he said, pretending he hadn't just named the animal.

Trouble was a description, not a name, he told himself.

What the hell was he going to do with a dog? He had nowhere to keep it but in the back of this pickup. If he took it to the county shelter, it would probably get put to sleep. If he let it loose somewhere, it could be picked up by Animal Control or hit by a car or shot by some farmer protecting his chickens or by some stupid yahoo out for drunken kicks.

He remembered a night from high school, drinking with some of the guys from the football team after they'd lost a game and spoiled their perfect season. Young men pissed up on liquor and anger and disappointment, howling at the moon. They had parked behind a falling-down barn out in the country to drink and curse and have their tantrums. Someone had produced a .22 target pistol, and a couple of the guys had taken turns shooting at rats and rabbits for no other reason than that they thought it felt good to make something hurt worse than their wounded egos.

All the commotion had scared up a raggedy calico cat out from under a rusted abandoned piece of farm equipment. They had shot that too, wounding the poor animal with their drunken piss-poor marksmanship. They had laughed at John when he expressed his disgust at their behavior.

Carver had handed him the .22 and told him to finish the job then—which he had done with one merciful shot to the head to end the cat's suffering. Then he'd handed the gun back to Andy Dodson and turned and punched Tim Carver in the face so hard he fractured a bone in his hand. He'd gone into such a blind rage it had taken both Andy and Bobby to pull him off their quarterback and knock some sense into him.

He thought now about Carver's threat earlier tonight to have this dog hauled off or shot as a dangerous animal, and his anger rose and swirled around with the rage from all those years ago.

What a dick, threatening a dog. Mr. Deputy Sheriff. *I'm gonna be the closest thing you've got to a friend here.*

John shook his head at the memory. What kind of friend had Tim Carver ever been to him? The kind who slapped him on the back after a touchdown and forgot who he was when the shit hit the fan. He had turned into worse than a stranger that summer Casey went missing, distancing himself and his sterling West Point reputation as far from John as possible.

Anxious from the memories, John dug his hand down into the deepest recesses of his most hidden coat pocket and pulled out a joint. Weed was about the only thing that took the edge off without making him feel like his brain was surrounded by a thick layer of wet cotton wool. The meds the VA docs had put him on had left him feeling like a zombie, struggling to function. This was better so long as he was careful about his intake. Too much and he could tip over the fine line and trigger his paranoia. Just enough and he could chill out and fall asleep on his own.

The act of smoking relaxed him. The intake of breath, the slow exhale, the rhythmic repetition. The tension left his muscles as the familiar sensation seeped through him. He looked at the dog. The dog looked at him, sighed, and laid its head on its outstretched paws.

They had a lot in common, John thought, him and this dog. Motherless strays with no real place in the world, with no one giving a shit what happened to either of them.

Starting to feel the chill of the night, he wadded up the burger bag, stuffed it in his coat pocket, and climbed out of the truck. He would leave the tailgate down. The dog could stay or go, its choice. At least now the animal had a full belly, a bowl of water, and a blanket to curl up on if it wanted to.

"Stay if you like," John said. "But no barking. The old man will come out here and shoot you."

The dog sighed and burrowed into the blanket.

John went in the house through the back door and into the kitchen. It was past eleven. If he was lucky, the old man would be passed out in his recliner by now, and he could slip down the hall unnoticed. He wanted a hot shower and a couple of pulls on the bottle of whiskey he kept hidden in his room. If all went well and nothing disrupted the sense of calm he was nurturing, he might drift off and sleep without nightmares—at least for a little while.

He assumed the voices coming from the living room were on television, some sports network talk show or redneck reality program. He assumed wrong. He had already stepped into the tiny dining room when he realized the voices were live. Three men were standing in the living room dead ahead of him: his father, Tim Carver, and a third man in a dark trench coat, medium height, heavyset, with a drooping mustache. They all turned and looked at John.

"Speak of the devil," his old man said.

"Hey, John," Carver said. "This is Detective Tubman. I told you he might be stopping by."

That wasn't what he'd said, John thought. He had said the detective wanted him to come into the sheriff's office. He hadn't said anything about invading his home, but here they were, standing in his living room, talking to his father. God only knew what the old man might have told them already. And why did Carver have to be here anyway? If all the detective wanted was to talk to him, why did he need a uniform backing him up?

Eyes narrowed, John looked from Carver to the detective to the old man. He could feel himself tipping over that delicate line the weed had put him on. He could feel the paranoia rising like a cold tide inside him. He wanted to bolt and run out the back door and just keep running. But he held himself in place like he was a dog on a leash. Running from cops was never a wise choice.

"I have a few questions for you, John," the detective said, coming toward him. He waddled like a pregnant woman, his belly preceding him into the room.

Carver came forward as well, maybe six feet to the right of the detective, effectively blocking the route to the front door. He had his hands on his hips, close to his service weapon, close to his baton.

John's pulse kicked up faster and faster. He was hot and sweating inside his jacket. He could feel his blood pressure rise. Inside his wounded brain, fight-or-flight hormones were running like water from a wide-open faucet.

"Some girl from the Grindstone got raped," his old man said, hanging a fresh cigarette from his lip and lighting up. "So, naturally, they come looking for you," he said sarcastically.

John could hear the Maker's Mark in his voice. He was more than half in the bag. He took a drag on the cigarette and started laughing and coughing.

"Maybe your next stop should be St. Theresa's rectory," he said to the detective, laughing. "The priest is a better suspect than this one. He only ever had the one girlfriend all through school. Of course," he conceded, smiling like a wolf, "she was a hot little tamale."

Tim Carver frowned at the comment. "Maybe we should all have a seat," he suggested.

"I'll stand, thank you," John said.

"Suit yourself," Tubman said, pulling a chair out from the table. "I'm taking a load off. It's been a long damn day."

"Then why are you here?" John asked. "It's the middle of the night. This can't wait until tomorrow?"

"Crime doesn't run on a time clock, Mr. Villante," Tubman said, settling in. "I've got a rape victim lying in the hospital. I need to find out who put her there."

"Wasn't me."

"Where've you been all evening, John?" Carver asked.

"Nowhere special. Why? Did something else happen that you want to try to hang on me?"

"Nobody's trying to hang anything on you, son," Tubman said.

John laughed under his breath and looked away, down the hall. If they decided to press him, tried to put hands on him, he could be down the hall and out his bedroom window in a matter of seconds. He'd done it enough times over the years to avoid a beating at the hands of his old man. *Down the hall, out the window, run for the woods . . .*

"So," the detective began, "how well do you know April Johnson?"

"I don't."

"Sure you do," his father said. He pulled a chair out, turned it around, and straddled it, leaning over the table to tap the ash off his cigarette into a beer can. "She works the evening shift. Mousey hair, cute ass, perky little tits."

"Maybe they should be talking to you," John said pointedly.

His father's eyes went cold and flat, like a shark's eyes. "Don't get smart with me, boy. I don't need to force myself on women."

"Neither do I."

"I understand you got fired from your job at Anthony's last

night," Tubman said, sending John's father into gales of laughter. The detective ignored him. "What did you do after that?"

"I came home," John said. He shot his father a glare. "If he wasn't too drunk to remember, he saw me."

"Yeah, I saw him come home," his father said. He took another long pull on his cigarette and fired the smoke at the grimy yellow ceiling. "And I saw him leave again after that."

"The hell you did!" John shouted. "You were passed out in your chair!"

"So you did leave again?" Tubman said.

Fuck.

"I went for a run," John said.

"And where did you run to?"

"Nowhere. I just ran."

"Unless you were on a treadmill, you ran somewhere."

"Down the road. I just ran. But I sure as hell didn't run all the way to the Grindstone."

Tubman looked at Carver. "How far is that from here?"

Carver shrugged. "Three or four miles."

The detective looked at John with a critical eye. "You look to be pretty damn fit to me, soldier. Three or four miles isn't so much."

"Unless you're built like Detective Tubman," Carver said, trying to lighten the mood.

John just stared at him.

"Did anybody see you running?" Tubman asked.

"It was the middle of the night. No. No one saw me."

"What time did you get home?"

"I don't know. I didn't look at a clock."

Tubman looked at his father. "Did you see him come home?"

"No, sir," the elder Villante said, giving John a cold look. "I must have been passed out. Too drunk to notice anybody coming into my house in the dead of night."

"What did you wear to run in?" Tubman asked.

John shrugged. "A sweatshirt, sweatpants, shoes."

"What color?"

"Black."

Tubman raised an eyebrow. "You went running at night in black clothes? Why would you do that?"

"Those are the clothes I have."

"Running in black at night," Tubman said. "In your experience, who does that, Deputy Carver?"

Carver sighed. "People who don't want to be seen."

"Burglars, thieves, rapists—"

"I'm no rapist," John said angrily. His head was starting to throb now. *Boom, boom, boom,* with the beat of his pulse. It felt like his brain was swelling, pressing against the inside of his skull.

"Could we have a look at those clothes?" Tubman asked.

"No."

"Why not?"

"Because fuck you; that's why not!" John snapped, the anxiety winding inside him like a spring.

Carver moved a couple of slow steps toward him around the end of the dining room table, hands out in front of him at waist level, palms down. "No need to get all jacked up here, John," he said. "If you haven't done anything wrong—"

"I haven't done anything wrong!"

"Then let us see those clothes and we'll be on our way," Tubman said.

His head was pounding like a drum. He was breathing too quickly but not getting enough oxygen. Carver came another step closer, an expression of phony concern on his face.

"Are you okay, John?" he asked. "You seem a little on edge."

"You come in my house and accuse me of raping some girl. Yeah, I'm a little on edge about that."

"Are you on something, John?"

"Me? Yeah. I'm high on life," John said sarcastically.

"Your eyes look a little funny is all. Tony Tarantino mentioned you had a head injury in the war."

"That could explain a lot," Tubman said. "Do you black out, John? Do you have problems controlling your temper?"

"Are you taking any medication for it?" Carver asked.

"He always did have a hair trigger," his father said, getting up from his chair. He dropped his cigarette butt in the beer can.

John glared at him. "Yeah, I always did have. I got that from you. Where were you last night when I was out running? Where were you when I got home—or after?"

The old man planted his big hands at the waist of his jeans. "I believe we established I was drunk."

"Like that ever stopped you from anything."

To John's right, Carver took a step closer, sniffing the air. John turned his body to cut off the angle, weight on the balls of his feet, knees soft, ready to spring into action. His senses seemed hyper-acute. Colors were brighter; sounds were louder; smells were stronger. The scent of fried onions and greasy burger coming from the crumpled bag in his coat pocket overrode his anxious sweat and the faintly sweet smell of what he had smoked.

"You're an ungrateful little shit," his father said, coming toward him from the other side.

John shifted positions, trying to keep an eye on each of the men coming toward him. He took a step backward.

"I let you live here in my house, rent free, and this is how you talk to me?" his father said, coming another step toward him. He was a couple of inches shorter than John, but thickset and heavily muscled. Even though he was near fifty, most people were afraid of him. The menacing energy that came off him was as strong as the smell of booze and sweat and cigarettes.

"You always did take after your mother," he said.

A red haze washed over John's vision. The roaring in his head was so loud now that Tim Carver's voice seemed to come from the far end of a tunnel.

"Mr. Villante, could you please go back to your seat? There's no need for this to get ugly."

John's attention was squarely on his father now as the old man took another step toward him, his face red and contorted, his white mustache twisting around his sour mouth.

"Pissy little bitch," he said, and he reached out with both hands and shoved John hard in the chest, pushing him back into the wall.

In that instant John seemed to separate his thinking brain from his emotional brain, as if the two were housed in different bodies. His thinking brain stood away from what happened, watching, taking it in like a prizefight on television. His emotional brain simply reacted and acted. His body responded to commands his thinking brain couldn't hear.

Springing forward like a big cat, he went after the old man with fists, connecting hard and lightning fast—right jab, right jab, left hook—instantly bloodying his father's nose and mouth.

Swimming through a haze of alcohol, the old man pawed at him like a dog as he stumbled backward. John grabbed the front of his shirt as he hooked a leg out from under him and rode him down to the floor.

He couldn't hear Carver or the detective shouting at him. He couldn't feel Carver pulling on him. All he could feel was the white-hot rage his father had unleashed. Then suddenly a weight pressed down on his back and a pressure pulled back against his throat and he couldn't breathe, and then blackness.

He came to on a big gasp, sucking air back into his lungs like a deep-sea diver just breaking the surface of the ocean. His surroundings reappeared through a black lacy spiderweb that cleared as he shook his head and rubbed his eyes. The raw wounds on his hands had begun to bleed again—or maybe the blood wasn't his.

He pushed himself up from the floor to sit back against the wall. Carver was helping his father onto a chair. For the first time ever, the old man looked like just that—old. His face was pale against the contrast of the blood coming from his nose and mouth. He suddenly looked so much smaller and less fierce than he ever had. He wiped his bleeding mouth on the sleeve of his denim shirt and stared at John.

"Get the fuck out of my house."

John said nothing.

"Get the fuck out of my house," his father said again, louder.

John got to his feet. "I'll get my stuff."

"No, you won't get your stuff," the old man said, standing up, one hand on the table for support. He used his anger to generate energy, reinflating his ego. His voice got stronger and louder with every word. "You will get the fuck out of my house before I tell these assholes to throw you in jail! Get out! Get the fuck out!"

"You don't want to press charges, Mr. Villante?" Carver asked. "It's your call, although I will say you laid hands on him first."

The old man made a face of disgust and waved the idea off.

Carver turned to John, shrugged, and spread his hands. "You heard the man, John. Go before he changes his mind."

Tubman finally hoisted himself to his feet. "Don't take any out-of-town trips. That's some temper you have on you, young man."

John looked from one to the other to the other. His father's nose looked busted. The hate in his eyes was caustic. This wasn't the first time in John's life they had come to blows, but it was the first time he'd ever done real damage to his father. No one deserved it more, but still there was a part of him that was a scared little boy afraid he had crossed a line he wouldn't be allowed to cross back over.

Pathetic, he thought.

"Come on, John," Tim Carver said, stepping toward him. "I'll walk you out to your truck."

John shrugged off the hand his old buddy tried to lay on his shoulder and headed for the back door.

"Wait a day or two, then come back when he's at work and get your stuff," Carver said as they walked around behind the garage. "Or maybe he'll come around by then and let you back in."

"Fuck him," John said. "I hope he drinks himself to death. The sooner the better. I'd pour it down his throat myself if I could."

"Not a good idea to suggest a manner of death in front of a deputy," Carver said. "Just for future reference."

John jammed his bruised, bleeding hands in the pockets of his coat and leaned back against the grill of his pickup.

"You shouldn't stay here tonight—if you're thinking of sleeping in your truck," Carver said. "Get off the property. I don't want to get called back here in an hour or two and find one of you shot the other. Do you have someplace you can go? A friend, a relative, a girlfriend?"

"I'm fine," John said. He had none of the above. He had his truck and a stray dog. But he'd slept in worse places than a pickup, and with worse company than a dog.

"Stay out of trouble, for Christ's sake," Carver said. "I'm cutting you a big break here, John, not taking you in. Tubman's going to ream my ass for it. So don't make me regret it."

"You think I'm a rapist and you're cutting me loose?"

"I never said I think you're a rapist. But even if you are, you'd have to be dumber than a sack of shit to go attack somebody now. Even with a head injury, you can't be that stupid."

"Thanks," John said with just enough sarcasm it was hard to tell if he was indeed thankful for the break or pissed off by the backhanded vote of confidence.

"He's a downright son of a bitch, your dad," Carver said. "If you were truly gonna kill somebody, I think you would have put him in the ground by now. Go on and get out of here. And don't say I never did anything for you."

John watched him walk back to the house. He went around to the back of the truck and closed the tailgate. The dog was still curled on the blanket.

"We're going for a ride," John said.

He drove to the truck stop and parked in line with a couple of big rigs that had pulled in for the night. He let the tailgate down to give the dog options, then walked into the wooded lot to take a leak. The dog followed him, lifting its leg on a tree. The night was alternately star filled and dark, with clouds scudding over the moon. The breeze was cold. He thought back to Afghanistan and some of the rough places where he'd had to sleep there, with the threat of death ever present. A night in a parking lot was no hardship by comparison. And yet he half wished he was back there. At least in a war the enemy wasn't a man's own father.

He thought about what his old man had said—about him taking after his mother. He wished he could remember enough about her to know if that was true. She had left when he was eight. He remembered thinking she was beautiful. He remembered how she had tucked him into bed at night. He remembered thinking he wished she wouldn't have left without him. He remembered the feeling of emptiness and fear that yawned open inside of him because she had left him behind with no one to protect him from his dad. Yet he had never managed to hate her. He had gone to bed every night with the secret hope that she would come back and get him, but she never had.

Back at the truck, he climbed into the cab, jockeying for a half-way comfortable position to try to sleep. He leaned his shoulder against the driver's door window and glanced out as the dog put its front paws up on the door and started to whine. Their eyes met in the dim light from the parking lot.

John sighed. He told himself no good would come from giving in, but he found himself opening the door just the same. He got out of the truck and stood back while the dog jumped in and settled itself on the passenger's seat.

"But you're still not my dog," John said as he got back in and shut the door. "Just so you know."

20

Mom, have you seen my feet?"

"Yes."

"Where?"

Dana's mother flipped a pancake and looked up from the stove. "What do you mean, where?"

"Where are my feet?" Dana asked impatiently.

"On the ends of your legs, last I checked."

"No!"

"Yes!" She looked down at the floor and pointed with the spatula. "There they are. I see two feet and ten toes."

Dana squeezed her eyes shut and groaned. "No. Not *feet*. Like feet. Goes on feet."

"Starts with an S," her mother prompted.

"Ssssss-shoes!" Dana said with a sense of mingled triumph and relief. Then came the familiar mix of disappointment and embarrassment. For God's sake, of course she knew the difference between shoes and feet.

"Don't be hard on yourself," her mother said. "I don't think you're getting enough rest. You have more trouble finding words when you're tired."

"I'm fine," Dana said, grabbing a plate, her bare feet forgotten.

"Dr. Burnette said I need to challenge myself with goals. I can't do that if I'm asleep all the time."

"If last night was an example of you pursuing a goal, I'm not for it. You can't just go off by yourself like that, Dana. I don't even want to think about what could have happened."

"Nothing happened," Dana said, ignoring the fact that she had been scared out of her wits with Detective Hardy, and just trying to follow the directions of the navigation system had stressed her to the frayed end of her last nerve. Her mother didn't have to know any of that. "I went to talk to the detective and I came back. If Frankie hadn't come by when she did, no one would've been the wiser."

Her mother gave her a look as they went to the table. "Dana . . ."

"Lynda . . . What?" Dana asked, taking a seat.

Roger peered over the top of his newspaper at her. Dana cut him a look, then turned back to her mother.

"You want to think you can just do everything like you did before, but you can't, sweetheart," her mother said. "Not yet. What if you had gotten lost last night?"

"I had my phone with my navigation app."

"And what if your phone died? What if you lost service?"

"What if a spaceship beamed me up?"

"My scenarios are realistic," her mother insisted. "We have to have a system. If you're going somewhere, I need to know. You need to text me or leave a note. Make a note in your phone that you have to tell me when you're going somewhere. Promise me you'll do that."

"I promise."

Dana took a bite of her pancakes. What if she forgot to look at her note that reminded her to leave a note? She kept the question to herself.

"What did the detective have to say to you last night?" her mother asked, as if that was normal breakfast conversation, as if she was asking about running into an old teacher from high school.

"He said he investigated Daddy's death," Dana said.

Her mother looked up. Roger lowered his newspaper.

"I thought you went to ask him something about Casey's case," her mother said.

"I did. He brought up Daddy. Why didn't anybody ever tell me there was an investigation?"

"You were a child," Roger said.

"Why would we have told you, sweetheart?" her mother asked. "We were all so devastated—you especially. The investigation was just a formality. Nothing was going to come of it. Nothing did come of it. Daddy had an accident."

"What if he didn't?" Dana asked. "That's why they had to investigate—to make sure somebody didn't push him off the bluff. Didn't I have a right to know that?"

"You were twelve," Roger said.

"I was fourteen," Dana corrected him, offended that he didn't care enough to remember.

He rolled his eyes. "You were a child. There was no reason to involve you."

"They never questioned me," she said. "What if I had known something?"

"Like what?" her mother asked.

"I don't know. What if I had overheard a conversation or witnessed something but didn't realize it might be important—"

"Because you didn't," Roger said flatly. "Because there was nothing to know or witness. Your father slipped and fell. No one pushed him. Why would anyone have done that? He didn't have any enemies. I would know. I was his best friend."

"Were you there?" Dana challenged. "Did you see it happen?"

"No."

"Then really, you don't know anything."

"There was nothing to know, sweetheart," her mother said. "The sheriff's office had to investigate because no one saw what happened, but no one ever believed it was anything other than an accident."

"That doesn't mean it wasn't," Dana said stubbornly.

"He went hunting alone," Roger said. "I always told him that was a bad idea, but he said it cleared his head to walk that property. He was probably trying to get hold of that damned unruly dog of his, got too close to the edge, and lost his footing."

"Then where was Moose?" Dana asked. "Moose never would have left Daddy. Never."

"He couldn't have gotten to your dad. Maybe he got lost trying to find a way down to him. We always figured someone probably picked the dog up off the road and just kept him."

"Yeah," Dana nodded. "Like maybe the person who killed Daddy."

"Think about that," Roger said, trying to be the voice of reason. "Do you really think that dog would have let somebody hurt your father?"

Dana sat for a moment, silent, recalling the big, exuberant Labrador and how much the dog had loved her father. Immediately a picture came to mind of her father with the gigantic Moose draped across his lap, both of them with huge smiles on their faces. As good-natured as the dog had been, he had also been protective of the family. It was doubtful he would have let anyone with bad intentions near her father.

"Unless he knew the person," she said slowly, looking at her stepfather.

Roger sighed and stood up. "I'm leaving now before you accuse me outright of killing your father," he said. "Eddie was like a brother to me. I loved him like a brother."

"Roger . . . ," Dana's mother started, reaching out a hand as if to stop him.

He waved off whatever excuse she had been about to make. "I don't want to hear it, Lynda. I have to go anyway. We're filming that interview at the nursery today and starting to set up for the party."

He left the room, and Dana's mother turned toward her, looking frustrated.

"Did he have an alibi?" Dana asked, all the finer emotions of the moment skimming past her.

"Dana, you have to stop this."

"Why? What if he killed Daddy?"

"Stop it!" her mother snapped. "He did not kill your father! They were best friends. Roger was devastated when it happened. We all were. The sheriff's office conducted a routine investigation of an accidental death, and they were very discreet about it and very considerate of our family. There was no conspiracy. Get that out of your head!"

Dana frowned down at her plate, cutting her pancakes with her fork into smaller and smaller pieces as she processed what her mother had said. But she still wasn't able to stop the questions that came to her.

"So where was he when it happened?" she asked.

Her mother put her hands over her face, took in a slow, measured breath, and let it out. "He was making calls on suppliers that afternoon."

Meaning he had been driving from one wholesale nursery to another. Unless he had taken someone with him who could account for every minute between stops, there had to be big gaps in his alibi. But the sheriff's detectives would have checked his story out, Dana knew. She thought of the timeline Dan Hardy had posted on his wall from Casey's disappearance. He would have done the same for her father's case, she supposed.

"It's been more than a decade," her mother said. "In all these years you have never once questioned Roger's character or motives. You were never close to him the way you were to your dad, but you always got along with him."

"I don't know why," Dana grumbled. "I don't like him now."

"That's new since your head injury. You liked him fine before. Maybe you're reacting to him this way just because he's a man. Maybe he reminds you of the man who hurt you—"

"I don't remember him."

"You don't consciously remember him. According to the doctors, that doesn't mean there isn't an impression of him in the emotional part of your brain."

One of the many frustrations of her condition: the memories that couldn't be accessed but still had the power to influence her emotions. How much of what she was feeling toward Roger was genuine and justified? Or was her dislike and distrust of him the result of the emotional hurt she felt because he had distanced himself from her during her recovery? How much was attached to the residual paranoia instilled by what had happened to her?

"Do you really think I would have married him if I thought he'd done something to your father?" her mother asked. "Do you think I'm stupid or a poor judge of character?"

"No."

"Or am I in on the conspiracy too?"

"No," Dana said, feeling contrite. She had never doubted that her parents loved each other. Her mother had fallen completely apart when her father died. Her relationship with Roger had developed slowly over the course of two years following the death of her husband.

"I'm sorry," Dana said.

"You don't have to apologize to me, but I think you owe Roger something. He loves you, sweetheart. He's done his best to fill in for your father. You and your dad were so close; it wasn't easy for him to try to take on that role. But think of all the events he attended when you were in school. Think of all the times he chauffeured you and Casey around before you were able to drive. Anytime I wasn't able to be there, Roger was there. Remember the big after-graduation party he organized for you and your friends? You need to go back through all your photographs of family events and holidays and remind yourself of your relationship with Roger before."

She had already spent many hours on her iPad and computer,

looking at photographs of family and friends, high school years and college years, photos of friends from places she had worked. She had filled much of her time in the hospital and at the Weidman Center doing just that, trying to connect the images together with fragments of memory with varying degrees of success. There seemed to always be a certain disconnect simply because she wasn't the same Dana she had been when those memories had been made.

Relationships were no different. The relationship Before Dana had with Roger Mercer was going to seem like it belonged to someone else, because it had. After Dana was her new reality, and After Dana saw the world through a much darker filter. Before Dana had been curious. After Dana was suspicious. Before Dana had believed in the inherent good in people. After Dana knew firsthand their capacity for evil.

The question was: Which perception was truth? Which reality was she supposed to believe? Maybe young, naïve Before Dana had seen the world as it should be, rather than as it really was. Maybe After Dana was right to question everything and everyone she thought she had known.

"He loves me?" she said. "He can't even look at me for more than two seconds since this," she said, pointing to her damaged face. "Haven't you noticed that?"

Of course she had, and still she made an excuse for him. "He doesn't want to accept what you went through and what it did to you."

"Neither do I," Dana said. "But I have to look at this face in the mirror every day. I could use the support of the people who are supposed to love me. You've been there every day for me, Mom, either physically or over the phone or on the computer. Roger couldn't be bothered to come visit me more than once a month."

"Roger has a very busy schedule, sweetheart—"

"So what? Daddy had a busy schedule too. Do you think he would have stayed away? You know he wouldn't have. He would have been there for me just as much as you were. You know that's true."

She did know. Dana could see her mother's struggle with the emotions that truth evoked, the truth that Roger Mercer wasn't the man Eddie Nolan had been. She lived with that truth every day and slept with it every night.

"He's not a bad man, Dana," she said. "He's a flawed man, but he's got a good heart. What happened to you impacted all of us. He's just having a harder time dealing with it."

"He should imagine how I feel," Dana said quietly. "He lost a pretty stepdaughter. I lost my identity. I lost what my life was and what it could have been."

Her mother reached over and touched her arm. "You'll build a new life, sweetheart. I wish you didn't have to, but I'm very grateful you're getting that chance. And you need to know you're not making that journey alone. We're all on it with you."

Dana nodded to appease her mother, but in her mind she thought: *Everyone but Roger.*

The alarm on her mother's cell phone went off. She glanced at it and sighed.

"I have to go. I've got a hair appointment. Do you want to come along?"

"I don't have any hair," Dana said, running a hand back over her short blond crop.

"You could get your nails done, have a pedicure."

"No, thanks. I'll rest," she said for no other reason than to make her mother happy.

"Good," her mother said, leaning down to kiss her forehead. "I'll see you later."

Dana sat at the table for a few minutes, staring at the breakfast she no longer had any interest in eating. A kaleidoscope view of memory fragments tumbled through her mind. Memories of herself and Casey here in this house, at this table, cooking in this kitchen, watching TV downstairs.

She could see Roger in some of those bits and pieces. Roger the chaperone, the chauffeur, the surrogate father. He had never had that ease around kids that had come so naturally to her father. Her dad had effortlessly balanced the authority aspect of parenthood with a sense of camaraderie that made all of Dana's friends love and respect him. Roger's attempts at connecting with the kids had always seemed fake and forced. Dana had appreciated his efforts and cringed at the same time.

Now as she looked back on those memories, she felt uncomfortable thinking about her stepfather. But according to her mother's theory, those feelings were attached to an event that had nothing to do with him.

Head throbbing from the effort to sort it all out, she went back downstairs to her room and opened the French doors to the patio, letting in the crisp, clean air. The sky was the incredible electric blue that seemed unique to fall. The colors of the grassy field and the woods beyond seemed extra-saturated.

Tuxedo immediately trotted outside to lie in the sun on the flagstone, purring and trilling as he rolled and stretched.

Dana walked out onto the patio, the stone warm beneath her bare feet, while the breeze was just cool enough to make her wrap her oversize cardigan around her slight frame. The day was so beautiful it was hard to imagine there could be evil in the world. As she looked past the low stone wall, down the grassy hill to the woods painted with the brilliant shades of autumn, she tried to recall the feeling from her first night home when she had the feeling there was someone watching from the woods. It seemed ridiculous in the light of a picture-postcard-perfect day.

But the day Casey had disappeared had been a beautiful day too. A hot summer day with fluffy white popcorn clouds floating in the sky. And at some point during that day someone had taken Casey Grant away from everyone who loved her. Dana wanted to know who and why.

Mind fixed on her goal, she went back into the bedroom, then

remembered Tuxedo. The cat was running along a row of chrysanthemums, leaping in the air every few strides, trying to catch a butterfly.

"Tux!" Dana called and clapped her hands to get his attention.
He paid her no mind, continuing in his pursuit of the butterfly.

Dana went back out on the patio and had no more luck catching
the cat than the cat had catching the butterfly. Playful, he dashed
from one part of the patio to another, to another, trilling and chirping, his tail straight up in the air, daring her to chase him.

Winded and dizzy, Dana finally gave up and went inside, leaving
the door ajar just enough for Tuxedo to slip through, hoping his
curiosity at where she had gone would quickly get the better of him
so she could close the door again.

She sat down at her desk and woke the computer up. Next to the
keyboard was the notebook she had taken with her into Detective
Hardy's house the night before. She pulled out the copy of her statement that Hardy had given to her and read it over, start to finish.

There wasn't much to it. Casey had spent the night. They had
gone the next morning for breakfast at the Grindstone, then continued on to the nursery. She said Casey had left because she wasn't
feeling well. Dana hadn't seen or heard from her again. Ever.

There had to be so much more to the story than a few dry para-
graphs, a collection of dull declarative sentences—*we went here, we
did this, she did that*. What had they been thinking? What had they
said to each other? Hardy claimed a witness had seen them arguing.
Dana swore she had no memory of it. Was that just another piece of
her past her brain had decided to delete for her own good? Or was
there truly nothing worth remembering? In the seven years since
Casey had gone missing, she hadn't come up with any relevant information. No one had.

She thought about Hardy's office—the timeline, the notes, the
photographs. It was like having his memory pulled out of his head
and tacked to the wall. He didn't have to dig for the details stored

in the far corners of his troubled mind. He could just look at the wall and see them.

Dana looked around her room at the built-in bookcases and the big upholstered headboard, the framed artwork on the walls and the interruption of doors. She went out into the hall and looked at a long stretch of uninterrupted wall directly across from her room. No one came down this hall but her for the most part.

She went back to her desk and dug a fat black marker out of a drawer, went back to the wall, and starting at the door to the utility room, drew a thick black line at eye level all the way to the door of the powder room, a good ten feet from end to end. At the starting point she wrote DAY BEFORE on the line, then a few feet to the right wrote DAY CASEY DISAPPEARED. Perpendicular to the horizontal line, she drew vertical lines above and below and scribbled what information was readily available in her memory—that she and Casey had gone to breakfast at the Grindstone, that Casey had come with her to work at the nursery, that Casey had left the nursery— adding the question: *sick?? or fight???*

When her memory ran out of information, she got her iPad and started going through the articles about Casey's disappearance, noting details on the wall. She used different colored markers for details given by different people—blue for John Villante, red for Tim Carver, green for Casey's mom, purple for her own statements.

She had no idea how long she'd been at it when she finally stepped back and looked at what she'd done. The clean, smooth beige wall had gone from blank slate to a chaotic work of art, a spiderweb of lines punctuated by bubbles of words, statements, and questions. She felt exhausted from the effort but lighter for having taken her memories and put them up where they could be seen, where they couldn't slip away into a dark, hidden cranny in her brain.

She was sweating. She was breathing hard, as if she'd been through a strenuous workout, but she felt good. She had accomplished something.

Hands on her hips, she started at the beginning of the timeline and read each notation slowly. Casey had spent the night. Dana had noted that her mother had been out of town, gone to Florida to help Grandma after her gallbladder surgery. Roger had been their chaperone. The next day she and Casey had left the house a little after nine and gone to the Grindstone for breakfast, then on to the nursery. Roger had stayed home with a migraine. Casey had left the nursery after an employee witnessed her having words with Dana. Casey had later called and spoken to Tim. She had also called John to set up a time to meet that evening. He claimed she was a no-show. Her car had been found in the parking lot at the truck stop on the far side of Silva's Garage, along the edge of the wooded lot that bordered the property.

There was too much open space on the wall, Dana thought. The picture painted by the lines and words was lopsided, weighed down at the beginning of the timeline. After that last day she had seen Casey, the line stretched on and on with the occasional notation of a supposed sighting that had dissolved into the nothingness of wishful thoughts.

Too much blank wall, she thought again. Then a dark stain appeared, growing slowly up the wall toward the far end of the timeline.

Dana's heart seemed to stop, then pound against the inside of her chest like a fist on a door.

Not a stain, she thought as her brain scrambled to make sense of what she was seeing. All in a matter of nanoseconds, recognition went from stain to not a stain to like a stain to the word that made her blood run cold.

Shadow.

The shadow of a man standing in her bedroom.

21

"Have you solved it, little girl?"

Dana spun around and ran backward, banging hard into the wall.

Dan Hardy stood in the doorway to her bedroom, his dark eyes shining bright with some kind of fever. *Madness,* Dana thought. He seemed bigger than he had last night, too large for the space, his broad shoulders threatening to strain the doorframe. The smile that turned the corners of his mouth was the smile of a cat with a cornered mouse.

"What are you doing here?" Dana asked. She wanted to sound outraged but knew she sounded exactly how she felt—terrified.

"I came to see you," he said. His tone was low and dark, the seductive purr of a predator enjoying the fear he was stirring in his prey.

"How did you get in the house?"

"I rang the doorbell upstairs. Nobody answered. Thought I'd have a walk around. See what I might see. You left your patio door open. You should be more careful. When you open the door to let the breeze in, anything might follow."

Afraid to move, afraid to turn her head, Dana glanced to her right. The hall ended in a utility room. No escape route. Even if she could get into the room and shut the door, there was no lock to keep him out. She tried to think of the things that might be in the room that she could use for a weapon. Christmas decorations. Maybe some hand tools. He would be on her before she could get to them. He would be on her before she could get to the door.

"You're a skittish little thing," he said. "I suppose you have more call than most. How many days did he keep you?" he asked. "Two? Three? I forget."

Meaning he knew her story. He had given it thought. Dana didn't answer. If he wanted to fantasize about her captivity and torture, she wasn't going to participate willingly.

Every cell in her body was trembling. Her fear was like a band around her chest. She couldn't seem to get a deep breath.

She glanced to the left, to the family room with its big stone fireplace and iron fireplace tools, a wall of doors that let out onto the patio, the stairs leading to the main floor of the house. All of it might as well have been a mile away. She would have to get past Hardy to get to any of it. He had only to step into the hallway to block her path.

She didn't have a choice. She had to try to run.

Her fingers closed tight around the marker in her hand. It wasn't much of a weapon, but it was all she had.

As if he had read her mind, Hardy stepped into the hall, trapping her.

"Did you follow me last night?" Dana asked.

"Why would I bother to follow you? I already knew where you live."

"To scare me," she said. "You seem to enjoy that."

Her mind flashed back to the story Tim had told her about Hardy and a young prostitute, how he had physically removed the girl from the house she had worked in, how she had disappeared and shown up days later, beaten and bloody.

"You caused quite a fuss last night," he said. "I saw it on the news."

"Everyone knows I went to see you," Dana said. "I told them. The sheriff was here."

"And Carver, your old boyfriend. He likes to get in front of a camera, that one," he said. "He'll make a politician one day."

"He knows I went to see you. If something happens to me, they'll go straight to you."

"Ah," he said, smiling. "Young Carver's been telling tales out of school. He told you a few stories about me, didn't he?"

Dana didn't know if it was better to mention the girl or not. She had no idea what might trigger him. She wondered what her chances were of getting past him. If she could kick him in the balls hard enough to double him over, maybe . . . Or he would get hold of her before she could land a kick, or kicking him would only enrage him . . .

"Why would I want to hurt you, little girl?" he asked. "You're gonna help me solve my case. I need you to come with me."

"I'm not going anywhere with you," Dana said.

He chuckled at that.

"You've got spunk. I'll give you that," he said. "Better to be smart, though. If I'm a bad guy, I'll do what I have to do to get you out of this house—knock you out, choke you out, tie you up. Or I'll decide you're not worth the bother, and I'll just do what I want, then kill you here now. It's all about risk versus benefit. If I can get you away from the house and control you, I get more of what I want, but is the risk greater getting you out of the house or doing you here? That's how a predator thinks."

Dana wanted to cry. Wave after wave of emotion washed through her, emotions attached to memories she couldn't access, memories of what another madman had done to her. Her instinct to flee had died with her opportunity to do so. Now she felt frozen in place, waiting. How would he kill her? With his hands? With a knife? How long would he play with her first? Would she be able to shut her mind down and escape the reality of what he was about to do to her?

"Hypothetically speaking," he said. "If I was a bad guy, you should pretend to be cooperative and compliant long enough to get me to step out of this hallway. Come along like a meek little lamb until we're out of this house. Then you bolt and run like hell.

"If I was a bad guy," he reiterated.

He let the possibility hang in the air for what seemed like minutes. Then he sighed and took a couple of steps back, releasing some of the pressure of the confrontation.

Dana was shaking like she had hold of a jackhammer. She wrapped her arms around herself and held on tight. The relief that he might not have come here to kill her was at least as draining as the fear had been. Her legs turned to jelly, and she slid down with her back against the wall until she was sitting on the floor.

"Please go," she whispered. "Please just go away."

"I need you to come with me."

"You're not a cop anymore. I don't have to go anywhere with you. I'm *not* going anywhere with you."

"You want to know what happened to your friend, don't you?"

Dana said nothing for a moment. The answer was more complicated than a simple yes or no. Did she want to know that her friend had died the same horrible death she herself had somehow managed to escape? No. Did she want to know that angry words she had spoken might have sent Casey away and into the direct path of a killer? No. Did she want a resolution and answers to the questions? Yes. Did she want justice for her friend? Yes. Was she afraid of where those questions would take her? Very much so. Was she afraid of Dan Hardy? Absolutely.

"We have a common goal, you and I," he said, looking at her timeline. "That's why you came to me. Now I'm coming to you."

"What do you want from me?"

"I want you to retrace your steps that day."

"I've been trying to do that. I close my eyes and I try to remember—"

"No," Hardy said. "I mean we go everywhere the two of you went that day. We go through it step-by-step."

"I'm not getting in a car with you," Dana said.

"If I wanted to kill you, I could have done it by now."

"Maybe you don't want to kill me," Dana said. "Maybe I'll be found naked and beaten, wandering down a dirt road in a couple of days."

His expression hardened. Dana wished she had at least gotten to her feet before sending him into a homicidal rage. She would have liked one last chance to at least try to get away.

"You only know what you've been told, little girl," he said, his voice a low growl, his dark eyes boring into hers. "You don't know me. You don't know anything about me. And you don't know anything about what happened."

Dana was afraid to blink. She tried to swallow, but her mouth was so dry she nearly choked.

"You don't need to be afraid of me," Hardy said.

"Why not?" Dana asked bitterly. "You're a man, aren't you?"

He looked at her for a long moment, his expression softening to something like sympathy. "You more than earned the right to think that way," he said quietly.

Dana still didn't trust him. "I've been told you used to live to fuck with people's heads."

He might have lunged at her and smashed her face with one of his massive fists. He might have leaned down and crushed her larynx in one hand. Instead, he laughed with a mix of amusement and bitterness.

"You're a funny little thing," he said. "Indeed I do live to fuck with people's heads. There isn't much else left for me. Except this case," he said, nodding up at the wall and the notes Dana had scribbled across it. "Are you gonna help me with it, little girl?"

"I'm not getting in a car with you," Dana said again.

"Suit yourself. We start here, anyway," he said, pointing at the beginning of the timeline. "Casey spent the night with you here. What do you remember about that night?"

"Nothing stands out. We slept over at each other's houses all the time. Well," she corrected herself, "Casey slept over here more than the other way around. Her mother had a boyfriend from out of town. When he would come for a visit, Casey would stay here so she didn't have to hear them having sex."

"Karl Florian," Hardy said. "He was an insurance claims adjuster from Terre Haute. He and Ms. Grant had gone up to Indianapolis for a long weekend. They had solid alibis. So Casey came here and . . . ?"

"I read over my statement," Dana said. "It didn't say we did anything special."

"The statement isn't worth wiping your ass on," Hardy said. "It doesn't mean anything. I don't want you thinking about what you told me seven years ago. I want you to close your eyes and imagine that night. What do you see? What do you hear? What do you smell? Who else was here?"

"My mom was in Florida with my grandmother. We stayed in that night. It was raining. We ordered pizza. We watched movies. Just normal stuff. Nothing worth remembering. We didn't know that would be the last time."

"What about your stepdad?"

"What about him?"

"Was he around? Did he hang out with you?"

"He was around. He had some pizza."

"Was he ever inappropriate in any way?"

"Roger? No. He was kind of awkward around my friends. He wanted to be the cool dad, but he just wasn't."

"Did Casey ever say she felt uncomfortable around him?"

"No," Dana said automatically, then took a moment to think about it, trying to remember any time she would have said his awkwardness had crossed a line. Nothing clear came to mind, but when she said no a second time, she said it with less conviction.

"Was Roger a suspect?" she asked.

"Everyone is a suspect," Hardy returned. "Until I find an answer in a case, everyone is a suspect. You're a suspect."

"Me?" Dana said, offended at the idea. "Why would I hurt Casey?"

He shrugged, indifferent to her feelings. "You were angry with her for something."

"I didn't like her choice in boyfriends, so I killed her?" Dana said, getting to her feet. "That's ridiculous!"

"People lose their tempers," he said, taking the black marker out of her hand and stepping up to the wall to add to her notes. "They lash out. They don't always mean it. Angry words get exchanged, a push, a shove, someone stumbles and falls, hits their head wrong. Just like that, you're a killer."

"And I'm such a criminal mastermind, I hid her body without a trace of evidence anywhere. How did I manage that?"

"You'd manage that with help," he said matter-of-factly.

"Who's my accomplice?"

"Your boyfriend, her boyfriend, your stepdad, your mom—except she was out of town. She's in the clear."

"You're out of your mind."

"I'm just saying. This is how a detective has to think," he said. "I can't worry about you getting your feelings hurt, little girl. I can't worry that your stepdad is a state senator. There's not a person on this earth that couldn't be guilty of murder in the right circumstances."

"Yourself included?"

He gave her a long sideways look but said nothing.

Dana looked at the wall, at the note he had added to the timeline saying that after leaving the nursery Casey had returned to the house and picked up her things. *Time undetermined.*

He capped the marker and checked his watch. "Let's go. I want to get to the Grindstone before the lunch crowd."

22

Dana drove her own car to the Grindstone with Hardy following in a nondescript older gray sedan. Not a pickup, she noted, though that didn't mean he didn't have one. She parked in the lot out in front of the restaurant and sat for a moment, rethinking the wisdom of coming here. She couldn't just walk into a place and go unnoticed. People would look at her, stare at her. They would recognize her and turn to each other and whisper.

She jumped as Hardy rapped his knuckles on her window.

"Let's go," he barked, pulling her door open.

"I don't want to," Dana said. "I changed my mind."

"Why? You think everybody's gonna look at you?"

"Yes."

"So what? You are who you are now. You can't hide for the rest of your life because you've got a few scars. If people don't have better manners than to look, fuck 'em. Come on."

"Gee," Dana muttered. "Why should I bother with a therapist when I can just spend time with you?"

"Don't know why you would anyway," he grumbled, reaching for her arm to pull her out of the car.

Dana jerked away. "Don't touch me! I'll get out when I feel like it. It's not like you're paying for my time."

"I'm dying," he groused. "I'd sooner not do it in a goddamn parking lot waiting for you to decide whether or not to risk your delicate sensibilities."

"Fuck you."

"Don't curse. It sounds ridiculous coming out of a little thing like you," he said as she got out of the car. "Unless you're strong enough to knock him on his ass, never tell a man to go fuck himself."

"You're just full of life wisdom," Dana muttered, pulling up her hood.

"Feel free to stitch that on a pillow."

Dana walked toward the restaurant as if she was walking to her execution. She hadn't been to the Grindstone in years. The building sat a little bit separate from the other facilities on the property—Silva's Garage, the island of fuel pumps, and the convenience store that also offered shower facilities for truckers. While the building itself was of simple concrete-block construction, the facade of the restaurant had been decked out with weathered board-and-batten siding and a wide front porch lined with old rocking chairs, giving it a down-home country look.

Dana's apprehension grew with every step. If she and Casey had crossed paths with Doc Holiday all those years ago, this would have been the scene of the encounter. He was known to have followed truck routes. He had snagged several of his known victims from areas just like this one, busy, high-traffic places where people came and went and were quickly forgotten, their faces blending into all the others that stopped there for ten minutes or an hour at a time.

"What are you thinking?"

She flinched at the abrupt sound of Hardy's gruff voice. "Just that we spent so much time here—Casey and I, and our friends. We always came here after football games and basketball games. We never thought that it might not be safe, that someone we might have met here for a few minutes could have turned out to be . . ."

She didn't want to say his name. She felt like if she said his name here she might somehow conjure him up, like calling up a demon at a séance.

"He was just a man," Hardy said as they climbed the steps to the porch. "Don't make him more than what he was."

He was just the man who ruined her life, destroyed her career, shattered her sense of self, damaged her brain and her face. He was just a man who had tortured and killed who knew how many young women.

"He got up in the morning and took a shit just like every other man on the planet," Hardy said. "And when you killed him, he bled like any other man. Don't give him superpowers just because he got the drop on you once."

Dana wanted to argue with him that there was a lot more to what had happened to her, that it wasn't that simple, but she swallowed her protest. What man could understand the terror of being absolutely at the mercy of someone bigger and stronger, someone who had a boundless capacity for cruelty and an insatiable hunger for the suffering of others? Not many men would ever experience anything close to what she had experienced. From what Tim had told her, Dan Hardy had more in common with her assailant.

He held the door for her to go into the restaurant. Dana stepped inside and immediately turned to the right, head down, pretending to look at the rack of tourist brochures that mostly advised people to keep on driving past Shelby Mills to Louisville and Kentucky's horse country. Hardy asked the hostess for a booth.

She kept her head down as a waitress led them through the restaurant, self-consciously tugging at the edges of her hood. Even then she believed she could feel the stares and hear the whispers of people who caught glimpses of her face.

"What are you looking at?" Hardy barked at someone.

Dana cringed and tucked her chin to her chest, pulling again at the hood, wishing it could swallow her whole. She slid into the booth, up against the corner, and made herself as small as possible.

Hardy took his seat across from her and ordered coffee for both of them.

"You defeat the point of the exercise if you spend the whole time staring at the tabletop," Hardy complained. "You need to look up, look around, listen to the voices, smell the smells."

The sounds and smells were inescapable. She was on the verge of sensory overload. The place was busy, nearly full. Conversation and the clink of silverware on plates was an assault on her ears. She imagined she could hear her name being whispered. The aromas of strong coffee and bacon grease filled her sinuses. She hadn't been in a restaurant in nearly a year, and her first outing was to be crammed into a truck-stop diner overpopulated with men, stuck in a place where she may well have first encountered the man who had brutalized her years later.

Her nerves were humming like high-voltage power lines. In her mind she ticked through the checklist to calm her thoughts and even her breathing, to push back the flood of emotions that would swamp her brain and send her into a meltdown.

She looked up at Hardy without lifting her head. "I thought you were supposed to have chemo today."

"I canceled."

"Why?"

"Look around," he said, dismissing her question. "Imagine Casey sitting here with you. You came for breakfast. What did you order?"

She took a slow, deep breath and released it on a slow count of four. "I always got the egg skillet with biscuits."

"Order that."

"I'm not hungry."

"Doesn't matter. Order it anyway."

"Are you buying?" she asked. "I forgot to bring money."

"I'm buying."

"You order it."

The waitress returned with the coffee. Hardy ordered the breakfast skillet. Dana kept her head down, counting out her breaths.

"You're Dana Nolan, aren't you?" the waitress said, a little breathless, like she was meeting a movie star. "I followed your case every night on the news! And now you're back. You're like our own celebrity in Shelby Mills!"

"Leave her alone," Hardy barked.

The waitress shied away like a skittish horse, hustling back toward the kitchen, where she would tell every single employee about her encounter.

"She'll probably spit in my food now," Hardy grumbled.

"A waitress from here was attacked the other night," Dana said.

"Yep. The night you came home."

"You say that like it's my fault."

"Could be. I don't believe in coincidence."

"I think the stock market fell that day. Was that my fault too?"

"You come home. It's all over the news. And that night a young waitress, who happens to work at the same place as your friend that went missing, gets attacked and brutalized.

"On the one hand, shit happens," he said. "This county averages a certain number of reported rapes a year. On the other hand, you coming back here is generating renewed interest in Casey Grant's case. That could be enough of a stressor to set somebody off.

"If her bad guy lives here, he's gotten away with a crime for seven years. He maybe had even stopped looking over his shoulder by now. God knows that asshat Tubman wasn't putting any pressure on the case. Then all of a sudden here you come, and everybody's looking at you and looking at that old case, and everybody has questions, and Casey Grant is in the news again, and the pressure starts to build for this guy. What if someone remembers something? What if someone finds something? And that pressure builds and builds until he needs to tap the valve. So he goes out and finds himself another young waitress from the Grindstone."

Dana followed his logic, her stomach turning at the idea that her return home could have been the catalyst for an attack on another woman. The cycle of violence fed on itself in ways she hadn't even imagined.

"I saw John Villante that night," she said. "He delivered a pizza. When he saw me he ran away like he'd seen a ghost."

"Maybe he had," Hardy said. "Or maybe Doc Holiday grabbed Casey. Maybe April Johnson was just in the wrong place at the wrong time, and her attack has got nothing to do with you."

They sat in silence for a few minutes while the possibilities chased one another around in Dana's head until her brain began to hurt. To distract herself, she pulled her phone out of the pouch of her sweatshirt and started taking pictures of the restaurant, catching some patrons eating and others staring at her, looking annoyed or surprised or perplexed. She pointed the camera at Hardy and captured his scowl.

Beneath the unflattering overhead light, his complexion was sallow, and the lines in his face were as sharp and deep as if they had been gouged out by a woodworker's tool. She remembered him as he had been when Casey had gone missing—younger, heavy, with hair. It was as if time and illness had stripped away everything that wasn't strictly necessary except for his thick mustache, his one remaining conceit.

When the food came, the waitress plunked the skillet down in front of him and left without a word.

"What did Casey order that day?" he asked as he took a fork and stirred the food in the small skillet.

The aromas of the dish escaped in a cloud of steam: fried egg and home-fried potatoes with onions and green peppers and chunks of bacon. Despite the fact that she wasn't hungry, Dana's mouth watered as she breathed in the scents. She could almost taste the biscuit as Hardy slathered it in butter and lifted it to his mouth. The memory of the taste and texture had been imprinted on her memory years ago, and even though she hadn't eaten this dish in a long, long time, that memory was still there, triggered by her sense of smell.

"What did Casey order that day?" Hardy asked again.

"Toast," Dana said, surprised such an insignificant detail just popped to the surface like an air bubble emerging from the thick soup in her head.

"Did she or you speak to anyone that you remember?"

"Wouldn't I have told you that seven years ago?"

"Not necessarily. Not if you didn't think it was important. What's a 'Hey, y'all' to someone on your way to the ladies' room? Probably nothing."

"Then it probably wouldn't stick in my memory either," Dana pointed out.

"It's all in there," Hardy said. "Buried in the back of a drawer in some mental filing cabinet. You just need the right trigger to shake it loose."

Dana tried to picture Casey making her way to and from the ladies' room, smiling, tossing her thick mane of dark hair. So many of the Grindstone's local patrons were regulars and knew Casey. She always said hello to everyone, had been friendly with everyone. Despite what Hardy said, Dana didn't think she would have paid any attention to Casey exchanging a casual greeting with anyone. There wouldn't have been anything remarkable in it.

But there was something in his mention of the ladies' room that struck her. Casey hadn't been feeling well that day and had made a trip to the ladies' room the instant the food arrived at the table. Dana closed her eyes and tried to call up the scene—Casey coming back to the table, all smiles, exchanging greetings with people on the way. Dana tried to remember the other faces but couldn't.

She turned her attention back to the screen of her phone and flicked through the photographs she had just taken, looking closely at the faces of the other diners without them being able to look at her. Had any of them been here that day seven years ago? Had any of these men been the one to put April Johnson in the hospital two nights ago? They all looked so . . . ordinary.

He was just a man, Hardy had said of Doc Holiday. He was just a man like any other man. Just like the men sitting in this restaurant. Tall, short, fat, thin, bald, bearded—they blended, one into the next. What made a killer remarkable was not what was in his looks, but what was in his head and in his heart. What made a killer was hidden in the places no one could see. The shells were interchangeable. No one could tell who the bad guys were until their demons emerged in the dead of night.

Her breath caught a little as a pudgy balding man with a dark beard filled the phone's screen.

"What?" Hardy asked. "Do you recognize someone?"

Dana stared at the photograph. Her hands were suddenly cold. Her face felt suddenly hot. Her heartbeat quickened.

"Who is it?"

"I don't know," she murmured, shaking her head. She felt sick to her stomach. "I don't know who he is."

Impatient, Hardy snatched the phone out of her hands and looked at the picture, then turned and looked directly at the man, who sat in a booth not far away.

"Oh my God," Dana whispered, mortified. "Don't look at him!"

Hardy was already out of his seat. Dana watched in horror as he walked up to the man and showed him a badge. She wanted to pull her hood over her face and slide down under the table as both men turned and looked at her. It felt like everyone in the restaurant was staring at her now. The din of voices and bang and clang of food being served and eaten faded to nothing. All she could hear was the roaring of her pulse in her ears.

Overwhelmed and panicked, she got up too fast, banging the tabletop with a hip and sloshing Hardy's coffee out of the cup. She bolted out of the booth, bumping into a waitress, causing her to drop a plate loaded with food. The woman turned on her, surprised and angry, her face contorting like something in a funhouse mirror.

Dana pushed past the woman and ran out of the restaurant, onto the porch, colliding head-on into a burly man who caught her by the upper arms with greasy hands strong enough to crush bone. She took in only impressions of him as she instantly fought to get free—a battered and bruised red face beneath a white flattop, a heavy Fu Manchu mustache bracketing a grimace of yellowed teeth and a fat lip, dark eyes like a shark.

"Hey!" he yelled as Dana kicked and struggled to tear herself out of his grasp. "I caught a feisty one!"

The men around him laughed. "Hang on, Mack!"

"Let go! Let me go!" Dana shouted, looking up at him.

His expression contorted with shock and disgust. "Jesus Christ!"

Dana kicked him in the shin as hard as she could.

"Ouch! Fucking little bitch!" he howled, hurling her away from him.

Dana stumbled backward, losing her footing and landing on her butt on the floor of the porch.

"Hey!" another male voice shouted. "What the hell?"

Then Tim was bending down over her, offering his hand to help her up.

"Are you okay?"

"I'm fine," Dana said, flustered and embarrassed.

He moved her to the side like a piece of furniture and turned to the men. "What the hell is going on here?"

"She kicked me!" the big man blustered.

"Mr. Villante, do you think you're a big man shoving a girl around like that?" Tim asked. "You think it's okay to lay your hands on a woman? That's not okay in this county. Not in front of me, it isn't."

He turned back toward Dana. "Are you all right?"

"I'm fine," Dana mumbled, fussing with her hood. "I just want to go. I have to go."

She hurried down off the porch and across the parking lot to her car, only to find the doors locked. Hands trembling, she searched the pockets of her jeans and the front pouch of her hoodie. No keys. Nothing but a vibrating cell phone.

She pulled the phone out and looked at the screen. Her mother was calling. The logjam of emotions in her brain prevented her from remembering how to unlock the screen. The call went to voice mail and a text message popped up: *Where are you???? Answer me!!!!*

Her frustration erupted like a volcano and she threw the phone at the car, punishing both at once. The phone ricocheted off the driver's window and landed faceup on the asphalt.

"You'd have more luck with these," Dan Hardy said, holding up her key chain, the Hello Kitty figure looking ridiculous in his big, rough hand.

"You want to run away, little girl?" he asked. "You can't run away from what's in your own head."

"Give me my keys!" Dana snapped, jumping to try to reach them.

Hardy raised his arm, holding the key chain well out of her reach. "That demon is in your head whether you put a face on him or not. You'll never be rid of him until you take him out and put him in the light of day."

"Hardy!" Tim called, hustling toward them. He was out of uniform, in jeans and cowboy boots and a blue oxford button-down. Off duty but still wearing the air of authority in his expression and the set of his shoulders. "May I ask what the hell you think you're doing?"

Hardy looked at him with a stone face. "Miss Nolan and I were reliving old times," he said. "Remember the good old days when your friend Casey went missing?"

Tim gave the older man a long, cold look. "Last I remember, you were retired. In fact, as I recall, you were specifically asked to leave the job. So what is this? You don't have anything else to fill your sorry, empty life but some demented idea of recapturing your past glory? Oh, wait. You never solved that case, did you?" he said, throwing Hardy's failure up in his face.

"You'd be smarter to mind who you're mouthing off to here, West Point," Hardy growled.

Tim Carver's face flushed red. "I think you should give the lady her keys back."

Hardy looked from Tim to Dana and back, his gaze inscrutable. He lowered his arm and Dana snatched her keys out of his hand.

"You think about what I said, little girl," he said. "You can't be free of the past if you don't ever face it."

He went around to the driver's side of his car, got in, and started the engine. Dana waited until he was driving away, then bent down to pick up her phone.

"Well, you are just the center of all unwanted attention these days, aren't you?" Tim said. "Are you all right?"

"I'm fine," Dana said. "What happened with the man on the porch?"

"Mack Villante? Nothing. Unless you feel compelled to file a complaint against him."

"John Villante's dad," Dana said, recognition only now clicking in. "I ran into him and he wouldn't let go. I panicked, I guess."

"It's okay. There's surely a long line of people who would like to kick him. Don't feel bad for being the one to do it. He is one mean, nasty piece of work. I watched him go after John last night—his own kid. Went at him swinging those fists like a pair of canned hams. But I'm sure that wasn't the first time that ever happened."

"Casey was afraid of him," Dana said. "I remember she and John hardly spent any time at John's house because his dad creeped her out. She said he was always looking at her like she was edible."

"He's a crude dude," Tim said. "I know he got a hard look from the detectives at the time Casey went missing, but he had an alibi. He was with some girlfriend over in Levine. The girlfriend corroborated his story. Hardy thought she was lying, that she was scared of Mack, but he couldn't prove it. And there was never any physical evidence to point in Mack's direction. The girlfriend died not long

after that in a house fire. A suspicious turn of events, but nothing ever came of that investigation."

He leaned back against the car and crossed his arms. In jeans and a shirt he looked more like the boy she had known, but a beefier and more serious version. The blue of his eyes was as intense as the fall sky as he looked at her.

"Dana, what the hell were you doing here with Dan Hardy? After what I told you last night, here you are with him? Seriously? What were you thinking?"

"He wanted me to retrace Casey's and my steps from that last day," Dana said. "He thought it might shake loose a memory."

"Did it?"

"Not the way he meant. Not yet, anyway. Maybe if we had made it to the nursery . . . He says Casey and I had an argument there. I don't remember it that way. Or I don't want to remember it that way."

She looked down at her phone as it began to vibrate again with another call from her mother. She declined the call and sent a text message instead: *I'm with Tim. All OK.*

"I've got a couple hours before I go on duty," he said. "I'll go with you if you'd like."

"Thanks. I'll take you up on that," Dana said. "After the morning I've had, a police escort sounds like a great idea."

23

Mercer-Nolan Nursery and Garden Center had been like a wonderland to Dana as a little girl, with all its terraces and pergolas and gazebos decked in twinkle lights. During spring and summer the place was as lush as the Garden of Eden must have been, with hanging pots overflowing with flowers and greenery, and topiaries made in the shapes of rabbits and unicorns and rearing horses. For the Christmas season it would become a winter wonderland, with every conceivable kind of Christmas tree decorated and on display, garland and wreaths everywhere, the smell of pine and spruce and hot, spiced cider perfuming the air.

With Halloween fast approaching, the nursery was bursting with fall colors—chrysanthemums everywhere, rows of young trees with turning leaves. Hundreds of pumpkins lay scattered on either side of the driveway, with happy scarecrow sentinels overseeing the selection of the perfect prospective jack-o'-lantern.

Out of long habit Dana took the side drive to employee parking behind the gift shop and greenhouses. Tim pulled his shiny silver pickup in beside her. He had always taken great pride in his vehicles, waxing and polishing every Sunday morning. This one looked like it had just rolled off the dealer's lot, buffed to such a sheen it was almost blinding when the sun hit it. *An extension of his perfect im-*

age, Dana thought as he climbed out of the truck and came toward her. It had always been important to him that people thought of him as perfect. She hadn't been much different, she supposed. "I spent many an hour here breaking my back for slave wages back in the day," he said with a grin as he came around the front of the pickup.

"I'm sure it built your character," Dana said dryly.

"I'm sure it did."

The nursery had always been a source of jobs for the local high school kids. As Dana's boyfriend, Tim had had an automatic in.

"As I recall, you talked your way into a sales job fast enough," Dana said as they walked up the path toward the buildings.

His grin only widened. "That gift of gab has to be good for something besides filling awkward silences."

It had always seemed so easy for him to ingratiate himself with adults. Roger had treated Tim more like a son than he had ever treated Dana like a daughter. It had been in part Roger's string pulling and calling in favors that had gotten Tim his nomination to West Point.

"How did Roger take it when you left West Point?"

He shrugged. "I never heard from him. I didn't come back here for quite a long time after that. My folks split up and moved, and I was up in Fort Wayne. By the time I came back to Shelby Mills, he acted like he had never met me before in his life. I guess maybe that's his way of expressing his displeasure. I no longer exist for him."

"I wish he'd pretend he didn't know me," Dana grumbled. "Mom says I used to get along with him. I don't like him now, so I can't make that work in my head. I can't believe that I ever liked him."

"He was never going to take the place of your dad. I just think you were more polite back then; that's all."

Dana frowned at him as they walked along the edge of the shade-garden display. "Are you saying I'm rude now?"

He laughed. "Hey, I like the new, unvarnished Dana. You're refreshingly unfiltered."

"It's strange," Dana confessed on a sigh. She took a seat on a park bench that overlooked the lily pond. "To think that I used to be someone else."

"We all used to be someone else, Dee," Tim said, sitting beside her. "We all change. The causes are different; that's all. Some people change because they want to, some because they have to. Sometimes it's a choice and sometimes it's not. You didn't get to pick.

"In case you don't remember, you were never good with other people making decisions for you," he said, trying to tease her away from the dark thoughts of what had happened to her. "That was when the temper came out. Hooo-weee!"

"Was I that bad?"

He laughed. "I think I probably still have some of your tooth marks on my pride."

Dana didn't laugh with him. She thought of what Hardy had said to her that morning. That a person could lose their temper, and a push and a shove and a bump on the head later, they were guilty of murder.

"Hardy told me I was a suspect back then," she said, still offended. Offended and just a little bit afraid.

"Well . . . yes," Tim said. "Statistically, people are killed by people they know. You were one of the last people with her. And you were seen arguing."

"She left here. I never saw her again."

He held his hands up in surrender. "I'm not saying you did! But Hardy had to look at you differently. That was his job. *Was.* I want you to get that through your head. You are not to have anything to do with him, Dee. I mean it."

"Let's walk," she said, getting up again. "I want to get on with this."

She wanted to walk around and remember that day and everything that was said between her and Casey, and see beyond all doubt that she didn't know a damn thing about what had happened to her friend.

A weekday in late fall meant there were fewer customers brows-
ing the nursery than there would have been that summer day seven
years ago. Dana led the way up to the terraces where the flats of
summer annuals would have been in full bloom. Pansies and other
cool-weather flowers had taken their place. It had been her job to
drag the hoses around, watering the plants. Casey had followed her
around, jabbering away about whatever their current obsessions
had been—pop singers, Hollywood heartthrobs, school gossip,
boys.

She stood there for a moment, trying to hear their conversation
from seven years past. Below them activity buzzed around the large
central gazebo. Workers were arranging bales of straw, moving potted plants, setting up picnic tables. People sat on directors' chairs in
the gazebo itself, a videographer standing off to one side behind a
camera on a tripod.

Roger had said something about doing an interview. And something about setting up for a party. Something to do with his campaign, she supposed, not that she was interested in the least. She
only hoped he would get reelected so he would be going back to
Indianapolis for days at a time, out of their house.

She looked over to the right, to an area where various trellises
were displayed along a tall, slatted, wood fence. From her vantage
point she could see beyond the fence to the utility building where
the restrooms were tucked away. For a split second an image flashed
in her memory of Casey coming out of the ladies' room and walking
toward her, and a strange leftover sense of anger and anxiety seeped
through her.

Dr. Burnette had explained the difference between emotional
memory and contextual memory. Dana had done some of her own
research on the subject. But knowing how and why and where in
the brain different kinds of memories were stored was of no help in
recovering those memories.

Now she remembered she had been angry with her friend, but for whatever reason the memory of what they had argued about had either never been implanted or had been shut down after the fact, dismissed as either not important or too traumatic.

"Anything coming back?" Tim asked.

"She came back from the ladies' room and I was angry with her," she said, trying to stare back in time, trying to hear their conversation. "We had words. Someone saw us arguing. I still can't remember what it was about."

"Probably about Villante," he said. "She probably told you she was taking him back again. That would have set you off. And why would you bother remembering that? Y'all argued about that at least once a month."

"Didn't she tell you?" Dana asked, looking up at him. "She called you after she left here that day. Detective Hardy told me you said she called you to complain about me."

"Yeah. Same as fifty other times," he said. "Dana's so bossy. Dana's being a bitch. Blah, blah, blah.

"Let me clue you in—in case you don't already know this," he said. "Girls' blah-blah-blahing to boys goes in one ear and out the other. She didn't say anything she hadn't probably said a hundred and twenty times before. And, no, I don't feel guilty about that because it wasn't in the least bit relevant to what happened to her after."

"I wish I could feel that way," Dana said.

"Can I put my hand on your arm?"

"What?"

He made a comical face of frustration. "I'm a toucher. You know that. I want to touch your arm before I make my point, and I don't want you punching me in the throat because I touched you. Can I touch your arm?"

Dana scowled. "Okay."

He put his hand on her upper arm and looked into her eyes. "Sweetheart, has it occurred to you that maybe all this angst over what happened to Casey is coming out of the guilt you feel because you survived what happened to you and she didn't?"

Instantly, Dana thought of the nightmare she'd had and the guilt she had felt afterward.

"Maybe."

He moved his hand to her face, cupping the side where nerves had been damaged. It felt like he was touching her through a thick blanket. "It's not your fault, Dee. Let go of that."

Easier said than done, Dana thought.

"We don't know for a fact that she isn't alive," she said. "She could still be out there somewhere. There was that girl in Northern California. She was gone for years and years. And those women in Cleveland were held captive for a decade or more."

"Those are rare exceptions to the rule."

"I know, but still . . ."

He checked his watch and grimaced. "I have to go. Will you be all right on your own?"

"I'm fine."

"I'll call you later."

He bent and planted a quick kiss on her lips—so quick she had no time to protest or react.

Not sure how she felt about it, she watched him hustle down the path, slowing at the big gazebo to wave and say something she couldn't hear.

Ducking into her hood to avoid the stare of a woman considering a flat of pansies, Dana started down the path herself. Slowly. It occurred to her that she was tired. Time to go home and have a nap. If she was lucky she would wake up in another lifetime.

And yet, as tired as she was, she couldn't quite turn off the mechanical churnings of her brain, still trying to pull together the pieces of the day she had last seen Casey.

They had had whatever words they'd had here on these terraces; then Casey had hurried down this very path, past the tomato plants and kitchen herbs, past the big gazebo. She had gotten into her car and drove away to a fate no one knew. They had been best friends forever, and the last conversation they had had been a fight. They hadn't known they would never see each other again. They had thought they had all the time in the world to make up, as they had many times before. They'd had their whole lives in front of them. The flaw in that theory was that no one guaranteed how long a life would be.

Dana could see Roger clearly now as she got closer to the gazebo. His face was animated as he went on about something to the woman interviewing him. He was a handsome man, Dana had to admit, even if she didn't like him. The camera loved him, with his square jaw and angular features. The Clark Kent glasses looked so good on him, it would have been easy to imagine they were just a prop to suggest serious intelligence.

The woman interviewing him was clearly enthralled by whatever he was going on about—state sales tax or business incentives or his position on school vouchers or some similarly scintillating topic of state government. She looked to be in her early thirties, a pretty brunette with dark eyes and beautifully painted red lips that stood out against a complexion like fresh cream.

Casey might have grown up to look like her, Dana thought, absently moving closer to the gazebo. In a trick of her mind she superimposed Casey's face over the interviewer's, eyes sparkling, a sweet smile.

"Dana, what are you doing here?"

She startled at the sound of Wesley Stevens's voice. He had come to stand beside her, looking very preppy with a V-neck sweater over his shirt and striped tie, tan corduroy pants and Top-Siders. His smile was pleasant enough, but it didn't reach his eyes.

"Enjoying a beautiful day," she said.

"That's wonderful," he said, "but we're shooting an interview here, so I'm going to ask you not to get so close. The mikes are very sensitive."

He put a hand on her shoulder to steer her away, and Dana shrugged him off, shooting him a glare. "Please don't touch me."

He stepped back with his hands up. "I'm sorry. I didn't mean to upset you. It's just that we have a bit of a time crunch here. And I don't want the interviewer to become distracted."

"I get it," Dana said. "Don't let the ugly stepdaughter attract attention."

He looked uncomfortable. "That's not what I was going to say."

It was already too late. The interviewer had spotted her and slid out of the director's chair to come to the gazebo railing.

"Dana," she said, as if they were old acquaintances. "It's a pleasure to meet you. Sue Peralta."

She extended her hand. Dana looked at it with suspicion, taking hold of it reluctantly. She knew the woman was looking at her as a possible interview exclusive. She knew because she would have been thinking the same thing in her position.

"It's such a relief to have you home," the woman said. "Senator and Mrs. Mercer must be so happy."

"Well, you're half right," Dana muttered, her attention on Roger coming toward her.

"It's been a long road," Roger said. "But of course we're so grateful to have Dana home."

"I realize you're just settling in," the woman said, "but I would love to interview you for the show—"

"No," Dana said automatically.

Sue Peralta's smile faltered only briefly. "Well, not right now, of course, but later—"

"No," Dana said again, anger rising. "I know I look like a freak show, but I'd rather not be on public display. Thanks anyway."

Roger's face flushed red. "Sue, could you give me a moment with Dana, please?"

"Of course. I'm sorry if I seemed presumptive, Dana," she said, backing away a few steps.

Roger tried to block her view with his shoulder. He looked down at Dana, angry with her interruption.

"What are you doing here?" he demanded in a harsh whisper.

"Well, my father owned half of this business," Dana said in a normal tone of voice. "So I feel like I should be able to come here and walk around if I feel like it."

"You know what I mean," he said. "We're busy here."

"I'm sorry. I'm busy too," she said. "I just have to ask you a question."

"Then ask it and go. Your mother is probably beside herself wondering where you are."

"Okay. The day that Casey disappeared, you stayed home because you had a migraine. Were you there when Casey went back to the house to get her things?"

"What?"

"She left here, and that was the last I saw her, but we know she went back to the house at some point to get her stuff, because we don't have it. Were you there when she picked it up?"

"Dana," Wesley Stevens said. Looking nervous, he tried to wedge himself between her and Roger. "This really isn't the time or the place for this conversation."

"He told me to ask my question," Dana said.

"You need to consider whether a question is appropriate or not before you ask it."

"Screw you," Dana said too loudly. "Who are you to tell me anything?"

"Can we discuss this over here?" he asked, looking at some point far away from the gazebo. He reached out and took hold of her arm, his grip unnecessarily strong.

Dana wrenched away from him. "I asked you not to touch me!"

Stevens jammed his hands at his waist, looking exasperated and angry. "I'm sorry. Can you please keep your voice down?"

"Oh, for God's sake," Roger muttered. He climbed over the railing to stand too close to Dana. He was in dark jeans and a leather bomber jacket over a blue sweater, trying to look like the slightly rugged but elegant everyman.

"Is your mike live?" Stevens asked in a harsh whisper.

Without waiting for an answer, he stepped behind Roger and lifted the bottom of his jacket to check the switch on the battery pack of the microphone that was clipped to the V-neck of his sweater. "You're clear now. We don't need anybody overhearing this."

"To answer your question, I never saw Casey that day," he said, his words terse. He was very angry. Dana imagined she could see the anger rolling off him in waves. He lowered his voice to a barely audible whisper. "You need to go now, Dana. Right now."

"But how can that be?" Dana asked as half a dozen more questions popped into her head. "If Casey—"

His face darkened to a deeper shade of red. "Go home. Now. Or I'll have Wesley escort you off the property."

He turned away before she could say anything and walked around to the gazebo steps, going with a smile to smooth things over with Sue Peralta. She could imagine what he was saying. *So sorry, Dana isn't herself. The head injury changed her. We're coping as best we can. Her poor mother. Such a tragedy. Blah, blah, blah . . .*

All true.

The woman glanced over at her, brows knit with concern or interest or both.

Wesley Stevens took a step toward her. Dana stopped him with a look.

"If you lay a hand on me, I will scream like you've never heard in your life," Dana said. "And I won't stop. How good will that be for the campaign?"

His jaw worked from side to side. He looked like he wanted to throttle her. "Nothing you've done since you got home has been good for the campaign."

"Really? I got you the lead on the local news two nights in a row. Free face time for Roger. You should be happy."

"Dana, you can't persist with this Casey Grant business. She's been gone for seven years, for Christ's sake. Wait until the election is over. People could get the wrong idea, draw the wrong conclusions. This race is too close to call. We can't afford to lose votes because of this nonsense."

"A missing girl is nonsense to you?"

He closed his eyes against the need to shout at her. When he opened them he spoke in a carefully measured tone. "Please go home now, Dana. Please."

"I'm going."

"Do I need to see you to your car?"

"You'd better not think so."

He backed away, raising his hands in surrender.

Dana backed up in the other direction, up the slope to the next terrace.

All around the gazebo, workers were being directed to arrange areas for the coming party. Her gaze caught on one man a few yards to her left as he hefted a bale of straw off the back of a flatbed truck. John Villante.

He was in an army-green T-shirt, jeans, and combat boots, sweating for his effort, the carved, bulging muscles of his arms on display as he hauled the straw bale into place. His expression was the same one he had worn every day she'd known him: serious—brows a straight line over narrowed eyes, mouth set in a semi-frown. He set the bale down on a pile of others, straightened his back, and looked right at her. Dana imagined she could feel his gaze hit her, full of anger and resentment. She walked toward him anyway.

"John."

He turned away and kept his head down, pretending not to hear her.

"John, can I talk to you?"

"I'm working," he said, reaching for another bale.

"Just for a minute."

He shook his head. "I already lost one job on account of you, Dana. I can't lose another."

"What does that mean? How did you lose a job because of me?"

He stacked the bale and reached for another. "Your mama called Paula Tarantino the other night and got me fired."

"Oh God," Dana said, shocked and embarrassed her mother would do such a thing. "I'm sorry, John. I never meant for that to happen."

"Why not?" he asked. "You never liked me."

"It's not that I disliked you," she said. "I didn't think you were right for Casey. Is there anything I can do? I can have my mom call Anthony's and try to fix it—"

"Please don't. What can you do? You can *not* talk to me right now. You can *not* get me fired from this job."

"I'm the boss's daughter. I think it's okay if you talk to me."

"You can't get fired from being the boss's daughter," he said. "But tomorrow morning when the foreman comes to the parking lot at Silva's, he will look past me and pick a Mexican dude who can't speak English. So please go away."

"I just want to ask you a couple of questions about Casey—"

"I don't want to talk about Casey."

"Do you get a lunch break or a coffee break or—"

He cut her a glare. "Girl, this ain't no union job. We're lucky if we get to take a piss, pardon my language."

"When do you get off?"

"When the boss man says so."

"Will you talk to me then?"

"No."

"Why not?"

"I don't see the point."

"Well, you won't know the point if you won't talk to me."

"I'm good with that. You already accused me of killing her."

"I didn't mean that," Dana said. "The wrong word came out. I have a head injury. I sometimes have trouble like that now."

"So you don't think I killed her?"

"I don't know what happened to her."

"So you don't think that I *didn't* do it."

"I'm just trying to figure it out, John."

"You can do that without me."

"Is there a problem over here?" the foreman called, rounding the front of the flatbed truck.

John swore under his breath and grabbed another bale of straw.

"No, sir," he barked like he was answering a drill sergeant.

"Hey, Mr. Kenny," Dana said. "I was just saying hello. John and I went to school together."

Bill Kenny stopped short, carefully managing his reaction to the sight of her face. "Miss Dana, I'm sorry. I didn't realize it was you."

"I don't mean to disrupt John's work," she said.

"He can take a minute or two."

"I don't want to find out later he lost his job on account of me. That won't happen, will it?"

"No, ma'am," Kenny said. "John's a hard worker. We could use more like him."

"That's good to hear," Dana said. "Thanks for the time, Mr. Kenny."

"He's all yours," the foreman said, backing away. "But not for too long. We have to get this place shipshape for your stepdad's party tonight."

Dana forced a smile and nodded.

"What do you want from me, Dana?" John asked, head down.

"I'm trying to put that day together in my head," she said. "I saw her here that morning. This is the last place I saw her. I keep thinking if I can just remember all the pieces . . ."

"If you can remember all the pieces, what?" he challenged. "You can't change the past."

"It's not really the past, though, is it? We don't know what happened. How can it be the past if there's no end to the story?"

He looked at her like she was the stupidest creature on the face of the earth. He drew a big breath and blew it out. "What do you want from me, Dana?" he asked again.

"Was Casey going to make up with you? Was she going to take you back? Again," she added, remembering how many times that scenario had played out back then.

He rubbed the back of his neck and laughed to himself. "You always did have your own version of history. You were the queen of Dana World."

"What's that supposed to mean?"

"I was never good enough for Casey because she was your friend, and you were queen of the freaking universe. That's what that means," he said. "Casey didn't break up with me. I broke up with Casey. And no, I wasn't taking her back."

Dana stared at him, trying to absorb his version of the truth, every cell in her body trying to reject it. "You never said anything about breaking up with Casey. You never told the detectives that."

"Why would I tell them that?" he asked. "Why would I tell them my girlfriend was cheating on me? Isn't that called motive? A bigger motive than they already thought I had. Yeah, let me double down on the motive. That's a good plan."

"I don't believe you," Dana said. "Casey wasn't cheating on you. I would have known. She would have told me."

"Really?" he said. "Well, you might want to think about why she didn't. Maybe she didn't want to be imperfect in front of Ms. Perfect.

"I have to go back to work now."

Dana stood there flat-footed as he walked away, half-afraid that if she moved the world would drop out from under her. Her head was swimming, overloaded. Because of that, it took an effort to find her way around the grounds and back to the parking lot where she had left her car. Dan Hardy was waiting for her, leaning back against the hood of her car with his arms crossed over his chest.

Dana stopped in her tracks, quickly checking around for other people. But at midafternoon, employees were doing their jobs, not sitting in their cars behind the buildings.

"You followed us here," she said stupidly.

"Did you think I wouldn't?"

"You need to go."

"Why? Because West Point said so? He wants to make detective. If that boy was smart, he'd be happy to see me. He might learn something."

"So far, I don't know anybody who would be happy to see you," Dana said.

Hardy laughed, banding an arm across his stomach as if it hurt him. "What'd you see up there, little girl?"

"Nothing," she said, not ready to share what John Villante had told her—not ready to believe it. She thought of what he had said about Casey not wanting to appear imperfect in front of her. Maybe she didn't want Casey to appear imperfect to the world. Was that so wrong?

"Nothing," Hardy said. "Nothing at all? Nothing came to you?"

"Maybe there's nothing *to* come to me," she said, looking away from him. "Maybe nothing that happened that day meant anything at all."

"You don't believe that."

"What does it matter what I believe? The only thing that matters is what's true. And I don't know what's true."

"Every second of that day mattered," Hardy said. "All of those seconds added up to Casey Grant being in the wrong place at the wrong time doing the wrong thing with the wrong person. All of the puzzle pieces matter. Are you gonna keep looking for the one we need, little girl?"

"Yes," she said on a sigh as she pulled out her car keys. "After I have a nap."

24

John watched Dana Nolan walk away and disappear through a gate that led to the back parking lot. The possibility of running into her had been in the back of his mind all day—her or her stepfather or her mother. He needed the job too badly to turn it down, especially if his old man was truly going to pitch him out of the house. He couldn't live in his pickup forever. He needed to make as much money as he could to either get a room somewhere or get the hell out of Shelby Mills before winter.

Then there she was, Dana Nolan, like he had conjured her up by wanting to avoid her. And now that she had stirred the hornet's nest inside him, she walked away and left him buzzing, his nerves on edge. He glanced around to see if anyone was watching, if they could sense his anxiety.

To his left, the other day laborers were minding their own business. Straight ahead, Roger Mercer was wrapped up in whatever he was doing down in the big gazebo. To his right, Bill Kenny was watching him like a hawk. He was probably now putting two and two together and coming up with nothing good. The foreman walked toward him, hands on his hips.

"She took quite a beating," Kenny said. "It's a wonder she's alive."

"Sir?" John said, turning to heft another bale of straw off the truck.

"You don't know what happened to her?"

Oh Jesus, John thought. Was he going to get blamed for something new? He hadn't seen Dana Nolan in years.

"No, sir."

"She was abducted by a serial killer up in Minnesota almost a year ago. It was big news. Where were you?"

"Iraq."

"Oh." Kenny frowned. "Well, she ended up killing the guy before he could finish her off. I wouldn't have said she had it in her. I guess you never know about people."

"No, sir."

It didn't surprise John that Dana Nolan could have killed somebody. He'd seen her temper. He knew firsthand how cold she could be if given a reason. Everybody thought she was so sweet because she was petite and polite and had a pretty smile. That girl had iron down her spine.

All the more reason to have nothing to do with her, he thought.

"I'll find a place for you, soldier," Kenny said.

"Sir?"

"I'll make room for you on a crew." Relief ran through John like a cold flash flood. "Yes, sir. Thank you, sir."

"You're a hard worker," Kenny said, slapping him on the shoulder like he was a horse. "And it never hurts to have the boss's daughter like you."

"Yes, sir."

The last John knew, Dana Nolan hadn't liked him at all, and that probably wasn't going to change after what he'd told her today. But he was going to keep that information to himself.

They worked past six, hanging strings of lanterns, setting up tables, and opening folding chairs. A uniformed catering crew came in and added to the chaos, scurrying around to drape the tables and place the centerpieces.

The party was to be some kind of fund-raiser for Dana's stepfather, who was running for whatever. John had no patience for politics. All he'd ever seen from politicians were empty pledges and broken promises. The politicians were quick enough to send guys like him to war, but they ground out every bill to benefit veterans.

The politicians didn't give a shit that veterans couldn't get jobs or that their health care system was a train wreck. No politician was going to come and help him straighten out the red-tape nightmare of the meager veterans' benefits he was owed—of which he had yet to see one red cent. They didn't want to hear about how he couldn't navigate the frustrations of the system because he had a head injury incurred in the war they had voted for.

Fuck politicians, he thought as he watched Roger Mercer walk around approving or disapproving of the work the day-labor grunts had bent their backs into all day. It had always been his opinion that Roger Mercer was a prick—even before he had become a politician. He was the kind of guy who would wear a sweater tied around his neck, the kind who complained about having to pay but was never willing to pitch in and help do the work himself.

Casey had always rolled her eyes and shuddered in distaste when Dana's stepfather was mentioned. He was one of those dads who mistakenly thought kids believed he was cool. John had never had to worry about anything like that with his old man. Kids had never come to hang out at his house. He had never wanted to hang out at his own house. The place was a depressing mess that stank of cigarettes and sour sweat and dirty dishes. Mack was always drunk and belligerent.

The couple of times John had brought Casey to the house, he had been embarrassed beyond belief by both the mess and his father. The old man had leered at Casey like a wolf looking at fresh meat. And he always managed to say something degrading or sexual or both. They had taken to climbing into John's room through the window if they knew that Mack was in the house.

John's bedroom had always been his sanctuary, always scrubbed clean and as neat as a pin. He had devised all kinds of hiding places for the few possessions he had that meant something to him. Nothing could be left out for Mack to get hold of and purposely ruin or somehow use against him. He lived like a prisoner of war in his own home.

Only he wasn't living there anymore.

His hands still hurt from punching the old man in the face. He had a pretty good fresh cut on the big knuckle of his left hand from catching the edge of a tooth. He didn't regret doing it. He regretted the consequences.

The foreman paid them their day's wages and drove them all back to Silva's on the flatbed. The garage was long closed by the time they got there. Mack's truck was gone. He had already moved on to his evening bender.

John had parked his pickup at the back of the lot between a pair of long-idle Peterbilt tractor cabs, as hidden from easy view as possible. He doubted his father would expend the effort to go looking for it, but he for sure would have messed with it had it been easy for him.

The dog stood up in the box of the truck, tail wagging as John approached. John shook his head. He had left the tailgate down, half hoping the animal would be gone by the time he came back from work.

And half hoping it wouldn't be, if he had to admit it.

He wasn't used to having anyone be happy to see him at the end of the day. The dog jumped down from the truck and ran a few steps toward him, then suddenly remembered to be afraid and stopped, tail down but still wagging, ears lowered, lips pulled back in a sheepish smile as it danced in place.

"I ain't gonna beat you," John said.

The dog spun around in a circle and gave a little yip of delight.

"You're a funny dog, Trouble," John said. "Why you'd latch onto me, I don't know. I got nothing for you or anybody else."

Nothing except the day's wages, which would buy them both a sackful of ninety-nine-cent burgers.

"Come on," he said, pulling open the passenger's door. "Let's go eat."

Whatever else the night was going to bring, at least he wouldn't have to face it on an empty stomach. Or by himself. He had to admit there was some comfort in that.

The dog jumped into the pickup and settled itself in the passenger's seat, panting happily. John went around to shut the tailgate, then got behind the wheel and coaxed the truck to life. He rolled slowly to the road, looking over at the parking lot in front of the Grindstone for his father's Avalanche. No sign of it. But as he turned out onto the road, he could see the black truck tucked along the side of the bar across the way.

His father had to look like he'd gone a few rounds. John could still feel the impact of his knuckles on the old man's face. He could hear his father now, telling his cronies how they should see the other guy. It was debatable whether or not he would tell them the "other guy" was his kid. Knowing Mack, he would probably take some kind of perverse pride in telling people he had a fistfight with his own offspring. He'd probably be hitting the Maker's Mark pretty hard to fend off the full-on aches and pains of his beating and the sting to his pride.

If he had settled in at the bar, then this was John's window of opportunity to go to the house and get his stuff out. He swung through the drive-through for the burgers and shared them with the dog as he drove home. It wouldn't take him long. He ran through the inventory of his few possessions, ticking off each of his hiding places, making sure not to forget anything. He had a feeling once he left this time, he wouldn't be coming back until the old man had breathed his last breath. Maybe not even then. There was no guarantee Mack Villante wouldn't leave the property to the fire department to be burned to the ground rather than give it to John. He was that spiteful.

To be honest, John thought, it would probably be a relief to be free of it. It wasn't as if he had a head full of happy childhood memories growing up in this house. For the most part he had raised himself once his mother had left. The only memories he had of being nurtured and loved were memories of her when he was small. And those memories were so old and faded they were more like half-remembered dreams. After she had gone, his life had consisted of figuring out ways to stay under his father's radar. He hadn't been a child so much as a tenant, given no more real consideration than if he'd been the stray dog now sitting on the far side of his truck.

His memories of his mother were of a fragile beauty and gentle soul trapped by some bad fairy-tale twist of fate with the ogre that was his father. John had been far too young to understand how or why she had come to marry Mack Villante in the first place, or why she had stayed with him as long as she had. He had no memories of his father that didn't include drunkenness and cruelty. But he supposed they had to have been happy once upon a time, before it had all gone wrong, and the drinking had unleashed the temper, and the violence had driven her away.

John had never blamed her for leaving. He had only wished she would have taken him with her. He had spent many lonely, scary nights imagining why she hadn't. In some scenarios she had meant to take him, but something had prevented her. In other scenarios her plan had been to come back for him and snatch him away in the middle of the night, or to pick him up at school and take off for their new life in parts unknown. But in the back of his mind he always suspected she had left him because he was a burden and she didn't want the reminder of the man who had made her life a misery.

He couldn't blame her for leaving, he thought as he pulled into the driveway and looked at the little run-down ranch-style house with its weedy yard and ratty old shed out back. He was going to be glad to see the last of this place himself.

The sooner the better.

25

In the dream the colors were so intense, so supersaturated, they made Dana's eyes hurt. She stood on the terrace at the nursery in exactly the same place she had stood that afternoon, but it seemed she could see for miles beyond, as if she was on a mountain. She could see the road winding down into town. She could see the rolling, wooded hills and the river.

Casey emerged from the ladies' room in the utility building and came toward her, smiling, laughing. She had no right to be so happy, so carefree. Dana felt her anger building like steam inside her head. Heat flushed through her whole body, hotter and hotter until sweat popped from her pores. She could see each bead of moisture as it emerged and swelled.

"You don't get to be mad, Dee," Casey said. "It's all your fault."

"That's not true. It's not my fault."

"I'm dead because of you."

"That's not true! I loved you!"

"You killed me."

"No!"

The pressure in Dana's head was so much that she had to open her mouth and scream to release it. And then her hands were around Casey's throat and she was squeezing and squeezing. Casey's face went red, then purple; then her eyes exploded. In the next instant she became a writhing snake that opened its mouth and hissed in Dana's face. Screaming, Dana let go and tried to run backward as the snake struck at her.

She fell with a thud to the floor of her bedroom, waking with a start, gasping for air, disoriented. She was drenched in sweat, dizzy, and nauseated.

Slowly she got up to her hands and knees and pulled herself into a tight ball on the carpet. Tuxedo hopped down from the bed and began rubbing himself against her, trilling and purring. After a moment, Dana rearranged herself, sitting on the floor, back against the bed, cat in her lap.

Images from the nightmare continued flashing through her mind like stark landscapes illuminated by lightning in the dead of night. She kept seeing the accusation in Casey's eyes. She kept hearing her voice—*It's all your fault . . . I'm dead because of you . . .*

It turned her stomach to think she might have played any kind of role in what had happened, even if her only part had been to send Casey away at that particular moment on that particular day.

She kept hearing what John had said about Casey not wanting to appear imperfect in front of her. God, had she really been that much of a bitch? Had she really been that controlling? When she thought of her relationship with Casey, she thought of her as a sister, as someone she loved absolutely. John's impression of her had to be colored by the fact that she had never believed he was good enough for Casey. But she had only been looking out for her friend's best interests.

She thought of what he'd said about Casey cheating on him, and she couldn't make herself believe it. She and Casey had shared everything, had known everything about each other. But even as she denied it, the emotion that burned through her was anger—not at John, but at Casey.

They had argued about something that day. The memory of the

emotions she'd had remained like a faint bitter aftertaste. Was the actual memory of the event still in there somewhere? Hidden by guilt, or blocked out by the need to forget? If John had dumped Casey, had Casey wanted him to take her back? Had that been the argument she and Casey had had?

She closed her eyes and pictured the scene at the nursery again. Casey returning from the ladies' room, a funny little smile on her face.

Anxiety grew like an air bubble in the center of her chest. In the next moment of that memory they would be arguing. To escape that moment, she went back to her memory of their breakfast at the Grindstone. She had ordered her usual breakfast. Casey had ordered toast. The memories of sounds and smells came back to her. The picture of Casey smiling and chatting with people as she came back to the table from the restroom . . . The memory of the man Dana had photographed today . . .

Had she seen him before? Did he look like Doc Holiday?

She thought of the panic and the embarrassment she had felt today as she had run out of the restaurant and into John Villante's father. She could feel his big hands squeezing her arms, see his battered, angry face looming over her, twisting with disgust at the sight of her disfigured face.

All of it—the physical sensations, the fragments of memories, the wash of emotions—swirled inside her head like floodwaters rising. All of it set off by the sight of a man she didn't know and the thought of a monster she couldn't remember.

She tried now to remember the instructions to calm her nerves and slow the maelstrom of emotions in her mind. *Breathe deep . . . four counts in, four counts out . . .*

Hardy said she was never going to get past her fear without confronting it. If she dragged Doc Holiday out of the shadows of her memory and looked at him in the light of day, would he lose his power to terrify her? Would the fact that he had put his pants on one leg at a time somehow negate the monstrousness of his deeds?

Would she look at Doc Holiday and somehow know that he had taken Casey? And if he had, would knowing that somehow bring a weird kind of relief? Would it bring a sense of closure to know that some foreign evil had reached into their lives, thereby absolving the people she knew, including herself?

Maybe it was time to find out. Maybe she was sick of hiding from it. Maybe, if she could look at Doc Holiday and know that he had taken Casey all those years ago, Casey would stop blaming her in her nightmares.

Setting Tuxedo aside, she got to her feet, went to the desk, and woke the computer. She knew as soon as she typed the name *Doc Holiday*, the search engine would cough up links to hundreds of articles. Literally hundreds of articles had been written about the serial killer who had tried to end her life. She knew that multiple books were in the works detailing his bloody exploits. The authors had contacted her parents and her colleagues from work to ask questions and angle for her participation.

It struck her as obscene that he had been made into a celebrity of sorts—just as Ted Bundy and Jeffrey Dahmer and a dozen other notorious murderers had been over the years. The public's fascination with killers seemed to be unquenchable. Was it because it seemed so inconceivable for a human being to cross that line—or because people wondered why they themselves hadn't crossed it?

What made a killer? Hardy claimed there wasn't a person on the planet who wasn't capable of it in the right circumstances. Dana couldn't imagine being angry enough to take another person's life, and yet she was famous for having killed Doc Holiday—not that she could remember doing it. What other terrible memories had she locked up in the deepest recesses of her mind?

She couldn't escape the images of the nightmare she'd just had, but at the same time, she wouldn't believe she could have harmed her best friend. The dream had to be some kind of metaphor. Or maybe it was nothing more than an electrical shitstorm in her damaged brain, lighting up random thoughts and emotions and throwing them into a jumbled mix of half-remembered random images.

She and Casey might have argued. Casey might have left the nursery because of it. And after leaving the nursery something had happened to her.

That doesn't make me a murderer.

She would never have hurt Casey. She wanted to believe she would never have physically harmed anyone. But she knew that thought was a lie. She had killed the man who tried to kill her. She had no memory of it, but she had done it. She had taken a screwdriver and stabbed it into a man's temple.

Maybe Hardy was right. Given the right circumstances, anyone was capable of anything. All a person needed was a reason that made sense to him or her, the need to end a threat, or the need to avenge some terrible wrong.

She stared at the icons on the toolbar of the computer screen. Instead of clicking on the search engine to go in search of Doc Holiday, she clicked on the photo icon, opening a screenful of photo albums and choosing the one from senior year. She watched as the slideshow played, one picture melding into another and another as her favorite sappy pop song of that year played in the background. Pictures of herself succeeding and being popular. Pictures of herself, pretty and bright eyed, excited about life. Pictures of Casey. Pictures of the two of them.

One jumped out at her, and she clicked on it and it filled the screen. Herself and Casey, side by side, cheek to cheek, each of them holding out the pendant of the matching necklaces they wore—two halves of the same heart, engraved with words declaring their friendship. They had worn those necklaces every single day of their lives. Casey would have had it on the day she went missing. Dana still had hers, stashed away in a box of memories, a heart forever without its missing half.

She started the slideshow again, sending more photographs sliding across the screen, spinning and bending, one dissolving into the next. Pictures of her and Tim, of Casey and John, of the four of them together going to the prom. Photos from an outdoor party a month or so after graduation—around the time she had broken up with Tim. He was off to the far right of the picture, sitting on top of a picnic table, hoisting a beer and grinning at the camera. Casey sat on the bench below him, facing away from the table, laughing. John sat to her right, a little separate, looking churlish.

The bubble of anxiety swelled again in Dana's chest. Two months after this picture was taken, Casey had vanished. What had happened in the interim? John said he had broken up with her. Why hadn't Casey told her? What had she been hiding? She had called John the afternoon of the day she went missing, asking to meet him that night. Why? It had to be because she wanted to get back together with him, Dana thought. Why? In another month they both would have been out of Shelby Mills and off to colleges in different parts of the state. On to new adventures. If Casey had been cheating on him, as John said, she couldn't have been that committed to the relationship.

Casey had been cheating on John. Dana couldn't bring herself to believe it. How would she not have known? He had to be lying. But why would he tell a lie that only gave him a greater motive to have harmed Casey? Was his male ego such that he couldn't admit she dumped him?

Restless, Dana clicked out of iPhoto, abandoned the computer, and went to her doorway to look at the timeline and the notes across the hall.

Her mother was upset that she'd done this—not so much because the wall would have to be repainted, but because it pointed to impulsive and obsessive behavior she didn't want to see in her daughter. She probably preferred the blankness of the adynamia that had plagued Dana during her months at the Weidman Center to this tunnel-vision focus on what had happened to Casey.

Dana stared at the notation regarding her alleged argument with Casey at the nursery, and the notation of the time when Casey had called Tim to complain about her afterward. She went and got a marker from her desk, returned to the wall, and drew a line from the circle around *Casey Called John* and wrote *John broke up with her??*

On his timeline, Hardy had made note of the fact that on the day of her disappearance Casey had at some point returned to this house to pick up her things. Dana moved to that point on the wall, drew an arrow upward, and wrote *Where Was Roger?* She couldn't understand how Casey could have come back here to get her stuff and not have run into Roger. How would she have gotten into the house if Roger hadn't been here? Had he gone somewhere and left the door unlocked? That wasn't normal for him.

"You're scaring your mother with this behavior," Roger said.

Dana startled. She had yet to fully regain the peripheral vision in her right eye. She hadn't seen him coming down the hall from the family room.

"I want to know what happened to my friend," she said simply.

"In seven years, three law enforcement agencies haven't been able to find out what happened to Casey. What makes you think you'll figure it out?"

"Nothing. I just have to try; that's all."

Hands on his hips, he looked at the timeline. Dana tried to watch where his eyes went, where his gaze lingered. His face was unreadable.

He was dressed for the evening's party in dark trousers and a brown suede jacket over a camel cashmere sweater. The casual, elegant man of the people.

"Dana, what happened today at the nursery can't happen again," he said, turning to face her. "Whatever the source of your sudden animosity toward me, you need to keep that here, in the house, between family."

"I had a question and you told me to ask it," Dana said, genu-inely not understanding why that was a bad thing. She had only done what he told her to do. She hadn't done it with bad intentions toward him.

A muscle flexed in his jaw. "Don't pretend you don't know ex-actly what you did there. You worked in news. In front of a reporter, you asked a question that implied I might have something to do with Casey's disappearance."

"I did not! I only asked if you were here when she came back for her things. I don't understand how she could have gotten her things if you weren't here. And if you were here and let her in, then you must have seen her. I'm just trying to put the pieces of that day into order. I never accused you of anything."

"You're more clever than that."

"No, I'm not," Dana said. "I have all I can handle just trying to function. Believe me, there's no cleverness involved. And if you didn't have anything to do with Casey's disappearance, why are you so worried people will think that you did?"

"Because people think whatever they want to think, and the ma-jority of them want to think something bad. They want to think there's a conspiracy, a cover-up, that someone with money and power can get away with murder. I don't have an explanation as to why I didn't see Casey come back here to get her things. Maybe I was asleep. Maybe I was in the bathroom. Maybe I was on the phone. Those answers are not alibis."

"But how did she get in the house?" Dana asked.

Frustrated and angry, he lurched toward her and banged a fist against the wall a foot above her head. Dana's heart leapt into her throat.

"Stop it!" he shouted. "I had nothing to do with what happened to Casey! Oh my God! After all I've done for you! After everything I did for your boyfriend! He took that opportunity and threw it away without so much as an apology. Now you come here and fuck up my reelection with this!" he said, throwing his hand in the direction of her impromptu marker board. "Stop it!"

Tears of fear flooded Dana's eyes. He must have seen them, must have read the panic in her face. He stepped back, working visibly to rein in his temper, breathing deeply and rubbing his hands over his face as if to scrub away his angry expression.

Calmer, he said, "Dana, I can't have you making people wonder if I did something to Casey Grant. I'm running for public office. Do you think that's going to help me in the polls? To have people suddenly doubt my integrity, to have them start wondering and speculating about my possible involvement in a horrible crime—do you think that's going to weigh in my favor?"

"I didn't think about it."

"That's a problem," he said. "You don't think first anymore. Or worse, you *do* think and you just say whatever comes into your head anyway. I can't have it. Do you understand me? I can't have it!"

"What do you want me to do?" Dana asked defensively. "It's not like I can predict how I'm next going to mess up because my brain doesn't always work right!"

"I'm sorry for what happened to you, Dana," he said. "I am. But I can't have you mess up my political career because you no longer have a filter and just blurt out these outrageous things!"

He shook his head in frustration. "You know, I tried to tell your mother you needed to stay at Weidman until after the election."

"Really?" Dana asked. "Because you seemed pretty damned happy putting your face in front of the cameras with my homecoming. What were your constituents thinking then? 'Oh, look, that wonderful, handsome Senator Mercer. What a loving father he is to the brain-damaged ugly daughter of his dead partner who he probably pushed off a cliff!'"

"Dana! Stop it!" her mother shouted, arriving in the hallway at the worst possible moment. She was also dressed for the evening's party in a flowing dark skirt and boots, a burgundy cowl-neck sweater, pearls at her throat. Her hair was done, her makeup perfect.

"I guess my party invitation got lost in the mail," Dana said, looking down at her sweat-limp T-shirt and baggy yoga pants.

"You are most definitely not coming tonight," Roger said. "If I had my druthers, you and your mother would be spending the next two weeks in Hawaii, starting tomorrow."

"Frankie and Maggie are coming over," her mother said, brushing past her husband's remark.

"I hope they have a lovely evening," Dana said. "I'm going out."

"Dana—"

"I'm meeting Tim Carver for dinner."

The lie was out of her mouth before she realized she'd thought of it. It was a good one. She secretly congratulated herself as she watched her mother's concern soften.

"Are you sure you feel up to it?"

"I just had a nap. I'll be fine."

She could see her mother reasoning through any possible objections. She knew Tim. She liked Tim. Tim was a responsible person, a sheriff's deputy. What could go wrong if she was with Tim? How much trouble could she get into?

"Lynda," Roger said, checking his watch. "We have to get going. I'll go start the car. I'm done here."

Dismissing them, he stalked off down the hall.

Dana's mother looked at her with concern. "This has to stop, Dana. You have to let go of all this paranoia. It's not good for you."

"It's not good for *him*," Dana said.

Roger's voice boomed back down the stairs, "Lynda! We have to go!"

"You'd better go," Dana said. "Duty calls."

Her mother bit her tongue on a retort. Dana saw her swallow it back. Instead, she leaned in and kissed Dana's cheek and brushed a hand over her hair. "Please be careful. And don't stay out too late."

Like she was seventeen and going on a date.

Just like old times.

Dana went back into her room and sat back down at her desk. She stared at all the little icons that dotted the home screen of her computer, tiny thumbprint pictures and little blue file folders with cryptic names. She opened and closed them one by one, taking glimpses into the past—term papers and book reports, collections of juvenile poetry and short stories, school projects and her personal journal.

She had forgotten all about it. She hadn't looked at it in years. She had named the folder *Days of Our Lives* so anyone casually snooping would assume it had to do with the soap opera she and her friends had all been hooked on at the time.

She had kept the journal all through school, recording all the triumphs and tragedies of middle school and high school in the overly dramatic language of a child. She opened the folder now to find a long list of documents. Her senior year was broken down month by month and big event by big event. She clicked on August and began to read, starting with the entry she had made the day Casey went missing.

As she read, a strange feeling of hurt and sadness washed over her like rain. She could see why she wouldn't have mentioned it to anyone. The argument she had had with Casey couldn't have had anything to do with her disappearance, but it had everything to do with her own wounded pride and hurt feelings.

Dana grabbed her phone and Tim Carver's business card. He answered on the third ring.

"Can we meet somewhere?" she asked. "I need to talk to you."

26

The old man had locked the doors. Not just the main locks in the doorknobs and the deadbolts, for which John had keys. He had locked the extra locks—the Fort Knox locks, John called them. The locks his father had installed for extra security when he was feeling paranoid that some of the low-life losers he associated with might come to steal his guns or murder him in his sleep.

Apparently he now considered his own son to be counted among the lowlifes—although John would have never killed him in his sleep. In his fantasies he choked the life out of the old man face-to-face, so he could see every emotion that went through his head as he realized he was about to die at the hands of the son he had tormented all these years.

John heaved a sigh and walked down off the back porch. The dog was roaming the yard with its nose to the ground, racing after rabbit trails, tripping the motion-sensor security lights Mack had installed all over the place.

Out of old habit John went around the side of the house and tried the window to his room. The latch had been broken for years. He had broken it himself, on purpose, knowing his father would never bother to fix it. He had used it regularly during his high school years, sneaking in and out to avoid the old man's questions and wrath. He had sneaked Casey in this way a few times when they had nowhere else to go to have sex. But she hadn't liked coming here because the old man made her nervous and she was always worried he would catch them.

He shoved up on the window, expecting it to rise, meeting resistance instead. Swearing under his breath, he tried again, able to budge it only an inch or so before it jammed hard, as if blocked by something.

The anger built quickly inside him, like a sudden storm blowing up, black and violent. All he wanted was to take his things and go. The old man didn't want him here, and yet he had to be so contrary as to make leaving more work than it had to be. The frustration wound and wound inside him like a spring. He could feel it in his head getting tighter and tighter. His pulse began to pound in his ears. He felt like his head might explode.

Fuck it. He'd spent his whole life tiptoeing around this house, trying to be quiet, trying to be invisible. What difference did it make now? What did he care now what his old man would think or do?

The dog came to check on him and jumped back with a yip as John wheeled around, cursing. He hustled around the corner and up the steps once again to the back door. He called on his army training and kicked the thing in, applying boot to door with explosive violence again and again until the old wood splintered like so much kindling.

Once inside, he stormed from room to room, memories from Iraq and Afghanistan flashing through his mind. His sense of the potential for danger dated back to his childhood but had been reinforced in war. The life experiences tumbled together now in his mind—his fear of his father in this house and his fear of the enemy as he and the other men from his unit raided buildings in war zones. His heart was pounding. His senses were achingly sharp. He wished for the security of a rifle in his hands.

Even though he knew his father was belly up to a bar, the old man's energy lingered here in the air like the stink of his cigarettes. There was no telling when he would return. It all depended on his mood, and his moods were subject to change in a heartbeat. He could be regaling his cronies with the story of how he beat his kid and threw him out of the house, but one imagined slight and he would be out the door in a huff.

The anxiety and anger swirled in an oily mix in John's gut as he went down the hall to his bedroom. The door stood open. The room was empty of personal effects—no clothes, no shoes, no duffel bag. A note had been left on the bare mattress: *keeping your shit. U owe me rent—$2,000.*

Un-fucking-believable, John thought. He didn't know whether he should laugh at the ridiculousness of it or fly into a rage. The spiteful, hateful, stupid son of a bitch would go to the trouble of locking up his meager possessions and believe that John would—*could*—pay him two grand to get the stuff back. Two grand—like this shit hole was the fucking Ritz-Carlton! If he'd had two grand he never would have been staying here in the first place. The absurdity was mind-boggling and aggravating.

He went to the closet and moved the extra leaves from the dining room table, which had never been used in his memory, revealing the hidden small section of drywall he had cut out and replaced long ago. He removed the piece, reached into the wall, and dug out the few things he kept stashed away there in plastic bags: his dog tags, a bottle of whiskey, a couple hundred dollars rolled up and bound with a rubber band, a little horse-head pin that was the only thing he had of his mother's. He took a swig of the whiskey, stuffed the rest of the things in a coat pocket, and left the room.

The dog was sitting waiting for him as he went out the broken back door, ears up, eyes bright with interest. It followed him to the garage and sat in the doorway, watching as John rummaged around for the tools he wanted—a crowbar, a flashlight, a hammer. When he emerged from the garage, the dog jumped up and loped ahead a few feet at a time, stopping and looking back as John strode toward the long shed at the back of the property.

The motion-sensor light popped on above the heavy metal-clad door, spotlighting the big padlock that kept thieves from stealing the worthless shit Mack Villante valued. John grabbed the lock and gave it a yank. There would be no picking it or prying it. It was a brand that boasted holding up to a gunshot. The frame of the door was another matter.

With no proper eaves on the shed, rainwater had run down behind the frame, softening the wood enough that he could work the crowbar in between the frame and the building. He put his back into the job, pushing and pulling, prying the frame away an inch or three at a time, the nails moaning as he wrenched them out.

The old man would call the cops on him for this. Breaking and entering. He'd file a complaint just to be a bastard. He'd sue for damages to this door and to the back door of the house, dragging him into court for what wouldn't amount to as much as his legal fees.

John fantasized that he might have the courage to use the crowbar on the miserable son of a bitch himself. The world would be a better place without him. It wasn't that hard to get rid of a body in these parts. There were gullies and sinkholes aplenty, and the river was known to have kept many a secret over the years.

Plenty of people hated Mack Villante. The trouble was that John would be number one on the top of that list, and he had no intention of sitting in prison for the rest of his life on account of his father. The life he'd lived here with the old man had been prison enough to last him.

The doorframe came away from the wall with a creaking and cracking, snapping off above the U-bolt that accommodated the padlock. Another planting of the crowbar, a heave and a pull, and the piece of wood with the U-bolt splintered away and the door swung inward.

John pushed his way inside and flipped the light switch. Nothing happened. The backwash of the security light spilled dimly across the floor from the doorway. It cut a second band of light across the middle of the room from the small barred window in the wall.

From the back waistband of his jeans John pulled the heavy flashlight he'd swiped out of the garage and flicked it on, shining it all around. It was a big Maglite, like the cops carried—half flashlight, half billy club. He carried it high, up by his shoulder, swiveling the light as he moved his head.

He hadn't been in this building in years. Not since he was twelve or thirteen and had discovered the old man's collection of dirty magazines one summer day when his father had been too drunk to remember to lock the door. His father's reaction had been swift and violent, out of all proportion to the crime. John had spent the next week telling people he had taken a bad fall off his dirt bike to explain away the signs of his beating. He had never set foot in the shed again.

The building was about ten feet wide by twenty feet long, lined with tool benches and deep plywood shelves that were crammed with boxes and crates, filthy old car parts and stacks of dirty magazines—the hard-core stuff full of S and M and bondage. Lawn mowers and weed eaters, shovels and spades and post-hole diggers cluttered the floor space. One shelf held boxes and boxes and boxes of ammunition, stockpiled for the apocalypse, going to ruin in this damp shed.

The place smelled of mold and mildew, dust and mice, grease and gasoline. The roof had been leaking for who knew how long. Part of the ceiling was peeling down like old sheets of wet paper in the far back corner. Everything that was piled and stacked below the bad piece of roof was wet and stinking. Water pooled in a low spot on the concrete floor. A fifty-five-gallon drum stood in the wet corner, rust eating away a wide band of the steel around the bottom of the barrel.

The dog came in and started poking its long nose into the nooks and crannies, sniffing for mice, trying to reach a paw into narrow openings between containers and piles of junk.

"Pee on whatever you like," John said as he shined the light around, looking for his duffel bag. "You'll probably improve the smell."

A row of tall, narrow cupboards ran across one end of the room like lockers, each of the individual doors secured by a small, cheap padlock. Swearing under his breath, John set the flashlight aside and went to work prying the first of the locks off with the crowbar.

He was going to dismantle the whole building if he had to. He was set on it now, even though a small voice of logic in the back of his mind had begun to whisper that he should just leave, that Mack had probably chucked his stuff into the back of his truck and this demolition would be all for naught, just a waste of time that would get him caught and tossed in jail. What did he have to take with him anyway? Old clothes and a few books, a container with mementos from his time in the army, and another with a few things he'd kept from high school—his sports letters and pins, a few pictures. But the bigger part of his brain wouldn't let go of the mission or of the idea that he wasn't leaving anything of himself behind.

The flimsy latch gave way, and John pulled the door open. The cupboard was crammed with old hunting gear—coats and boots, a blaze-orange vest. A pile of stocking caps and gloves and camouflage masks tumbled out. John moved to the next door and pried the lock off.

The figure that lunged out at him as the door fell open was dark and tall. John's reaction was swift and instinctive, honed in combat. His right arm came up to block the assault as he struck with the crowbar still in his left hand.

The bar landed with a dull thump against dead weight. John jumped back in a crouch, his arms out in front of him. The duffel bag fell to the floor in the shaft of light that poured in through the open door. It had been stuffed in the cupboard, on end, on top of a stack of junk.

Heart pounding as the adrenaline rush crashed, John stepped back and leaned against a workbench littered with tools. He felt the familiar watery rush of weakness run through his body as he let go of the tension on a big exhale. His hearing came back to him as his pulse slowed. The dog was whining and digging at something at the other end of the shed.

"Come on," John said, pushing away from the bench. He grabbed the handle on the duffel bag and hefted it up. "Let's get the hell out of here."

The dog whined and yipped, pouncing at something. John shined the flashlight back into the corner, the wet corner with the bad patch of roof and the rusted oil drum. The dog was scraping at the base of the rusted-out barrel. Mice had probably got inside of it.

"Come on," John said again, more insistent. "Or I'll leave you to deal with the old man."

Intent on its task, the dog ignored him and continued to pounce at, dig at, scratch at, and bark at the barrel.

John swore under his breath and set the duffel bag down.

"What you got back there? A rat?" he asked as he climbed over boxes and busted lawn mowers, the beam from the Maglite bobbing up and down.

The dog had hold of something and was trying to pull it through a rusted-out spot in the barrel.

"What the hell could be in there you want that bad?"

He squatted down beside the dog, shining the light at the bottom of the barrel. The dog shied sideways, out of the way, and the light fell on the last thing John would have expected to see in this shed in a million years. As bad a man as he believed his father to be, he had never imagined him doing anything like this.

Protruding from the crumbling base of the oil drum was a bone.

Every animal had bones, John told himself as he crouched lower, getting closer to the barrel. Maybe something had crawled into the barrel and died. But the bone sticking out through the hole was too big to have belonged to a raccoon or a possum or anything else that would have found its way into this shed. Much bigger.

He shined the light through the lacework of rusted steel and his breath caught in his throat.

Staring back at him with empty eye sockets was a skull. It sat in the midst of a pile of bones that had once constructed a human being.

The hair rose on the back of John's neck. The dog began to growl.

"I told you never to come in this shed." The voice came from behind him. "Now you're gonna end up just like her."

27

Dana met Tim at the Grindstone.

"My home away from home," he said, grinning as he held the door for her.

Dana hesitated. "I kind of made a spectacle of myself here this morning."

"That's the beauty of a truck stop. Most everyone from breakfast is two states away by now." He put his hand on the small of her back and herded her along to the dining room. "Next time I'll let you pick the restaurant. I can get away with being here while I'm on duty."

The restaurant was quieter at this time of day. Breakfast and lunch were the big meals. The dinner crowd took up only half the table space.

Tim guided her to a corner booth, where he had a vantage point of the entire restaurant. Dana slid in opposite him, readjusting her hoodie to close out the curious glances of patrons near them, who all seemed to know Tim.

"Any word on who did that to our April?" the waitress asked as she came to take their order. She cut Dana a hard look. Dana bent her head and stared at the tabletop.

"Not yet," Tim said. "We're working a couple of leads. But you ladies here should be careful going out in the parking lot at night. You never know what might be lurking out there. The world's a dangerous place."

"I carry my bear spray," the waitress said. "Works on bears and truckers alike."

"There you go," Tim said, grinning up at her.

He ordered the chicken-fried steak. Dana asked for a cup of chicken soup. He frowned at that.

"You need to eat, Dee. There's nothing to you."

"I can't eat and think at the same time," she said. "I have a lot on my mind."

"Too much. You know, your mama called me after you did. She's worried about you."

Dana put her head in her hands and groaned. "Oh God. That's so embarrassing!"

"She's just being a mom. And she's probably right," he conceded. "Casey's been gone a long time, sweetheart. There's no sense in you running yourself into the ground like you seem to be doing. I mean, where's the fire, right?"

"I can't stop thinking about her," Dana admitted. "I'm having nightmares about her. I spent months in rehab with my brain stuck in neutral, not able to care about anything. Now it's running non-stop and I can't seem to turn it off. I don't want to turn it off. I want to remember what I can. I want to know what happened. My mother wants me to sit and do crossword puzzles and watch television all day."

"She almost lost you. She just wants to keep you safe."

"I know she means well," Dana said. "The Dana she got back isn't the same girl she had before. I know that's hard for her. It's hard for me, too. But I'm not going to let go of Casey until I have some answers. I can't now."

"Have you given any more thought to the Doc Holiday possibility?"

"I'm working my way toward it. I've been told I should just confront the issue and get it over with, that I'm giving him more power by not dealing with it."

"There's some wisdom in that. Pull the Band-Aid off and get it over with. You say the word and I can show you a photo array."

She pulled her phone out and opened the photo album. "You probably don't have to. There was a man here this morning. I didn't know him, but something about him upset me."

She scrolled through the pictures to the bearded man and showed it to Tim. He looked at the photograph, then looked her in the eyes, his expression carefully blank.

"He looked like this, didn't he?" she asked.

"Could be."

"I still don't remember—not in a way that could be helpful to anyone. I wish I did. I wish I could look at a picture of him and say I saw him right here in this restaurant the day Casey went missing. I wish I could say he spoke to us, that he flirted with Casey. That would be so much easier," she said.

"Give yourself time, Dee."

"Time for what? To make up a memory of something that probably didn't happen?"

"Nobody wants that."

"It would probably be a better story than the truth will turn out to be."

"Why do you say that?"

"You said yourself—most murder victims are killed by someone they know," she said. "You and I know everyone Casey knew. Do you want to think any of those people did something to her?"

"Well, I might not want to think it," he said, glancing off to the side as the waitress approached with their meals, "but John was a pretty good suspect—from a detective's point of view."

"I gave you extra biscuits and gravy," the waitress said cheerfully, setting his plate down in front of him.

He flashed the big smile. "You're gonna make me fat, Charlene!"

"Well, I can think of ways to help you work it off," she said sweetly.

She plunked Dana's cup down, sloshing soup over the sides without apology, and flung down a couple of cellophane packets of saltine crackers like she was throwing down a gauntlet.

"Charlene is a little bit in love with me," Tim explained as the waitress walked away.

"Right down to her bleached-blond roots," Dana muttered, staring at her soup, wondering what the odds were that Charlene had spit in it. She pushed the cup aside and opened a packet of crackers.

"I saw John today," she said. "He was working at the nursery."

He chewed a piece of his steak and swallowed, looking somber. "You be careful, Dee. That boy's got a hair trigger since he's back from the war. He beat the shit out of his old man last night before I could pull him off. Not that the old man didn't have it coming. But I mean to say, the look in John's eyes was like nothing I ever want to stand across from. He went to a dark place in his head. God only knows what lives in there.

"The detective in charge of this sexual assault case with the waitress is looking at him," he said.

"At John?"

"He doesn't have an alibi. Says he went out jogging that night all dressed in black like a goddamn ninja. He wouldn't give us his clothes to look at. The guy's full of rage and post-traumatic stress. He's got a head injury—"

"Well, there you go," Dana said sarcastically. "He might do anything."

He realized his misstep too late. "You know what I meant. It's not the same thing."

"Isn't it? He suffered a traumatic head injury while someone was trying to kill him. If that makes him homicidal, then I must be homicidal, too. Or does that just make him crazy and unpredictable?"

"Stop it," he said, annoyed with her. "He has a long history of violence. You don't. And considering how hard they looked at him when Casey went missing . . . We have to take a look at him for the waitress attack."

"He told me Casey was cheating on him," Dana said.

She watched Tim's reaction, looking for . . . what? Surprise? Shock? Wariness?

"Really? I don't believe it."

"He never told anyone back then because it would only make him look worse."

"Well, that's a fact," he said. "He looked bad enough when we all thought Casey dumped him."

"You don't think it's true?" Dana asked.

"She was your best friend. What do you think?"

"She never told me she was seeing anybody else. I was so used to her and John breaking up and getting back together. When she told me they broke up, I assumed . . . I was always pushing her to break up with him; it never would have occurred to me he would break up with her."

"Tubman—the detective in charge of the case now—he'll want to talk to John about this."

"You didn't answer me. Do you really think John was lying?"

He shrugged as he mopped up gravy with a biscuit. "I don't know."

"I think maybe you do," Dana said quietly.

He sat back and pushed his plate away as if she had just ruined his appetite.

"That day—the day she went missing—we argued about you," Dana said. "I found my old journal tonight. I read the entry from that day. Casey asked me if I would be all right if she went out with you."

He looked across the room and sighed, unhappy with being caught out—if not lying, then skirting the truth. "You and I had already called it quits, Dee. You broke up with me, remember?"

"That's right. My choice. We'd been broken up for a while. I guess it shouldn't have bothered me that my best friend for my entire life wanted to go out with the first boy I ever loved. Maybe teenage boys operate that way with their friends, but girls don't. Not if they want to stay friends, they don't."

"You were pissed," he said.

"I thought you said that conversation you had with Casey went in one ear and out the other that day."

"It was seven years ago, Dee. What's the point of me telling you now? You and I had split up. Casey was there for me. And maybe I thought I wanted to hurt you a little bit."

"Good job."

"You took the first swing."

"I was just trying to be practical."

"Yeah, that's a comfort," he said sarcastically. "I had served my purpose."

"You were awfully busy being you at the time," Dana said. "You wouldn't have even noticed I was gone if you hadn't needed a pretty girl on your arm for all those events celebrating you."

"I had a lot to be proud of," he argued. "Including you. Losing you stung, Dee. I'm not gonna lie. A young man's ego is a fragile thing."

"And Casey wanted to soothe the hurt?"

"She was my friend, too," he said defensively. "And a shoulder to cry on. Nothing came of it. She asked your permission, for God's sake! And then she was gone. There wasn't any point in talking about it. Why would I talk about it? Just to make it all hurt worse?"

"I told Detective Hardy that Casey and I didn't argue that day," Dana said, "because I was embarrassed."

"It had no bearing on what happened."

"My best friend wanted to date my ex-boyfriend and I was angry about it. Don't you call that motive?"

He made a face. "If I didn't know you."

Dana looked down and picked at the wrapper on the second packet of saltines. What if she had been that angry? Angry enough to shove her friend, who might have fallen and hit her head . . . She had berated Roger for possibly having been in the house when Casey had come to get her things. What if she had been there? What if that was what Roger had meant when he'd said *After all I've done for you* . . .

"I keep having these nightmares," she whispered, staring down at the saltines crumbling between her fingertips. "Casey keeps saying it was all my fault."

She put her hands over her face and started to cry as silently as she could.

She heard Tim get up from his seat; then his hand was on her arm.

"Come on," he murmured. "Let's get out of here."

Dana kept her head down as they left the restaurant and went out into the cool night air. He walked her to the far end of the long wooden porch with its row of rocking chairs. She looked past the side parking lot for the restaurant, past Silva's Garage, and to the dark wooded lot beyond. Casey's car had been found parked along the edge of that lot. Had she been taken from her car? Had she been lured into the woods? The same woods where the Grindstone waitress had been attacked just a few nights ago.

"Look at me," he said, tipping her chin up.

She looked up at him through a wavy sheen of tears.

"I don't believe you could have hurt Casey, Dee," he said. "I mean, you had a temper, but . . . Hell, I know you. You would have wrote that in your journal, too."

He meant for her to laugh. She couldn't quite manage it.

"I'm gonna hug you for real now," he said. "So don't knee me in the groin or anything."

He pulled her close as the second wave of tears came. She let him.

"Let it go, Dee," he murmured. "Let it all go. It doesn't matter now. The past is gone. Just let it go."

"I wish I could," she whispered. "I wish I could."

28

John spun around at the sound of his father's voice, shining the flashlight up to blind the old man just as he pulled the trigger. The sound of the explosion was deafening in the small shed. The shot caught him across the top of the right shoulder, gouging out flesh and chipping bone as John dove the other way. The impact felt like a strike from a white-hot poker. But there was no time to think about the pain. A massive wave of adrenaline carried him past it.

He crashed hard against the plywood shelving and used it to propel himself forward, launching himself at the old man, driving his good shoulder into his father's midsection and running him backward into the cupboards.

Stars burst behind his eyelids as something hard struck the side of his head again and again—an elbow or the butt of the gun.

Mack Villante was a big man. Broad and strong and heavily muscled, he was fueled by rage and alcohol and a hatred that had burned inside him every day of his life. He'd been fighting in bars and back alleys for years. Twisting his body to the side, he deftly turned John back up against the cupboards and brought the gun up, inches from John's face.

John grabbed hold of his father's wrist and forced the old man's arm out to the side, and the gun went off again with a flash and a *boom*! He brought his weakened right arm up and hit his father in the mouth with his elbow, then swung a hard left hook, catching him just above the ear and staggering him sideways. But the old man caught himself and swung backhanded as hard as he could, catching John across the face with the body of the gun.

John turned with the motion, lessening the impact but still stumbling to his knees. He scrambled to get his feet under him, grabbing blindly at the shelves in front of him, catching hold of something hard and irregularly shaped—some part of an engine. He hurled it at the old man, buying himself a second or two as he turned back around and launched himself up and forward.

The old man grabbed onto him as they collided, and, feet tangling, they went down in a heap. They rolled on the floor throwing elbows and knees and fists, crashing into boxes and toppling rakes and weed eaters, John's right arm losing strength with every second. As they rolled, the old man gained top position and dug an elbow into the wound, and what vision John had in the dimly lit shed went black.

With all the power he could muster, John twisted his hips out from under his father's weight and reversed their positions. As he straightened up, pulling his left arm high, fist balled, the old man brought the gun up with both hands, screaming.

John twisted his body and flung himself to the side as the gun went off again. His hand closed on the nearest thing—the wooden handle of something, a shovel, a spade, a rake. He didn't know. It didn't matter. He grabbed it and turned and swung as hard as he could.

The head of the spade caught the old man in the face, snapping his head to the side, blood and teeth spewing across the concrete floor.

"Fuck you!" John shouted at him. "I hate you! I hate you!"

Staggering to his feet, he drew the spade back to swing again. He wanted to hit him again and again and again. He wanted to obliterate the face, hit the head so many times it would come free of the body. He was capable of that much violence. The years of abuse had primed him for this very moment. He could end it all forever now.

And then the moment was gone. The dog was in the way, barking at him, jumping at him. John's head was ringing like a bell from the blows he had taken and from the noise of the gun. He could only see that the dog was barking. The sound was lost.

He took a step back and leaned back against the shelves as the adrenaline ebbed. He gulped in the cool night air to soothe his burning lungs. He was drenched in sweat, every muscle in his body quivering from the effort of the fight. The pain in his right shoulder began to burn and throb. The pain had weight, as if he was being struck again and again and again with a ten-pound hammer.

The old man lay motionless on the filthy floor, groaning and gurgling.

John tossed the spade aside as he looked down at his father.

"That's enough," he said. "I'm not going to prison for you."

Feeling weak, using only one arm, he struggled to turn the old man's unconscious body onto one side to keep him from drowning in his own blood and saliva. Then he dug the cell phone out of his old man's pocket and dialed 911.

29

I just came to get my stuff," John said. He couldn't tell if he was whispering or shouting. His ears were still ringing from the noise of the gun in the close quarters of the shed.

He sat on the tailgate of his truck, watching as the EMTs loaded his father into the ambulance. John had tried to minimize the severity of his own wounds. While he was pretty sure the bullet had fractured his collarbone and had drilled a nasty trench through the flesh and muscle along the top of his shoulder, he told the EMT it was "just a graze" and could wait for attention. The wound was ugly but not fatal. He held a thick gauze pad against it to absorb the last of the blood. The pressure kept the throbbing to a minimum.

Unable to quite take a deep breath, he knew his ribs were badly bruised if not broken. He thought his nose was busted and possibly the orbital bone around his right eye where his father had back-handed him with the gun. The eye was nearly swollen shut. The cut the gun's sight had sliced across his cheek would need glue.

But worst was the constant pounding inside his skull from the blows he had taken, jarring his already damaged brain. He had to fight to keep his focus on the task at hand. Nausea curdled his stomach.

"You're sure you want to do this now, John?" Tim Carver asked again. "I can run you to the ER and we can take your statement later."

"I'm fine."

Carver's eyebrows sketched upward. "Fine might be a stretch. But you've still got all your teeth in your head, which is more than we can say for your old man."

John wanted this interview over before anything else happened. He wanted the cops to hear it from his lips before they heard his father's version. He would walk them through it step-by-step and blow by blow if he had to because he could already imagine his old man fabricating a tale of his own self-defense with his son as the aggressor. He was going to end up wishing he'd killed the son of a bitch after all.

The yard was lit up like Christmas with the strobe lights on the ambulance and half a dozen Liddell County Sheriff's Office cruisers and unmarked cars. They had already set up a bunch of portable halogen lights on stands in and around the shed. John had told them about the skeleton in the barrel. They would probably be here for a day or more to process the scene.

The dog lay right beside him on the bed of the truck, big head down on his outstretched front legs, watching the scene with intelligent eyes.

"I thought you said that wasn't your dog," Carver said.

John shrugged with his good shoulder. "Guess I was wrong."

"So you came to get your stuff," the detective prompted. Tubman. Wrapped against the night chill in a heavy trench coat, he was the size of a small refrigerator. He swiveled his belly in John's direction, turning away from the scene in the yard. He looked over at the house, at the back door, which was hanging cockeyed on broken hinges, the wood doorframe splintered. "And the old man wouldn't let you in?"

"He wasn't here. He was at the Roadside drinking his dinner. That's why I came back when I did. He had locked me out."

"So you kicked the door in. That's breaking and entering."

"I just wanted my stuff."

"You could have asked us to help you with that, John," Carver said.

"Well, I didn't."

"So how did you end up in the shed?" Tubman asked.

"My stuff wasn't in the house. I figured he locked it up in the shed, 'cause that's what he'd do."

"So you broke into the shed, too."

"I just wanted my stuff!" John said again, aggravated. "It's okay for him to steal from me, but I can't take my own stuff back?"

"You can't destroy property to do it," Tubman said.

"He fucking tried to kill me!"

"He shot at an intruder," Tubman countered.

"He knew it was me!"

"In a dark shed?"

"With my truck sitting right here," John said. "And him knowing he locked my shit up in that shed. He knew damn well it was me! He said, 'I told you never to come in this shed.' Who else would he say that to?"

"And we saw the other night how the two of you treat each other," Tubman said. "I would have taken a gun with me, too, if I was him."

"And shot your own kid for going in a shed to get his own stuff?"

"Him being your father didn't stop you beating his face in with a spade."

"He shot me!" John shouted, incredulous, pain exploding through his head. "And if I'm the bad guy, why didn't I finish him off?" he asked. "Why didn't I just fucking kill him and be done with it? Then my story would be the only story. Why didn't I do that?"

Christ knew he had wanted to. If he'd had a dollar for every time in his life he had wished the old man dead . . .

"'Cause I'm *not* him—that's why!" he shouted, as much for himself as for the detective. "I'm *not* him!"

Tim Carver intervened. John hadn't realized he had moved toward the detective until Carver's palm hit his chest and stopped him, keeping him from coming off the tailgate of the truck.

The dog jumped to its feet, growling.

"Let's all calm down here," Carver said, one eye on the dog as he took a step back. "It's pretty clear to me John didn't shoot himself. He didn't pistol-whip himself in the face. I think we can all agree a struggle ensued. Right?"

"He knew I saw what was in that barrel," John said. In his mind's eye flashed the image of the skull staring out at him through the ragged side of the rusty steel drum, the crowning piece on a pile of bones that had once been a human being.

"Any idea who that might be?" Tubman asked.

John didn't answer. He knew the only name that came to their minds was Casey Grant. And they already believed he had killed her. It was his luck that he might have just given them the evidence to prove them right.

30

Dana stared at the television screen, riveted to the scene. Tim had gotten the call while they stood on the porch at the Grindstone—reports of a shooting at an address he had recognized as the Villante residence. The blond girl, Kimberly Kirk, was reporting, standing out at the edge of the road in front of the Villante property. Behind her, the scene was a circus of lights and activity. Sheriff's office vehicles were parked everywhere. Deputies in uniform and other personnel crisscrossed the yard, going back and forth to a long shed in the background.

"Sources close to the investigation are reporting the discovery of a human skeleton found inside a barrel in the building at the back of the property," Kirk said. "Liddell County deputies first responded to a 911 call from the residence regarding a shooting, and we have confirmed that one person has been transported to Liddell Regional Medical Center, while a second man is being questioned in relation to the incident. The property is owned by John Villante Sr., a local mechanic.

"While it is, of course, too soon to speculate as to the possible identity of the skeleton, viewers may well remember the prime suspect in the disappearance of Shelby Mills High School graduate Casey Grant, seven years ago, was her onetime boyfriend and Shelby Mills High School standout athlete, John Villante Jr."

"Well," Roger said dryly, "looks like I'm off the hook for one murder, at least."

Dana shot him a glare. "That isn't funny."

"Roger," her mother said with disapproval.

They stood in the kitchen, Roger and her mother just back from their evening festivities. Dana sat on the long table with her feet on a chair and her arms wrapped around herself against the internal chill of fear. Her mind was racing—thoughts, questions, and emotions tumbling over one another in a tumult. She kept trying to remind herself of the steps to take to slow it all down, but she couldn't seem to pass the second step before the emotions overwhelmed her.

A skeleton in a barrel. The idea brought a rush of terrible questions. Was it Casey? Casey, who was supposed to have met up with John the evening of the day she disappeared. He swore he hadn't seen her. He swore he hadn't hurt her—the girl he said had been cheating on him.

Dead inside a barrel in some long-forgotten shed. Had she been dead when she was put in the barrel? Or had she died inside of it? Had hours or days gone by with her awake and aware in the terrible stifling blackness, waiting for someone to save her? Waiting for death. Praying for death.

The mental images seemed to open a door on memories that consisted entirely of emotion: panic, terror, dread, desperation. Tears flooded her eyes and she began to shake.

Her mother was beside her in an instant, arms wrapped around her.

"That's enough! Roger, turn that off!"

Her voice sounded far away.

Dana felt as if the essence of her being had shrunk down to a small sphere floating deep inside the shell of her body. She was aware of her body climbing down from the table, walking beside her mother, still wrapped in her mother's embrace. They went together down the stairs, down the hall, past the crazed graffiti of the timeline she had scribbled over the wall trying to answer the questions of her best friend's disappearance.

All for nothing, she thought. The answer to the question was in a barrel in a shed a mile away. And she didn't have to wonder what her friend had suffered, because she knew firsthand. Even if she couldn't see the details in her memory, she felt them. She had survived them. Casey had not.

"We don't know that it's Casey," her mother said. "We don't know that it's her."

They sat on the bed in Dana's room. Dana curled into a ball against her mother's side, trembling violently, holding on to her mother as if she was her only anchor to reality, terrified that if she let go her mind would take her to a place she might not escape a second time—the madness that had tried to seduce her away from the pain and terror of her ordeal at the hands of a killer.

Nothing and no one had saved Casey.

An enormous wave of guilt came with that thought.

She cried for her friend. She cried for herself. She cried, lost in a sea of emotion, until she couldn't cry anymore.

Exhausted, she lay still, her head on her mother's shoulder, her mother's arms around her, her mother's voice coming to her as if from far away, singing a song from long, long ago.

"Blackbird singing in the dead of night. Take these broken wings and learn to fly . . ."

SHE SLEPT THE SLEEP of the drugged. Her body felt too heavy to move even a finger. Even the images in her mind drifted in slow motion through a fog. Casey smiling. Casey crying. Casey dead, her face decaying bit by bit, the flesh turning gray and sliding off the bone, the eyes dissolving. As badly as Dana wanted to turn away, she couldn't move her head because it felt as heavy as the earth itself. There was no escape.

There was no escape from truth. There was no escape from reality. There was no escape from the images conjured by her mind.

She woke more exhausted than she had been when she had finally fallen asleep. Her mother lay asleep beside her on the bed, both of them covered with the soft pink blanket, both of them still wearing the clothes they had had on the night before.

Dana slipped from the bed and padded across the room, shivering. She grabbed a thick chenille throw off the back of a chair and wrapped it around her.

The light that seeped in around the draperies was the gray of predawn on a day that promised gloom and rain. Fitting, Dana thought as she pushed back the drapes at the French doors.

Someone had written in the moisture on the glass panes: *Hugging U, T.*

Tim. He had to assume she had watched the news. He must have stopped by on his way home or back to the sheriff's office at the end of his shift.

A sad mix of emotions stirred through her as she unlocked the door and slipped outside onto the patio. The flagstones were cold and wet beneath her bare feet. She climbed onto the small wrought-iron table, put her feet on the seat of a chair, and rearranged the thick throw around her like a cocoon.

A thin fog shrouded the yard and the field beyond that rolled down to the woods. In the absence of sunshine, the leaves were a muted palette of muddy browns, dull gold, and maroon. There was no sign of the buck deer she had seen in the field before. For a moment it seemed to Dana she was the only living thing awake on the planet, sitting alone in the cold and damp.

Tuxedo emerged then from the open door and trotted over to join her, jumping up onto the table and rubbing against her, purring. Dana snuck her fingertips out from under the throw and scratched his head absently as her mind wandered.

Every murder had a motive, sometimes known to the victim,

sometimes known only to the killer. Doc Holiday had tortured and killed his victims for reasons that existed only in his cold, dark heart. If the body in the barrel was Casey, she had died for a reason known to her, whether it was John's jealousy or his father's sick attraction to his son's girlfriend. Either was possible.

Mack Villante had provided an alibi for the night Casey went missing. He was supposedly with a girlfriend in another town. The girlfriend had corroborated his story, though Dan Hardy hadn't been convinced. Casey had been supposed to meet John that night. Her car had been parked along the wooded lot that bordered the truck-stop complex. Mack Villante worked right there at Silva's Garage, not more than fifty feet from her abandoned vehicle. Had he seen her there and grabbed her? Dragged her into the woods or thrown her inside his truck?

Or it was possible John had been lying when he said she hadn't shown up. Casey had been cheating on him, he said. Cheating on him with Tim.

Cheating on me, too, Dana thought, although she supposed that wasn't strictly true. She and Tim had already broken up. But if Casey had thought she wasn't doing anything wrong, why hadn't she brought it up?

Even though Tim said nothing had come of it, that Casey had gone missing before their relationship could begin, Dana wondered how long it had been going on. Casey had asked her that last day if she would mind her going out with Tim, but John said Casey had been cheating on him—past tense—as if it had been going on for some time. Dana had broken up with Tim shortly after graduation—the first of June. Casey had gone missing the ninth of August.

Casey had been Tim's friend, too. Had she offered him comfort in the wake of the breakup, and one thing led to another? Tim had told Dana he might have wanted to hurt her for hurting him, and what better way to do that than sleeping with her best friend? Had he been taking his revenge all summer? Had Casey been seeing him all the while she pretended to want Dana to take him back?

It had never occurred to Dana at the time. In reading her journal entries leading up to that day, she had never suspected anything between Casey and Tim. She had suspected Casey of secretly seeing John—as if she had no right to make her own choices independent of what Dana had wanted for her. Had she been seeing Tim all that time, while Dana, the imperious teen princess, had been busy thinking she was in charge of everyone in her circle?

A mix of amusement and shock and embarrassment had tumbled in an endless loop through Dana's mind as she had read the journal of the girl she had once been. That Dana, Before Dana, had a good heart ruled by the naïve, self-absorbed brain of a pampered, privileged, well-loved child. Her world, and everyone in it, had revolved around her. She was the beautiful, benevolent monarch manipulating her subjects as she thought best for them. Meanwhile, her real-life Barbie and Ken dolls had been mounting an insurrection, with her none the wiser.

That wasn't entirely true, she thought now. She had suspected Casey was hiding things from her. She had suspected her friend was secretly seeing John again. In the days leading up to her disappearance, Dana had even begun to suspect Casey might be hiding something else from her. Casey suddenly wasn't feeling well. She would never quite look Dana in the eye when she said it was nothing.

Dana looked into her memory now and recalled once more the image of Casey walking toward her that morning at the nursery, coming from the ladies' room with a funny little smile on her face . . .

She felt sick in the pit of her stomach as she considered the possibility. If she was right, the tragedy doubled.

Casey had made a plan to meet John that night to tell him something. Had John been building a rage all summer that might have spilled over that hot August night? It wasn't difficult to imagine him that angry. He had always been a boy with a chip on his shoulder the size of Ohio. He had always resented Tim's golden-boy status. But Casey had been his prize. Regardless of his troubles and his faults, having Casey for his girlfriend had meant something to him. Dana remembered thinking of them as Beauty and the Beast. Sweet, beautiful, kind Casey and brooding, tormented John from the wrong side of the tracks.

If Casey told him she was dumping him forever for Tim Carver . . .

It wasn't all that hard to imagine him putting his hands around her throat and choking the life out of her. He had a violent temper.

Last night someone had found a skeleton in a barrel in the back of a shed at the back of the Villante property.

The rest of that story had still been a jumble at the time of the eleven o'clock news. Someone had been shot. Someone had gone to the hospital. Someone was being questioned. Too much was left to the imagination. Dental records would solve the biggest part of the mystery. They would likely know today whether or not the body in the barrel was Casey's.

"What are you doing out here?" her mother asked, padding across the damp flagstones in her bare feet.

"Thinking," Dana said.

Her mother wrapped her arms around her and kissed her cheek. "Come do that inside before you catch pneumonia."

Dana climbed down from the table and they went back into the house together, Tuxedo tagging along at their heels.

"You should go back to bed," her mother said. "You're not getting enough rest."

"I can't. I'm awake now. I can't stop thinking. It's all going around and around in my head like a swarm of bees. I can't make it stop."

Her mother's face was a mask of concern. She started to fuss, touching Dana's hair, damp from the fog, trying to rearrange the throw wrapped around her, her hands fluttering like the wings of a small distressed bird.

"You should take your anxiety medication."

"No," Dana said, shrugging off her touch. "I don't like how it makes me feel. I know you gave me some last night. I feel like I'm walking through molasses."

"You were so distraught—"

"I had good reason to be. That might be Casey, dead in a barrel for seven years. That's horrible! I *should* be upset. *Everyone* should be upset."

"Of course we're all upset."

"I don't want to take a pill to make it stop. Because it *doesn't* stop. The truth doesn't go away because you take a pill. It all just keeps happening in slow motion, and I can't feel it, and that's wrong. I don't want to go through life as a zombie.

"That's what he wanted me to be, isn't it?" she asked, the memory striking her hard.

Her mother looked stricken. Tears filled her eyes. She put her hand across her mouth to keep the pain from escaping as a sound.

"Doc Holiday," Dana said. "He didn't want me to die. He wanted to leave me a zombie. Is that what you want, too?"

"No!" her mother said. "I want you not to hurt. I want you not to have to remember it or feel it. I want none of it to have ever happened!"

"But it did happen, Mom. It did happen, and here we are," Dana said. "I'm not a broken doll you can glue back together and pretend I'm the same as before. I'm not the same. I'm never going to be the same. But I have to accept that and go on the way I am; otherwise, he might as well have killed me."

As her mother began to cry, Dana reached out. In that moment she realized it was her turn to offer comfort, to console her mother for the child she had lost. She would never be the same girl she had been before that cold January morning in a Minneapolis parking lot. Doc Holiday had taken that girl away from herself and away from everyone who loved her. They would all have to start again with the damaged young woman who had survived, and part of that process was mourning what they all had lost.

They held each other for a long while as that truth settled over both of them.

31

It was dawn by the time John walked out of the ER. Despite his protests to the contrary, his body had betrayed him in the end. After more than an hour of questioning by the detective, Tubman, he had excused himself to go piss blood and had passed out five steps from his truck. He had come to quick enough, but the decision was out of his hands by then. Carver had driven him to the ER.

There was no sign of him now as John walked out into the gloom. Another Liddell County cruiser sat at the curb. A young bulldog of a deputy he didn't know got out of the car and called to him across the roof.

"Can I drop you someplace, Mr. Villante?"

"Home," John said.

The deputy shook his shaved head. "Can't take you there. The whole place is a crime scene. It's still being processed."

John tried to sigh, pain stabbing him in his cracked and bruised ribs, catching his breath short. "I just want to get my truck."

"'Fraid that's not happening either. It's part of the scene."

He had nowhere else to go. Home, such as it was, or his truck. Beyond those two choices, he had nothing and no one. All he had were the clothes on his back, filthy and stained with his own blood and the blood of his father.

He had refrained from asking after the old man while he was in the ER. That hadn't stopped him hearing, just the same. Multiple facial fractures and a skull fracture. He would live to fight another day. That figured. The son of a bitch was too damned mean to die, even if John had made a better effort. Belligerent and combative, the old man had been put in some kind of twilight state to keep him quiet through the worst of his concussion.

John had fared little better. The bullet had indeed fractured his collarbone. His right arm now hung useless in a sling. He didn't want to know how many stitches it had taken to close the trench the bullet had dug through the flesh of his shoulder. He had badly bruised and cracked ribs and a kidney that felt like it had been pounded with a mallet. The right side of his face was like something from a horror movie, the eye swollen nearly shut, the cheek glued together, all of it filled with fluid and discolored like a rotten peach.

Even though his head was banging like a bass drum, he had refused the head CT against the doctor's wishes. His brain was already a mess. He didn't need a test to prove he had a fresh concussion in addition to the damage he'd already had. What difference would it make what Mack had done to him? If he was lucky, he would get a blood clot and die from it. But he was never that lucky.

He heard the distant crackle of the cruiser's radio and watched the young deputy speak into the remote unit on his shoulder.

"Detective Tubman suggests you come in to the sheriff's office to wait," the deputy said. "We can make you comfortable there."

What good would it do to protest? He had nowhere else to go. As much as he would have liked to get on the first bus out of town, no one was going to let him do that either.

Resigned, he eased himself into the backseat of the deputy's car and closed his eyes against the pain as the car pulled away from the curb. His last thought before he passed out was to wonder what might have become of his dog.

He came back around as the deputy took hold of his damaged shoulder to shake him. John's roar of pain sent the kid running backward.

"Hey! Sorry, dude!"

John said nothing as he worked his way out of the car.

He was "made comfortable" in an interrogation room with no windows and nothing but a hard chair to sit on. John ignored the chair in favor of sitting on the floor, propped up in the corner, facing the door. The deputy brought him a bottle of water and a couple of stale doughnuts and left him. He drank the water, ignored the doughnuts, and drifted in and out of consciousness, welcome, at least, for the quiet when it came.

When he was awake, he worked to keep his mind quiet, to keep the flashbacks of what had happened from replaying over and over. He wanted to think nothing, to feel nothing. He tried to picture absolute darkness, but the blank screen was sporadically interrupted by blasts of sight and sound and feeling, so loud and so intense it made him flinch. Memories of last night, memories of his father, memories of war, memories of death— *Bam! Bam! Bam!* Flash-bang bright. So loud he wanted to cover his ears, but the sound was in his head, and there was no escape.

Eventually, exhaustion overtook him, and he dozed for a while. He had no idea how much time had passed when Tubman showed up.

"You should have stayed in the hospital," the detective said as he pulled out a chair and seated himself next to the tiny round table. He promptly ate one of the doughnuts.

"When can I go home?" John asked.

"Remains to be seen."

"What does that mean?"

"Means it won't be anytime soon."

The detective munched on the second doughnut and stared at him. John let his eyes drift shut.

"You want to tell us about that barrel?" Tubman asked.

"No, sir. I don't know anything about that, sir."

"How long has it been in that shed?"

"I don't know."

"Why don't you know? You grew up there. You live there."

"I don't go in that shed."

"Ever."

"Ever."

"I'm supposed to believe that."

John said nothing. He didn't give a shit what this tub of lard thought, but even with a concussion he knew better than to say so.

"You don't know who that skeleton is," Tubman said.

"No, sir."

The detective opened the cover of a thick file and looked down through the lenses of his little wire-rimmed glasses at a typed page of something John couldn't make out.

"How is it nobody looked inside that barrel seven years ago when Casey Grant went missing?"

"I don't know, sir. You'd have to ask one of your own."

"Fucking Hardy," Tubman muttered under his breath.

Detective Hardy, John supposed. He hated the very name. Hardy had made his life a misery. It was half Hardy's doing that he had ended up in the army. He might have thanked the man for that— right up until the moment the IED had gone off, flipping the Hummer he was in, scrambling his brain like an egg.

"What's the deal with you and your old man?" Tubman asked.

"How do you mean?"

"You clearly hate each other. Why is that?"

John said nothing. He didn't know how to begin to explain his relationship with his father. Looking back to his childhood, he knew that he had both loved and feared the old man. Even as a teenager, as much as he had hated the man, he had still known a pathetic need to make his father proud of him—something he had managed every once in a while on an athletic field. He might have thought his father was proud of his service in the military, but he had never heard it from the old man's lips.

Even last night, even after every other disappointment in his life, a little part of his heart had died looking down the barrel of his father's gun. Surely he had known long before that his father didn't love him in any sense of the word, and yet some small part of him had held out a tiny scrap of hope, secret even to himself.

He didn't have the energy to try to explain any part of that to Tubman.

"How was he around your girlfriends?" Tubman asked. "Did he express an interest? Was he inappropriate in any way?"

A strange wave of shame washed over John as he considered his answer. His father's leering and inappropriate remarks had been the reason he had rarely taken Casey to his house. His lack of ability to do anything about his father's behavior had left him feeling less of a man.

"Yes, sir. He was a pig, sir," he said.

"Did he ever threaten Casey Grant? Did you ever see him make a physical advance on her? Did she ever express a fear of him?"

"He made her uncomfortable," John said. "I didn't bring her around him much."

The detective referred back to his notes, licking the tip of a thick finger and paging through the file.

"You think it's Casey Grant in that barrel?" Tubman asked.

He had considered the possibility. He had wondered over the years if his father could have had something to do with Casey's disappearance. Her car had been found in the parking lot between Silva's Garage and the woods. The old man had just laughed at him when John had confronted him about the possibility. He'd had an alibi. An alibi who had died in a fire a month later.

"I don't know, sir," he said.

"You sure about that?"

And so it would begin again, John thought. The endless questions, the accusations, the twisting and turning of his words and deeds, the scrutiny of the media. The inevitability of it swarmed over him, sapping what little strength he had. He had barely weathered the storm seven years ago when his brain had been whole. In the intervening years he had grown from boy to man. He had been battle-tested and survived two wars. But he was so tired now, his body and his brain so beaten, the idea of having to face it all again made him want to cry.

He hated Casey Grant in that moment—as he had hated her that summer seven years ago. She had been the one pretty, perfect thing in his otherwise ugly life. She had been his reward after a childhood of abandonment and abuse, finally someone to love him when no one else ever had or ever would, it seemed. Too good to be true, he had thought at the time, every time he looked at her as she held his hand or smiled at him or kissed him. Too good to be true. And so she had been. A pretty little liar, tired of his drama, done with her community service of being kind to the poor boy with no mother. He had ceased to be her charity, and she moved on to a brighter future with no real understanding of what that meant to him.

She had broken his heart, had ruined his life, and she was about to do it all over again.

"Sir?" he asked. "Am I under arrest?"

"No," Tubman said. "But it's in your best interest to cooperate here."

With great effort and great pain, John pushed himself to his feet.

"No, sir," he said. "I don't believe it is. I'll be going now."

32

The waiting was terrible. Every minute was like a bubble that grew and grew, filling with anticipation only to burst so that another might begin to form and grow and grow. Dana had texted Tim with the single question: *Is it her?* And then waited and waited for him to text her back, only to receive: *will let u know*. An answer that wasn't an answer.

The story was all over the news. The local television stations all had reporters and cameras live at the scene. Each crew had staked out a patch of weedy ground outside the yellow barrier tape that cordoned off the Villante property on the ragged edge of town. They stood in the rain, bundled in their station-logo storm jackets, reporting the news of no news, regurgitating everything that had happened the night before.

The one revelation of the day was the name of the person who had been hospitalized. John "Mack" Villante Sr. was in serious but stable condition with a head injury of some kind. John Jr. had been treated and released. There still had been no official explanation of the reported shooting that had initiated the call to the sheriff's office.

Dana sat at the kitchen table watching the coverage and checking her phone, checking the time, checking to make sure no messages had managed to sneak into it unnoticed, as if that was even remotely possible. She watched the recounting of Casey's disappearance, the rerunning of old footage from news stories seven years ago.

There they all were, players in the drama—herself and Tim and John, their friends from school, Casey's mother, the people in her life who wanted her found, and the people in her life who might have wanted her dead.

It seemed so strange to see herself, Before Dana, just on the brink of going out in the world, trying so hard to seem like an adult, as frightened as a child at the sudden loss of her friend. And there was Tim, tall and straight, already carrying himself like the military cadet he was about to become. His hair thicker than now and combed just so with a razor-sharp part on the side. He seemed so serious and so earnest in his answers to the reporter's questions about Casey. And there was John, lean and sullen, brows tugged low over his narrowed dark eyes, his broad shoulders hunched against the weight of accusation.

All three of them had left Shelby Mills, left that time, and left the story of Casey Grant behind them. And here they were, seven years later, back in the town that had grown them, back in the wake of Casey's vanishing.

The television screen was full of still and video images of herself seven years ago, and a year ago, and three days ago. A photo chronicle of her growth and her tragedy. Then John took her place, and the photos were of him in a football uniform, then in an army uniform, then in the desert camouflage of a war half a world away. Images of Tim completed the segment. A still photo of him at eighteen was planted in the upper left of the screen as video rolled showing him today, in uniform, directing other sheriff's personnel around the scene at the Villante property.

There was no real neighborhood where the Villantes lived. Curbs and gutters ended a quarter of a mile from their driveway. Properties were irregular in size and shape and set apart from one another with no sense of community intended. The houses had been built in the fifties and sixties and neglected in recent decades, cracker boxes and ranch rectangles in aluminum siding and cheap brick. Detached garages and ramshackle sheds were the norm out there. A thick woods ran right up to the back of the Villante yard.

Dana imagined John as a boy growing up there with no mother and a brute for a father. She remembered him as a third grader, always having bruises but never having much of anything to say. She had kept her distance from boys like John. She was the queen of the class, hosting tea parties for her circle of little ladies-in-waiting.

Her mother brought a steaming cup of tea to the table now, set it down in front of her, and ran a hand over Dana's hair.

"No word?" she asked.

"Not yet."

They both sighed and stared at the television. They jumped together when the doorbell rang. Dana popped out of her chair like a jack-in-the-box and hurried to the front door.

Tim stood on the front step looking like he hadn't slept in days, dark half-circles sagging beneath his blue eyes, the lines around his mouth etched deeper than his years accounted for.

Dana's heart caught in her throat and fluttered there like a trapped bird. She put her hand over her mouth to prevent herself from asking the question. She didn't want to hear the answer.

"We haven't heard," Tim said. "There's some snafu finding her dental records."

"Oh my God," Dana's mother said, putting her hands on Dana's shoulders. "Come in, Tim. You look like you could use a cup of coffee."

"Yes, ma'am. Thank you."

He took his cap off and shrugged out of his rain poncho and left both in the foyer to drip on the tile next to his wet boots.

"Can you tell us what's going on?" Dana asked as they went back to the kitchen.

"Not really," he said. "I'm not allowed to say much more than what you've probably seen on the news—if that much. We haven't pieced it all together yet ourselves, at any rate. We haven't been able to speak to Mack Villante yet."

"But you've spoken to John?" Dana said.

"Yes. He apparently went to the house to get his stuff and move out. He ended up in that shed at the back of the property. His father—we don't know if he mistook him for an intruder or what. John says his father knew it was him. Anyway, he took a shot at John and there was an altercation. That's what we know."

"Oh my God," Dana's mother said, bringing a cup of coffee to him at the table. "He shot at his own son?"

Tim made a pained face. "That's what you might call a bad family dynamic there."

"Casey always said John's father made her skin crawl," Dana said.

"But he's the one in the hospital?" her mother asked. "I'm confused."

"John got the better of him," Tim said. "You know, he's a trained commando—Special Forces and whatnot in the army. He's got a box full of medals. I wouldn't want to be on the wrong side of a fight with him."

"What does John have to say about the skeleton?" Dana asked.

"Nothing. He denies knowing anything about it. But I have to say I don't think he's telling us everything he knows. He walked out of an interview with our detective just a little while ago."

"He just walked out?" Dana's mother said. "How can he do that?"

"It was what we call a noncustodial interview," he explained. "He's not under arrest. That makes him free to get up and leave."

"He put his father in the hospital!"

"His father shot him. Winged him pretty good. It looks like John was defending himself. He made the 911 call and was reasonably cooperative at the scene. We didn't have grounds to arrest him. Not at that point, anyway."

"And now?" Dana asked.

"And now things are getting complicated," he said.

He took a sip of his coffee as if to fortify himself. Dana could feel him holding something back. There was a tightness around his mouth like he was trying not to swallow medicine that was bitter on his tongue. He made a little gesture toward the television on the wall.

"As you've seen, we've been going over the place with a fine-tooth comb."

"And what have you found?" Dana asked.

"Something I need to have you look at," he said.

He reached into a big pocket on his coat and pulled out a clear evidence bag with chain-of-custody notes scribbled on the front of it.

"I have to leave it in the bag," he said. "But I think you might recognize it."

He flipped the bag over, notes side down, on the table and pushed it toward Dana.

"We found this in the house," he said.

Dana stared at the piece of jewelry in the bag, every inch of her body suddenly ice-cold with dread. Just last night she had looked at the photograph of herself and Casey, each holding up the pendant of their friendship necklace. Two halves of the same heart, inscribed with a saying only complete when the halves were joined together.

"Oh no," she said in the tiniest voice.

"Of course, this by itself doesn't necessarily mean anything," Tim said. "She could have left it there by accident . . ."

"No," Dana murmured, fingering the necklace through the plastic bag. "We wore these every day. She had it on that day. We both did."

She could see it in her mind as she squeezed her eyes closed against the tears. She had taken her necklace off that day and put it away because she was angry. She had written about it in her journal.

I'm not going to wear a friendship necklace shared by someone who isn't a true friend.

There couldn't be an innocent explanation for Casey's necklace being in the Villante home. Casey would never have left it anywhere voluntarily. John had said again and again that he never saw her that day. But someone in that house had seen her. Someone in that house had probably killed her.

The tears welled up and spilled over Dana's lashes. She turned to her mother. "Mom . . ."

Her mother wrapped her up in a hug and kissed her hair and murmured, "I'm so sorry, sweetie."

Tim waited for a moment before clearing his throat discreetly.

"I need to get going with this," he said as he got up. He tucked the bag back into his coat pocket. "Thank you for the coffee, Mrs. Mercer."

"Anytime."

Dana followed him to the foyer, wiping her cheeks on the sleeves of her sweatshirt.

"I wish I hadn't found it," Tim said, glancing up at her as he pulled his boots on.

"I guess the truth works its way out eventually," Dana said. "Like a sliver. Sometimes it hurts worse coming out than it did going in."

"I think sometimes things are better left unknown," he said. "She's just as gone as she was before."

"But she'll get justice now."

"If that's her in that barrel. If we can prove John killed her."

"Or his father," Dana said, thinking of what Hardy had told her about Mack Villante's so-called alibi for the day Casey went missing.

Tim shook his head. "My money's on John. He told you his motive. Casey was dumping him for me. He always was jealous of everything I had."

True enough, Dana thought. Poor John Villante from the wrong side of the tracks. He had always worked twice as hard for half as much, while the sun rose and set on Tim Carver. How angry he must have been to know the only girl he'd ever loved was setting him aside for the golden boy of Shelby Mills.

"But if the body in the barrel is Casey, and John put her there, why would he call 911?" Dana asked.

"I don't know. Maybe that makes him look innocent while it makes his old man look guilty."

"Maybe his father *is* guilty."

"We'll know soon enough if it's Casey in that barrel," he said. "As soon as her dental records turn up. Then we'll figure out who put her there."

"God," Dana said, hugging herself against an internal chill. "Now I want to hope some poor person I don't even know died a terrible death."

"Somebody died. It's a sad story no matter what."

He pulled his rain poncho over his head, sending little water droplets scattering.

"I'd better go."

Dana went to open the door, pausing with her hand on the door-knob. "Can I ask you a question?"

"Sure."

"When did you and Casey get together?"

His eyes narrowed slightly, but he didn't look away.

"Just then," he said. "Like I told you. Why?"

"John told me Casey had been cheating on him," Dana said. "Past tense."

He shrugged. "I don't know."

"You might as well 'fess up," she pressed. "What does it matter now?"

The muscles in his jaw flexed. "If it doesn't matter, why are you asking?"

"It matters to me, not to anyone else," she said. "I've been going back over my journal, and it just looks to me like something had been going on with her for a while. I thought that something might be you."

"We'd seen each other a couple of times," he confessed. "She didn't feel right about keeping it from you. That's why she decided to just come out and talk to you about it. You and I had split up, Dana," he said with an edge to his voice.

"You and I," she clarified. "Casey was still supposed to be my best friend. Best friends don't lie to each other. We had never kept a secret from each other until that summer. Then she had a couple doozies."

"Let it go, Dee," he said, weary of the conversation. "Just let it go. Remember the good times. We were kids, for God's sake. We made mistakes. We shouldn't have to pay for them for all eternity."

"Had she told you she was pregnant?"

"What? No!" He shook his head. "Did she tell you that?"

"No, she wouldn't have. She would have known I would go ballistic. But I think she might have been. Something was wrong that summer. She was sick a lot. I made a remark one day—a joke—that she'd better not be pregnant. She laughed it off. I let it go. I never told anyone because I didn't know. But looking back on it, I think she might have been."

"Not by me, she wasn't," he insisted. "We'd only just started seeing each other. Besides, you know I was careful. I never would have risked that. Did we ever have sex without a condom? Ever?"

Which was all but an admission that they had slept together before Casey's big attack of conscience. Salt in the already raw wound.

"No," Dana admitted. "Well, one more strike against John, then. Casey had arranged to see him that night. Maybe that's what she was going to tell him."

"Jesus," Tim muttered, driving a hand back over his thinning hair. "I don't understand you, Dee. You don't have enough bad shit in your life with everything that just happened to you? You have to go and stir all this up from the past, and guess that it was even worse than it really was? Stop it!"

He took hold of her by the shoulders and said it again for emphasis. "Stop it. Casey loved you. Don't think ill of her because she made a mistake. We were all human, Dee. Even you. Let it go."

He checked his watch and heaved a sigh. "I have to go. I'll see you later. In the meantime, please don't torment yourself. There's no good going to come of it. The story is sad enough the way it is. Leave it be."

Dana turned away as he went to kiss her cheek. He gave her a long look, but whatever he might have been thinking, he kept to himself.

She watched him dash through the drizzle to his county cruiser and waved at him as he backed out of the driveway.

"I'm going to go take a nap," she said, sticking her head into the kitchen, where her mother had started gathering ingredients to make dinner.

But when she went downstairs she didn't go to bed. She stopped in the hall and stared at the timeline, then took a marker and ran the line backward from the day Casey had disappeared. She wrote *June* and *July* a few feet apart on the line. She made notations referring to things she had read in her journal, things she had looked at one way when she was eighteen and the center of her own universe, things that looked different to her now. Things that Casey had said, times when she hadn't seemed herself. She went to the other end of the line and noted the discovery of the barrel in the Villantes' shed and the discovery of Casey's friendship necklace in the house—half of a heart, incomplete without its partner.

Dana went into her bedroom, to the shelves behind her desk, and started poking through mementos accumulated since childhood— odd little trinkets and toys from county fairs and family vacations, renaissance festivals and high school fund-raisers. She went through her desk drawers and the cupboards in her closet.

She found it, finally, in a small, shell-encrusted jewelry box in the bottom drawer of her nightstand. With great care, she extricated the chain from a tangle of other necklaces and held it up to watch the pendant twist and turn, catching the light. Half a heart, incomplete without its partner. Half a heart with half an inscription.

She imagined Casey sitting beside her, shoulder to shoulder, as close as sisters, sharing everything, including a heart. She imagined them fitting the pendants together and reading the inscription out loud.

> *2 Lives*
> *1 Heart*
> *4-Ever*

As girls they had believed their friendship would transcend everything, that nothing would ever come between them, not time or distance, not parents or boys. Friends forever. Pinky swear it. And dot their i's with hearts.

Dana touched the pendant to her lips and closed her eyes and saw them as they had been—two little girls, one light haired, one dark, hand in hand, smiling the secret smile of friends.

What could matter more than that? What could she need more than that now, when she felt that so much had been taken from her—her innocence, her youth, her optimism, her career, her beauty, her*self*. The friend she needed now would never be with her again. The hole in her heart felt a mile wide.

With the necklace wrapped around one hand she dug her phone out of the pouch of her sweatshirt with the other, opened her contacts, and touched a name.

The call went straight to voice mail. "Hardy."

33

John made his way home in the rain, taking alleys and back streets, avoiding people in general and sheriff's deputies in particular. He kept his head down and his collar up, shoulders hunched against the miserable drizzle. His pace was slow, every step jarring, setting off explosions of pain all through his body.

He felt sick, the specific kind of sick that comes after a hard physical beating, when the body is trying to process and dispose of the toxins of tissue breakdown and internal bleeding. Every cell ached with it, and his head just kept pounding and pounding and pounding. He stopped a couple of times to puke up the meager contents of his stomach—bile and water. He stepped once behind a shed to take a piss and watched the rusty stream of blood-tinged urine exit his body, draining his damaged kidney.

He approached his home from the woods behind the property, moving quietly among the dark trees and rain-softened brush. He had spent many hours back here as a boy, exploring, pretending he was in a faraway world, avoiding his father. He would watch from the cover of the woods as the old man worked on cars and bottles of bourbon in the backyard, getting drunker and louder and more belligerent as the afternoons wore on. John would wait until he had gone back into the house, knowing just how long it would take for him to pass out, and that it would then be safe for him to slip unnoticed into his bedroom.

Finding a vantage point, he hunkered down, sheltered by a thick tangle of blackberry bushes, and waited. From there he could see the forensics people and the deputies swarming over the yard like ants, going in and out of the house and the garage and the shed, back and forth to the big mobile crime scene unit.

He could see a section of the road that led back toward town, crowded with news vans with rooftop satellite dishes, people in rain gear walking up and down. The Villantes were big, bad news today. He could only imagine what they were saying about him. John Villante Jr., once and future murder suspect with a psych discharge from the army. The deranged PTSD poster boy, so violent and unstable his own father had felt compelled to shoot him, then got his brains beat in for defending himself.

That was how the story would go. That was how the old man would spin it as soon as he had the chance.

The media might put a sympathetic slant on it. The sad plight of the forgotten veteran: good enough to send to war, then cast aside like everything else that was disposable in American society. But in the end he would still be considered violent and crazy no matter how many medals the army had pinned to his chest.

All his life he had wished he could be someone else, somewhere else, never more so than now, as he sat alone in the woods in the rain contemplating a future with nothing good in it.

He needed a plan, but he couldn't focus on the task for the pain in his head. He had to live from one moment to the next moment to the next moment. Breathe in, breathe out. He dug his good hand through the pockets of his coat, searching every crease and corner, praying to find what he eventually found—the short end of a joint. He had a bottle full of pain pills but nothing in his stomach to help keep them down. A couple of hits might help the pain subside a bit for just a little while.

He fixed the joint between his lips, flicked his lighter, and hoped that he could take a deep enough breath to get it going.

The dog found him as the gray of afternoon darkened from battleship to charcoal. It approached him with caution, head lowered, tail down, belly skimming the ground. John just watched. He had nothing but time. But it wasn't until he turned his attention back to the goings-on in the yard that the animal settled on the ground beside him.

The forensics people were packing up and clearing out, apparently satisfied that they had examined, bagged, and tagged everything of interest to them. The TV newspeople followed suit. Vehicle by vehicle, the crowd dispersed until the road was empty, yellow barrier tape and the mud-churned yard the only remaining signs that anything had happened here at all.

Still, John waited—just to be sure no one had forgotten something. He didn't want to be caught because of an afterthought. The last shade of darkness fell, and Mack's security lights popped on. There were no lights on in the house. If the sheriff's office had posted a deputy, John couldn't see him. And if John couldn't see a deputy, then the deputy, if there was one, couldn't see him.

Bent in a low crouch, he hurried as best he could from the woods to the back of the shed. He made his way around the side, scanning the yard for danger, seeing nothing. Still wary, he made his way from the shed to the old cars that had sat there for years, forlornly awaiting refurbishing. From the cars he made it to his truck.

The doors were locked. That wouldn't be a deterrent to him when he wanted to leave. He had learned long ago how to pop a lock on a car door and how to hot-wire an ignition, when it came to that. All he wanted now was a place to lie down, a hot shower if he could manage it, and a dry change of clothes. To the latter end, his duffel bag was gone, confiscated for no good reason he could imagine. Of what possible interest could his meager belongings be to the Liddell County Sheriff's Office?

No matter, he decided. He could steal a change of clothes from the old man. As long as he had a belt to hold up his pants he would be fine.

As he suspected, the back door to the house was still broken. The deputies had pulled it shut and run three long pieces of DO NOT CROSS tape from one side of the frame to the other, but John could see the hinges were still broken and the door was hanging so it couldn't latch properly even if the frame wasn't splintered.

He ducked under the tape and shoved the door open with his good shoulder. The dog refused to follow him, sitting just outside the door, softly crying its dismay.

"Suit yourself," John muttered. But he left the door ajar in case the animal changed its mind.

He turned on no lights. He didn't need them. He had found his way around this house in the pitch dark many times. The backyard security lights gave plenty of illumination through the window above the kitchen sink for John to see his way to a spoon and a jar of peanut butter, which he stuffed into a coat pocket. In the refrigerator he found a deli package of lunch meat. He tossed the meat out the door for the dog, then grabbed a jug of water and made his way to his father's bedroom to steal a blanket.

The shower would have to wait. He needed sustenance and rest.

He went to his own room, toed off his boots, and carefully lowered himself to the bed, propping himself up against the headboard. He was exhausted; just lifting the spoonful of peanut butter from the jar to his mouth seemed like a Herculean effort.

He forced the issue because it was necessary. He had learned in combat to eat what he could when he could because his body needed fuel to function. So he choked down the peanut butter and washed it down with water. He was going to need his strength later.

34

Dana picked at her dinner, a casserole that had been her childhood favorite. Comfort food. But there was no comfort to be had. Her stomach was in knots as she waited for the phone to ring with news of the identity of the skeleton found in the Villantes' shed.

Despite her mother's protests, she begged off after a few bites, pleading exhaustion. Her mother let her go with a kiss and a concerned frown, wishing her a good night's sleep.

Dragging, Dana trudged down the stairs to the lower level, pausing in the hall to look again at the timeline and the madly scribbled notations and arrows. All that mess boiled down to one likely, sad truth: that Casey was probably dead, and no one would ever be able to bring her back.

"Dana?"

Heart in her throat, she spun around to see Roger filling the end of the hallway.

"Can I have a word?" he asked.

"Can I stop you?"

He huffed a sigh and tipped his head, silently acknowledging that he would take that one on the chin and not lash back at her. The muscles in his jaw flexed.

"I want to apologize," he said.

Dana doubted he wanted to apologize. It was probably more a case of her mother telling him to apologize. She said nothing, waiting.

"I'm sorry," he said, coming toward her. "I've had a short fuse with you since you've been home. I probably don't have a clear understanding of your brain injury, and I need to adjust my expectations."

"Maybe if you had come to any of the family sessions at Weidman you would have been better prepared," Dana said quietly. "I guess you didn't feel obligated to do that, but it would have been nice."

Temper flashed in his eyes. He tried to keep it out of his voice. "Dana, I'm a busy man—"

She nodded. "I get it. I do. You married my mother and you got a pretty, perfect stepdaughter in the deal. You didn't sign up for Brain-Damaged Barbie. I'm a disappointment now, and I do things that embarrass you and piss you off because I can't always think before I act. I'm sorry for that."

"Dana . . ."

"I wish I didn't have to be here, you know," she said. "I wish I could go back to the life I had and live in my own apartment and have my career back, but I can't do that right now. I don't know if I'll be able to have a job again. I don't know who will want me. You're certainly off that list."

He looked away, hands on his hips, unable to contradict her. At least he had the grace to look embarrassed.

"I'm sorry I'm a problem for you," she said.

"It's just that there's so much at stake," he said. "But you know now I didn't do anything to hurt Casey."

"I don't know that. Nobody knows what happened to Casey. That might not even be her in that barrel. Even if it is, we don't know how she came to be there. Did John kill her? Was it his dad?

For all anyone knows, Mack Villante might have killed her for someone else or hid the body for someone else. He's a bad man who's done a lot of bad things."

Roger's expression darkened as his temper strained its boundaries. She wasn't cooperating. She wasn't reciting the lines he had played out in his head.

She turned back to her timeline, reached up, and tapped a finger on the note indicating that Casey had come back to this house the day she went missing.

"I don't understand how she could have come into this house to get her things without you being here, or without being seen if you were here. Please explain that to me in a way that makes sense."

Roger groaned and turned around in a circle, his hands clamped to his head, and gritted out her name between his teeth. "Dana—"

"I'm not going to let it go," she said. "No one should have let it go."

He had never been considered a serious suspect. While the sheriff's office had conducted a search of their home, nothing had come of it, and Roger's name had never been a part of the larger conversation regarding Casey's disappearance. Dana wondered how he had managed to pull that off, then remembered Sheriff Summers was Roger's old friend.

He rubbed a hand across his mouth as he tried to decide what to say. "All right," he said. "All right. Maybe the door wasn't locked—"

"Bullshit," Dana said, locking her eyes on his. She saw a flash of anger in his, then something like fear.

"Fine," he said as his resolve crumbled. "I let her in."

A chill swept over Dana from head to toe.

"I let her in," he confessed. "But that was all I did. I let her in to get her things, and I went back to bed. I never touched her."

"Why did you lie about it?"

"Come on," he said, giving her a look. "You worked in news. A grown man home alone opens his door to a teenage girl who then goes missing? I didn't do anything to her. I don't know what happened to her. There's no way I'm saying I might have been the last person to see her alive when it would serve no purpose.

"You have to let this go, Dana, *please,*" he said. "At least until after the election. If not for my sake, for your mother's. Do you want to see the press go after her? Because you know they will. And there's nothing to be gained by it. After the election, we can quietly go to the sheriff and set the record straight. I promise."

Dana considered the options. He had told her something he could have continued denying. Out of frustration? To shut her up? To stop her digging at the question? All of the above? She thought about her mother and how upset she would be with the press tearing at her with questions and accusations. Dana didn't want to be the cause of that.

"Do you really think I could have hurt Casey?" Roger asked softly.

That was the trouble, right there. She didn't know what to think he might be capable of. After Dana didn't have a good impression of him. Before Dana had never said a word against him.

"All right," she said. She wasn't at all sure she was doing the right thing. The thing she was sure of was that she wanted to get away from him, and telling him what he wanted to hear seemed a good way to do it. She would talk to Hardy about it the next day.

Roger breathed a sigh of relief. "Thank you. Truce?" he asked with a contrived hopeful look.

Dana nodded, quite sure she didn't look overjoyed. Roger seemed not to notice. As usual, the thing that mattered to him was that he had gotten what he wanted.

"Can I give you a hug?" he asked, as if he'd ever been that kind of parent.

"No."

He didn't press it. "Good night, then," he said, and left her.

Dana watched him disappear up the stairs, then went into her room and locked the door behind her.

For the first time she wondered if there might be some connection between Roger and Mack Villante. The idea that John's father might have killed or hidden Casey for profit had just fallen out of her mouth with no forethought whatsoever. Was it a possibility? She didn't know. All she knew was that someone in the Villante household had had something to do with Casey the day she disappeared.

Even if the call came and the dental records didn't match, that wouldn't change the fact that Casey's necklace had been found in the Villante house. There was no innocent explanation for that. Casey wouldn't have given the necklace to John. She couldn't have left it at his home if she wasn't seeing him anymore. She had been wearing the necklace the last time Dana had seen her.

A shudder passed through Dana as she remembered her collision with Mack Villante on the porch at the Grindstone—his battered, angry face looming over her, his big, meaty hands grabbing hold of her. *I caught a feisty one!* She could hear his rough voice, his crass laughter. She remembered the feeling of her foot connecting hard with his shin, and his instant fury as he cast her away from him. *Fucking little bitch!*

There was no reason for Casey's necklace to be in the Villante house other than someone had kept it as—what did the detectives call it? A token? A silver? A reminder? Her tired brain searched for the word, finding words that were similar in sound or similar in meaning until the right one finally tumbled out—*souvenir*. A souvenir, something the killer kept to remind him of the victim and the crime. A thing to trigger the memory and allow him to relive every detail.

A chill went through her as she looked over at her nightstand, at the butterfly necklace she had sorted out of her jewelry pouch the other day. She picked it up and let the delicate filigree butterfly hang down. Her mother said she must have been wearing it when she was brought into the ER that terrible night in Minneapolis. One of the emergency room personnel had cut the chain to remove it from around her neck.

The tremors of fear started deep inside her and worked to the surface until the hand that held the necklace was shaking and tears blurred her vision of the butterfly.

This wasn't her necklace. This was something meant to evoke a memory. A souvenir of her experience with a madman.

Something Hardy had said the night she had gone to his house came back to her now—that cases get broken all the time on small details that might seem to mean nothing . . . a photograph, a cigarette butt, a piece of jewelry . . .

This wasn't her necklace. This was a piece of evidence from some other young woman's death. This was something Doc Holiday had taken from one victim and gifted to another victim. She could imagine his sick amusement at the idea that the necklace would be nothing more than an insignificant oddity to her or to the family that survived her had she died.

A vague memory floated at the back of her mind: photographs of jewelry being shown to her by the detectives. Did she recognize this, had she ever seen that . . . ? She hadn't understood the significance at the time. Now she did.

Dana flung the necklace away as if it were a live snake, a sound of distress tearing up her throat. She ran into the bathroom and turned the faucets on full blast and started washing her hands with the fervor of a zealot, scrubbing and scrubbing until the skin was red.

She had touched something *he* had touched. He had taken that necklace from around the throat of a dead girl and put it on her, giving her a souvenir of what had happened. His own sick joke. He was probably in hell laughing as she tried to wash away the idea of his touch.

Dana turned off the hot-water faucet, bent over the sink, and splashed cold water on her face to cool the flush of rage and wash away the tears that came with anger and fear. The water went everywhere, soaking her hair, soaking the sleeves and the front of her sweatshirt.

She stood in front of the mirror, faucet still running, and stared at herself, at the face a demon had carved for her.

"You son of a bitch," she muttered. "You son of a bitch! How dare you do this to me?"

Furious, she yanked her sweatshirt over her head and tore the wet garment off, flinging it aside. Her chest rose and fell as she gulped air and huffed it out. She stared at the mark he had etched into her flesh, the number nine carved below her collarbone, the tail of it dipping between her breasts. She was his ninth victim by the count of law enforcement, though they suspected there were many more.

She was nothing more than a number to him, one of many. Yet this number was the souvenir he had given her to remind her every day of her life of what he had done to her, so that even if her memory didn't allow her to recall the horror in detail, she still had something tangible to tie her to him forever. The skin across her chest was tissue-thin and nearly transparent. The plastic surgeons had been unwilling to even attempt to remove or minimize the scar, saying they would only make a worse mess. Dana didn't see how anything could be worse.

She went to her closet and pulled on another of her endless supply of hoodies, this one soft black velour that swallowed her up, the sleeves falling nearly to her fingertips. She shoved the sleeves up as she went to her desk and woke up her computer. Her heart was pounding as she typed the name into the search engine: *Doc Holiday*.

She hit enter before she could think twice and held her breath as she stared at the screen, waiting for his face to appear. Her heart was pounding like a trip-hammer.

"You can't own me anymore," she said. "I won't let you."

When the photo came up, she expected to scream, to run backward in horror. She gripped the arms of her chair to hold herself in place. Then there he was, and she didn't move, and she didn't cry out.

She was struck by how much he resembled the man she had photographed in the Grindstone. He was pudgy, balding, in his mid- to late thirties. He wore a beard and a pleasant smile that made him look like some lovable cartoon hobo. He didn't have horns or fangs. He wasn't frothing at the mouth.

No one would have looked at him and thought he might be evil incarnate, yet that was exactly what he had been. And at the same time, he was just a man, like Hardy had said. He was just a man who had gotten up in the morning and put his pants on one leg at a time . . . and then he'd gone out into the world and kidnapped young women and tortured and killed them. This ordinary man.

There was no telling, looking at them, the dark thoughts that lurked in the hearts and minds of men like Doc Holiday. By all accounts he had been a friendly sort, always upbeat, the kind of guy who talked to everybody. Dana had been that person too. Friendly, outgoing, happy to engage in conversation with anyone. She had been told she had met him the day before her abduction at a convenience store. There had been video surveillance tape of them exchanging pleasantries by the coffee station.

No woman went willingly with a man she believed might kill her. Not Doc Holiday's victims, not Casey Grant. And yet it happened all the time.

Most murders were committed by people known to the victim—a spouse, a lover, a brother, a friend. It was only after the fact that anyone claimed they saw it coming. No one expected to die at the hands of someone they knew, but it happened every day, everywhere. It had probably happened to Casey, whether her demise had come at the hands of John Villante or his father.

Dana checked her phone, as if a message might have snuck in without the alarm alerting her. Nothing. She glanced at the muted television, looking for a splashy news-bulletin graphic. There was none. There wasn't likely to be one now, she realized, seeing the time. It was nearly midnight.

There wouldn't be any more news tonight. For law enforcement there was no real sense of urgency to identify a victim long dead. A skeleton would still be a skeleton in a day or a week or a month. The urgency came for the loved ones, who, no matter how long their friend or family member had been gone, were instantly transported back in time to the intensity of those first days of the search as they waited for words that would either raise or dash their hopes.

Dana tucked the phone into the pouch of her hoodie and walked away from the desk. Going back into the bathroom, she turned off the faucet she had left running and found tweezers in a cup among her makeup brushes. She grabbed a tumbler off the vanity and went back into the bedroom, on a mission.

Tuxedo appeared from under the bed, bounding out to bat at the necklace as Dana picked it up from the carpet with the tweezers and dropped it in the tumbler. She set the glass on the desk, then scribbled a note and placed it on top of the tumbler: *Send to Mpls PD.*

She would send the necklace back to the detectives, Kovac and Liska, and hopefully, it would be the one small, seemingly insignificant piece that would complete the puzzle for another victim. That small action gave her a welcome sense of accomplishment as a step in the direction of defeating the monster who had occupied her mind all these months.

"One small step for Dana," she whispered, bending over to scoop up the cat.

Tuxedo dashed away like a crazy thing, white-tipped tail straight up in the air. He stopped short by the drapes, meowing with a question mark at the end of it, arching his back and rubbing back and forth against the draperies.

"You can't go out," Dana said. "It's late."

The cat flopped down on the carpet and rolled onto his back, batting at the drapes, purring and chirping. He rolled again and disappeared beneath the curtains.

Dana smiled for the first time in what seemed like days. Silly cat.

She went to the drapes and pulled them apart, expecting Tuxedo to jump up and scurry across the room. But the cat was gone, out the door, which was open just an inch.

"Oh God," Dana muttered.

She didn't remember having cracked the door open, but then that was the problem, wasn't it? Just like she didn't remember leaving the faucet running or turning the stove on when she meant to use the microwave.

She didn't want to go out after him. Her nerves were still on edge from her encounter with Roger in the hall, and the additional questions that had arisen because of it. The patio lighting was still on, but the timer would cut it off at midnight, just minutes away.

Tuxedo had trotted out to jump up on the little wrought-iron table. Dana called him. He just looked at her, very satisfied with himself and content to stay where he was.

She couldn't leave him out there. Coyotes and foxes roamed the wooded countryside here, happy to make a snack of a little house-cat. Cursing under her breath, Dana padded out onto the flagstones, barefoot. The rain had finally stopped, but the stone was still wet and cold. Heavy clouds scudded across the moon, and the wind rattled the trees like giant maracas. She hunched her shoulders against the chill.

"Come on, you."

The cat arched his back and purred loudly, kneading his paws on the table. Happy to have made his human bend to his will. Dana picked him up and held him close, closing her eyes and burying her nose in his fur for just a second.

In that second she heard the click of the landscape lighting going off. She opened her eyes to absolute darkness. The streetlights from the cul-de-sac didn't reach back here behind the massive house. The land beyond the yard was wild and wooded. Only a sliver of light escaped from between her bedroom drapes.

Dana's heartbeat raced as she turned to hurry back inside. She felt like the darkness was a living thing behind her that was reaching its bony hands over her shoulders to grasp her by the throat.

At the door, she pulled the drape back with one hand and set the cat down with the other.

"Dana, what are you doing out here at this time of night?"

Dana spun around, her heart in her throat, to see Tim emerge out of the darkness near the family room doors.

Without thought, she launched herself at him, hitting him in the chest.

"Damn it, Tim!" she said, her voice angry but soft, the automatic whisper remembered from her adolescence when she had snuck him into her bedroom on many occasions. "What are you doing here? You scared the hell out of me!"

"Ouch!" he yelped, catching hold of her wrist before she could hit him again. "I told you I'd see you later."

"And I told you not to sneak up on me!"

"I wasn't. I was coming down to see if your light was still on; then I would have texted you," he said. "It's late. I thought you might be asleep by now. I didn't want to wake you."

The adrenaline drained out of her abruptly, leaving her feeling weak.

"I couldn't sleep," she admitted. "I couldn't even think about it. Come in. It's cold out here."

"I'm sorry if you were waiting on news from me," he said. "We're not going to hear anything until tomorrow."

"I figured as much."

She sat down on the arm of the upholstered chair and hugged herself. "I keep thinking about her being in that barrel, wondering if she was alive when she was put inside of it. To think of that, of being stuffed inside there in the pitch black with the lid sealed . . . it makes me want to throw up."

"Don't think about it," Tim said. "We don't know what happened. Whoever that was, I choose to think was dead first. The barrel was just a convenient container. Who would ever look at it or give it a second thought? It was tricked out, anyway, rigged so it could hold about fifteen gallons of battery acid in the top third or so of the barrel. The skeleton was below a false bottom. That's why the victim was never found when they executed the search warrants back when. They opened the barrel, saw the acid, closed it up."

Dana shuddered at the thought. "I so hope it isn't her. Bad enough that she's gone, but I can't stop thinking that if someone killed her, then they killed her baby too."

"Stop thinking about it," he said, scowling. "You don't know that she was pregnant."

"I don't know for a fact, but I think I'm right," she insisted. "She would have gone to the free clinic in Louisville if she was. That's where she went when she wanted to go on the pill and her mother wouldn't let her.

"There must be some way to look at their records without breaking confidentiality," Dana said. "Even if you have to get some kind of waiver from her mom or something."

"You don't think her mother would have told the investigators back then?"

"Casey wouldn't have told her until she absolutely had to. Her mother would have had a fit. She would have hustled her off to have an abortion. Casey would never have gone for that. Not in a million years. She loved kids. She always talked about having her own family one day."

"Jesus, Dee," Tim muttered as he settled himself in her desk chair on a long sigh. "You're like a dog with a goddamn bone. You're giving me a headache talking about it. Leave it be for tonight, will you? This has been a hell of a day as it is. If we need to find out, we'll find out."

"A hell of a day is right," Dana said. "Roger confessed to me tonight that he was here when Casey came back that day to get her things. He let her in. He says he didn't tell anyone because it would have made him look bad for no good reason."

"You don't think he was involved, do you? Arrows don't get any straighter than Roger."

"I don't know what to think anymore. I look at people I've known my whole life, and it's like they're from an alternate universe. Those memories belong to someone else. Before Dana, I call her. After Dana looks at the same pictures and sees everything in a different light. I don't know what's real."

"I think reality is highly overrated," Tim said, glancing away. He looked tired. He looked like he had aged as the day had gone on, which was exactly how Dana felt.

"We can't find John," he said. "He walked out of the interview this afternoon and managed to disappear."

"Do you think he left town?"

"I don't know. Maybe. Not in his own vehicle. We know that much. No one saw him at the bus depot. But he could have hitched a ride out at the truck stop. Or he's hiding out somewhere. He doesn't have any friends in town that I know of, so I don't think anyone is helping him out."

"Would he go home?"

"That'd be stupid. The place is sealed as a crime scene. Even after we were done processing it, we had a deputy parked out front for a couple hours, and we've been cruising past all evening."

"Who knows what might be going through his head," Dana said.

"We've all been through some crazy shit," he said, swiveling around to look at the stuff on her bookshelves—the photographs and other things she had collected over their years in school.

He reached out and plucked down the framed picture of the four of them ready for prom and stared at it, frowning, lost in his own memories.

Dana had spent enough time looking at that photo in the last few days to have every detail crystal clear in her mind. The four of them in their best-dressed glory. She and Casey had had their hair and makeup done at the Cutting Edge salon that afternoon. They had fancied themselves to look like Greek goddesses. Tim was in his rented tuxedo, posing with a James Bond swagger. John stood looking uncomfortable in a suit that didn't quite fit him, looking like he would rather have been anywhere else on the planet.

They seemed so young and so blissfully clueless, so full of the absolute arrogance of innocence. There they were, on the brink of becoming adults, thinking they already had it all figured out. Except for John, Dana thought. John had the troubled look of a boy who had already seen the cruel truth of the real world.

Tim set the photograph aside on the desk and absently toyed with the computer mouse, bringing the screen to life. Doc Holiday smiled at him like a long-lost friend.

He turned to Dana with a questioning look.

"I decided I had to get it over with."

"And?"

"Turns out he was just a man. He was a man who did monstrous things, not a monster from another world. He was just a bad man who did bad things, and I stopped him. I don't remember it. I don't know how I found the strength to do it. But I killed him. He didn't kill me."

He stared at her for a long moment, digesting what she had said and what it meant, nodding.

"Are you okay?"

Dana laughed. "No! I'm not ever going to be okay. Not the way people who have never been through what I went through are okay. Whether I ever remember the details or not, that experience is a part of me now. It changed me. But I'm alive. I won. I'll take that over the alternative."

"You're something special, Dee," he murmured, getting up from the chair. "I want to hug you for real. Can I?"

Dana nodded, sliding off the chair and into his arms. She pressed her cheek into his shoulder and felt his heart beating beneath her ear. A reassuring sound, she thought.

"Like old times," he said softly.

She could see their reflection in the mirror above her nightstand. Their eyes met in the glass.

"I'm a little worse for wear," she said.

He turned her to face the mirror and tucked her back against him, wrapping his arms around her from behind.

"It's a shame," he said. "I'm sorry, Dee."

As she looked at his reflection, something changed. Something in his eyes went dark, and an ice-cold rush of fear went through Dana, the emotion coming seconds before her rational brain could understand why.

"I'm so, so sorry," he said as the crook of his right arm came up underneath her chin and pulled back, and his left hand cupped the back of her head and pushed forward.

Before she could even form the thought to fight, it was too late. The last thing she saw was her own disfigured face, her eyes wide with shock as Tim Carver choked her unconscious.

35

He was worried he had killed her, which seemed a stupid thought on the face of it. He was going to kill her. That outcome was inevitable. She knew too much, had guessed too much. She wouldn't let bad enough alone. Her obsessive digging was hitting too close to the truth, and he couldn't have it. He had worked too hard to rebuild his life after Casey had all but ruined it.

Tonight he had the perfect window of opportunity to pull this off, but the timing had to be right. He knew too much about forensic science to fuck this up on a stupid mistake. She needed to be alive going into the house. She needed to die there so there could be no questions about other possibilities.

There could be no questions as to where she had been killed or if her body had been moved. She would be found lying where she died so the patterns of lividity—the settling of the blood in the corpse—would match the position of the body. The inevitable leaking of bladder and bowel content that took place at the time of death would take place at the scene. He had considered every detail.

This was the riskiest part of his plan: getting her from her house to the destination, and so far luck had been with him. The rain had stopped, but the heavy cloud cover remained, allowing him to carry her off the property to the little-used service road that ran behind the low stone wall on this backside of the development without danger of being seen by any insomniac that might glance out a bedroom window.

He had pulled the cruiser onto the little-used road, lights out, creeping slowly along, knowing that the car was pretty much hidden from view by the wall and the heavy landscaping that bordered it, keeping the riffraff out—symbolically, at least. He had placed a tarp across the backseat of the car and wrapped her in it to contain her DNA and any trace evidence—hair, clothing fibers, and so on. He had left the car running so no one could be awakened by an engine roaring to life. He backed over any tire tracks that might have been left on the thinly graveled trail.

Now he only had to pray he didn't get a callout in the next half hour or so. But nothing much ever happened in Shelby Mills on a weeknight. The murder of one of its best-known citizens would be a rare exception.

SHE THOUGHT SHE HAD died. Her body was moving, but she wasn't using her arms or legs. She opened her eyes and saw nothing but blackness.

But she was breathing. Her heart was beating. She was uncomfortable. She tried to move, but her hands and feet were bound.

The sense of panic was immediate and huge, like an explosion going off inside her body. Her heart was galloping. Tears flooded her eyes. Her pulse was roaring in her ears. She wanted to scream, but he had taped her mouth shut.

For a few chaotic seconds, Dana didn't know where she was or who had taken her. She wasn't entirely sure this wasn't a nightmare conjured up by the image of Doc Holiday. She shouldn't have looked at him. This was the thing she had feared, that by looking at his photograph she would give a face to the monster of her nightmares and plunge herself back into an experience best left in the dimmest corners of her memory.

All of the brain chemistry, the hormones and neurotransmitters that create emotion and capture memory, flooded her brain, threatening to drown her. She couldn't capture and hold more than a scrap of a thought or a snippet of a memory. She had to fight to remember the steps she had been taught to tame the storm.

Breathe deep. Four counts in. Four counts out. Concentrate on the individual parts of her body. Be aware of the tip of each finger, the tip of each toe. Breathe deep. Four counts in. Four counts out . . .

Slowly the flood eased and the memory came back to her—the image of her and Tim in the mirror above her nightstand. The way his eyes had suddenly gone dark. The sound of his apology just before he started to choke her.

Dana's heart sank.

Oh my God. Tim.

It had never entered her head that he could do something like this. It had never entered her head that he could have killed Casey. He had only just started to see her— But no, Dana thought, she didn't really believe that was true. For all she knew they had been seeing each other all summer. She had broken up with Tim shortly after graduation. She would have never pegged Casey for a stone-faced liar. She had always been so sweet and kind and honest. But looking at it now, Dana had to believe her friend had been an accomplished liar indeed.

She had to have lied to Tim, as well. She had been on the pill since they were sixteen. And Tim was meticulously careful. He never would have risked unprotected sex, pill or no. He had his whole big future to consider.

Dana's stomach turned.

Tim Carver had had his whole big future ahead of him—his acceptance to West Point, his career in the military. He had been a star. The golden boy of Shelby Mills. The apple of his parents' eyes. He'd had so much at stake. He'd had so much to lose.

Oh my God, Tim.

No one had ever suspected him. They might have—if Dana had given Detective Hardy the one piece of information she had been too embarrassed to give him: the fact that her best friend had asked that fateful day about dating her former boyfriend.

It wasn't his business, she had thought at the time. It wasn't anyone's business. It certainly had nothing to do with Casey's disappearance. Or so she had thought. She had believed Casey had secretly been seeing John. She had been so focused on her disapproval of that relationship. It had never occurred to her that her dearest friend would betray her . . . or that the first boy she had ever loved could be a murderer.

36

The dog barking woke John. The sound was in the distance, but it was enough.

He had fallen asleep sitting up on his bed. He startled awake, then went very still as he listened and tried to remember where he was and why.

Was he in Iraq? Afghanistan? Home?

The smell of cigarettes burned his nostrils. It was coming from the blanket he had thrown over himself.

Home. He'd taken the blanket from his father's room.

He was in pain. Why?

He had been shot. He had been beaten. Who . . . ?

His father.

The dog barked in the distance.

Years in war zones had trained him to sleep lightly, to never totally give himself over to the deepest, most restful phases of slumber. To sleep deeply in enemy territory was to die. The ability to be attuned to his surroundings at all times was paramount to survival.

He set aside the jar of peanut butter, which had fallen in his lap, and eased his body off the bed. It would be his luck that the old man had checked himself out of the hospital and come home.

And here I am, trapped in the one room where the only window is nailed shut.

In his bare feet he padded silently across the room to stand, back up against the wall, next to the door to the hall. His head was still hurting, but the incessant pounding had subsided to a dull throb that at least allowed him to hear. He tried to listen without imagining sounds. He fought to clear his mind of the memories of other situations in other countries in other wars.

He thought he could hear someone moving around in the vicinity of the kitchen. Possibilities ticked through his mind. If it wasn't the old man, then who? A deputy? A vandal? A thief? It made the most sense to think the sheriff's office would send a deputy by to check on their crime scene.

John had left the back door ajar in case the dog wanted to come in—the dog that wasn't his dog. That would have prompted a deputy to cross the crime scene barrier. Now he was going to be found out because he had left that door open when it should have been shut.

He thought about escape routes. The house was small, and the common areas opened into one another, affording no cover. The room next to his was the only bathroom. The window was high on the wall and too small to get through easily. Across the hall was his father's bedroom, with the only window looking out on the street in front of the house.

He didn't like the idea of going through that window or making a dash for the living room and going out the front door. If there was a deputy coming in the back door, there should be one out front waiting for any quarry to be flushed out.

If he wanted to exit via the back door, then he would have to wait until whoever it was made it to the living room before he could make a move to get past. Another bad option. In his current condition, he didn't want to test his ability to outrun anyone.

He was trapped.

37

No one would question the Liddell County sheriff's cruiser in the Villante yard. The place was a crime scene. Tim was the deputy on patrol in this area tonight. He belonged here. He would be the one to discover the terrible scene. Having stopped by the property to make sure no one had disturbed anything, he found the door ajar and broke the seal to investigate . . .

As he pulled the car in behind the house he could see he wasn't going to have to lie. The back door was ajar.

John.

With little more than a glance in the backseat, he got out of the car and drew his gun. The phrase *killing two birds with one stone* was about to take on real significance.

Hyperalert to his surroundings, he made his way from the car to the house, eyes scanning back and forth from the house to the garage to the junker cars in the yard to John's truck to the shed where Mack Villante had shot his own son and a skeleton had been languishing in a barrel for God knew how long.

He could hear that damned stray dog barking, but he couldn't see it. He had to hope the thing wouldn't come running. He didn't want to have to discharge his weapon any sooner than necessary.

The Villantes didn't have many neighbors, but he didn't want to risk one of them calling in a report of shots fired.

He pulled the yellow tape down and slipped into the house through the open door. The kitchen was clear. The refrigerator humming was the only sound.

From the doorway into the dining room he could see the front door and most of the living room. He worked his way around both rooms, noting nothing but the acrid stench of thirty years of cigarette smoke.

A narrow hall led down to the bedrooms and bathroom. His senses were heightened to the point that his eardrums hurt and his eyes burned. He could hear a faucet dripping slowly like a hammer banging on a lead pipe. His heart was racing, his pulse whooshing over his eardrums. He could hear himself breathing in and out like he was fucking Darth Vader. Adrenaline. Nerves.

The first bedroom had been made into a home office and was so messy, so crowded with shelves and boxes and stacks of papers and magazines and whatever other crap Mack Villante thought worth keeping, that no one could have been hiding in the room.

Across the hall, he pushed open the door to the bathroom. Empty.

The next room on the right had to be the old man's, judging by the smell—cigarettes and stale sweat and musk. Tim stepped into the room and made his way around the piles of dirty laundry and dirty magazines and the unmade bed. The small closet was knee-deep in an avalanche of clothing beneath the rod of shirts and jackets Mack Villante had bothered to hang.

The last room, he knew, was John's. He had been in it just that afternoon to find absolutely nothing but bare furniture. Every dresser drawer was empty. There was not one hanger with one shirt in the closet. The bed didn't even have sheets. It was as Spartan as a monk's cell. More so.

But somebody had opened that back door, Tim thought as he

pressed his back to the wall and inched his way toward the bedroom door. He gulped a big lungful of air and went into the room, gun first, to find . . . no one.

DANA LAY STILL on the backseat of the cop car. A cage separated the front seat from any unwilling passengers in the back. The doors could be opened from the outside only. She was trapped.

She had no idea where they were. A dog was barking in the distance. There was no other sound but the occasional crackling of the radio. No traffic noise. She couldn't decide if it would be better to sit up and try to get her bearings or continue to play dead. Even if she knew where they were, her feet were bound. She couldn't run.

This must have been what it had been like in the back of Doc Holiday's van, she thought. Forced to lie motionless, helpless, waiting for a sadist to determine her fate.

She had somehow gotten free of her bonds that night. Now plastic zip ties bound her hands, digging into her wrists, which were already scarred with ligature marks. She brought her hands up to her mouth and pulled the duct tape loose on one side, then tried to chew at the ties around her wrists, an exercise in frustration and futility.

He hadn't taken as much care binding her feet together, looping one long tie around both ankles. When she realized she had room to maneuver, she began to wiggle and wriggle and twist and turn her feet, trying to work her way free.

At least the action gave her some hope.

Where there's life, there's hope. Where there's life, there's hope . . .

38

John lay on top of the trapdoor in the attic. Anyone pushing up at it from the closet below would likely think it was sealed or somehow locked. If they even bothered to look up at the ceiling inside the dark closet.

He could hear the intruder moving around in his room, and he hoped the person wouldn't have a look inside the doors of his nightstand, where he had hastily stashed the peanut butter jar and the water jug. But he heard only footsteps, no drawers or doors being opened, not so much as the click of the light switch.

That struck him as odd. A thief would search the drawers. A cop would turn the lights on. His old man would have been muttering to himself.

Who the hell did that leave?

No matter, he thought, so long as they weren't moving in. Let them look and let them leave. He wanted to clear out of here before dawn. He wasn't under arrest. They didn't have any cause to hold him—unless his father could somehow manage to convince the sheriff's office that he was the victim, in which case John wanted to be long gone from Shelby Mills and Liddell County. He would take his truck and go as far as he dared, then abandon it somewhere it wouldn't be easily found and start hitching rides south and west. If he was going to be homeless, he was going to be homeless on a beach in California.

For now, he had to wait. He could still hear his visitor moving through the house, going back toward the kitchen.

The air ducts served as a kind of sound system. As a boy, he had spent many hours up here in this dusty, stifling space, avoiding the wrath of his father. The old man never had figured out this hiding place. There was too much effort involved in considering it. He would never bother to go get an actual ladder and investigate. Climbing a ladder was not high on the list of things to do for drunks. He knew nothing of the rope ladder John had devised to get up and down.

The climb had been awkward tonight. He had been forced to use his right arm, setting off explosions of pain in his damaged shoulder. But he had made it up into the attic and got the hatch closed, then collapsed in agony on top of the door, panting and sweating until the barrage faded.

The drawback of the attic as a hiding place was the lack of light and the lack of visual vantage points. He had a flashlight with an age-old battery and weak beam to see his way around the low, cramped space. A small louvered vent at either end of the house afforded little in the way of a view outside. Still, as he heard the intruder exit the kitchen, he made his way carefully, bent uncomfortably in half, moving joist to joist to the garage end of the house, to the space over the living room and dining room, and tried to see out.

The security lights illuminated the swatch of ground below. What he could see was mud and dead grass. Somewhere to the right, on the back side of the house, he could hear the crunch of gravel under boots and a car door opening.

He could imagine kids thinking it would be a kick to sneak into a crime scene and have a party. But what he heard next disabused him of that idea.

What he heard next made his blood run cold. He'd heard it all the time in one war and then another—the abject terror of someone about to face death.

39

Dana heard his boots on the gravel as he came back to the car. She felt sick with panic, choking on tears. The storm of emotions coursing through her threatened to overwhelm any rational thought she had.

She had to get hold of herself. She had to be able to think or she was going to die in very short order. She had managed to work one foot free of the zip-tie loop around her ankles. If she got half a chance, she would try to run.

He pulled her out of the car still wrapped in the tarp, then stood her on her feet and peeled the tarp away.

Dana had no idea where they were. The house and its surroundings were unfamiliar. Coming out of the darkness of being covered, she felt assaulted by the security lights situated over the back door of the house. As she blinked and turned away, she was vaguely aware of wooded surroundings, a run-down garage, a dog barking somewhere nearby.

She didn't know if they were in town or in the country. She didn't know if there were neighbors to run to or if the barking dog might run her down. But she knew if she didn't do something, Tim Carver was going to finish the job Doc Holiday had started nearly a year ago. If he got her inside that house, he was free to do whatever he wanted to her. She knew all too well what that could mean.

The duct tape hung loose, stuck to only one side of her mouth. If she could talk to him . . . If she could reason with him . . . If she could keep him aware that she was a person and not just a problem to be disposed of . . .

"Don't do this, Tim," she said. "There's no need."

His expression was cold. "What? You're going to pretend none of this happened? I should trust you never to speak of it?"

Dana's eyes filled. "I loved you, Tim. Don't do this. If you ever cared for me—"

"You dropped me like a hot rock when I needed you. Do you know how that made me feel?"

"I'm sorry! I'm so sorry!" she said, hating the sound of desperation in her own voice. "But we were kids. We made mistakes. You said yourself we shouldn't have to pay for all eternity."

"Too late for that," he said, his mouth twisting on some sour amusement. "Let's go."

As soon as he put his hands on her and leaned in close to move her, Dana brought a knee up as hard as she could, catching him square in the crotch. He doubled over with a hard grunt, and she bolted.

She had no idea where to run. She only knew she had to.

She bolted, screaming, her voice shrill with absolute terror. "Help me! Help me!"

She hadn't taken three strides when she caught her foot in the loop of the zip tie that had bound her ankles together. She went down hard, barely able to break the fall with her arms, an animal sound of panic escaping her with her breath.

Tim was on her in seconds, turning her over and straddling her hips.

"You fucking bitch!"

He gritted the words out between his teeth and punched her full in the face, his knuckles smashing her lips against her teeth. The copper taste of blood filled her mouth and she turned her head to the side to spit it out as she tried to bring her arms up to protect her face.

He struck her again and again, swinging his fist like a hammer, banging her head off the ground, striking her left ear so hard she lost hearing.

Her consciousness dimming, Dana went limp. He slapped her across the face with an open hand.

"Look at me. Look at me!" His voice was a harsh rasp.

Dana opened her eyes and saw three of him. He looked like a stranger. There was nothing in his face that related to the Tim she had known growing up or the man she had known for these last few days, the man with the easy charm and the aw-shucks country-boy grin. She didn't know this animal that lived inside him. It was a thing with a feral grimace and black eyes. A creature bent on hurting her.

"You'll pay for that," he said, leaning over her. "You'll pay for that. I could have made this easy for you. You just made it hard. You did this to yourself."

He had come into her bedroom and choked her unconscious. He had brought her to this place for the express purpose of killing her. And somehow he twisted the intentions around to make it her fault. It was her fault he was punching her in the face. It was her fault he would now make her death as painful as possible.

He hauled her up off the ground and pushed her ahead of him toward the house, shoving her so hard she stumbled and fell.

He kicked her hard in the side. "Get up!"

Dana's breath left her and she pulled herself into a ball on the ground like a turtle pulling inside of its shell. Tim dragged her up to her feet, his hand clamped like a vise around the back of her neck. He pushed her up the step and shoved her through the door, banging her forehead on the door's frame so hard she saw stars. Blood instantly flowed from the fresh gash above her right eyebrow.

She heard the word *no* over and over and over, only dimly realizing it was coming from her own mouth as he manhandled her through the dark kitchen and a dining room. He grabbed her with both hands by the back of her hoodie, lifted her off the ground, and chucked her into the next room like a bag of garbage.

Dana hit the floor with a thud, landing on her stomach, landing on something hard and rectangular in the pouch of her hoodie.

Her phone.

Her heart sank. If she had remembered she had it when she was alone in the car, she could have somehow managed to call 911. She wouldn't get that chance again.

THE NOISE COMING THROUGH the air ducts sounded like a barroom brawl—knuckles pounding flesh, bodies crashing into furniture. The fear in the woman's voice told a different story.

John listened, flinching at every sound, emotions from childhood stirring in a corner of his mind he had shut away long ago—memories of his mother's voice begging, pleading, crying. His stomach turned as the images flashed like explosions in his mind—his father's face twisted with rage, his mother's tears, the physical force of violence.

As a child he had no choice but to hide. As a man, he couldn't listen and do nothing. Not even if it meant risking himself.

MOANING, IN PAIN, DANA struggled to turn over and propped herself up with her back against the side of a recliner that reeked of smoke. Her left eye was swollen nearly shut. Her lips were split and bleeding. She couldn't breathe through her nose. She pressed her tongue against her teeth and felt several of them move.

Tim stalked her, his hands on his hips. The filtered light coming in through the sheer curtains was cold and blue, making him look like a monster from science fiction.

"Is this what you did to Casey?" she asked.

"No," he said, looking down at her. "Casey made it easy. All I had to do was hold that choke a little while longer. She never knew what happened. She thought I loved her. She thought I would marry her. She died thinking that. She died happy, I guess."

Dana wanted to cry as she thought of her friend. Sweet Casey, always the first one to offer comfort. That was how it would have started between her and Tim. Poor Tim, cast aside by his college-bound girlfriend, Miss Ambition. Casey had always cared more about having a family, settling down. She would have offered him a shoulder to cry on. He would have taken advantage of that. He had always been an opportunist.

"She would have ruined everything for me," he said. "She did it on purpose, too. She had to have. Or the kid was John's and I was just the better catch. I couldn't have it. I had plans. I was going to West Point."

And his plans had been more important than the life of a girl who had been his friend for years, and more important than the life that had only just taken root inside her.

"I couldn't have a wife," he said with disgust. "I didn't want a kid. She wouldn't get rid of it."

So he had gotten rid of his problems himself in a two-for-one killing.

"No one knew about us," he said. "Not even you. You were too busy looking down your nose at John."

"Why couldn't you just have left it alone, Dee?" he asked. "All these years with no one the wiser, no one even looking. I told you to leave it be, but you had to keep digging and digging."

"Why would you even come back here?" she asked. He was going to kill her. All she could hope to do was stall for time and pray for a miracle. If she died, at least she died with answers.

He smiled like a crocodile. "Why wouldn't I? I got away with murder. When I made detective, this case would have been mine."

Like Hardy had said, Dana thought. He had gotten some kind of sick charge out of coming back to the scene of his crime and going to work in the very sheriff's office that hadn't managed to even consider him a suspect.

"Where are we?" she asked, glancing around the room. There was nothing familiar.

He came forward, straddling her legs, and lowered himself to his knees. The smile that curved his mouth made her skin crawl. He placed a hand on either side of her head and leaned in close.

"We're at a crime scene," he murmured, amused at some secret joke.

A chill shuddered through her as she began to think of what he might do next. He was so close she thought he might try to kiss her. His breath was warm against her cheek. The memory of all the times she had kissed him back turned her stomach now.

"I wish I had time," he said as he closed a hand around her throat.

JOHN CREPT DOWN THE hall, straining to hear the voices—one male, one female. He hadn't been able to make them out well enough to understand who these people were or why they would be here in his father's house, but it was clear the woman wasn't here by choice.

He had come down from the attic and grabbed the first thing he saw he could use for a weapon—the short length of galvanized pipe he had always used to prop open his bedroom window. He would have preferred a firearm, but his father's guns would have all been confiscated in the search. There was no time to go digging for anything the old man might have hidden.

His thumb rubbed up and down against the metal pipe as he crept down the hall, nearing the living room.

"Is this what you did to Casey?" the woman asked.

"No," the man said. "Casey made it easy . . ."

Casey.

John felt like he had fallen into a surreal dream. Maybe he had. Maybe his brain was bleeding and he was in a coma and this nightmare was his new reality. The disembodied voices drew him into a story like he was walking in on the middle of a movie, except that he knew the players: Dana Nolan and Tim Carver.

He paused in the hallway just short of the living room.

Is this what you did to Casey?

No. Casey made it easy . . .

He slipped out of the shadows of the hallway and stood at the edge of the living room, staring at a grotesquely battered version of Dana Nolan. Leaning into her, his hand around her throat, was Tim Carver.

"I wish I had time," Carver said. "You were a sweet little fuck back in the day."

Rage and hatred burned through John, old fuel for his old friend. He thought of the summer Casey had gone missing, of the hell law enforcement had put him through while all of Liddell County celebrated the poster boy that was Tim Carver. Tim Carver, local hero, West Point cadet. Tim Carver, killer.

Dana Nolan looked at him with pleading eyes.

"John," she said, her voice barely more than a tremulous whisper. She looked right at him over the shoulder of her tormentor. "John, help me. Please."

"Nice try," Carver said. "There's nobody here to help you, sweetheart."

"Think again, asshole," John said.

Carver came to his feet in an instant, stepping away from Dana, drawing his weapon and pointing it at John.

"Well, shit," he said. "This is my fucking lucky day. I'm about to happen upon a tragic murder-suicide."

The gun was not his service weapon. The filtered light from outside touched the chrome barrel like moonglow as Carver crossed the room with it pointed at John's sternum. "With your old man's gun."

"Let's start with the suicide," Carver said.

"Let's not."

John spun sideways and struck out with the pipe, knocking Carver's aim wide as the gun went off. He followed through on instinct and adrenaline, calling on his army combatives training, stepping in and catching Carver in the face with his right elbow.

He felt the broken shaft of his collarbone give and the flesh of his shoulder tear free of sutures. The pain was like a white-hot ball of fire that dimmed his vision and buckled his knees for a second. In that second, Carver swept his feet out from under him.

John hit the floor on his backside and rolled to the left, using his good arm to start to push back up to his feet. Carver came with a knee to his already damaged ribs and dropped him again, catching him with a second knee to the chin, snapping his jaw shut hard enough to crack teeth.

As John fell to his side, he swung the pipe, cracking Carver's ankle, knocking the leg out from under him, dumping him on his ass. The gun flew free of his hand and skidded across the floor.

They came up onto their knees together, John swinging backhanded with the pipe. Carver caught hold of the pipe and twisted it out of John's grasp, turning it back around on him with a vicious strike to his bad shoulder. John felt the collarbone collapse. A second blow sank directly into the wound his father's bullet had cut through his flesh. Pain exploded through him, and everything went black.

JOHN CRUMPLED TO THE floor, his face contorted in agony. Tim turned and kicked him like he was a soccer ball, hard and repeatedly.

"Stop it!" Dana shouted. "Stop it!"

Tim turned around, looking across the floor, looking for the weapon he had lost in the brawl.

Dana struggled to cock the hammer back on the gun. The sound seemed abnormally loud in the otherwise silent room. The weapon was awkward in her bound hands, too big for her, cumbersome and heavy. Her hands were shaking as she pointed it at him.

Tim stared at her, his face carefully blank. They weren't more than a few feet apart. She could hear him breathing. She could smell his sweat. He had been her first love. He had murdered her best friend. He would have killed her. He still would.

He didn't bother saying she wouldn't shoot him.

He started to move toward her. She raised the gun.

"I'll do it in a heartbeat," she said.

He stopped, hands out at his sides, his eyes trying to read her, looking for a tell. Would she really? Would she hesitate? Would she fumble the gun, which was too big for her awkward grip?

"Where is Casey?" she asked. "She's not in that barrel. What did you do with her body?"

He said nothing.

"Answer me," Dana said. "Answer me!"

His eyes were fixed on hers. "If I answer you, you won't have a reason not to shoot me."

"Casey's dead," she said. "She's never coming back to life. I don't have a reason not to shoot you now."

The tension of the moment stretched as taut as a guy wire.

"You're not a killer, Dee," he said.

"Yes, I am. I've done it before."

"You won't kill me."

He started to turn away, to walk away, as if he thought he could do that—kill Casey, try to kill her, try to kill John, then just walk away.

I should shoot him now, she thought. But she hesitated. What if she couldn't hold on to the gun? Holding on to it, she had the upper hand. If she dropped it, she was screwed.

He stopped and looked down, then knelt to attend to a bootlace.

Dana glanced at John as he stirred on the floor. A dark stain spread across the right shoulder of his shirt. He held his right arm close against his body as he struggled to get up to one knee. He looked up at Tim. His eyes widened and his mouth tore open to shout: "*Gun!*"

It seemed to happen in slow motion and in the blink of an eye at the same time.

Tim pulled a revolver from a holster strapped to his ankle and leveled it at her.

John launched himself not at Tim, but at her, knocking her flat as the revolver fired.

They tumbled across the floor, Dana losing hold of the bigger gun, John grabbing it. He came up to his knees firing.

Bam! Bam! Bam!

The look on Tim's face was stunned surprise as he stumbled backward, struck twice in the chest. The slugs buried themselves in the bulletproof vest he wore under his uniform shirt. He sat down hard on the floor, banging the back of his head into the wall.

The third shot had hit him in the forehead. Dead center. Blood trickled down between his open eyes.

Just like that, it was over. Seven years of wondering and waiting and searching. All the complicated pieces of who they had been as children, and how their lives had fit together, and how they had impacted one another . . . Just like that, it was over.

Casey was gone.

Tim was gone.

She turned to John as he dropped the gun to the floor and fell on top of it, blood spreading out on the carpet.

"Oh my God!"

Dana scrambled to his side, fumbling to get the phone out of the pouch of her hoodie, the zip ties cutting into the flesh of her wrists.

"Hang on, John! Hang on! Don't you die on me too!"

She managed to punch the numbers and make the call, then pressed her fingers to the side of his neck and felt his pulse. It was weak, but he was alive.

"Where there's life, there's hope," she whispered like a mantra, like a prayer. "Where there's life, there's hope. Where there's life, there's hope . . ."

40

He dreamed he was in heaven with his mother. He could see her, dressed in a beautiful sky-blue dress, standing on white stone steps, maybe twenty feet away. She waved at him, smiling a sad, sweet smile. Her dark hair was down, loose and wavy, hanging past her shoulders. She was so beautiful. He had always thought she was the most beautiful woman in the world.

He had been eight years old the last time he'd seen her. She had taken him to lunch at the diner downtown and bought him an ice cream sundae for being a good boy while she did her shopping. He remembered she had bought two suitcases at the Goodwill store—one for her and a little one for him.

She was going to take him with her, but she never had.

In his dream he reached out toward her. He tried to walk toward her, but no matter how hard he tried, he couldn't get any closer. Even when he tried to run straight at her, he couldn't get any closer. He banged his fist against an invisible wall. She just looked sad as she waved good-bye and turned and walked away.

John opened his eyes and saw nothing but white. White walls. White ceiling. White sheets. But he knew he wasn't in heaven because heaven wouldn't let him in.

*   *   *

"DENTAL RECORDS HAVE CONFIRMED the identity of a skeleton found in a barrel on the Shelby Mills, Indiana, property of John Villante Sr. to be that of Villante's wife, Rachel Longo Villante, missing for nearly two decades. Foul play is suspected.

"In other news, a memorial service for a Liddell County sheriff's deputy—"

Dana used the remote to silence Kimberly Kirk. She knew all she wanted to know about the memorial service of Tim Carver. Despite the details surrounding his death, there were still plenty of people in Shelby Mills who remembered Tim the star athlete, the West Point candidate, the affable man with a badge and a ready smile.

They didn't want to believe that he had murdered Casey Grant and her unborn child, that he had covered it up all these years, that he had planted evidence in the Villante house to try to turn the spotlight back on John or his father. They didn't want to know that he had tried to kill Dana and John.

Until someone convinced them otherwise, Tim Carver's death was a stunning tragedy at the hands of a former schoolmate, an army veteran with documented psychiatric problems and a former suspect in the disappearance of Shelby Mills sweetheart Casey Grant.

"They'll believe the truth when they see it on *Dateline*," Dan Hardy had said.

Dana had told Wesley Stevens to call the *Dateline* people and make it happen. As much as she hadn't wanted to tell her story about Doc Holiday, she wouldn't let this one go. She would expose herself to the stares and revulsion of viewers, but they would come away knowing who the hero was in this story.

The news had yet to break that Tim Carver was now also being considered a person of interest in the attack on Grindstone waitress April Johnson and that authorities in Liddell County, Fort Wayne, and the area surrounding the military academy in West Point, New York, were reviewing similar cases for possible connections.

Hardy's theory that after Casey's murder the pressure would have built inside Tim until he felt a need to lash out was looking more than plausible.

Even though she had experienced Tim the monster herself, there was a part of her that didn't want to believe it either. The better part of him had been her first love, her first lover. Before Dana would mourn his loss. After Dana would move on, even more disillusioned than before, as impossible as that seemed. After Dana would mourn the loss of the naïveté that had allowed her to believe in the inherent goodness of the people in her life. Tim. Roger. She had yet to tell her mother about Roger's confession that he had lied all those years ago about the day Casey had gone missing. She didn't see the point in telling her now. What purpose would it serve to ruin her mother's belief in her husband over a sin of omission that hadn't changed the outcome of anything? None.

She stood up from the table and slung the strap of her purse over her shoulder. The better part of a week had passed. Her face was still swollen and the bruises had turned putrid colors. She didn't care. She had something important to do.

"Are you sure you want to do this by yourself?" her mother asked as Dana dug her car keys out of her bag.

"Yes," Dana said. "I'll be fine. Turns out he's the good guy, remember?"

"I'll never forget," her mother said, tears rising.

She hugged Dana and found a spot on her cheek without a fading bruise and kissed it. She was clingy these days. Dana didn't blame her. As close as she had come to death for a second time, Dana had decided to welcome all the hugs she could get.

"Call me if you get lost."

"I will."

"Text me when you get there."

"I will," Dana promised.

They both knew she would forget.

JOHN WAS WAITING ON a bench outside the ER entrance of the hospital, looking uncertain and uncomfortable. All he had was the clothes on his back—gray sweatpants and a zippered hoodie and a pair of too-white sneakers—courtesy of the hospital auxiliary. He still wore the bruises and lacerations of his life-or-death struggles with his father and with Tim. His right arm was in a sling.

"You didn't have to do this," he said as he eased himself awkwardly into the passenger seat. He moved as gingerly as a brittle old man. He had served tours of duty in two wars and managed not to get shot, only to be shot in his own home.

"You saved my life," Dana said. "The least I can do is give you a ride."

He was uncomfortable with the idea of someone feeling beholden to him.

"It's not just a ride."

"You need a place to stay and we have a place to offer you," she said. "Don't look a gift horse in the mouth."

Even if he had wanted to live in the home he had grown up in—which Dana couldn't imagine, considering the events that had transpired there—he wasn't going to be allowed to. Even from a jail cell his father was a son of a bitch. He had made it known via his attorney that John was not welcome to stay there.

A caretaker's cottage on the Mercer-Nolan nursery property had been vacant for some time. It had been Roger's suggestion for John to live there and to assume caretaker's duties when he was able. The gesture would garner him favor with voting veterans, but Dana happily let him have that.

"It's charity," John said.

"It is not," Dana argued. "Charity is something for nothing."

"I'll start work as soon as I can."

"Nobody's worried about it but you."

"I'm just saying. That's all."

Dana looked over at him with frustration.

"What's harder for you?" she asked. "Believing I could be a nice person or believing you deserve to have anyone treat you well?"

Both, she thought, but he didn't answer her. He was a man with less than nothing and less than no one, and Dana knew she had certainly done nothing in her past life to deserve him risking his life for her, but he had done so, nevertheless. Whatever her younger self might have believed a long time ago, John Villante was a hero in every sense of the word.

"I'm sorry about your mom," she said. "It was on the news this morning."

He looked out the window. What was he supposed to say? The tragedy of his life was so much bigger than the Band-Aid of a polite apology could begin to cover. His mother dead at the hands of his father all those years ago . . . No one caring enough to look for her or to look after the child she had left behind, taking Mack Villante's word for it that she had abandoned him and her son . . . It seemed that everyone on the face of the earth had failed John Villante.

"I'm sorry about Casey," he said softly.

"Me too," Dana said, tears and emotion rising. "I wish we knew where he left her so we could bring her home."

John looked over at her and said, "She's in your heart. That's all that matters."

Dana nodded, not trusting her voice.

They rode the rest of the way in silence. When they reached Mercer-Nolan, Dana took the employee entrance to the nursery and drove to the cottage that was tucked back by the apple orchard. John's old red truck was parked alongside. The tailgate was down. Dana watched his face as he saw the dog—surprise he tried to hide and happiness he didn't want to let show.

"I hope that's your dog," she said as they got out of the car. "He wouldn't get out of the truck, so we just brought him along."

The dog danced with joy at the sight of him but stayed at the front of the truck box, too shy to come greet him.

"I guess that's my dog," John said, leaning against the pickup. "He picked me. I don't know why."

"He's smarter than a lot of people, then, I guess," Dana said, standing beside him.

"John, I owe you an apology for a long time ago," she said.

He shook his head, but he didn't look at her.

"It's funny how smart we think we are before we know anything at all," she said. "Now, after everything that's happened to me in the last year, I look back and it's like that girl was someone I used to know. I'm not who she was."

"We're who the world makes us," he said. "For better or worse."

"No," Dana said. "The world made me a victim. I won't be what the world made me. I won't be what happened to me. I'll be what I become. So will you. Life can try to break us. We don't have to stay broken. And if we help each other with that, that isn't charity. That's humanity. That's friendship."

He gave her a long look then, inscrutable as always. His life had taught him to show nothing or risk having what he held precious taken away. He couldn't even admit to wanting the dog that had chosen him.

"However we got here," he said, "I guess this might be a good place to start."

Dana smiled. "Yes. Yes, it is."

Author's Note

When I was a child of ten, I got bucked off a pony and landed on my head in the street. In those days, no one wore helmets when riding anything—horses, bicycles, motorcycles, whatever. I was incredibly lucky not to have been killed. I was doubly lucky in that my head is as hard as a block of granite. I lived in a very rural place with no hospital, no helicopter to whisk me off to a trauma center. We had a cranky old town doctor who was none too happy to be called to his office on the Fourth of July. He came in complaining and smelling of what I would later come to recognize as whiskey. He held fingers up in front of my face and asked me how many I saw. I guessed two, and he sent me home. No X-rays. CT scans and MRIs were the stuff of science fiction. My mother sat in my bedroom that night waking me up every time I started to fall asleep because that was what she had been told to do with someone who had taken a bonk on the head.

The reality of that situation was that I had a concussion, something that was regarded very differently in 1969 than it is today. I had suffered a mild traumatic brain injury (TBI) that was never diagnosed, let alone treated, and I have suffered with the effects of that injury my entire life. While the severity and frequency of my headaches have lessened over the years, I still get them. I have one right now as I write this note. Over the decades I sought help from a number of doctors, none of whom diagnosed me with TBI. My headaches were blamed on allergies, sinuses, eye strain, stress, hormones, and, my personal favorite, my imagination. I don't deny having a vivid imagination, but I don't know anyone who would choose to imagine the feeling of an axe cleaving his or her skull for hours and days at a time.

The fact is that many people who suffer mild and even more serious traumatic brain injuries often go undiagnosed and misdiagnosed even today. Closed head injuries are not always obvious. They may present themselves in ways that can be minimized or rationalized away. After all, the person has no outward signs of injury, and they can be very clever in compensating for the cognitive deficits caused by the injury. Every TBI is as unique and mysterious as the brain it impacts. A fellow competitor of mine in the equestrian world took a fall on soft footing that would not have been considered serious by any of us but for the fact that she bumped her head. She was in a coma for weeks and suffered severe physical and cognitive deficits that ended her riding career, which she struggles to overcome to this day, years later. Meanwhile ol' Ironhead here was thrown with force onto concrete, and the only lasting aftereffects I have are headaches.

The good news is that great strides have been made in the study of TBI in the past ten years. The bad news is the major reason for these advancements: war. The U.S. Department of Defense reported new TBI cases among military personnel in 2013 alone at 27,187, with many of those injuries incurred by deployed active-duty personnel. I have personally witnessed the result of TBI incurred in war by a friend's husband. The ongoing struggle of the wounded warrior is a heartbreaking thing to watch. The post–brain injury person is often not—and often never will be—the pre–brain injury person remembered by friends and family, and the reality of that is difficult to accept for all involved.

Compounding the struggles of those injured in war is post-traumatic stress disorder, as if one or the other affliction is not hell enough by itself.

While I was writing this book, and had already immersed myself in the research of both TBI and PTSD, a serendipitous thing happened. I had taken a break one evening to watch my passion: mixed martial arts. One of the fighters in particular caught my attention as he was being introduced. MMA fighters don't wear shirts in competition, and the majority of them have often-elaborate body art in lieu of a uniform. This particular fighter had a lot of script taking up the full length of his back. I couldn't read the fine print, but I was so intrigued, I decided to do some research to find out what the tattoo was all about. The fighter's name was Shane Kruchten. The tattoo was a list of nineteen names and dates, bracketed by the words ONLY THE GOOD DIE YOUNG. The names are of the United States Marines he served with in Iraq, along with the dates they were lost in the war.

As I read Shane's story, I realized that Shane's experiences with PTSD and the military bureaucracy mirrored the experiences of my character, John Villante, and the experiences of my friend's husband. As a nod to Shane, I gave John a similar tattoo on his back, the names of fallen comrades and the dates their lives were ended by war. Shane's story is one of tragedy and struggle with PTSD, drugs, and alcohol, and ultimately his triumph over a tremendous amount of adversity. I encourage readers to look up Shane's story for a true account of what can happen to our soldiers fighting this terrible internal battle long after the war is behind them. There are tens of thousands of veterans in this country who each have a story of their own and struggles that will plague them for the rest of their lives.

Thankfully, there is help available to these men and women through various organizations, some of which I've listed at the end of this note. It's also important to know that PTSD is not exclusive to veterans of war. PTSD is an equal opportunity affliction that torments victims of crimes and other tragedies. People like Dana Nolan, who have suffered and survived unspeakable evil but who will forever live with the memories and nightmares. The following is a list of just a few of the many organizations helping victims of crime, PTSD, and TBI, including several organizations that provide service dogs to veterans struggling with PTSD.

About PTSD organizations: http://search.about.com/?q=-
   PTSD+organizations

Brain Injury Association of America: www.biausa.org
Defense and Veterans Brain Injury Center: www.dvbic.org
Fisher House Foundation: www.fisherhouse.org
Intrepid Fallen Heroes Fund: www.fallenheroesfund.org
National Center for PTSD: www.ptsd.va.org
The National Center for Victims of Crime: www.victimsofcrime
   .org
Office for Victims of Crime: www.crimevictims.gov

The Battle Buddy Foundation: www.tbbf.org
K9s for Warriors: www.k9sforwarriors.org
Paws for Veterans: www.pawsforveterans.com

And for veterans struggling to find employment post-service:
   www.hireheroesusa.org

TAMI HOAG

"Tami Hoag is simply one of the best."

—*New York Times* bestselling
author Lisa Unger

For a complete list of titles, please
visit prh.com/tamihoag